# TROUBLE WILL FIND YOU

## A Novel by
## Ed Bonner

Copyright Ed Bonner 2023

ISBN: 9798391862543

Imprint: Independently published

My grateful thanks to Felix Hodcroft (creative writing department Hull University at Scarborough) whose insightful critiques, encouragement and practical comments improve everything I write; to my wife and best friend Adrianne for her unending encouragement and support; to Shyama Pereira who gave me belief that I could write a full-length novel with oxygenated characters.

"Success is a lousy teacher. It seduces smart people into thinking they can't lose."

*Bill Gates*

"Well, you know, there's depression and depression. What I mean by depression in my own case is that depression isn't just the blues. It's not just like I have a hangover in the weekend ... the girl didn't show up or something like that. It isn't that. It's not really depression, it's a kind of mental violence which stops you from functioning properly from one moment to the next. You lose something somewhere and suddenly you're gripped by a kind of angst of the heart and of the spirit.

"I've taken a lot of Prozac, Paxil, Wellbutrin, Effexor, Ritalin, Focalin. I've also studied deeply in the philosophies and the religions, but cheerfulness kept breaking through."

*Leonard Cohen*

"Time after time, wicked scrape after bloody fall,

I ask, How is there returning from this?

I return to the most fundamental of all:

This world has a place where ruin and redemption kiss."

*"The Reformed Philosopher"*

# Contents

Book 1   The Road to Perdition ---------------------------- 1
  Chapter 1   Leeds 2009 --------------------------------- 2
  Chapter 2   The Portuguese Goalkeeper Leeds 2004 --- 7
  Chapter 3   A Woman's Illness   Ballarat 1985 ------- 12
  Chapter 4   Ballarat   1975 - 1987 -------------------- 16
  Chapter 5   Sydney   1988 - 1994 -------------------- 24
  Chapter 6   Post-grad London   1995 ----------------- 29
  Chapter 7   Meeting his Match   Leeds 1999 ---------- 37
  Chapter 8   Taking the plunge   Leeds 2002 ---------- 46
  Chapter 9   The Black Dogs   Leeds 2005 ------------ 52
  Chapter 10   The shitshow begins   Leeds 2009 ------ 62
  Chapter 11   Coming apart   Leeds / London 2010 --- 70
  Chapter 12   Dr Susan McDonald   Suffolk 2010 ----- 75
  Chapter 13   Mr Bernard Finch, Barrister   London 2010 ---------------------------------- 83
  Chapter 14   Dr Stanley Wethers   London 2010 ----- 87
  Chapter 15   The Train Crash   London 2010 --------- 94
  Chapter 16   Puglia   2011 ---------------------------- 99
  Chapter 17   The Missile   London 2011 ------------- 106
  Chapter 18   Head beaten   Manchester 2011 ------- 111
  Chapter 19   The Hearing ---------------------------- 116
  Chapter 20   The second half ------------------------ 119
  Chapter 21   A Consummate Stitch-up Manchester - 121
  Chapter 22   A Sad Farewell ------------------------- 132

Book 2   The Road to Redemption --------------------- 137
  Chapter 23   Johannesburg   2012 ------------------- 138
  Chapter 24   White River   2012 --------------------- 144
  Chapter 25   White River Hospital   2012 ------------ 151
  Chapter 26   Snakes alive!   2012 -------------------- 156
  Chapter 27   The Lofty Giraffe 2012 ----------------- 160
  Chapter 28   Bokkie   2012 -------------------------- 164

| Chapter 29 | The Hard Man | 169 |
| --- | --- | --- |
| Chapter 30 | Gardener Stories 2012 | 174 |
| Chapter 31 | African Adventures | 177 |
| Chapter 32 | Carotid blowout | 182 |
| Chapter 33 | Raichie's 2013 | 187 |
| Chapter 34 | Shabbat Dinner 2013 | 192 |
| Chapter 35 | The AIDS Clinic 2013 | 199 |
| Chapter 36 | Enjoying Mpumalanga 2013 | 204 |
| Chapter 37 | Slender Fingers, Deep Pockets 2014 | 208 |
| Chapter 38 | Closure: Manchester 2014 | 213 |
| Chapter 39 | Denver and Australia 2014 | 216 |
| Chapter 40 | Randfontein 2014 | 221 |
| Chapter 41 | The Bar Mitzvah 2015 | 232 |
| Chapter 42 | Samson 2015 | 239 |
| Chapter 43 | The Eye 2015 | 243 |
| Chapter 44 | Expert Witness 2016 | 248 |
| Chapter 45 | *Schadenfreude* 2016 | 271 |
| Chapter 46 | Winston Rabada 2016 | 261 |
| Chapter 47 | Sipho & Dube 2017 | 268 |
| Chapter 48 | The River 2017 | 271 |
| Chapter 49 | Shleps 2017 | 284 |
| Chapter 50 | Cape Town 2017 | 287 |
| Chapter 51 | Lunch with Vultures 2018 | 295 |
| Chapter 52 | Bokkie 2018 | 300 |
| Chapter 53 | The Birthday Party 2021 | 304 |
| Chapter 54 | The Best Laid Plans | 311 |
| Chapter 55 | White River 2022 | 319 |
| Chapter 56 | Epilogue Sydney 2023 | 326 |
| Acknowledgements | | 329 |
| About the Author | | 330 |

# Book 1
## The Road to Perdition

# Chapter 1

## Leeds 2009

It was in the operating theatre that Dr Nick Simpson came alive. This was where all manner of human drama took place, where his golden hands took centre stage in that red zone under the bright surgical lights. This was where the nurses and junior doctors were his supporting cast, each with their own essential role to play. Risks had to be weighed. The outcome was everything.

It was there that his talent met his ambition.

Since arriving in Leeds ten years earlier, his reputation had burgeoned, and he was justifiably regarded by his peers as being a highly talented and skilful surgeon and excellent teacher. He had carried out operations many others would simply not have attempted, and each had been successful beyond expectation. He had every reason to feel content with what he had achieved thus far, and on that bright Tuesday morning had no reason to feel that anything was about to change. Had he ever studied philosophy, however, he might have come across the words of Goethe:

"Wherever a man may happen to turn, whatever a man may undertake, he will always end up by returning to the path which nature has marked out for him."

Dr Nick Simpson was about to discover his preordained path.

Allison had just left for her legal practice and Nick too was about to depart for the hospital when the doorbell rang. He was a little surprised to find the postman there with a registered letter – he did not usually arrive that early. Nick was slightly more surprised to see the buff-coloured envelope bearing the return address of the Medical Board of Control. He was sure he had paid his annual registration fees, and his Continuing Professional Development was well up to date. Well, if it wasn't that, what other mundane reason might the grey men in grey suits have for writing to him? Surely not a registered letter to inform him of their upcoming AGM? He slit open the envelope.

He might as well have slit his throat.

20th July 2009

Dear Dr Simpson

Following a routine investigation into the prescription records of several pharmacies local to your hospital, we have found an abnormally large number of these prescriptions bearing your signature. All matters relating to above average prescribing of addictive drugs / medication are of concern to the Medical Board of Control.

We wish to inform you that it is the intention of the Medical Board of Control to hold a formal hearing to investigate your conduct in respect of the issue of these prescriptions.

As yet, we have set no formal date for this hearing but advise you in the meantime to contact your indemnity organisation, to whom a copy of this letter has been sent. We have also sent a copy of this letter to the Administrator of the hospital at which you are lead surgeon of the Department of Head and Neck Surgery, and you will no doubt be hearing from them too in the very near future.

With regret, we are obliged to warn you that should the allegations against you be found proven, criminal prosecution may follow because there is a strong likelihood that many of the abovementioned prescriptions in the names of patients you have treated were intended for personal use by yourself, thereby taking this matter into the realms of fraudulent drug prescription and thereby egregious conduct.

Sincerely yours
Graham Thesby
Clerk to the Medical Board of Control.

Nick felt the blood drain from his head. He began to reel and dropped the letter. He felt as if he had just walked into a wall. The room began to spin. He must have come very close to passing out but managed to remain vertical until he was able to lower himself slowly onto the floor and lay on his back. Then his head started pounding as the blood gushed back into his brain. As he filled his lungs with deep breaths, the drumming in his head began to diminish.

When he felt a little easier, he rose slowly to get himself a glass of water, and then another. He waited for a few more minutes till his head cleared and then headed for his car. He had a busy schedule ahead of him and could not afford to be late. Whether he should be driving, indeed whether he was capable of operating at all, was another matter entirely because his mind was in turmoil.

The letter was as unexpected as it was unwelcome. A hearing? He'd heard of colleagues being summoned – in some cases one might have said with some justification, they had it coming. But not in his worst moments would he ever have thought it could befall him. How had he, an intelligent and well-educated man, allowed this to happen? Since leaving Australia and starting his days as a surgical registrar in London, his career had maintained an unerringly upward trajectory, yet he had remained modest and relaxed. Had this made him over-confident?

When his career came crashing down, as cataclysmic an event as being told one had cancer, it was almost beyond belief. It was not a slip of the scalpel that brought him to his knees. It was simply hubris.

In those dark months following his fall from grace, Nick had ample time to reflect on the reasons that he had been found wanting. It took a good while before he came to the realisation that it was not that he had *failed*. On the contrary, he had been successful with everything he had ever attempted. He concluded that, *because* of that continued success, when he came to be tested by difficult challenges, he did not have the experience of self-doubt to deal with them. He had never thought of himself as being anything other than unquestionably ok, so he had never considered questions as to whether he might not be.

Now he was asking himself, what if he had not been the boy in school that his mates most admired? What if he had not been 'quite handsome' (not *his* opinion)? What if he had been a less talented surgeon? Might he have been better equipped to manage life when difficult questions were asked?

As these thoughts replayed endlessly in his mind, he arrived at the inevitable conclusion that he was not adequately prepared for dealing with adversity when it arose. Had he been, he might have coped better. The intelligent person learns from failure, but this was the first and only time Nick had failed an exam. The fact that it was not a school or university exam that had brought him low – he had always distinguished himself in those – but one that he himself had set was what he found most galling.

He remembered the advice of his professor at Sydney Medical School those years ago when Nick suggested a complicated technique for a relatively simple operation:

*'No need to look for shit, Nick, I can assure you that trouble will find you in any event.'*

Dr Nick Simpson had sought trouble and found it, and he should have known better. He should have known that after the Shipman debacle (that man had caused so much trouble for the medical profession), every action, every prescription was being monitored by those sharp-eyed people on the Medical Board of Control. He had known but had not cared.

Trouble had found him. And it was all so unnecessary.

# Chapter 2

## The Portuguese Goalkeeper

## Leeds 2004

The dramatic case five years earlier that really cemented Nick Simpson's reputation with his peers was an unusual one.

He had arranged leave and booked aeons ago to watch his beloved Wallabies play England in an international rugby match. The Wallabies had been playing well and had every expectation of beating England on their own hallowed turf. The thought of being at Twickenham under floodlights that Saturday evening really excited him. He had left ample time to get there, share a beer with old mates and savour the atmosphere. The weather in London was reported to be significantly better than it was that day in Leeds. It was great to be able to have a day off and to get away from the constant demands of hospital work and the unremitting rain.

He was parking his car at Leeds Station to take the express train to London when his bleeper sounded. The light on the bleeper was a bright red in the grey of the early afternoon. The message was unequivocal: *"Level A1 Surgical Emergency – all staff - repeat all staff - required to attend hospital immediately. Mr Simpson to lead."*

'Bugger,' he thought ruefully, 'that's one person who won't be watching rugby today.....'

THE ROAD TO PERDITION   CHAPTER 2

Like many cities in the north, Leeds was rarely short of rain, but on this particularly wintry weekend it had poured with all the energy the heavens could muster. In fact, so much had fallen that a lunch-time Championship League football match between Leeds United and Birmingham City had to be called off due to the pitch being waterlogged and unsafe. Forty thousand disgruntled spectators had to be sent home.

This information obviously hadn't been passed through to the official in charge of a minor league match scheduled to take place a few miles away on a pitch that could only be described as a quagmire.

Despite the pleas of the team managers, the referee (who was a craggy Tyke) was dismissive. He decided that the game would go on.

'We'll give it go, lads. Boogered if I'm going to give oop game for bit o' rain!'

An ex-army man, he clearly didn't cater for softies. It was apparent very early on that the pitch was unsafe but still the gung-ho official was determined that no game on his watch would be called off by mere rainfall, not even a deluge akin to Noah's great flood. Come hell or high water he was going to get his fee, and all he had to do to get it was to keep the game going for a minimum of fifteen minutes. So, he blew his whistle and the match commenced. Within five minutes it was difficult to distinguish who was in which team because all were equally caked in mud. The referee was not concerned. Just fifteen minutes, call off the game, be paid.

Ten minutes into the match, five more minutes to pay-time, it happened.

The attacking winger squared a ball from near the touchline hoping to reach his striker whom he could see sprinting forward at great speed. At the same time the defending goalkeeper, a young Portuguese immigrant, had seen the danger and run forward from his goal, also at great speed. At exactly the moment the ball stuck in the mud, the two sprinting men approaching from opposite directions slipped. Slipped, but did not lose momentum. They continued to slide at pace towards each other, the striker on his back with his legs splayed forward, the goalkeeper on his stomach leading with his head. Two trains on the same track heading towards each other.

As the goalkeeper reached the ball, the striker reached the goalkeeper, both still moving inexorably forward. The impact of the attacker's knee meeting the defender's face could be heard by each of the thirty-four spectators still sitting in the stands. It was an irresistible force meeting an immovable object. The immovable object lost.

The attacker rose. The goalkeeper remained prostrate. The ambulance arrived seven minutes later to transport the unconscious man to the Yorkshire County College Hospital. Throughout that high-speed journey the paramedics bathed the injured man's face with ten litres of saline to remove bits of debris that were potential sources of infection that might prove life-threatening. The victim was ferried straight into the x-ray room to have x-rays and a CT scan and to have blood types matched.

When Nick saw the grey x-ray images on the computer monitor, even he retched. The man had suffered no less than eight fractured facial bones, some of these in several places. There was a box of cornflakes beneath the skin, which was turning darker by the moment as his face engorged with blood. He was struggling to breathe. What remained of the nose was embedded in the lower bone of the right eye socket, which was fractured in four places. The front six teeth had been re-located in a solid block a centimetre backward into the palate, and the lower jaw was hanging at a very odd angle. The poor man's face was a jigsaw box, with all the pieces somewhere inside, but lots more pieces than were there originally, and those pieces were not where they were supposed to be.

While the goalkeeper's stomach was being pumped (he was conscious and in excruciating pain), the surgical team assembled, scrubbed and ready. Nick called them together to discuss and plan their approach.

'OK guys, in surgical terms, this is a tsunami. There's already massive swelling and oedema causing blockage of the victim's airway. The anaesthetists will keep him alive, but we've got to make bloody damn sure *we* don't kill him.

'We will have to deal with poly-fractures, join those pieces of bone that can be joined and remove those fragments that can't. Where there has been excessive loss of bone our orthopaedic surgeon will have to recreate the framework with fine Kirschner wires and hope that the natural bone cells will do what they're supposed to do and reconstruct the lost bone so that we can remove the wires later.

'We will have to manage uncontrolled bleeding in a highly vascular region. So, nurses, you've got a big job. You have got to control the flow of blood to enable us to see what we will be intending to repair. What you do will be as important as what the surgeons are doing. This is the perfect storm, and each of you will have to be at your best and then some. We're going to be in close proximity to cranial nerves that can easily be permanently damaged, so we need to be very careful. This is landmine territory. But we can do it, ladies, guys, and we will.'

Fortunately - if one can use such a word in the context of this catastrophic accident - it was the striker's knee and not his grass-laced boot that had made contact, so although the impacting force was greater, there were few splits of skin to allow ingress of mud and grass. Nevertheless, the risk of infection was still very high. Despite his bravado, Nick knew there was a high probability that the patient would not survive. Still, he had not yet lost a patient on the operating table, and he really did not want this to be the first.

At 4:30pm, the operation began. It did not cease until the final suture was placed in position at 6am the following morning. Two maxillo-facial surgeons, two plastic reconstructive surgeons, an orthopaedic and an ear, nose and throat surgeon had interchanged throughout as required. Three teams of nurses had assisted. Nick, as team leader, had been present throughout, and not for a moment had he given thought to anything other than the job in hand. Not even the rugby.

Twelve titanium implants and eighteen metal strips that resembled flattened bicycle chains in miniature had been screwed into those pieces of bone to re-unite those bones that had not been crushed. Each of those metal strips required fixing with half a dozen screws – this was building a Meccano set on a live patient. Close on a hundred sutures. Fifteen litres of blood had to be transfused. Bleeding had been a problem throughout, gushing everywhere until Nick lost sight of his operating field, but through the skill of his nurses he was able to regain dominance. The nurses had performed magnificently, and Nick told them so. As the last instrument was being laid down, the patient's face, which had long turned purple, had to be swathed in iced bandages to limit the swelling. But he was breathing. The vital signs were there. They had kept him alive. They would keep him alive as long as infection, an ever-present risk, didn't kill him.

# Chapter 3

# A Woman's Illness   Ballarat 1985

When Nick returned to the staffroom, one of his assistant surgeons was keen to learn more about the man whose concentration had not waivered for a single moment of those fourteen hours. As they sat with the pot of steaming black coffee in front of them, Dr Sally Stubbs quietly commented, 'That was some performance in there!'

'Yeah, the team was brilliant. They all did their job, and I reckon our man is going to make it.'

'A team is only as good as its leader, and I have to say, you were amazing. You never seemed to lose control for a moment.'

'Thanks, Sally, but I can tell you there were times when I could see bugger all – the team was magnificent but i'm bloody exhausted now', mused Nick.

'Did you always want to be a surgeon, Nick?'

Nick contemplated for a moment, as he always did, before responding to the younger woman. He doubted Sally would remain awake for long, but she had asked the question.

'Nah, I wanted to play professional rugby when I was at school in Australia. I was sixteen when my mother took ill, and I guess that's what caused me to change my mind.'

He related how Gladys, always a healthy woman, had started to lose weight, and her energy with it. Her way was to shrug it off, but she was clearly deteriorating. His dad, Tommo, eventually insisted on calling the doctor.

'I can still remember how serious Dr Mason looked as he explained to us that she had a tumour growing in her womb. My first thought was, "womb" - what an old-fashioned word. Then the message sank in. My mother had cancer.'

Dr Mason said there was a chance it had spread. If it had, that would be very serious, but he hoped it had not yet progressed to any other part of her body. Only one thing was certain: she would need to go into hospital urgently.

'You can imagine how devastated we felt', said Nick wryly, 'we were certain she was going to die.'

Tommo had driven them to Ballarat General Hospital where she was immediately admitted and examined by the surgeon on duty. He confirmed that a lump (he called it a "mass") was indeed present, and it required urgent removal. There was no other option. The following morning the surgeon did what he had to do. Tommo and Nick sat in a small side room, each glad the other was there. As the hours ticked by, the tension became unbearable, but there was little conversation between the two. Idle chit-chat was not the Simpsons' way.

When the surgeon came out of the operating theatre some six hours later, he was smiling even though obviously exhausted. He was optimistic that they had caught the disease in time, saying 'I think we've removed all the cancerous tissue. I don't think it has spread and I'm really hopeful it won't recur.'

'That really impressed me', Nick told Sally. 'This man could stop people from dying. He had that power.'

Sally did not respond. Nick looked at her. She was still sitting, but so deeply asleep.

When Nick checked in on his patient later that day – he had granted himself five hours' sleep - the patient's face was still swathed in bandages, and he looked more like a mummy than a goalkeeper. Unlike other mummies, this one could breathe. He was alive. What was going on beneath the bandages would only be revealed in the coming weeks. The concern at that moment was to keep him breathing and the prevention of infection and sepsis. Careful as they were and would be, superbugs were an ever-worsening problem, and he did not want to abuse the prescription of just-in-case antibiotics.

Fortunately, the goalkeeper was young and fit and managed to avert that particular complication. Nevertheless, he remained in intensive care for three weeks, and in hospital for two months. During that period, he had many visits from friends and team-mates. The referee was not one of them.

Six months later, the metal plates that could be removed, were - the others had to be left in situ. Beware metal detectors at the airport, thought Nick. At the end of it all, although by no means as handsome as he had once been, the patient still had a face that still resembled a face, albeit very scarred and with a nose set at an odd angle. Nasal breathing was a problem. His right eye had lost significant vision. He still required two more operations, but he could not have been more grateful to the surgical team and their leader. He presented his laundered goalkeeper's jersey to Nick: *'Estou muito agredecido. Muito, muito obrigado, Doktor.* Me is much grateful.'

Nick had little doubt that the patient would survive. He was delighted that the goalkeeper was going to be able to get on with his life. Hopefully it would be a long one, although probably not in football.

With that one performance Nick Simpson had become legend to everyone in the hospital – to everyone else but not to himself. It had been the most demanding task he had ever undertaken but the operation itself had not meant much more to Nick than a job well done. Somehow Nick remained modest and his feet remained firmly rooted to the ground. The adulation of others was not what turned him on - he had always had it - but recreating order from chaos was always his spur.

At that moment, how could he possibly have anticipated the shitstorm that awaited him five years down the line?

# Chapter 4

## Ballarat  1975 - 1987

Gladys was more than a competent dressmaker and seamstress – she was an artist. In a different place and time, with her skill with needle and thread, she might have been able to match the best of surgeons. Who knew the subconscious influence that had on Nick? Farfetched? Perhaps.

Tommo, from the time he left school earlyish, had worked his way up to senior manager of the local supermarket.

They were salt-of-the-earth, decent, law-abiding, hard-working citizens, passionate supporters of everything Australian. They had already lost two children soon after birth, a boy to meningitis and a girl by cot death, but the third survived, and they doted on Nick. His early years were happy, carefree and (except for his mum's illness) untroubled.

He loved playing sport, especially rugby and cricket; as much as possible, all day and every day. He dreamed of playing one or other (or preferably both) for Australia, but that was true for all other Australian boys – they were all sport-crazy.

Ballarat was a growing town and the newish suburb where they lived in their semi-detached bungalow was full of young kids. Nick and his mates would never miss an opportunity to get a game going in the nearby park, never short of guys to make up two teams of whooping ten-year-olds. Nick was always captain of one because he was without argument the most natural sportsman and leader out there, and most of the guys wanted to be in his side. Even then, he displayed something that was a bellwether of the type of person he would become – when it was his turn to choose a player for his team, he would always choose the least talented kid first.

Nick didn't have to be competitive – it was for the rest to compete with him. He never made any other boy feel inferior, and just got on with being a normal kid in a group of normal kids. The one word that always appeared on his school reports was "well-balanced."

Where he differed from the other boys was that once he got back indoors, all sweaty and smelly, he would shower and then knuckle down to get his homework done. He actually enjoyed doing it, whereas for most of the other boys it was a chore often left uncompleted. He was quick to take advantage of the public library and could often be seen cycling there to look for material for one of his history or geography projects. His efforts were reflected by very good grades. This bode well for the future, although he gave little thought to what that might be.

Nick never stressed his parents, nor did they bother him or each other in any way. Their relationship was one of a family at ease. His parents were not by nature loquacious, so the art of conversation was an art unlearned and underpractised in the Simpson household. The evenings were not generally given to idle chatter, with first radio, later telly filling the hours before sleep. Nick read voraciously, and particularly loved the burgeoning school of Australian writers of whom Peter Carey later became his favourite. As a consequence of all of this, Nick acquired not only the tendency to listen rather than speak, but possessed of a sound general knowledge.

At senior school, Nick played the more popular Australian Rules football, and showed prowess as a speedy defender. His strong physique allowed him to tackle fearlessly, and his name was always the first to be added to the team selection list.

He enjoyed most of his school subjects, but although he found the logic of Latin constructions moderately stimulating, he found the Latin tribes tedious. He stuck at it for one reason only, and that was his Latin teacher, Dr Thomas, an Italian woman who called herself Dottore Tomasso. She had researched her PhD in "Italian Football Culture", which she loved to tell everyone was a contradiction in terms. She was a woman of the world. Dr Thomas smoked endless rounds of unfiltered cigarettes, and whereas Nick generally found the smell unbearable on others, on Dotttore Tomasso he found the aroma alluring. She kept telling Nick that if he was unable to imbibe the culture of Europe (and Italy in particular) he would spend his whole life being a BORE.

'Why am I a bore, Dottore Thomasso?'

'Have you ever read Oscar Wilde? Obviously not, but you should. He wrote, *'A bore is someone who deprives you of solitude without providing you with company.'* Are you good company, Simpson? Do you need to up your game, maybe read more?'

Nick went home feeling pretty dejected. Who the fuck was Oscar Wilde?

This conversation sowed a seed in his mind that would bug him for years but would bear fruit later in his life.

At a parents' evening, the headmaster approached Tommo and Gladys. 'Good lad you've got there, Mr and Mrs Simpson! He's got an exceptional brain and doesn't let sport get in the way. Doctor Thomas reckons he's super-bright. Nick is not driven to achieve more than others - he just seems to do so anyway.'

Despite the pride welling inside her, Gladys looked concerned. 'Yeah, Mr Tompkins, that's nice to hear, but isn't there the risk they'll think he's a smart-arse?'

'Clever kids are not always popular, but he never seems to rile the other kids, they just let him be. We were concerned that his classmates might be jealous that everything seems to come so easily to him, but that has not been the case. It seems no one has a bad word to say about him. Also, there's something the other teachers have noticed – Nick's always ready to help the other children who have learning difficulties.'

The parents beamed. They positively glowed. The headmaster continued: 'By the way, we're thinking of putting him up to train with the senior footies squad.'

Tommo was sceptical. 'Mate, they're two years older than Nick – he'll get murdered!'

'We don't think so, Mr Simpson. He's fast on his feet and a quick thinker – he'll know how to protect himself. Oh, by the way, I'm glad he got over his stomach bug quickly and only missed the one day of school. I appreciated the note you sent, Mrs Simpson. Anyway, I must go and chat to the Johnsons, or they'll say you're hogging all my time. Thanks for attending tonight.'

As he reached the Johnsons, Gladys and Tommo looked at one another. 'What was that about, Glad?'

'Search me, Tommo. I didn't write anything.'

When they returned home, they confronted Nick. 'Explain yourself, son. Have you been bunking off and forging notes?'

Nick did not even think of denying it.

'Jason and I decided that the weather was so perfect we should go for a swim in the lake. Then we rode out to old Horgan's orchard and picked some peaches. They were literally falling to the ground there were so many. He wouldn't have minded. Not like we were stealing or anything, Dad.'

'It's *exactly* like you were stealing. Not only that but you bloody forged a letter from Mum. If Mr Tompkins had been less gullible, mate, you would have been right up shit creek without a paddle, because we wouldn't have been willing to support your ridiculous story.'

'I'm really sorry, Dad, I won't repeat it.'

'You're bloody damn right you won't or I'll report you to him myself and you can forget about training with the seniors. Do I make myself clear?'

Nick could but nod. It was very rare to see Tommo riled up, but Nick knew he had crossed a red line.

As predicted by his headmaster, Nick survived his promotion to the seniors intact, and cemented his place in the senior team.

Nick was comfortable with his mates, and as he grew into his early teens, with girls as well. He preferred to be one of the crowd rather than committing to any girl in particular, although chances were he could have paired off with anyone he chose. He never had to break up with a girl, simply because he never 'went steady'. At the Saturday night parties, he really enjoyed dancing, but would rarely spend the evening with one individual. He did not seem highly motivated by sex, and getting off with one of his numerous girl-friends was less interesting to him than enjoying the company of the crowd. The loss of innocence seemed to apply more slowly to Nick than to his mates. He was more desired than desirous. Yet, for all that, he was never unhappy to be on his own. Well-balanced.

When his mates - all offspring of working-class parents - spoke about the future at all, it would be about training for a trade like plumbing or getting a job as a builder. Going onto a sheep ranch was another option, or they could follow whatever their fathers were doing. Following Tommo to Westins had never appealed to Nick. He was not particularly ambitious or aspirational at that time, but he knew he had the ability to seek greater challenges than had been available to his father, greater than his mates were contemplating. He had little idea what those challenges might be until the hospital experience determined the course of his life.

Surprisingly, it was the first time Nick had ever been into a hospital, - they had always been an exceptionally healthy and hardy Australian family. Others seemed to get ill, but not these three Simpsons.

The place was spotlessly clean. You could have eaten your lunch straight off the floors. The nurses in their immaculate white uniforms moved about quickly and assuredly, wielding a variety of silver instruments that gleamed in the sunshine. The nurses seemed to be extremely respectful of the doctors, sometimes almost in awe, eager to carry out every instruction given *(this was the mid-eighties after all!)* The doctors wore white coats that were starched and crisp. The ever-present stethoscopes around their necks were amulets to ward off the evil spirits and were also symbols of power. They spoke with confidence of diseases about which mere mortals knew nothing. The aura they exuded was one of invincibility. What made the deepest impression on Nick were the looks on the doctors' faces: serious, purposeful, always in control.

So, Nick decided he would become a surgeon. Simple....

And that was the thing about Nick – if he liked and wanted something, all that was required then to do was whatever it took to become a doctor and after that, a surgeon. That it would take him ten years to get there was no reason to hesitate.

He recalled going to discuss his future with his parents.

'I've been considering what I should do when I leave school.'

Tommo smiled contently - in his mind it had long been mapped out. This would be a short conversation, as it usually was unless they were discussing cricket or footies.

'Well, Nick, glad you brought that up. I was reckoning that you'd follow me into Westins. I've spoken to the owner of the supermarket, and I know they'd be bloody happy to have you – they're looking for good young managers.'

Nick got straight to the point. 'Not for me, Dad. What would you think about me becoming a doctor?'

You'd think Tommo would have leapt off his chair with joy, but he looked more than a tad crestfallen. No one in his family had ever been to university, let alone medical school. Good white-collar working-class stock, yeah, but going for a profession? Beyond his capacity to comprehend, but Tommo knew his son. 'If that's what you want do, mate, that's ok with me!'

'I appreciate that, Dad. And don't worry about the cost, because Mr Tompkins reckons I'll be able to get a bursary. He's very pleased with my decision, by the way.'

Gladys simply beamed. 'Imagine that, Tommo - our own doctor!' Her son, her very own boy, her only child, would be not just the first doctor but the first professional in their family, a family that had been in Ballarat for nearly two hundred years.

The last year of school began. Most of the boys and girls in Nick's class were excitedly making their plans and looking forward to a gap year or two in England and Europe. Many of them had never been out of their state of Victoria, let alone Australia, and this was going to be the time for growing up and having a bloody good time. His buddy Jason approached Nick.

'Hey, mate, I wanted to get to you first, how's about we put together a group of guys and start saving to buy a Combi when we hit London? We can do building site work, no problem - good money. We might even get to like their piss-tasting beer, and their dollybirds apparently like us Aussies. I hear they fuck like rabbits. Then we head for Spain. Torremolinos is the scene – you get high there just breathing! After that, it's Ibiza, party-time. Then St Tropez. Think about those topless French chicks, mate - just the thought gives me a hard-on!'

But Nick wasn't thinking parties and pot and nubile females. Unlike his mates, he was not about to do the England and Europe VW Combi/ working on building site/ Foster's beer-and-parties rites-of-passage experience – that scene would have to wait or be forgotten. His response was unequivocal. 'No, sorry, Jayso, I've got plans to study medicine and I wanna get on with it.'

Jason stared at him blankly. The leader of the pack not joining his mates? Medicine?! What the fuck!! Jason said nothing, for there was no point. He knew that once Nick made up his mind to do something, that was it - no mind changes, no turning. That single-minded determination was what had made him top dog.

Supported by glowing testimonials from his headmaster and Dottore Tomasso, Nick applied for a scholarship to study at Sydney Medical School. Even Tommo exploded with pride when the letter arrived informing Nick that the scholarship had been granted. A new chapter was about to begin.

# Chapter 5

## Sydney 1988 - 1994

Moving from Ballarat to Sydney proved an exciting step. Sydney was different to Melbourne and certainly to Ballarat - faster, more aggressive, more competitive. It had an energy about it that was clearly a gear or two higher than the laid-back towns of Victoria. Nick was unfazed by this and took to life in residence with great brio, thoroughly enjoying the experience of being away from home and independent of his parents for the first time.

Although his departure left a void in their lives that could not be filled, the pride his folks took in his achievement provided some degree of compensation. At least he kept in touch and wrote regularly.

When he got to Sydney, he made the decision to switch from Aussie Rules football to rugby union, and once again he established himself without excessive effort. To his regret, there was little time anyway to develop his prowess as a sportsman. His career in rugby came to a grinding halt when he suffered a cruciate knee ligament injury, and that was that. He was disappointed but philosophical. Nevertheless, he took every opportunity he could to go and watch his medical colleagues and especially his national team. as the knee recovered, he turned to tennis and then, when it was strong enough, to squash. To his surprise, being in charge of himself only and not reliant on the efforts of a team where you were only as good as your weakest link seemed to suit his personality perfectly well. He was able to turn adversity into opportunity and quickly became very competitive at his new sport.

The early years of study were extremely demanding. If a student was going to fail at medical school, the complex subjects of anatomy, physiology and pathology would be most likely to bring one down. Nick took these at a canter, by no means an easy thing to do given the sheer volume of facts that were required to become etched into one's mind.

Nick proved adept in dissecting the female cadaver in whose company he spent an entire year. He and his three colleagues named her Lola – 'she was a showgirl.' Medical students rarely forget their first encounter with a sanitized, preserved human body lying on a stainless-steel table covered in a formaldehyde-soaked drape, just one of many in a room crammed with corpses. The stench of formalin filled his sinuses at first but after a while seemed less noticeable until it became normality. As the weeks passed, the students became less queasy until they had no problem eating their sandwiches as they pored over their manual looking to see where the next incision had to be made. Then it was just a case of you vs. the dead body. For many students the dead body won, but not with Nick.

Each of the six hundred preserved muscles was carefully teased aside ("reflected" was the technical term, but it was more like an unzipping) to reveal the nerves and blood vessels that ran beneath; every organ was precisely elevated and displayed, every bone (two hundred plus) bared. A budding surgeon was evident. When a fellow student struggled to achieve the same degree of skill, Nick was never unhappy when asked to lend a hand and he became the go-to person if you wanted to see a neatly dissected kidney or radial artery or heart or psoas muscle.

To Nick, who from a practical viewpoint was in no way religious, seeing how intricate and miraculous the human body was in all its form and functions was a transcendent experience.

Nick was blessed with a very retentive memory, able to recall the multitude of information hurled at him about the attachment of each of those six hundred muscles, the names of every bone, the hormones each gland secreted and their chemical composition and function; what each organ looked like when you examined slides under a microscope. He had an ability to break complex issues down into digestible chunks, and this served him well in his exams.

When Nick moved on to the clinical years, he found being in the wards far more interesting, and proved an able diagnostician; but what really got his energy and enthusiasm flowing was observing or assisting in theatre, which more often than not he did voluntarily. He appeared to have endless stamina and concentration and seemed to require little sleep. He so enjoyed the rarefied atmosphere of the operating theatre. With no view of the external environment, it was a world apart, a cocoon of drama where the stage was an operating table and the actors doctors and nurses. The props were operating beds, surgical lights, ventilators, and a variety of silverware laid out on a table covered in green towels. The surgeons, whom he observed and was then allowed to assist, were surprised by his manual dexterity.

The prestige of being a medical student afforded ample opportunity although little time for enjoying numerous unserious relationships with trainee hospital nurses, and gradually he became known for reasons other than his agile brain. There was more than one young lady who would cheerfully have considered a more serious involvement than just a roll in the hay with this gifted and handsome man. Nick was not for the taking.

He was much amused when from a distance he overheard a conversation between two young nurses, one of whom he recognised. They were speaking softly, but loud enough for their voices to carry.

'You know what? I reckon Nick Simpson could be a poofter.'

'Why d'you say that?'

'He just doesn't seem that interested in us. At least not like the rest of those randy dickheads.'

'Well, I can tell you absolutely 100% he is not.'

'Really? Personal experience, or you've heard?'

'Personal. Very personal.'

'Wow, you're the quiet one! Is he hot?'

Nick saw the familiar face smile. 'Babe, that's for me to remember and you to find out – if you're lucky! I'd be very happy to make it a regular event, but that man is so into his work! Committed about surgery, totally commitment-phobic with women.'

Nick enjoyed the parties at nurses' residence, and although generally casual in dress, he took pride in dressing up for Medical Ball when that annual event came round. His few leisure hours were taken up with squash, surfing and barbies on Bondi or Coogee beach, or a day up in the Blue Mountains and even an occasional concert or opera at the iconic building at the harbour - he was trying very hard to broaden his horizons and not be a BORE. But he never deviated from his mission, which was to pass (and pass well) each exam at the first time of trying.

Once again, he sailed through with first-class exam results. That he ended up being top student each year was no surprise. Nor did any of his college mates complain when in final year he was awarded the gold medal for achievement in surgery. This had his parents bursting with pride, and the medal took centre place on their mantelpiece. They thought back wryly to his short-lived abortive experience at attempting to learn the piano. It ended after two lessons when his boring teacher (who smelt of mothballs and cigarettes, not a good mix) told them that he would be better off choosing an activity that didn't involve the use of hands.....

A bore? Don't use your hands??

Nick set about seeking opportunities for the specialism he had chosen. The references he received from Sydney Medical School led to another scholarship offer, this time from University College Hospital in London. Now, at last, he was ready to go abroad. So, seven years after Jaso and the boys had drunk their way around the pubs of London, that was where Dr Nick Simpson would be heading.

The end of the academic year in Australia (December) and the commencement of the English one (September) differ by roughly nine months, so Nick decided to spend six of those doing a locum general surgery stint at the hospital in Ballarat. He was happy to be able to spend decent time with his parents, but unsurprisingly found little in common with his former school friends who, if they had not resented him previously, now seemed to do just that. As his parents had feared, he had become a tall poppy, and tall poppies in Australia were there to be cut down to size.

At the end of June, Nick once more said farewell to his parents, even more difficult the second time because he knew and they knew it would be a long while before they would be together again.

# Chapter 6

## Post-grad London 1995

Nick arrived in London to be greeted by an unusually glorious summer. He found comfortable if cramped lodgings on the east side of Regent's Park, close enough to walk to UCH, also close enough to the park to go for his early morning jog. His small bedsit would be barely big enough to house the library of fiction and technical books he was to acquire, that would account for more of his income than he could afford but he would spend it anyway.

He spent his first four weeks exploring the parks and historic buildings in and around London, the pubs and narrow lanes of Dickens - places he had read about in books borrowed from Ballarat library.

He frequented the theatres in the evenings, and never ceased to be surprised when it was still light as he emerged on a summer's night after a stimulating play. And then of course there was the open-air theatre in Regents Park - a short walk away - which that year featured Shakespeare's Richard III. Little did Nick know that the story of the Machiavellian rise to power and subsequent short reign of King Richard was a grim portent of his own future career.

He took a train to Aviemore in Scotland, hired a car and explored the lochs and hiked the mountain trails. The sun continued to shine and he loved the lengthy days. From there to Edinburgh and heady dips into the arts festival between the showers. The time passed quickly, but he could not wait to commence his postgraduate programme.

University College Hospital had been re-sited in a huge new chrome and green-panelled facility that displeased the architectural fraternity, who awarded it the 'Carbuncle of the Year' prize. Nevertheless, the doctors appreciated the state-of-the-art equipment.

At first while at UCH Nick tended to keep a rather low profile academically. He would be quite happy to listen to the opinions of others but, unusually for an Aussie, did not often venture his own, preferring to let his hands do his talking. Most of his colleagues were extremely well spoken, many from elite public schools, so when he did chat, he found himself mellowing his antipodean accent. He was by no means ashamed of his humble background, but he realised it was hardly likely to be advantageous to his career. He thought of the words of George Bernard Shaw: *"The reasonable man adapts himself to the world; the unreasonable one persists to adapt the world to himself."*

After the first year, his attitude changed somewhat. He decided that if his colleagues liked and respected him as he was, that was fine, and if they did not, that too was fine. He learned quickly that whereas at home he had tried not to stand out more than was absolutely necessary, here in the UK it was no great advantage to be the small poppy. He neither sought approval nor played down his talents. Well-balanced. Did his colleagues like it? Hmm...

Nick was never short of company when he wished it, and he was a regular figure at medical social events. Australian nurses were exchanged for British and others from countries further afield, but none could claim sole propriety rights. He was happy to keep it that way.

He took pleasure in enjoying the limitless cultural life of London, always on his own. When time allowed, he swopped the operating theatre for the one that had a stage, usually picking up a single ticket at the last minute. He even stood in the rain outside the Royal Opera House in Covent Garden and scored a returned ticket to hear and see Lucia di Lammermoor, which would forever remain his favourite. This was certainly not the only opera he saw, and he developed a particular liking for the Italians Verdi, Puccini and Donizetti *(if you could see me now, Dottore!)* He was never to lose that passion for opera and promised himself that one day soon he would visit Italy. He kept that promise but later than he had hoped, and not in the circumstances he would have chosen.

Nick found the quality of teaching to be high but not daunting. Over the three years he proved once again that he not only had a talent for imbibing knowledge but also great skills with a scalpel that in his supple hands became a paintbrush - no line too fine to draw, to be made to blend imperceptibly with its surroundings.

Facial reconstruction in particular interested him. It was one of the few types of surgery where the end-product was always visible, not like cardiac or gall bladder repair that were always internal. So it was in that area of specialty that he devoted his time and energy, and he found himself in the company not only of doctors but dental surgeons as well, most of whom were looking to specialise as maxillo-facial surgeons, maxilla being the technical term for the upper jaw. Their scope of operation did however extend well beyond the upper jaw. For Nick, everything above the neck with the exception of the brain was his fertile field.

One type of operation that he frequently found himself carrying out when he was studying in Sydney was the removal and repair of basal cell carcinomas, commonly known as BCCs or rodent ulcers. BCC is a form of skin cancer that arises in the lining of the skin's top layer, the epidermis. It was a common precursor of skin cancer, often associated with frequent or prolonged sun exposure.

More than 4 million cases of BCC were diagnosed each year in the U.S. alone. If there was anything good one could say about BCC, it was that most cases were manageable, a slow-growing cancer that seldom spread. Also helpful, BCCs usually occurred on the skin where they could readily be seen. BCCs can vary greatly in appearance but people often first become aware of them as a new lump on the skin that may or may not have tiny red blood vessels running across it, or as a scab that bleeds and does not heal completely, or as a small crater. Most BCCs are painless but can feel itchy and often bleed.

If left untreated, BCCs can eventually cause an ulcer, hence its better-known name "rodent ulcer." Surgical removal is an effective treatment, and the first thing that Nick learned back in Sydney was that excision was dependent on size. A small ulcer presented little challenge to a surgeon and could literally be scooped out and left to heal uneventfully, but it was the more advanced lesions that required special techniques for removal and reconstruction by facial plastic surgery. A botched job could easily leave someone permanently disfigured.

One of the first cases that Nick had to treat was Jen, a dancing instructor and former surfer from Byron Bay in Queensland. Jen had spent many hours on her board in the sun and had not always been liberal with nose-protective sunscreen. After a particularly nasty wipe-out, she decided to trade in her surfboard for dance shoes and travelled to Barcelona and then to London. Some years later she qualified as a Latin dance instructor and acquired a position in a chic dance school in the heart of London's fashionable Mayfair. Soon after her forty-fifth birthday, she could hardly miss an unpleasant-looking ulcer on the side of her left nostril which she had ignored in the hope it would disappear. It didn't. Her GP referred her to UCH where Jen came under the care of the expat surgeon from Sydney.

Nick carried out a small biopsy - the presence of a quite advanced but benign BCC was noted. Nick was relieved because it could have been a malignant *squamous* cell carcinoma that was fast growing and very invasive. Nevertheless, surgical removal was the only option.

Placing stitches in the skin around the nose can sometimes distort features by forming unaesthetic or rank ugly scars or pulling the eyelid down causing a lopsided appearance. To avoid this, it is often necessary to borrow some skin from somewhere else, for example the cheek. This was usually adjacent skin which has more 'give'. The loaned tissue is partly detached and swung into the gap but stays joined to its blood supply. This is called a local flap. The site from which a local flap is chosen depends upon where there is spare skin, and the colour, shape and position of this is chosen to minimise distortion and to hide the scars in natural skin creases where possible.

Doing this type of operation was relatively easy – doing it *well* required extreme skill and dexterity.

In Jen's case, the BCC was large, about 6mm in diameter. Nick and his surgery team offered Jen a solution. First, she'd undergo surgery to remove the large basal cell carcinoma under local anaesthesia. Immediately afterwards, he would repair Jen's nose in the first of two stages. The first stage would be a flap procedure under general anaesthetic, surgically moving a section of living tissue from Jen's skin beneath her eye to cover the opening left after the cancer was removed. Then, once the flap had taken hold, he would rebuild Jen's nose, using his skill to maintain its form and function. Jen felt very comfortable in Nick's care and having been given full information of what would occur and what might possibly go wrong, she agreed to proceed.

The two-stage operation took place uneventfully, and despite a fair amount of bleeding, swelling and bruising,

## THE ROAD TO PERDITION  CHAPTER 6

Jen's nose healed beautifully. When Jen presented a month later the swelling had gone down considerably. Nick asked Jen to relate what she had experienced since the operation. He would never forget her graphic description.

'It was really weird, Doc. I had hardly any pain, in fact quite the opposite. The skin on the flap went as numb and rubbery and white as a piece of calamari. I thought maybe the blood supply hadn't re-connected, you mentioned that as a possible risk. But then, after about five days, the dancing spiders arrived.'

'Dancing spiders?'

Well, that's what it felt like anyway. First in were the rumba spiders, Gentle as can be, they began to dance across the flap, and if just felt weirdly itchy. You can imagine those thin legs and tiny little feet in their tiny shoes. Then they were replaced by the cha-cha spiders, lots of movement, intense passion. Of course, I couldn't scratch, and it was driving me fucking demented. Finally, the salsa spiders pitched up, practically jiving on my nose. And then they pushed off, and took the calamari numbness with them, but I still feel the tingling, which is a relief given how wooden the area in general feels. What was all that about, Doc?'

Nick could but smile. Only an Aussie ex-surfing dance teacher could be so descriptive. 'Quite simple really, Jen. You were feeling the tiny little nerves in the areas that were knocked out by the skin transplant which were slowly reconnecting. They will continue to do so for another year until the scar tissue disappears. By the then the woodenness will also have disappeared and colour fully returned.'

'Do you mean I'm going to be bloody Pinocchio for an entire year?'

'If you're lucky....'

Jen did succeed in planting a tiny seed in Nick's brain, and he did consider enrolling for dance lessons, but the pressure of his course soon overwhelmed everything.

Nick found the quality of teaching to be high but not daunting. Aside from learning advanced surgery techniques, he made it his business to sit in with the maxilla-facial dental surgeons to learn the skills of wisdom teeth removal and the repair of cleft lips and palates. When the defect was too large to repair with bodily tissue and bone, it had to be replaced by a prosthesis. He was fortunate to find on the staff a brilliant dental prosthesis technician, from whom he learned innovative methods of repairing body defects using prosthetic materials such as acrylic and latex. These skills would one day prove very useful to him, but he was not to know this then.

He decided to write his doctoral thesis on tumours of the parotid gland. This gland that we all have in our cheeks is responsible for providing much of our saliva. Occasionally the little tube exiting from our cheeks, which you can just feel with the tip of your tongue, would become blocked. Remedying this was not difficult unless the thing causing the blockage was a tumour. Surgery on the parotid gland would have been relatively easy, except for the fact that the facial nerve and two important facial blood vessels pass through it, and unfortunately parotid tumours have the tendency to envelop themselves around the big nerve and blood vessels. The tumour would then have to be oh so carefully dissected away from the nerve and vessels without damaging either, by no means an easy task.

Damaging the facial nerve could result in transient and even permanent facial palsy, which was psychologically if not physically disastrous, not to mention the potential for accusations of surgical negligence. Removal of the parotid gland could cause hollowing of the cheeks. Other problems might include numbness of the lower lip, drooling, drooping of the eyelid and numbness around the ear. This was jungle territory. One did not want to mess up.

With that in mind, Nick set out to develop a surgical technique that minimised risk, caused least damage to the face and brought about acceptable function and aesthetics. He proved to be very proficient at this specialised type of 'niche' surgery and documented his technique with precision and care. On completion, his dissertation received the praise it deserved, and he was awarded his masters degree *cum laude* and another gold medal that was soon on its way to Ballarat.

He had proved once again that he not only had a talent for imbibing knowledge but also great skills within his supple fingers - no line too fine to draw, to blend imperceptibly with its surroundings. His specialisation in facial surgery had been achieved painlessly (for him at any rate) and honourably.

Nick was happy to continue for a period on the staff at UCH while he considered his options. That was until he went up to Leeds.

# Chapter 7

## Meeting his Match   Leeds 1999

Nick had travelled north to compete in the inter-county squash championship held that year in Leeds. He played to the peak of his ability, just managing to overcome a skilful and tricky opponent in the final. As he walked onto the club veranda where he was soon to be awarded a trophy, he noticed the attractive woman wearing large sunglasses sitting there in the setting sun. He had earlier watched her win the ladies final, and she looked an outstanding player who might well have been able to give him a very good game. He made his way slowly towards her and when he reached the table, he paused and said in a quiet voice, 'Are you alone?'

She looked at him through her large sunglasses, weighing her options, before responding. 'I am, although I may not be for very long because my Significant Other has arranged to meet me here in just a few minutes.'

'The story of my life, there's always a significant other...... May I keep you company in the meantime, till he or she comes along?'

She gave him a smile that made his entire body tingle, that made him feel as if a gentle pianist was playing sonatas in his brain and centipedes were doing the cha-cha on his spine. *(Thanks, Jen!)*

'Feel free! Do you always approach strange women sitting alone?'

'Only the ones who look interesting.'
"My lucky day, then. Please join me!'
'Why, are you broken?'
Corny as it was, she laughed.

He sensed she was ready for a different type of gameplay, something he had found advantageous as an undergrad in Sydney. He smiled at her. 'My name, by the way, is.. er... um... GianLuca.'

'What a lovely name! Are you Italian?'

'Australian, actually, but I am named for my maternal grandfather who came from near Sienna.'

'What a coincidence! My grandmother came from Pisa! I am named after her – er, Alessandra.'

'Very pleased to meet you, Alexandria.'

'Alessandra.'

'Alessandra, of course it is. Funny we should meet in Leeds of all places!'

Another more than generous smile, white teeth gleaming in the late afternoon sun.

'Do you believe in serendipity, Alessandra?'

'Absolutely, GianLuca, all the time!'

He felt his throat grow dry as he looked into the large lenses of her sunglasses – this woman was quite something. 'Are you sure your S.O. won't be upset when he or she finds me sitting with you?'

'No, he's very generous that way. Actually, she is.'

Damn, thought Nick, a guy he could compete with...

Then she said, 'Actually I am lying, she isn't ...'

'Isn't generous that way?'

'No, just isn't. Doesn't. Exist. Doesn't exist. I'm here alone – no significant other, *Da solo,* as my maternal grandfather used to say.'

'Alone? How fortunate!'

He saw her book on the table. 'What are you reading, Alessandra?'

'A novella about unrequited love.'

'I hope that will not be our experience.'

'Are you not jumping the gun, GianLuca? – we've only just met!'

'Yes, but life is too short for people of our age to waste on idle chitchat – let's cut to the chase, as the British like to say!'

'To the chase we will indeed cut, GianLuca! As men go, you are not bad looking and you appear to have a fertile imagination– I could get to like that. '

Nick's spirits soared. 'Do you believe in love at first sight?'

'I believe in love at *every* sight. One should always be in love, all the time.'

'How romantic!! Do you believe in passion?'

'Passionately!'

'Do you believe in lust, Allesandra?'

'Lasciviously,' said Alessandra in her armada-launching voice.

Nick, who rarely had much to say, now let loose all his feelings for the dramatic. 'We are so compatible! Our stars must be aligned in total congruence! As Shakespeare said, *'there's a tide in the affairs of men, when taken at the flood leads on to fortune.'* This could be the start of something big! Massive!! …. Let's away!'

(When he thought about this conversation later, he cringed.)

Just at that moment, a young woman in front of them rose, came over to their table and said, 'Hi, Allison or is it Alessandra, do you always play those games with a man you've only just met?' The wink she gave Allison left no doubt that she approved.

Allison and Nick danced together at the party that followed the prize-giving, and both were aware that something very special had occurred and that their stars were indeed about to be aligned.

Allison had developed a thriving law practice in the centre of Leeds. She was born in Yorkshire, the only child of aspirational parents. At school she too was known to be aspiring and ambitious, excellent at netball and tennis, popular and unpopular in equal measure, neither of which bothered her. After attaining excellent A-levels, she'd gone on to study law at Liverpool University. There, she'd had her share of boyfriends, but no relationships lasted; from her part because of boredom, from theirs because although physically somewhat unmotivated, she could be quite overpowering in other spheres. She was an ardent follower of Margaret Thatcher, which did not endear her to many of her Liverpudlian socialist classmates, especially so because being Leeds born and bred, she loathed Liverpool Football Club.

She decided to write her dissertation on '*Important Women in Law*' and chose to highlight women whom she found admirable for their courageous achievements and intellect. They included Ruth Bader Ginsberg, who rose to become an Associate Justice of the US Supreme Court; also the Canadian Louise Arbour, the UN High Commissioner who was Chief Prosecutor in the criminal tribunals for Yugoslavia and Rwanda. Allison was an admirer of Helena Normanton, who became the first female barrister in the UK. Rose Heilbron, who had preceded Allison at Liverpool Uni became the first woman to lead in a murder case in the infamous 'Cameo Trial', and the first woman to be appointed King's Counsel. Allison decided to complete her quintet with someone whose political principles were far removed from her own: the socialist Ruth Hayman, an anti-apartheid campaigner in South Africa who was placed under house arrest for her activism (she had defended the parents of Peter Hain), but was allowed to leave for the UK where she established a school for teaching English as a second language to people not born in the UK, and was lauded and honoured for that.

When Allison returned to Leeds with a law degree in her satchel, she initially worked as an Associate in a middling-sized practice but found her colleagues either stuffy and pretentious or downright boring, and most were both. So, after three years, she decided to take the plunge and set up on her own as a commercial lawyer. It wasn't long before she acquired a reputation as a no-nonsense negotiator and became as busy as she wished to be, but not so busy that she could not devote time to a different type of court, where she proved to be as competent at squash as she was at law.

Allison was tall, raven-haired and slim, and few women looked as lithe as she on a squash court or, as Nick was later to observe, in a bedroom. He and Allison had much in common, both taciturn but earnest, both driven by their careers and their sport. For the first time in his life, Nick found himself caring intensely about one particular woman. She too was much taken by this confident, outgoing and quite cultured colonial.

He began to travel regularly by train to Leeds on weekends when he wasn't on duty. Immediately after qualifying as a specialist facial surgeon, Nick applied to a number of hospitals in Yorkshire, this despite a plethora of offers to join private practices in London's prestigious Harley and Wimpole Streets. His first post was at a small hospital unit near Leeds, and he found himself in a part of verdant England that could not have been more different to the arid countryside in Victoria where he had grown up. The weather was testing, but when your working environment is entirely within the windowless room that is an operating theatre, this did not seem to matter too much. He distinguished himself not only by his surgical skills but his willingness to do any job that was asked of him, so it was no surprise to anyone when he was promoted to head the surgical department at this hospital.

Allison was particularly thrilled because the possibilities this offered for both of them was limitless.

Although Allison could be delightfully pleasant, as he had discovered that night on the veranda, she was not by nature a warm person, and when dealing with opposition lawyers, the 'not warm' became icy cold. If Nick had spent any time at her office, he might have seen her other face and hesitated, for Allison was formidable and totally driven by the task to be completed rather than the feelings of anyone involved in the process. "Kind" was not a word that anyone who dealt with her would ever have used to describe the ambitious, uncompromising and uncompassionate solicitor.

As with Nick, outcome was everything. For all that, she never deviated from established principles of law, and ensured she could never be accused of shady or underhand practise; she had nothing but scorn for those colleagues who were so inclined. She could spot sharp dealers from a distance and fought them ruthlessly. If you wanted a result, you went to Allison; if you wanted nice, you went to someone else.

Allison's parents were both professionals, dad an accountant and her mother a lecturer in psychology. They did like Nick a great deal, even if he was a tad too profession-orientated in his banter. Nick wasn't a chatty sort of guy, indeed rather reserved. At times he seemed almost aloof, but that was Nick - when he did say something it was usually sensible and rarely nasty. He seemed a man without malice and utterly confident within his own skin. He was always respectful of them and their adored daughter, who, like Nick, was an only child.

Nick received an offer to join the most respected private practice in Leeds that might have tempted someone with a greater commercial sense of priorities, but that was not what Nick was about. Financial remuneration did not figure high on his scale of values, if at all. He worked for his patients' wellbeing and his own satisfaction. He turned it down with ne'er a second thought. Allison's parents were a little disappointed but accepted Nick's decision, wondering only how long it would be before they committed fully in their relationship. Neither Allison nor Nick was in any hurry, so absorbed were they in their individual careers.

Over the next couple of years Nick competently but unobtrusively cemented his reputation as a facial surgeon and was happy for the opportunity to pass his knowledge and experience on to the medical students. In the ten years since he had studied in Sydney, teaching had changed. There was more reliance on 3-D models and computer-generated simulation and less on cadavers, which were in short supply. Nick felt that from the viewpoint of surgical training, something valuable was being lost.

Much of the work he carried out was routine, but from time to time he performed a tricky piece of complex surgery that left those who assisted him awe-struck. Although easy going and affable when at leisure, the operating theatre was his domain, and he reigned supreme. Watching him in action was art and harmony manifest. Every performance was carried out with total focus, consummate skill and perfect precision. The operation and its outcome were everything, and woe betide any nurse, assistant surgeon, anaesthetist or student who fell below his exacting standards. His credo was, 'If you don't perform perfectly, you will end up performing badly.' Most of his colleagues were happy to settle for 90%, and even to attain that level was hard work.

One case he would remember was a middle-aged gentleman who presented with a hard swelling of his inner cheek that, being a high-powered businessman, he had ignored. At the time he had become aware of what was initially a soft lump, David McKealy had been involved in a high-profile purchase of a block of successful health clubs in West Yorkshire. David was keen to effect a takeover of these clubs that would double the number of gyms that he already owned and at the same time eliminate his most serious opposition. The negotiations, as one would expect from hard-dealing men of coal miner stock who had made their own way in life, were protracted and were dragging on interminably.

Because of this intense activity, the growth in his cheek was ignored. A small and completely painless lump was not going to get in the way of a deal that David hoped would provide the pathway that he hoped would end with the takeover of the once mighty Leeds United football club. He had supported United since a child, but the club was now far from its glory days and struggling for promotion to the Premiership from where it had been relegated too many years ago.

So David ignored the soft lump till it became a hard mass that he found himself chewing and that was beginning to ulcerate and become painful. Eventually the penny dropped. Although he could have afforded the best of private treatment, he had great faith in the National Health Service. He presented himself at the small hospital where he was fortunate enough to be attended by one Mr Nicholas Simpson. Nick had immediately organised an MRI scan and biopsy that had shown the mass to be malignant. A muco-epidermoid carcinoma was not to be trifled with and in need of urgent excision.

The seven-hour operation the next day proved difficult, but at the end of it Nick was confident that he had cleaned away every last bit of cancerous tissue that had entwined itself along the pathway of the facial nerve. Whether there would be concomitant damage to the nerve only time would tell, but this proved not to be the case. Although there had been initial numbness, it settled quicker than expected.

'I'm extremely grateful to you, Nick. Without your skill I'd be in a sorry state. I'd like to express my gratitude by offering you a sizeable parcel of shares in my health club business.'

'Thanks, mate, but I'd much rather you made a donation to the creation of a new glandular surgery unit at the hospital.'

The new unit bears David McKealy's name.

# Chapter 8

## Taking the plunge   Leeds 2002

He was still making the time to correspond by letter and later more frequently by e-mail and phone with his parents, and they had received and admired the photos he had sent of the pretty Allison. Nick, realising that he was now unlikely to be returning to live in Australia, decided to apply for British citizenship, and this proved a demanding process.

Allison was leafing through the Sunday Times travel section when an article drew her attention. 'You know, Nick, we haven't taken a holiday since we met, and this hotel they describe here really appeals to me.' Nick took the paper from her and read about the luxurious boutique hotel in Majorca. The accompanying picture showed two tanned adonises jumping from a rocky pier into the azure sea. His face took on that naughty look she had loved since they first met. 'It looks great, but I'm not sure I want to go to a place where you're going to wear out your eyes ogling at these guys. Where will it end?'

Alison's eyes twinkled. 'You know the expression, a change is as good as a holiday? Well, who knows, maybe I will strike lucky and get both.'

'Touche! Ok darling, I'm up for it, but can you afford the time?'

She responded, 'No, but if I don't have a break soon it'll be someone's neck that I'll end up breaking!'

So Nick and Allison gave themselves time to organise locums, ensuring that their absence would not be calamitous.

Nick decided to use his recently acquired British passport for the first time. The hotel exceeded their expectations. There weren't many men jumping from the rocks, and those who did were large-bellied and balding. No risk of Allison's straying in that direction! The couple spent their days doing very little, enjoying the sun, the superb buffets and each other. As their last night neared, the manager understood Nick's very poor Spanish well enough to organise a guitarist to serenade them at their candle-lit dinner table as Nick casually suggested to Allison that it was time to seal their relationship. Allison accepted the invitation and the little box that accompanied it without a moment's hesitation.

Her aspirant parents were thrilled – a lawyer daughter and a surgeon son-in-law! Couldn't be better! Preparations for the wedding commenced. For Nick, this presented the best possible opportunity of seeing his parents again – it had been a long while, and once again he realised how much he missed them. His folks were more than grateful to accept the offered trip to celebrate the nuptials. It would be their first journey ever in an airplane, but in their small bungalow they were already flying high, grateful and proud that their only child was fulfilling their every dream.

On arrival, they were exhausted after a thirty-hour five-leg journey but were overjoyed to see Nick and Allison waiting to greet them. They took to Allison immediately – she seemed a steady, reliable woman with a winning smile, oh so pretty. Allison's parents were their hosts on the first evening when Barbara prepared a scrumptious if simple roast. As they chatted over the superb Tasmanian *pinot noir* that Tommo had bought at the airport, the Greigs found they had little in common with Nick's folks.

Nevertheless, they were pleasant enough to the Aussies, as they would be throughout the couple of weeks they spent in Yorkshire.

'So this is your first visit to England?' asked Gerald.

'I'm gonna level with you Gerald, the furthest we have ever travelled is to Melbourne! That's a two-hour drive in our ute, that's a pick-up truck in English. We go there every year for the Melbourne Cup.'

Gladys joined in the conversation. 'Most of my earnings come from making outfits for the Ballarat ladies to wear in Melbourne the evening before the Cup and on the big day.'

Tommo added that the men too dressed in their once-a-year suits, ties and fedoras - it was a time for friends to be together, to enjoy the spectacle, to share a few tinnies of the golden nectar but never to get drunk. It was just too good a day to waste.

Nick listened quietly, thinking to himself that much as he loved his parents, he had moved on from their parochial world.

Gerald, being what he was, was ever so slightly concerned about his future son-in-law's provenance – Nick had spoken little about it - so he raised the question of when Tommo's forebears had arrived in Australia. He was rather relieved to learn that they weren't stock of the notorious unmentionables sent to Botany Bay by the infamous Hanging Judge Jeffreys on one of his rare amiable days instead of to the gallows. It was the Victorian gold rush in the mid-1850s that enticed Tommo's great-grandparents to leave their home in a small, poverty-ridden English country town and undertake the then perilous sea journey to Melbourne, and from there by ox-waggon to Ballarat.

Tommo described how the quest for gold was not particularly kind to his forebears, as the best of it was over by the time they arrived. Nevertheless, they loved the heat and sunshine and decided to remain in Ballarat and set up home. The summers were fierce. The small bungalow home they bought for two-and-flumpence-ha'penny was a furnace when the sun beat down, but sun beats rain any day of the week. Best of all, it was theirs. In England they had been beholden to the goodwill or otherwise of the local land baron.

Tommo's great-grandparents had found their neighbours rough but hospitable, and they did as well as they were able, she finding work in one of the assortment of small factories that were springing up, and he at a nearby sheep farm. Their children and grandchildren were born there, as was their great-great-grandson, Nicholas, by which time Ballarat had transformed from a small sheep station to the third largest inland city in Australia with a present population of around a hundred thousand.

At the end of the evening, Barbara and Gerald were pleased to have learned more about Nick's origins and to have met Nick's parents, but there was only so much you could hear about the Melbourne Cup or about the hardships of old Ballarat, and they were pleased too that the senior Simpsons would be very infrequent visitors.

In a quiet moment, Gladys asked Allison, 'Will you be able to continue working when the kids come along?'

She was rather taken aback when Allison responded in a manner that was respectful but designed to ensure that the subject would not be raised again.

'I don't want to disappoint you, Gladys, but it's not our intention to have children. Having kids squalling around one's knees will not be our default choice. My friends' children are all so annoying, so why would ours turn out any better? If Nick were available to share duties, it might be one thing, but I have already learned about the life of a surgeon, and I am too much of a career woman to give up my law practice to spend my time wiping babies' bottoms at home. Our weekends are for squash and for cycling in the countryside. Children? No thank you!'

If Allison was aware of the disappointing effect of what she was saying was having on her future mother-in-law, she might have tempered her message, but that was not Allison's way.

Later, when Gladys spoke to Nick, he seemed in accord with Allison's expressed viewpoint. 'We have discussed this, Mum, often, even spoken about having an *au pair;* but even allowing for help through the infant stage, if I am to continue to be a successful surgeon, I cannot afford interrupted sleep every night. And even after that, we would constantly be having to deal with childhood emergencies, and we would lose focus on our careers. Ally's practice is really doing well now, so I can't see there's much chance we will be adding to the world's population.'

Disappointed as they were, his parents retained an undercurrent of hope that Allison might change her mind later. If they had known Allison better, they might not have kindled such notions, because, like Nick, once Allison chose a path, she would not easily deviate from it. Like the woman she admired so much, Margaret Thatcher, the lady was not for turning.

The wedding was a quiet affair at a small church in a small, quiet village near Leeds. Only their family, closest colleagues and a few select squash-club friends were in attendance to enjoy the ceremony and sumptuous meal at Leeds' best. Allison's father proposed the toast and was not surprised when Tommo raised his beer glass and not the one filled with champagne.

After the wedding, goodbyes were said by the parents. The Simpsons said they looked forward to returning soon, and the Greigs hoped they wouldn't.

The newlyweds drove Tommo and Glad to Bourton-on-the-Water in the lush Cotswolds where the older folk really enjoyed seeing the model village and the gorgeous stone homes. This was the England they had seen on so many magazine covers, although those did not have the multitude of tourists milling around.

Then on to London for a short visit that included a day at Lords cricket ground when they revelled in seeing a rampant Australian team demolish a pitiful England. Tommo was a great fan of Glen McGrath even though the bowler was from New South Wales. He was especially thrilled to see the fast bowler claim his 500$^{th}$ test wicket, and for that reason alone would have considered his trip to be worth the effort.

After taking in a couple of West End musicals - *Miss Saigon* and *The Lion King* were the rage of the day - they said farewell at Heathrow Airport.

'Thanks for an amazing trip. It was a great pleasure to meet you and your folks, Allison,' said Tommo.

'We wish you both a happy life together! Come and see us soon,' said Gladys, embracing each in turn. The parents had thoroughly enjoyed seeing the mother country for the first time, but in their hearts felt it might be a while before they would see Nick again. They were right, but not for the reasons anyone expected.

# Chapter 9

## The Black Dogs   Leeds 2005

For the most part, Nick took life as his parents had done, with an easy nonchalance and laid-back casualness. He did not have strong opinions about anything except Australian rugby and surgical operations. Not much seemed to faze him. Best of all, his relationship with Allison seemed rock-solid, and he felt complete. Their squash was improving in spite of finding limited time to get onto the court. Nick would win most times, but Allison had the ability, fitness and determination to run him close and occasionally beat him.

Nick had moved on to bigger things workwise and had been appointed head of facial surgery at the Yorkshire County College Hospital, one of the largest in Leeds. He thrived in this position and was respected not just as an innovative surgeon but also an inspiring lecturer to the hospital students. Was it easy to be one of his students? Not if you were a slacker. He was exacting in his pursuit of high standards of technique and cleanliness. Nick realised that he loved teaching surgery almost as much as he loved the practise itself. He would be quite happy to spend as long as it took to get a student to understand a concept he was attempting to put over, and his patience seemed infinite as long as he perceived they were trying their best. He could not abide shoddiness in any shape or form, and the students soon learned that under-performance was not an option.

His surgical department was blossoming. Allison's legal practice was booming. They were content, but contentment breeds complacency. The shit was soon to hit the fan, and they didn't see it coming.

To prove that success doesn't always bring happiness, as his thirty-fifth birthday approached and for reasons that may one day be better understood than they are now, Nick began to experience an increasing sense of unease, of disquiet; a sense that life, despite everything it had brought, was not quite working for him. He would awaken in the morning an hour earlier than usual with a heavyish head that he would attribute to a worrisome dream that he could not quite remember or that he may not even have had. There was this feeling of low-level internal discord. Not doubt, not fear. Nowhere near turmoil. Those words were not part of his vocabulary. Just something not quite in tune. The worst part, the not knowing quite what it was.

He mentioned this to Allison one morning over breakfast, but she barely raised her eyes from her legal journal. 'Don't worry, darling, I'm sure it'll pass.' Hmm. There were many wonderful things he could say about his wife, but emotional reassurance when required obviously wasn't one of them. Perhaps she was correct – maybe if he didn't worry about the worrying, it would indeed pass.

An article in a professional magazine that caught his attention had spoken of 'high-function anxiety'. Well, he thought, high function is definitely what I do, but anxiety? Had he ever been beset by doubt about making the wrong diagnosis, or by fear of an operation going wrong? Certainly nothing that stuck in his mind. In fact, quite the opposite – his colleagues had often commented on how calm he was before even the most difficult of operations, how assured he always seemed.

It had always been his opinion that if a surgeon wasn't sure about the route to travel, or had doubts about the technique to be employed, then they ought to be involved in another sphere of medicine where a wrong step would be less likely to lead to the early demise of a patient. He had great respect for physicians, but if they got their diagnosis wrong, they could always reset the route planner. A surgeon didn't have that luxury.

If he were honest with himself, he would admit to having become exceedingly bored professionally. Everything was coming too easily to him. He was no longer experiencing that thrill of carrying out a really tricky operation and doing it well. It just seemed more of the same. Yet, where were opportunities for diversification? Nick had devoted as much time to serious study as ever he wished and had no interest whatsoever in hospital politics. He wasn't motivated to carry out new research or write erudite papers.

Winning at the squash club was so regular that it had become routine, and when he strained a muscle in his back, he decided to give that sport and all others a complete rest for three months. To his chagrin he found himself putting on weight from the lack of activity. Golf? No chance, even without the injured muscle.

Pastimes? Most of his colleagues were obsessed with the fortunes of Leeds United, but for Nick English football was a monumental waste of time. He realised how testy he was becoming when one of his colleagues inquired, 'Interested in putting a few quid on Leeds to beat Liverpool in the Cup?' He responded by saying he had better things to do with his money than piss it away on poxy Leeds United. Although not a serious misdemeanour, that remark was quite typical of the snappy kind of response that was becoming commonplace and that his colleagues were noticing. The air of insouciance, that lightness that was his aura, was clearly being replaced by something less pleasant.

Eventually this malaise was noticed by Allison. 'Are you feeling okay, darling? You would tell me, wouldn't you, if anything was wrong?' Nick smiled wanly - what was there to say? When he had mentioned it previously, she had seemed less than concerned. Even at the best of times, he and Allison rarely spoke a great deal, but these days, in the moments when the dark feelings descended, he found himself unable to say anything at all. He realised he lacked the emotional maturity to articulate his feelings adequately, so he spoke little and just got on with matters professional as best he could, hoping the black dogs would cease their baying sooner rather than later. There were articles and journals to be read and he began to hide behind these. Allison would simply shrug and get on with her legal work.

So much in his life had become pedestrian, not least their physical relationship that had become perfunctory at best. At times, even the occasional touching of one another was conspicuous by its absence. Nick looked at his wife across the room. Even in the half-light, she had the golden glow of success. And yet as he looked at her, he suddenly felt he hardly knew her. It was as if they were railway lines rather than the carriages of the train, and the lines seemed to be going in different directions.

His Australian upbringing had ingrained in him that men should not show themselves to be vulnerable - vulnerability was a sign of weakness. Even if you don't feel strong, behave as if you do. That was why Australia so often triumphed against other sporting nations despite its relatively small population. How you set your own value would determine how other people valued you, and up to this point he perceived that he had always been respected. Now he no longer believed it. He stood in the bathroom staring at his face in the mirror, examining it minutely. It belonged to someone else. His life felt turned upside down by a facial tear that couldn't be seen, yet made every deed feel lopsided and out of balance.

His wife's face appeared in the mirror behind him. She was standing at the door, watching him. They were always watching each other these days. Watching, but not speaking. After half a minute, faced yet again by his silence, Allison's patience finally snapped. Almost hissing, she burst out, 'I really wish you'd pull yourself together', and turned on her heel.

Thanks for nothing, thought Nick.

They saw little of her parents, indeed little of anyone. He said nothing. Restaurants? Rare. Cinema? Hardly. Theatre, never. They rarely took holidays, hardly ever went further than a few miles from Leeds. Occasionally they would go cycling on a weekend and would have a pub lunch in the country, but these excursions were becoming fewer and further between.

'What the hell is wrong with you, Nick? You're so listless. You don't want to do anything anymore. I have to keep making excuses for you to our friends.'

Nick did not respond.

On one rare expedition, Allison decided to broach the issue once again. 'You've been very moody lately, Nick, and it's beginning to piss me off. What's bothering you?'

Unusually, he decided to discuss his feelings with Allison. 'Hard to explain, Ally, but I feel like I've kind of hit the wall. To be honest, I feel sort of depressed. I'm just not enjoying much at the moment. It's not that I have problems – there've been no disasters at work, and we're financially secure, but I've completely lost my enthusiasm. A successful outcome, something that used to give me pride, has become commonplace. What used to excite me a while ago bores me now. Do you think this is what they mean when they talk about burnout? Or maybe midlife crisis?'

'You're hardly midlife, darling! You're probably the fittest man I know. Maybe a holiday would be the answer, we haven't been abroad for ages. How would you fancy celebrating your birthday with a cruise round the Caribbean?'

He grimaced. 'I don't think I could stomach being on a ship for two weeks with a bunch of octogenarians.'

'Ok, I get that,' she said, but when she mooted the alternative of a big birthday bash, Nick found the notion entirely unappealing and turned that down too. Sanguine Allison thought that it would all sort out given time and let the matter rest.

It did not.

Nick had carried out an operation that initially appeared to be relatively straight-forward, but he had learned a long time ago that no operation was ever simple. Certainly, the oral cavity could be a minefield for the unwary. What had seemed a small cancerous growth on the left side of the patient's tongue had spread and engulfed the lymph nodes of the neck. By the time Nick and his team had completed the commando-style clearance of the nodes of this heavy smoker, seven hours of an operation scheduled for three had elapsed. He knew that the eighty-five-year-old patient would not live for many more days, but he felt safe in thinking that if and when the man departed this mortal coil, it would be for any reason other than a cancerous tongue; until then he would be able to eat. But so bloody what if a lonely elderly man lived with half a tongue for a few more months, or worse, years? Would they be happy months? Was it worth the effort? The cost? The construct Nick had created in his mind was that little he did was worth anything.

At the end of the procedure, Nick felt tired more than elated. Had he thought deeply enough about what he was experiencing, he might have seen signs of gross burnout.

He had simply been working too hard, doing intense work in a demanding environment, thinking too much of his patients' wellbeing and nothing of his own – not a healthy balance. There lay the seeds that gave meaning to the term 'vicious cycle.'

For the first time in his life, his mind began to fill with negative thoughts. In his mind, his work milieu was too aggressive, competitive and frankly, too masculine. Perhaps he was indeed spending too much time doing microfine work on a small area of the body in a room devoid of natural lighting. Was this what they called going stir crazy? He had begun to worry about feeling stressed and found this stressful. Being a medical man, he thought it might be a case of incipient endogenous depression, of chemicals that were going out of kilter. Well, there were ways of getting unkiltered chemicals back into shape.

Nick decided to consult a psychiatrist. Rather than selecting one at the hospital where he worked, lest someone should see him attend and put two and two together, he googled and found a therapist with an impressive cv in York, some thirty miles and an hour away from Leeds. Manageable. He did not tell Allison about this – why get her worried?

He spent a number of sessions with Dr Margaret O'Connor ('please call me Margie') but decided not to inform her that he was medical. When she asked him what work he did he was vague. He said he did complex repair work. He seemed reluctant to say more and she did not press him. He would later come to regret this.

He did however ask if she enjoyed opera. When she responded in the affirmative, he said to her, 'Do you know Verdi's Don Carlo?'

Margie nodded vaguely. Nick continued, 'King Felipe of Spain was a man who had everything, not least power, success and a beautiful wife.'

Margie, now remembering the king beset by dark thoughts, said 'Yes, but he allowed the black dogs in his mind to take control.'

'Yes, and that's exactly how *I* feel.'

'Let's try to find out why. Not what you feel, but how you see yourself. Who are you, Nick?' Margie probed.

Nick seemed to have difficulty in providing an answer. Because he had withheld from her the most pertinent information of all, that he was an overworked surgeon too dedicated to his profession, he was now unable to communicate to her the fundamental source of his inner turmoil. Was he the person who brought happiness to other people's lives by removing their pain and restoring their health? Or was he simply a machine for cutting straight lines and sewing the parts seamlessly together? Just a competent technician - a tailor. Had he become his mother?

Was he the person who made Allison laugh (or at least used to), whom she looked forward to finding at home, or was he just the provider of goods?

He felt vindicated if not pleased when Margie concurred with his self-diagnosis. He definitely seemed to be suffering from depression, and she did think it was endogenous. She suggested he needed to turn all his negative thoughts around, re-focus, and become more reliant on who he was, rather than what he was.

Margie prescribed a mild anti-depressant for a period of months and seemed to have selected one that not only worked but had no discernible side effects. Nick was beginning to see the light - he sensed he could do it, he could reframe his thoughts, turn it around. Although accompanied by a degree of detachment, after a few days he began to feel lighter and more relaxed, something that was noticed immediately by Allison, with whom he had still not shared the information that he had visited a psychiatrist and was on medication.

Too many secrets…...

After another couple of sessions with Margie, and another couple of months on the medication, they decided it was job done. 'Well done, Nick, you seem much improved, but it is possible that you may feel signs of relapse. If so, be sure to give me a call.'

Nick began to feel a sense of relief. His relationship with Allison did indeed improve, and so did that with his colleagues and students. His weight began to drop. His ailing back began to feel better. He was soon back on the squash court and performing better than ever. And not just on the court.

Unfortunately, depression isn't usually a one-off episode and eighteen months later, the feelings of unease began to rear once more. Nick didn't fancy driving to York again and starting a whole new course of treatment. The hour-each-way journey was a waste of good time, he thought. He decided that he would self-prescribe, a decision that would send his life increasingly out of control, his marriage and his profession careering into tailspin.

The pharmacist whom he was using, who was not local, began to feel ill at ease about dealing with self-prescribed medication and after a month refused to supply him.

'Sorry, but they've really tightened up on regulations and I don't want to draw attention to either of us.'

The warning to Nick – *to either of us* – went unheeded.

So, rather than going back to Margie, Nick simply found another pharmacy and rather than self-prescribe in his own name began to use imaginary ones or those of his patients, never more than once each. He began to use several pharmacies, then many. For a man in whose judgment others placed their lives, this was very poor thinking indeed. Yet Nick somehow believed that as no one was being harmed, including himself, there was no risk to anyone, and he continued his prescribing. He saw himself as untouchable.

By this time, and without mincing words, Nick had become addicted to his medication. Most antidepressant abuse is typically someone increasing their prescribed dose when they feel like the drug isn't working fast enough. This wasn't the case with Nick – his medication was working just fine. He had no intention of either increasing it, nor of seeking anyone else to prescribe it, nor of giving it up. It wasn't that he couldn't, he simply did not wish to. He felt he didn't need the medication to make him feel better, but felt worse when he was not using it.

That what he was doing was unethical and improper did not enter his mind. He was harming no one, least of all himself. He saw no need to share his actions or thoughts with Allison. Growing up as an only child gave him little experience in sharing anything much – his parents, kind though they were, were not the sort you could go to for emotional assistance and he had learned that Allison was not more easily approachable.

The doctor should have known better. He should have realised that the prescriptions of all addictive drugs are monitored by the NHS watchdogs, and it was not long before a red flag appeared at the echelons of control, raised by the high level of prescriptions within a ten-mile radius of his workplace. It was no surprise to the watchdogs that the overwhelming majority of prescriptions were being signed by one person, and the one person was Dr Nicholas Simpson BMed MD (Syd) MCh (UCL).

Now, one thing about the watchdogs is that they observe carefully, collect evidence, but do not react in haste - they wait until they have a case that is entirely cast-iron and shatterproof, one that cannot fail. Then they act.

# Chapter 10

## The shitshow begins   Leeds 2009

The day of the fateful letter. Nick read and reread it and then read the letter again. 'Unfortunately, we also have to warn you that should the allegations against you be found proven, criminal prosecution may follow because there exists a strong probability that many of the abovementioned prescriptions in the names of patients you have treated were intended for personal use by yourself, thereby taking this matter into the realms of fraudulent drug prescription.'

Criminal prosecution? Have they gone raving fucking mad?!

When he got to the hospital he sought and quickly found a colleague who could cover a relatively simple operation that required wiring of a fractured mandible. He headed off to Allison's office just a couple of blocks away. Allison was about to interview a client but was momentarily free.

'What brings you here, darling?' she said, looking up from one of the many files on her desk.

'This.' He could barely bring himself to speak. He showed her the letter, took a deep breath and explained as briefly as he could what had led to its sending. She was not pleased but did not vent her displeasure. Yet her whole demeanour changed. She pursed her lips but did not comment other than to say, 'I'm extremely busy, Nick, there will be plenty time to discuss this at home tonight.'

What upset Nick as much as anything else on that awful day was Allison's utterly cold response – she did not offer words that might have comforted him, did not extend an arm round his shoulders. It did not enter his mind that she was herself hurt and shocked that this man who hitherto had seemed invincible but was now facing ruin had not ever shared the reasons for it with her, his wife and soulmate. He left her office, thinking that for the first time ever when he had really needed her, he found her wanting, and that hurt almost more than anything else.

What she did add, as she turned away and picked up her file, was 'You're going to need a good medico-legal lawyer, and you know where to find one.'

He did indeed know, and telephoned DIG, the Doctors Insurance Group to which he had been paying monthly subscription fees for 16 years and to whom he had never had cause to speak, let alone ask for assistance. He was requested to come down to London as urgently as possible, and a conference was arranged for the following day. He returned to the hospital and despite his mind being elsewhere began to operate.

Later that day an inspector from the NHS Investigative Services arrived at Nick's hospital department. He was accompanied by a police officer. Nick was about to conclude an operation when the duo became a threesome as they were joined by the Hospital Chief Executive. No sooner had Nick shed his scrubs than the NHS man repeated that Nick would be required to defend himself on allegations of misconduct and fraud at a hearing sometime in the future.

Then the knockout blow. The CEO told him that he was under immediate suspension from duty on full pay pending investigation and was to leave the hospital premises immediately.

Why suspension? Who could possibly stand in for him? The letter had already informed him that an inquiry was pending. Wasn't someone innocent until proved otherwise? Why did this relaying of information already delivered require three men? Were they scared he would become violent, attack the CEO? Do a runner? All these questions spun through his mind.

Whatever the reasons, Nick was seriously embarrassed. He was only too aware that his surgical colleagues were staring, watching these events unfold without the slightest idea of what was going on, but they would learn soon enough and be shocked. Yes, he had been a trifle tetchy of late, but a police officer with the CEO? What on earth was happening? Nick had never experienced shame before, and he could not have conceived how humiliated he felt; the taste in his mouth was of undiluted bile.

That was the easy part.

The unpalatable part was having to tell Allison that evening of what had been going on for the past two years, of which she had had not an inkling of suspicion; to tell her that he was an addict, and as near as made no difference had been fired; that he would be brought before a tribunal, that he faced suspension or even erasure and potential criminal charges.

Allison did not take kindly to this. For the first time in their relationship, she questioned his integrity. If he could not be open and honest about this, what else might he be shielding?

'Why didn't you say something, Nick? You never mentioned that you'd seen a psychiatrist, that you were on medication. What were you thinking?'

She could barely hear his response. 'The medication was working, and I didn't see the need to burden you with what I knew was a temporary issue and completely under control.'

'I'm not sure you were the right person to pass judgment on that - why didn't you get a doctor to prescribe?'

His response of 'I *am* a doctor' made her realise that he had failed completely to see what ethical conduct was required of him, or of what the consequences of abusing those ethics might be.

He explained about Margie and his reasons for not returning to her. Allison simply shook her head in disbelief. This was all so out of character of this man she thought she knew: a thorough, take-no-risks, avoid-short-cuts person every bit her match. She was deeply hurt that he had not confided in her - surely she would not have allowed him to be so careless. She was angry that his stupid actions now seemed about to destroy the hitherto smooth passage of their relationship. No, angry doesn't cut it, she was livid. But Allison doesn't do tempers and tantrums, she simply bottles it inside herself where it will fester and corrode. She didn't express her anger, she kept silent, and silence can be sharper than a scalpel blade.

Allison reluctantly postponed her scheduled meetings for the following day and accompanied him on the two-and-a-half-hour train journey to London. They did not speak much, each waiting for the other to open a conversation that didn't wish to be opened. Then a taxi ride to the swish offices of the Doctors Indemnity Group, the DIG in Mayfair, its residence for the past sixty years.

Nick and Allison were whisked straight into a large office, more like a boardroom, where sat the legendary head of DIG, Dr Sir James Clifton, as well as a barrister plus one of DIG's most senior solicitors and her two assistants, a secretary and another doctor. No one was smiling. The barrister resembled a ferret, or perhaps a weasel, Nick wasn't sure which, but he disliked the thin man on sight.

Nick would quickly realise that this large group was not large for nothing.

THE ROAD TO PERDITION   CHAPTER 10

Dr Sir James Clifton was not one to mince words and certainly did not on this occasion. As his half-moon spectacles slid down his nose, so the huge bushy moustaches above his eyes rose in the opposite direction and pulsated fearfully. He was a large man with a mass of salt-and-pepper hair. Had he been a singer (which he was) he would have been a Russian bass (a bass he was, although not Russian) and his voice resonated two fathoms deep through the room. On occasion, it would roar throughout the entire building. Not undeservedly was he known as 'The Rottweiler'. He was, to say the very least, intimidating and when driven, ferocious. Nick Simpson was about to experience the full range of Dr Clifton's vocal capacities.

'Mr Simpson, let me begin by informing you that the plain facts of the matter are indisputable. Not only have you abused your right to prescribe medication, but you have committed fraud and potentially brought your profession into serious disrepute. The Medical Practice Supervisory Committee will most certainly take a lively interest in you. The police may also. The duty of this organisation is to defend you to the limits of its ability.

'We have four objectives: the first is to keep you in your job; the second is to keep your certain suspension period as minimal as possible; third, to prevent you from being struck off the medical register; and finally to prevent you from going to prison. No one here feels confident that any can be achieved.'

For the second time in two days, Nick felt as if he had been hit with a blunt but very heavy object. His mouth instantly dried and his head pounded. Was this for real? Weren't they over-reacting? He had after all harmed no-one, stolen nothing – he had paid for each prescription privately, and there had not been a single incident where his professional performance could be considered less than excellent. On the contrary, he was doing work considered by his peers to be innovative and life-changing. After all, what could be more life-changing than to repair a harelip and unite a cleft palate that was separating a child's face into two distinct halves? Skill that would spare that child from a lifetime of misery and avoidance of others? Did that count for nothing?

Unfortunately for Nick, that was not the way the people massed in this room saw it.

Dr Clifton continued, 'Having spoken to Counsel sitting opposite you *(Nick had decided Counsel looked more like a ferret than a weasel)* we must warn you that it is a fight you are most unlikely to win. I repeat, *most* unlikely. The duty of this organisation is to support you. We ask if you intend to contest the allegations. If the answer is yes, we will still support you to the full. But if the powers that be find against you, they are likely to conclude that you lack any semblance of insight and that you have learnt little from your egregious conduct, and the risk of erasure will increase.'

Once again, Nick felt his mouth go dry and he drained the glass of water before him. Was this really happening?

'If on the other hand, you accept the charges and embark immediately on a process of rehabilitation, there is the possibility of concluding this with a short period of suspension, perhaps three months, and then you can return to work, albeit at a lower level than you are at present. In short, we are suggesting what the Americans would call plea-bargaining.'

Nick thought about this briefly – far too briefly, and once more without discussing the situation with Allison – before he somewhat tartly responded, 'I do accept that I have probably erred, but I think the whole thing is being grossly exaggerated. I've hurt no one. My professional record is unblemished and exemplary.'

Sir James's glasses slid once more, and his eyebrows melded into one hirsute mass. His voice became menacing. 'Once the press gets hold of this, as they surely will, rather than a paragon of virtue you will be seen to have brought your profession and yourself into disrepute.'

Nick wasn't having this, no way. 'My colleagues all respect me and will speak for me. My patients think highly of me and will provide excellent testimonials. So, Sir, I've decided I want to fight this all the way and I hope you will defend me. I'll go further - I *expect* you to fight this all the way. I haven't been paying DIG subscription fees for seventeen years for you to take the easy way out.'

Allison winced – was this the usually taciturn, easygoing man she had known these years? He seemed to resent that his presence was required there at all. Biting the hand that protected you was probably not the best way to go about avoiding a possible allegation of criminal impropriety. Sir James Clifton pursed his lips (he did this often), and then in a voice six fathoms deep *(those about him knew the deeper his voice got, the more one should approach with great caution)* said:

'Think on this: a wise man knows how not to get into a situation that a smart man knows how to get out of. I fear you are being neither wise nor smart. You are making a mistake that bodes ill. Our organisation will do its utmost for you, be sure of that, but you are in serious trouble and getting you out of it is going to be a long and difficult journey.'

No one present, least of all gung-ho Nick, could foresee just how difficult it would prove to be.

If little had been said on the train journey down, that back home took place in frosty silence. Still stung by her lack of sympathy, Nick was in no way ready to apologise to Allison either for his actions or for his deception in excluding her from any knowledge of what he had been doing. How would it have helped for her to know? It wouldn't have helped him to feel better (the tablets were doing that rather well) but might conceivably have upset her on a matter that he considered fairly trivial anyway.

For her part, she was sure he had made another very ill-considered and poor decision by ignoring the advice of the DIG. She had always known him to be a proud man, on occasions arrogant, but had always felt these were positive traits in his character – he was a fighter who had never been known to accept defeat. Better to tread than to be downtrodden was his credo. But on this occasion, bearing in mind her extensive experience in the slings and arrows of legal practise and of seeing proud people humbled, she was in no mood to offer her unqualified support unless and until he was ready to reconsider his determination to take on the Medical Practice Supervisory Committee.

He was not.

So it began.

# Chapter 11

## Coming apart   Leeds / London
## 2010

In the dark days that followed, Nick contacted no one. Not his friends. Not his in-laws nor his parents. Sitting at home doing little of importance made him feel impotent, and there was only so much he could read. Evenings were the worst. On one occasion, Allison, who had become as tense as a guitar string, finally lost it. 'Bloody hell, Nick, don't you think it's time you stopped sulking? You're like a bloody child!'

Nick's response was, 'If you weren't so damn cold to me, I might find it easier to talk. For fuck's sake, I'm not one of your criminal clients. You can see I'm going through hell - can't you be just a little bit kind?'

'I would be if you were prepared to take responsibility for what you've done.'

'What have I done? I didn't harm anybody.'

'You've harmed us, Nick, and I'm not sure it can be undone.'

As the days went by, the anger and confusion occupying Nick's mind through every waking minute was not abating, rather the opposite. Did the bloody suits on the Medical Practice Supervisory Committee have nothing better to do with their time than crucify an outstanding surgeon? He hadn't killed or maimed anyone, not even left an unnecessary scar. He had an unblemished record and had never received a complaint nor even a semblance of one. On the contrary, every operation he had ever carried out was praised by staff and appreciated by patients. The only thing he was quite certain of in his mind was that he was being hung out to dry because he had allegedly "brought his profession into disrepute". How??

He had not mis-claimed expenses from the NHS, though he knew for certain a couple of well-respected if less competent colleagues were routinely doing exactly that. He had not racially abused staff. No-one had ever accused him of sexism or sexual harassment, something he witnessed on a daily basis in theatre. Why pick on him? Because he was a colonial? Because he was a tall poppy that needed cutting down to size? Yes, he knew he could be arrogant on occasions, but since when did arrogance need punishing by a fucking Medical Committee? Would that "protect the public?" Had he ever not protected the public, not operated skilfully, not been considerate?

The process of establishing his defence was arduous. The DIG solicitors, two most pleasant young women, were diligent and meticulous. Another practitioner might have found one or other of them attractive, but not Nick, especially surprising given that his significant other was practising chilled avoidance. He was interested only in their performance in the line of duty. The boxes of files grew with each passing week; Nick perceived quickly that nothing was going to be left to chance, and that his monthly subscription was proving to be worth every penny after all.

First of all, letters were exchanged with Dr Margaret O'Connor. Margie expressed surprise that Nick had not come back to her for further support and medication. She might have understood him better if he had shared that they were medical colleagues. Although she did not feel his medical condition was anything other than transient, an early midlife crisis if you will, she was distinctly unimpressed that he had not informed her that he was a surgeon. 'I'm quite peeved that you felt unable to be open and honest with me, Nick, so I don't think it would be appropriate for me to carry on working with you. I suggest you look for someone else closer to your home to assist in your rehabilitation process.'

Nick shuddered. He was not blind to her hostile reaction. He saw any support coming from her disappearing over the horizon - support that he would surely need.

Accordingly, Nick found himself attending a second psychiatrist, this time in Leeds. Dr Wilfred Barnes was as unemotional, non-committal and inspiring as a coffin. Indeed, he had the pallor of a corpse and the personality of a marshmallow. Dr Barnes spoke little, which was just as well - his voice was so monotonous that he would have lulled an insomniac into slumber. He said very little, never even a raised eyebrow, and at times Nick thought Barnes should have been reported missing. His suit, shirt and tie were unmatching – squares, stripes and dots - nondescript, haphazard. Dottore Tomasso would not even have bothered calling him a bore, so comatose was he.

Dr Barnes's main job was to get Nick to undertake to abstain from his drug habit and from all alcohol, and to authorise expensive hair tests every second week to ensure that he was complying. Nick loathed Barnes and dreaded their weekly shrink sessions but did cooperate in full. Although never a heavy drinker, he did miss a relaxing glass of cab sav, and now more than ever he needed relaxing.

The process of writing to colleagues asking their support did not prove as simple as Nick had imagined, not to mention how degrading and humbling he found the process. Although many supported him, it was with slightly less enthusiasm than he had anticipated. Worse, a few but not an insignificant number had found him arrogant and condescending, One or two had hinted at racist attitudes, and one nurse had even said she felt sexually threatened by him and did not want ever to be alone with him (Nick had no memory of her whatsoever). He was quite stunned by these responses, as his perception of self was at a higher level of positivity altogether. No matter – there were more than enough who thought him outstanding.

Nick's patients were far more supportive, some even attributing celestial powers; but those few whose names he had used on the prescriptions felt violated - yes, violated! - and this was what worried the lawyers. Nick began to realise he should indeed have taken responsibility for his actions as Sir James Clifton had earlier suggested, but by now the Medical Practice Supervisory Committee was preparing its case, one it was not now going to let pass by with simple plea-bargaining. To use a medical metaphor The MPSC panel were sharpening their scalpels and going for the jugular. The public had to be protected. The good name of the profession had to be preserved.

By complete contrast with his earlier complacency, Nick began to get paranoid, and with just cause: an arrogant Australian immigrant would make an excellent sacrificial lamb to take to the slaughter, and those who would be judging him were licking their lips in anticipation of the blood to be let and tasted.

As Nick was to learn, the lip-licking process was tedious and rarely took less than 18 months. Any chef will tell you it takes time to prepare a dish properly and they were determined to have him skewered and kebabbed. The Yorkshire County College Hospital, however, was not going to hang around for 18 months paying someone his full salary while he idled his time not in work. Their CEO set up a fast-track institutional hearing. He was an anal bureaucrat, an *apparatchik who* didn't like anyone who was talented and had never liked Nick. Nick liked him even less. Despite the testimonials of several colleagues at the hospital and the insipid evidence of Dr Barnes attesting to his full compliance in rehabilitation, Nick was found to have acted in a manner unbefitting a departmental head or indeed any medical person.

The hearing was little more than a kangaroo court. Nick was found guilty of gross misconduct and summarily dismissed, with the proviso that if the allegations of the Medical Practice Supervisory Committee were not found proven, the salary that was about to be terminated would be reimbursed in full, and he could re-apply for his post. The CEO knew they were on very safe ground.

Nick was however free to seek work as a general practitioner or specialist surgeon elsewhere in the UK.

# Chapter 12

## Dr Susan McDonald   Suffolk 2010

Nick, who had never before had to deal with a setback of epic proportions, was now faced with a full suite of them in spades. He seemed no longer to exist to Allison, so complete was her shut-out. Not one of his former friends or professional associates contacted him to ask how he was doing. He did not reason that they might have found it difficult. He just thought they were shits. Although in the past he had never felt he needed other people's company, he was intelligent enough to understand that this was because it was always available. Now that he really did need someone with whom he could share his feelings, he found he was utterly and completely alone, and had never felt so lonely and bereft.

He was out of a job, and the process of seeking employment was proving to be arduous, painful and demeaning. He lost count of the number of phone calls that were not returned, emails and letters left unanswered. No hospital was willing to employ him in Yorkshire. Was this what he had spent ten years of his life studying for? To be treated like an odious piece of detritus, as if he were a common criminal? He had got to the point where he was feeling that the case was not worth fighting and was seriously considering the nuclear option of taking his own life. He thought of his parents, how devastated they would be.

Nevertheless, his thoughts began to centre not on whether he should, but how best to do this.

Then, almost when he had reached his nadir, he was offered a junior surgical post in Suffolk, some 200 miles and four hours away. Hobson's choice - he at least had to make one more attempt to salvage what was left of his career and his life. He had no choice but to accept.

The thought of moving out of his comfortable home was galling, but he would at least be free for a while of the unexpressed but very real hostility of his once adoring wife. They were already in separate bedrooms, so living in separate residences was almost preferable, even if his was a small bedsit in a small Suffolk town.

So, six months after his last major surgical operation at his former hospital to remove a virulent malignant jaw cancer that had spread to the neck, Nick found himself mostly performing tonsillectomies - this was akin to a bridge teacher having to play Happy Families. There was the occasional demanding case, but for the most part it was pretty much pedestrian fare. His salary was just over half of what he had been earning previously. He was lonely, and even though there was more than one nurse who seemed interested in sharing his company, he had no inclination to follow this route.

There was one other surgeon on the staff, by name of Susan McDonald, who was in her early forties and who prior to his arrival had been complaining constantly about her onerous workload. You'd think she would be relieved to have him to lessen her load, but when he first arrived, she barely spoke to him; and when she did, it was merely to remind him of his lowly position in the departmental hierarchy. She cared nothing for his skills but a great deal about keeping him in line. He assumed this was because, before he invaded her patch, she was head honcho of the surgical unit (although she would have thought that description far too masculine and sexist) and here was this drug-taking upstart (everyone had had to be informed of his story) taking the few more difficult cases away from her. She would show him she was his superior and in charge.

After a couple of months, she realised that he was no real long-term threat and intended to be away from there at the earliest opportunity, and she began to thaw. Over the next six months, the temperature changed from iciness to over-heated as she began to view him as a man who might satisfy her frustrated libido, and later perhaps more.

Nick, however, was quite indifferent to her. No, more than simply indifferent – he actively disliked her. For Nick, this was quite an unusual emotion. So, when she suggested that they might meet for a drink after work at the Carpenter's Arms, he politely refused, citing his recently acquired state of teetotalness. He could of course have countered this with an invitation to go out somewhere local for a meal instead, but would have preferred to eat live wasps. Later, when he mulled this over in his mind, he thought of their first encounters and remembered that she had been downright unpleasant when what he needed was a little touch of kindness. Nick did not have a "can't stand you" shelf in his mind and his subconscious reaction was to put her into his "can't be bothered to have much to do with you unless I have to" category. More than that, though, he had no desire to blot his escutcheon by having an affair with anyone, least of all surgeon Ms Susan McDonald - not that she had the appearance of a stewed tea bag, but there was a sourness about her that spoke of tea that had been steeped for too long. So, as far it was possible to do so, he avoided any more contact with her than was absolutely necessary.

Dr McDonald took umbrage. She felt she was not unattractive, so she rationalised that the reason for his aloof attitude must be that one of the younger nurses was benefitting from his presence and his highly desirable body. We know, as William Congreve had written three hundred years ago, hell hath no fury like a woman scorned, but Nick did not rate her even worthy of scorn. So into his own issues was Nick that he was oblivious to the machinations of this woman's mind.

The nights were lonely times. The small Suffolk town did not have much going in the way of entertainment. Sitting in a pub drinking a couple of pints each evening was not an option, as this would have shown up in his testing, and he really needed to be cleaner than clean. Was Nick optimistic that when his hearing was eventually over, and it seemed to be taking forever to arrive, he would still be a surgeon able to practise his skills? In a word, no. Bernard Finch and Sir James Clifton were continuing to scare the shit out of him.

As he lay in his rented room, in his mind there was time and space in excess to replay the awful allegations against him and the more he dwelt on them the lower his spirits sank. The black cloud had become a black sky. It was utterly pervasive, and his spirit was sinking by the day. The real irony of his situation was that he had been knocking back anti-depressives when he wasn't really depressed, but now that he was, he was unable to do so.

Nick had been travelling back to his Yorkshire home, if he could still call it a home, every weekend when he was not on duty, but Allison was clearly not happy to see him. Had he been prepared to take responsibility for what he done and the changes that this had brought about, she might have been warmer and more kindly disposed to assist. Nick, being Nick, was not, and so she was not. Fortunately, her profession was providing more than enough income for this not to be a problem for her, and when Nick found that he was not even required to contribute from his comparatively meagre current earnings (most of which was in any case being spent on very expensive hair tests), he found this most demeaning. He had become unnecessary.

He made a decision. On one particularly frosty return, when not more than twenty words were exchanged, he went to the cupboard to haul out a suitcase. He said nothing, she said less. The only question in Nick's mind was, small suitcase or large? He settled on a medium-sized one, because that at least implied that their separation would not be for just a night but possibly not forever either. It was all rather eerie. It wasn't as if he had been thrown out or even asked to leave. Half the house was his, even if the other half was not. He seemed to have just drifted out, almost by accident. No not by accident, that implied a chance event, and truth was he has been heading out of that door for months, too many months to remember or to want to remember.

He definitely would also not wish to remember the excruciating loneliness of those following weekends in Suffolk. There was an active am-dram group, but Nick, even if he had wanted to, could not have committed to regular rehearsals – the life of a surgeon did not lend itself to routine. He was an avid reader, but the books in the local W H Smith store were limited, and those he could find were not written for a mind like his. There are only so many books a person can read, so he took many walks on Aldeburgh Beach (miles away). When all was said and done, he was wretchedly alone. Yet, for all of that, he never felt as lonely as he had the last few months when they were together, when the silence was deafening.

Nick decided to pass his spare time in the evenings by increasing his knowledge of music. He'd always enjoyed listening to both classical and jazz but understood little of either. So he purchased a cd player and found that there was a small shop nearby where he could drop in to select some second-hand discs. As he listened his way through the pile that he was accumulating, he would google for information on the composers and artists (*are you watching, Dottore Tomasso?*). It was a rare night that he did not fall asleep with the chords of Chick Corea or Herbie Hancock or the music of Mahler, Dvorak or Rachmaninov in his ears. He found particular enjoyment in his growing collection of jazz pianists, and on his frequent visits to London and DIG, he would try to attend a jazz gig at Ronnie Scott's or a concert at the Royal Festival Hall.

The only moments of occasional cheer that he enjoyed were on the rare occasions when, not exhausted after a day of surgery, he took himself out for a meal. The best restaurant in the town was the local tandoori, the Yak & Yeti (what a delightful name). Once a week or so Nick would drop in for a tasty and filling Indian meal.

He would be lying if he did not admit that one of the reasons he chose to return there was Anili. Anili Gupta was a young, completely anglicised Indian woman from a humble background. She was a lively, pretty, precocious flirt. It wasn't that she didn't have a partner, who it turned out was the local purveyor of noxious substances, but the only thing that Anili wanted and thought she lacked was a touch of class. In truth, she didn't need it, she was delightful enough exactly as she was, but she was aspirational. She did not wish to remain the long-time partner of her dealer friend whose future was at best precarious, who would sooner or later end up in prison. Ironic, really, when one considered that Nick was facing a similar fate for drug-related issues. There are drugs and drugs …

When her shift at the restaurant wasn't busy, Anili would sit with him at his table. She had taken a shine to this man whom she knew to be a surgeon (of course not just because he was a surgeon) and made not the slightest effort to hide her availability. She sensed that this rather pensive doctor might provide the status upgrade she craved, and she in turn the love that he was obviously lacking. Her ambition was to travel to New York, and she couldn't imagine anyone whose company there she would enjoy more than this troubled but obviously sensitive doctor. Another irony – he was where he was because of his insensitivity.

When he consistently refused her advances, she questioned his reasons. In her forthright way, she asked him whether it was because he couldn't get his soldier to stand to attention – if so, that wouldn't be a problem, and she would be quite happy to be entertained by his surgeon's fingers or even a pneumatic tongue. Or was his problem that he arrived at the station too early?

No those were not the reasons, at least he didn't think so. It had been a good while that he had been celibate as well as clean. In his own forthright way, Nick explained that it was just that he was so up his own arse with worry about his prospects that he couldn't think of anything else. Perhaps in the future, if there was going to be one …..

'It's a shame, beautiful Nick, but it seems to me you've lost the habit of happiness. What do you think?'

'I'm sure you're right, Anili – I really have forgotten how to enjoy life. Pathetic.'

Nick realised that Anili was someone that he could indeed open to. Without embarrassment, he explained to her that he was in disgrace with his wife and he was just an old-fashioned guy who believed that once one had made a decision, one should stay with it and he was not yet ready to be unfaithful to Allison. In any case, he did not deserve anyone as lovely and intelligent as Anili. Eventually, Anili stopped pushing, but the warmth and humour they shared was special and was the only good memory he would have of his time in this small Suffolk town.

What Nick was unaware of was that one night as she passed by, Dr Susan McDonald had seen the two of them sharing a joke at his table, and this cut her to the quick.

An Indian waitress in preference to an English surgeon? What was he thinking? By the same token, what was she, Dr Susan McDonald, thinking? How could she even have considered that such a pathetic man, a dishonest drug-taking professional and seeker of lowlife sex, could become a suitable partner? Well, if that was the way it was, so be it - her time would come, and he would learn a painful lesson.

# Chapter 13

## Mr Bernard Finch, Barrister London 2010

A year had elapsed since the first meeting at DIG, and there had been a dozen more group discussions in London during that period. Nick's barrister, reputed to be the best defender of errant or plain unlucky medical professionals in the legal arena, was the small, scraggly, sharp-tongued, ferret-faced and seemingly very spiteful man named Bernard Finch. Mr. Finch had the hangdog appearance of one who had known misery in the past but had made peace with it. Everything in his demeanour spoke not of present sadness or anger, merely of world-weariness and condescension.

His suit (it appeared he only had one that had probably originated in a charity shop) was always dishevelled although always clean. His once white shirts were matched in their dullness by the paisley tie that never varied. For some undeclared reason, Bernard always wore red tartan socks, but the cherry on the bottom was the hole in the sole of his right shoe. Bluntly put, it was a 'fuck you' shoe that was always resting on rather than under the table. The message his shoe conveyed was that he cared little how poorly you thought of him, he thought less of you.

If one tried to imagine why he was the way he was, one only had to imagine what his childhood must have been like: pushed around mercilessly by his rugby–playing older brother, despised by his ex-military father who thought him a runt, and bullied by the much bigger but far less clever boys at school. His mother was somewhat kinder, but over the years had been reduced to a nonentity by her overpowering husband especially when he was fortified by a couple of glasses of scotch. It was not an unusual event in their home for dishes to be thrown or even for the dining table to be upturned when the bully perceived his food to be overcooked or undercooked or poorly cooked. His father was not a soldier who took prisoners.

Shrimpy runty little Bernard had only two weapons in his arsenal – a razor-sharp tongue and the intelligence and ability to use it venomously. It mattered little how many times he got punched or shoved, the deliverer was always left wondering if he really was as stupid as Bernard made him feel. So it followed that year after year Bernard was top scholar, and the law was his natural destination.

It was not long before he decided that being a solicitor was adequate for his sharp mind but not for his sharp tongue, so in the shortest time possible he was called to the bar. There, he found he was at worst on equal grounds with the latest set of bullies to oppose him, and at best two leagues ahead. His incisive mind was as unforgiving as his razor tongue, and he became known as one of two barristers above all others one would least want to have in opposition. Why did he choose the medico-legal field? Well, contract law was boring, financial issues were of little interest to him, property disputes even less so, and marital matters not at all. At least in the medico-legal arena he could see quickly and clearly which issues were beyond the pale and which were winnable, and his special ability was to convert the former to the latter.

Bernard looked at his papers as he addressed Nick. 'The list of allegations against you is far worse than I could ever have imagined.'

He read them out, pausing after each one:

- *conduct unbecoming of a professional;*
- *withholding relevant information from a fellow professional;*
- *drug abuse;*
- *fraudulent self-prescription;*
- *fraudulently falsifying prescriptions in others' names for personal gain;*
- *breaking the trust of patients;*
- *putting patients at risk;*
- *bringing the hospital into disrepute;*
- *bringing the profession into disrepute;*
- *working while under the influence of drugs;*
- *deception of colleagues;*
- *deception of pharmacists;*
- *putting pharmacists at risk;*
- *dishonesty.*

On and on and on. Nick was left with little doubt of the barrister's disdain.

'A three-week hearing has been scheduled a year from now. Three weeks, Nick. They really mean business, I'm sorry to say.'

Nick winced, but said nothing, for there was nothing to say. A year from now. Another year of Suffolk and tonsillectomies and Dr Susan McDonald. Another year of Mr Bernard Finch and his viper tongue and his holier-than-thou hole in the shoe. Another year of Dr Sir James Clifton and his pursed lips and vibrating eyebrow moustaches. Another year of Dr Wilfred Barnes the living corpse and hair tests every second week. Worst of all, another year of not going home on weekends to Allison's stony silence. He was filled with dread feelings of existential disaster. The nuclear option seemed to be edging closer.

Bernard Finch saw from the off that unless he could get

Nick to accept his shortcomings, the case would not go well. Although it was taking a bit longer than usual to lick his client into submission, he had no doubt that when the hearing began, the man in the dock would seem like one of life's saddest victims who had been systematically bullied by his English colleagues only because he was from the colonies; an unfortunate casualty who had only developed the nefarious habit of abusing a medication drug because his dedication to work rendered it difficult to cope with life.

That Nick had acted fraudulently was undeniable, but if it could be shown that by the time he misappropriated the use of his patients' names he was already a victim (albeit self-inflicted) of a drug addiction beyond his capacity AT THAT TIME to control, then the case would swing from a *criminal* problem to a *medical* one.

This was not a nicety, but of major importance.

Not for one moment did Bernard believe that the Medical Practice Supervisory Committee would be any more kindly disposed to forgive Nick's misdemeanours at a hearing deemed *medical*, but it was one of the accepted conventions that whereas *criminal* wrongdoings including dishonesty and fraud were automatically punishable by erasure, the worst sanction against *medical* misdemeanours was an indefinite suspension. This would be held in force only for as long as it took to prove rehabilitation was complete and there was no risk to the public of re-offending. This of course might take some time, even years. His medical masters would not be in a hurry to reinstate until they were sure. However, as Finch pointed out, no matter how long it took, it was a great deal better than the alterative of erasure.

The second big advantage was that medical hearings were conducted 'in private' and not open to the public, and so could not be reported; and if there was anything that would really gut Nick, it would be to have his case brought into the public domain.

Yet still he demurred.

# Chapter 14

## Dr Stanley Wethers  London 2010

Bernard might have been Nick's only barrister, but Nick was by no means Bernard's only client to be defended. He suggested to Nick that it might be very helpful to his cause if Nick sat with him on a case that was about to be heard. This would include attendance at the pre-trial discussions at the DIG's offices. For once Nick did not offer resistance. He arranged to take a week's leave that was due to him and travelled up to London to sit in as an observer at the case of a dentist, Dr Stanley Wethers.

Wethers had been 'requested' to appear before the Behavioural Panel of the Dental Practice Committee. The allegations against him related to issues including inappropriate conduct towards patients, and rudeness to and in front of staff.

A psychiatric report noted that Stanley Wethers had showed a tendency to a schizoid disorder possibly related to excess use of recreational drugs and alcohol in the past. It was also suggested he might suffer from Asperger's syndrome. It referred to other reports relating to a narcissistic personality disorder. Wethers seemed to lack empathy and social skills and was unaware and uncaring of other people's feelings. All in all, thought Nick, a potent cocktail.

Stanley Wethers was an unprepossessing man in his early thirties, slightly overweight, somewhat dishevelled with his tie not quite fitting under his collar. If Nick was uncharitable, he would describe him as 'slobbish.' Wethers did not see himself as being at all slobbish, if anything rather dashing. He was rather unwilling to listen to anything Bernard had to say that did not meet his elevated self-estimation. Not for a moment did he accept the need for counselling. Bernard Finch opined that this, together with an unwillingness to shift his point of view to accommodate others and a tendency to see others' shortcomings rather than his own, might collectively be characteristic of Asperger's, a condition he had learned much about over the years.

Nick felt very uncomfortable. Had he not at times shown some of the same tendencies as Wethers? And, unpalatable thought, could he possibly be on the narcissistic spectrum himself? Was this why Finch had suggested he attend this particular case?

Mr Finch advised his client that, by making appropriate admissions, Wethers would show that he had reflected and show a level of insight. If they could have their expert psychiatrist's report disclosed, they might also be able to persuade the Behavioural Panel to refer the case to the Health Committee.

'This would be in your best interests – not least because it would remove the risk of erasure', advised Bernard.

Wethers was having none of this. He wrote a short note to his legal team:

*'I accept that you believe you are making this recommendation in what you believe to be my best interests, but I do not want the case referred to the Health Committee. This would be tantamount to an admission of mental illness, which I do not accept I have. I believe that my case is strong, and that we can show there has been a concerted and on-going conspiracy against me by the staff at my former practice.'*

Bernard was livid. Sir James was apoplectic with rage. They knew that there was more chance of them both falling pregnant than of Stanley Wethers getting off with a conspiracy defence. Strange how often medical defendants wished to play the conspiracy card!

Yet Stanley Wethers was absolutely correct about one point made in his note – his former staff hated him. No that is no way strong enough. They utterly loathed him. He was the kind of individual who made going into work every day something seriously to be avoided for those about him. They detested him sufficiently to lodge a serious complaint to the Committee. As events would show, they had very good reasons for loathing him.

At a meeting the day before the hearing, Wethers left the room to go outdoors for a cigarette (not a pleasant habit for a dentist). Finch lowered his head into his hands as he said to Nick, 'Unfortunately, there has been some heat but little light generated in this case. Essentially Dr Wethers continues to reject psychiatric evidence obtained, preferring to pin his defence upon an illusory conspiracy theory. He leaves me with little ammunition for the fight. I still hold out a glimmer of hope that we will convince him to adopt the psychiatric evidence that may give him a chance of avoiding erasure, but I'm not holding my breath.'

They met at 8:30 on the opening morning of the hearing. For Nick, this involved not only attendance at the hearing but also access to the defence room for private discussions. It would be a first time for him and turned out to be an eye-opener of the first order.

The defence room was small and airless - too small to hold five occupants. It was filled to the eaves with the countless boxes of files of the two female solicitors. That they were young women did not surprise Nick – medicine seemed be going the same way. And of course, he was reminded of his wife whose face seemed in the distant past. It had been months since they last spoke.

Finch gave Wethers a detailed overview as to how the hearing would be conducted. It was due to commence at 10am. At 9:35, Dr Stanley Wethers finally realised he did not have a leg to stand on, and acquiesced. He agreed to accept the use of a diagnosis of an individual with schizoid and narcissistic tendencies and probably suffering from Asperger's Syndrome to explain his bizarre behaviour. A number of allegations were now admitted rather than denied. At last he was beginning to show some insight. The hearing was immediately designated as a Health Matter to be conducted in private.

As they walked in tandem to the hearing room, Mr Finch whispered to Nick, 'Thank the bloody heavens for that!'

When they entered and seated themselves, the chairperson of the committee introduced himself and the four other members of his committee. They appeared a serious lot.

The prosecuting counsel acting for the Dental Conduct Committee, Mr Tam Grove, made his opening remarks. He spoke of a number of little actions carried out on a daily basis that when added together added up to exceedingly poor conduct. If it was found to be so, that was sufficient for counsel to demand that Dr Wethers be suspended at best, and at worst to have his licence to practise withdrawn. He was not a person who brought credit to an honourable profession, said the barrister.

When Dr Wether's nurse was examined, she spoke of his overwhelming frequency of poor behaviour in the form of belching, breaking wind ('farting', as she bluntly put it), sexist and racist jokes and comments, all of which she said were done in the presence of staff and occasionally of patients. She used terms such as 'a daily occurrence', and 'all day long'.

Wethers had admitted performing such acts in the presence of staff but only because he thought it 'amusing'. He denied doing this in front of patients. He did admit to flashing v-signs behind patients' backs when they annoyed him, which was frequently, but did not think this was anything other than 'silly'.

His nurse said he was rude, sarcastic and arrogant. He denigrated foreign and ethnic patients as well as the elderly and disabled. She had complained to the practice Principal, who seemed to do very little in response. All he said was that associate dentists were difficult to obtain, and bad as Wethers was, he was better than nobody.

It was time for patients to give evidence. The first two complained of the abrupt and uncaring way they were treated. One, a new patient, was particularly annoyed by being told three times to be sure to pay before leaving. He was offended by being asked whether his "smelly breath was not offensive to his partner". The patient, a lonely man, would have given much to have a partner that he could offend!

The final patient of several to give evidence was, from Stan Wethers' perspective, damning. A woman in her thirties, she had come as a new patient with a fractured tooth and was given an emergency appointment at lunchtime. She said Dr Wethers was extremely rude about having to work through his lunch hour. No nurse was present. He administered local anaesthetic without her permission and without discussing options other than extraction. He then sent her downstairs to pay for her treatment, which, as treatment had not yet been carried out, upset her greatly. She broke down in tears on several occasions while giving evidence, adding substantially to the overall negative swell of opinion of an uncaring practitioner.

Nick found this whole saga depressing, the only ray of sunshine being that he was sure none of his own patients would ever complain of him being anything less than kind and pleasant. He felt relieved that none of his staff (or at least none that he was aware of) would be likely to level complaints of boorish conduct against him. Or was that really true? Self-doubt was beginning to replace all sense of assuredness in his self-evaluation. Would his nurses turn on him? Would his patients? If they did, he would be doomed.

This was precisely the reason that Bernard had invited him to attend: to reflect not on how he saw himself but on how others might see him.

At the end of day 3, Nick and Bernard were sitting alone in the small Defence room, the others having left for the day.

'What do you make of this so far, Nick?'

'Well, he's certainly a one-off. I've worked with many dentists and they couldn't be kinder or more dedicated. Makes one wonder how he ever got through his dental training. I'm no expert, Bernard, but it seems that Wethers' professional career is about to go up shit creek without a paddle. He doesn't seem to want to help himself, and he's making it difficult for you to do much for him. What do you think?'

'I'm sure you're right, so what do we have to do?'

'Well. I think you've got to convince Wethers that his best hope lies in not trying to justify his conduct but to accept responsibility for constantly upsetting his colleagues and patients, and grovel.'

'Hmm, that's very astute. Unfortunately, he's very reluctant to do that because he simply cannot see he has behaved unprofessionally. But here's a thought, Nick: might that not reflect your position too?'

Nick winced and said nothing but Bernard knew that his words had hit the target smack in the middle of the bull.

The Defence case was about to begin, and following a couple of hours of discussion in the Defence room, Prof Denis Troughton gave evidence. He was Clinical Professor of Psychotherapy at a leading UK university. He said Wethers' condition was characterised by three problems: communication difficulties and poor social interaction were two. His behaviour was also characterized by being unaware of another's feelings and by an inability to read and appreciate expressions and signals from others. As children, individuals such as he tended to be restricted in play and preferred being alone, playing repetitive games and routines.

He thought Wethers did exhibit a significant lack of empathy and social skills and did not know how to get people on his side because he was unable to place himself in their shoes. He said inappropriate things at inappropriate times. His perceived negative experience of some black or elderly patients had led him to think poorly of them, but he did not think Wethers was fundamentally racist or ageist or elitist.

Prof Troughton noted that Wethers had suffered from stress when he was overloaded, and this was exacerbated by the high-volume flow of patients. Alcoholic drink and drug intake may or may not have been directly related to professional work patterns but may have increased anxiety.

Was Wethers on the autistic spectrum? Troughton thought it highly probable that he was.

When asked if Dr Wethers was fit to practise, Troughton said that although the man clearly had serious issues, given time and with appropriate help Wethers could return as a responsible member of the dental community.

# Chapter 15

## The Train Crash   London 2010

As the hearing moved towards the end of the first week, NIck decided to make a checklist of the positives and negatives of his own case compared to the one he was attending. In his entire medical career, he had never knowingly been rude to a patient. Tick. He had never treated poorer patients differently. Tick. He had never demanded money from a patient, tick, or been motivated by money, another tick.

He enjoyed alcohol occasionally, had never knowingly been drunk; had never got himself hooked on recreational drugs – tick – but he had become dependent on medication – cross cross. Which was worse? He had forged prescriptions. Cross cross cross cross cross. Throughout the past week he had seen himself as being a better practitioner than Wethers, but as he scanned his list, he began to have serious doubts. The big test for Wethers was still to come, and the auguries were not good. What would they be like for him?

Dr Wethers would be next to give evidence on his own behalf. Bernard had pleaded with him *not* to do so, but Wethers wasn't about to miss his opportunity to show that he was a far better person than his staff had led the Committee to believe. He was determined to have his time in the sun. Finch knew that this would be a walk to the scaffold, but Wethers was adamant. You know that feeling you get when you give someone sane advice and they choose to do exactly the opposite? Bernard once again asked Stanley to reflect carefully on the testimony he would offer and advised him to use the psychiatrist's diagnosis as his only possible get-out-of-jail card. Wethers finally acquiesced in respect of the last point.

Before opening his questioning, Bernard apologised on behalf of Wethers to those patients whose feelings had been hurt. Then he focused on minimising damage rather than blanket denials. He attempted to show that although there were instances where Stanley had behaved bizarrely, there were reasons for this behaviour that could be explained and understood although not defended by his diagnosed medical condition. When Wethers was asked if he made negative remarks to his nurse regarding black patients, he responded that he had inquired if they were black simply because it had implications for their treatment.

Finch completed his examination by mid-afternoon, and it seemed that Stan Wethers had at last managed to take given advice on board and to avoid the temptation to go off piste. Finch was happy with the manner in which Wethers conducted himself but knew, knew absolutely, that imperilment would follow the moment Mr Groves began cross-examination.

After a brief adjournment, Tam Groves began questioning Dr Wethers. His defence team experienced feelings of dread trepidation. They had coached him to keep his responses short and to the point; not to volunteer information unless specifically requested to do so; not to answer questions with questions; not to speculate; and not to allow himself to be baited. But they knew that the first time one his many buttons was pressed by Mr Tam Grove he would explode.

It was apparent quite quickly that Wether's attitude had begun to deteriorate. Low blood sugar? Highly likely. With each passing question, he seemed to become more testy, as Bernard knew he would, and began to respond to questions with questions of his own until he was warned twice not to do so by the chairperson.

Unfortunately, nobody foresaw the moment when he would metaphorically shoot himself not in the foot but in the head. He did so by uttering a hideous gratuitous comment. When asked whether he had made his remarks about black patients because he had issues about them, his response was that he did not have such issues.

Then he added for no apparent reason, "Black people can't be trusted".

Bang.

This was the domino that sent all the previously precarious but still upright dominoes tumbling. Nick passed a short note to Bernard simply saying "suicide." Bernard smiled wryly – was Nick beginning to show a glimmer of insight at last? After another 45 minutes of questioning, the chairperson put a premature end to an utterly disastrous session. Erasure now appeared to be inevitable.

The following day, the Committee went *in camera*. The atmosphere in the Defence room was akin to what it must have been like in days past when waiting with a criminal charged with murder, knowing with absolute certainty that the death sentence was imminent. Bernard and Nick tried unsuccessfully to make light banter, but the only person who seemed unfazed was Wethers. He thought he had done rather well, and nobody in the room was in the mood to disabuse him of this notion.

After eight hours of deliberation, the Committee on the following day returned a verdict of impairment of fitness to practise due to misconduct.

Then came the bombshell.

The degree of Dr Wether's misconduct was "so egregious" that it was of sufficient magnitude to eliminate the possibility of mitigation even on health grounds. Even though it was not an action they would normally have considered, an order was made to erase the name of Stanley Wethers with immediate effect.

The sword had fallen.

Not at any time since the hearing began had Wethers really understood what he had done, but he did understand what had just happened to him. So did Nick. What Wethers said to Finch as he walked into the defence room does not bear repeating, but he departed to an extremely uncertain future that no one thought would end well.

Later, Nick said to Bernard 'I think the sanction on Wethers was extremely severe. You said he couldn't be struck off if the case was medical, didn't you?' Bernard just shrugged and explained why Wethers' name has been erased: issues of lack of insight and aggressive and generally poor performance in the witness stand pushed the situation towards suspension, but the tipping point was undoubtedly his racist rant that led to its final result.

'In this day and age in the UK, many things could be forgiven, but one that cannot is overt racism. It might have been different had Wethers accepted advice given, listened and cooperated. There was no need for him to go into the witness box and I advised him not to. A tragic case, and we could see it coming', concluded Bernard. 'A really unpleasant and quite nasty man. What he needed was the help of a psychiatrist. What he got was erasure. What he faces is a life of bitterness and alcoholic abuse.'

Stanley Wether's defence team had done everything possible to save him, but he would not be saved. Bernard did not want the same thing to happen to Nick. He knew better than to ram that point home. It was something to be dealt with in the near future, but not at that moment.

'Nick, can I make a suggestion? I think it would be sensible for you to take a few days off, go abroad and reflect on the hearing you have just witnessed. I'm quite sure it would do you a lot of good. You've been under tremendous stress for quite a while now, so you deserve some away time.'

Nick thought this did indeed make sense, but where to go? Decisions didn't come easily for him at that time, least of all choosing a holiday - especially when his thinking, looming large at that moment, was of his own erasure. But he still had another week of leave due to him, and the thought of a week away from all of this became irresistible.

# Chapter 16

## Puglia 2011

Nick scanned the travel section of his newspaper. One advert leaped out at him – Chitalia! He had always wanted to see Italy, especially because of his love of Italian opera, but work had always taken priority. Well, he thought, why not now? He phoned the company to inquire what was available for Rome or Milan or Verona. The answer was *niente*. Another disappointment – he was beginning to expect this. A pause. Then the agent said they did have a cancellation for a week-long coach tour in Puglia leaving in a couple of weeks. Where was Puglia? It didn't really matter. Anywhere in Italy would do - he just needed to refocus while not under pressure.

He was informed he could, if he wished, bring a companion at little additional cost. He e-mailed Allison. He did not expect a positive response when he asked, 'Do you fancy a break in Puglia with me next week? I think it would be good for us to start mending fences'. He was correct in his supposition – in her own mind she barely managed to add the word 'thanks' to the 'no'.

As one can imagine, Susan McDonald was not well pleased that her precious schedule would have to be rearranged at such short notice, but the nurses were only too happy to have their workload eased if only for a few days.

The flight to Bari was uneventful. Three hours after their departure, they were on a sleek air-conditioned tour bus heading for the town of Ostuni. Nick soon realised that, with one exception, he was the youngest in the group of sixteen by at least thirty years. The other younger person was an attractive and vivacious American woman. Jesse was a well-known travel correspondent (well-known in America anyway) on a review experience for a network of American newspapers and a tv channel in Denver, Colorado.

They struck up an immediate friendship, so much so that they would have difficulty later in convincing the rest of the group that they were not an 'item.' For Nick, being with someone who did not treat him as a leper with halitosis was blissful.

Ostuni is known as the White City, and the scenic Old Town sits on a hill. As Jesse sat sipping cocktails and Nick a soda on a piazza in the centre of the old town, the setting sun had turned the white walls a radiant gold. It was a glorious and unforgettable sight, the first of many on this short holiday.

At dinner on the first evening in the modern boutique hotel that was to be their home for the next few nights, Nick sat with Jesse and six others. The rest of the group included a couple, Wilfred and Mary, aged eighty-five and eighty-two respectively, who both turned out to be very well-known semi-retired thespians. Although now acting only occasionally, they were both fully in control of all their faculties, not least memory, and the luvvies had a wealth of humorous stories about behind–the–stage events. Many of these concerned highly rated current actors and actresses, and the stories ranged from indiscrete dalliances to scabrous misconduct. The elderly couple were themselves somewhat less than discrete, and their stories were endlessly light-hearted and often hilarious. Nick laughed as he had not done in months, laughed till he had to rush to the toilet to avoid wetting himself. The more wine the older couple drank, and they drank copiously, the bluer their stories turned.

As he was to discover the following day, Mary and Wilfred were as agile physically as they were mind-wise. Nick smiled wryly as he thought *'If only I can be like this in forty years' time ......'*. And the next thought that flashed through his mind was, *'The way my life is going, I'll be lucky to be alive in forty months' time'*. Then he smiled - just three weeks ago he was contemplating not seeing his next birthday.

The tour guide was a small but solidly built Venetian barrister-at-law named Marco. When not on a major international finance case in Naples or Rome or Florence, Marco spent his time sitting in the front of a luxury tour bus imparting his voluminous knowledge about the history and architecture of Ostuni and the surrounding towns. A barrister working as a tour guide? Certainly not for the money. No, it was as prosaic as simply enjoying the company of interested and often interesting strangers and being able to share his knowledge and love of his fatherland. Although Marco's Italian accent was so thick that it would have taken a hacksaw to remove it, he was a bottomless well of information about local churches, old towns, industry, and not least, Puglian cuisine.

Nick resisted the opportunity to discuss his own legal case with Marco – he was there to forget about it, if only briefly.

There are more olive trees than there are people in Italy, and many of those trees are in Puglia. Most of those sturdy gnarled trees, beautiful in their squat green-and-grey ugliness, were several hundreds of years old. The group was taken to an olive oil producing farm where they were introduced to the process that resulted in the production of top-grade extra-virgin olive oil. To their surprise they observed that some of the crushing machines were massively large stone wheels dating back a multitude of generations, whereas others were brand new machines, shiny like Italian knives and just as sharp. They were able to taste the fresh peppery oil and appreciated for the first time that purchasing olive oil needed as much care in selection as a good vintage wine or a quality balsamic vinegar.

To each place they travelled Nick and Jesse sat together, thus reinforcing their 'item' status.

They visited a small town called Alberrobello, famous for its Trulli homes unique to Puglia. Trulli, small houses with funnel-shaped roofs dating back hundreds of years, were postcard perfect. They looked like they should have been inhabited by Hobbits, but were increasingly being bought up and zhuzhified by the wealthy, especially Brits wanting a foothold in Italy - and where better to have a foothold than in its heel?

Next on the itinerary was an experience in making *orecchiette,* the little pasta discs shaped into tiny ears by nimble fingers. They visited an *agritourismo,* a farmstead with a traditional restaurant attached. There they learned to mix the dough using just spelt and water, roll this into thin long sausages, divide into small cubes and shape these into the little ears. That was the work experience. The pleasure part came in boiling what they had just prepared, lathering the *orecchiette* in fresh tomato paste, and eating their own little ears with freshly baked *focaccia.* Heavenly!

The normally uncommunicative surgeon found himself engaged in discussions with the older group members about every conceivable subject. One fellow of eighty, David, had written no less than thirteen books about Southampton football club. The most recent one was about players who had fought in the First World War. Many never returned. Nick marvelled that an octogenarian was still capable of such erudite pursuits, and then remembered that many conductors and composers were only reaching their prime in their ninth decade. Maybe he should stick around life for a bit longer!

The evenings were spent in local *osterias* and *albergos* enjoying the local cuisine prepared simply and to perfection using locally harvested produce served with delectable seafood. The tomatoes even tasted like tomatoes! Simple local wine was in plentiful supply for the others if not for Nick, which wasn't easy but he did not as much as once sneak a sip.

He and Jesse found themselves chatting endlessly and sharing more and more of their life experiences but that was as far it went. Although both were experiencing marital issues, neither was prepared to complicate them. Later Nick would wonder about this and wish he had, but came to the conclusion that had he pushed it and been rebuffed, it would have ruined a heart-warming relationship, and he was certain he could not have withstood another knock-back.

They did however discuss and share their marital tribulations. Nick wryly commented, 'I've learned something interesting: it took my wife to dump me to make me realise how many friends I never had.'

On Jesse's side, her architect husband's career had hit a serious slump after the prime mortgage debacle. When the whole US property market went into tailspin, it knocked not only their finances but his self-esteem and their relationship into a downward spiral. As many of his colleagues had done, he had dealt with the issue by hitting the bottle very hard indeed. There were nights when he came home drunk as a polecat, and others where he did not come home at all. Despite all that, and more, Jesse had stuck by her Randy, and eventually with a lot of help from her and from AA, he seemed to be on an upward gradient and was not only abstaining but also finding new projects. Their relationship, although badly damaged, was making a recovery. She had come on this trip to recover her own badly dented spirit.

Nick on the other hand was on a slippery slope downwards, and Jesse, by contrast with Allison, was a lot more understanding, although, as she herself said, it was a lot easier to be sympathetic when you're on the outside looking in, especially in the idyllic setting of Puglia. She advised him not to surrender hope of resurrecting his relationship with Allison, but then she had not met Allison.

They visited the ancient city of Matera, allegedly the world's oldest city, where inhabitants had lived in caves with their animals for fifteen thousand years on a steep rocky outcrop until the late nineteen-sixties when the habitations were declared unacceptably unsanitary. Around them they saw some signs of cinematic activity but were completely unaware that this was to be the opening scene of the next James Bond epic, *No Time To Die,* something that even the omniscient Marco was unaware of.

The group walked through the labyrinthine caverns of Castellana with its multitude of steps that were not too much for the eighty-something-year-old youngsters Wilfred and Mary, who also found no difficulty in exploring the narrow streets of beautiful old Ostuni every evening. By the time the coach-trip ended Nick would remind himself of two current aphorisms: age was just a number, and life was to be lived.

He would remember the afternoon they had sat on the hotel patio, Jesse with a glass of white wine, he nursing a soda. He was observing two builder-decorators at work on a scaffold, patching the crumbling masonry of an aged bell-tower opposite the hotel. The builders were dressed in shorts, T-shirts and trainers and were well weathered by sun and wind. Their only concession to the ravages of solar rays were large handkerchiefs secured around their greying heads. They smoked as they scraped out and then plastered the cracks of the aged facade to the strains of popular Italian tunes coming from a paint-decorated and probably birdshit-spattered radio. They worked quickly and neatly, and in a short while one wall appeared transformed.

Nick thought their work was not dissimilar to his – cut out what's defective, close up and allow to heal. Then he thought, they might well die one day of skin or lung cancer, but they were never going to succumb to the stresses of whether their building lived or crumbled. Their work was not subject to the scrutiny of some governing board, only to their employer's. When the sun set, they would return home to a delicious *pasta al pomodori* and a glass of chianti, and their only worry would be whether it would rain the next day or not. Would he trade jobs with them? At that moment, he thought he definitely could.

The days passed quickly, too quickly, and for the first time in many months, Nick did not give Leeds, Suffolk, Bernard or Allison much thought. He was deeply saddened to say farewell to Marco, Wilfred, Mary, and most of all to Jesse, whom he had grown to love in the space of a week. *C'est la vie*. Addresses were exchanged in the sure knowledge that no-one would ever contact anyone else ever again.

Unfortunately, this was the only pleasure Nick was to enjoy for a long while.

## Chapter 17

## The Missile  London 2011

On his return, Nick continued in his work at the small hospital in Suffolk. It was mundane and boring. He continued to be disinterested in forming any relationships with the nursing staff in general, and with the forty-something year-old doctor in particular, who by now had returned to her former icy ways. He was certain of few things, but one thing he knew with absolute clarity – he could not wait to get away from working with this sour woman, and if he never saw her again it would be too soon.

The Wethers case was a tipping point, The bell had finally tolled, and Nick realised that a change of attitude was essential if he was not to suffer the same fate. For too long a time, Nick had resisted accepting the notion that he was the architect of his own misfortune. He had persisted in his belief that he had harmed no one, not even himself, and therefore the whole affair was being overblown. He had simply refused to see himself as a certified addict. Bernard Finch's remorseless persistence and the positive experience of his week with Jesse finally tilted Nick to give way to the relentless assault on his pride.

He had been an ass, a stupid one at that. A big step forward as far as Bernard was concerned; at last Nick agreed to accept most, if not all, of the allegations, thereby not forcing Bernard to defend the indefensible.

When eventually Nick decided to take ownership of his actions, albeit reluctantly, that break-through did help also to ease tension between him and Allison, if only to a limited degree. When he informed her a few days later of his change of attitude, she simply said 'That helps everybody – I'll assist where I can.'

It did not bring him back to her bed, nor to their home, but at least they began to talk. They did not discuss their future together, or even their future apart although that was becoming a distinct probability. What they did talk about with each other and with his legal team was how to minimise the severity of his punishment (his 'sanctions' as it was termed by the legal people) at the forthcoming hearing.

Using her legal letterhead, Allison threw energy into obtaining testimonials for Nick. This was by no means an easy task – most of his patients praised his surgical skills, but too many used expressions like "he seemed quite remote at times" or "he didn't really to seem to care about anything except getting the job done", even "he wasn't much concerned about my feelings." Allison could well understand this. Of the five hundred people she wrote to, only eighty responded, and only twenty were usable; but twenty good testimonials would go a long way, and the Committee would not need to know about the other 480.

However, as Bernard kept reminding him, all this would not be worth the paper on which it was written if Nick himself didn't show up as a reformed, insightful and caring individual, beyond whose lips no alcohol, drugs or medication, not even aspirin, had passed for two years. For the first time, Nick began to appreciate the wisdom and tenacity of his barrister. And to learn that there was a much kinder side to Bernard as well.

His *locum tenens* in Suffolk came to an end, he'd said goodbye to his nurses and his colleagues, even including

McDonald, He'd reluctantly also said goodbye to Anili, who wept like a baby. He did, however, leave her with an envelope containing a voucher for a return ticket to New York at a time of her choosing, and he departed with lipstick and mascara in equal measure all over his face.

Had Allison witnessed this touching farewell, would she have been upset? Little chance of that. She had settled back into the life of a single woman as if she had never left it. She was enjoying the luxury of closeness to her family and friends once more, enjoying her squash as much as ever, and missing bodily contact not a jot. Her law practice was thriving, and she was earning more than enough to have no concerns about her future. Most of all, she did not miss the debilitating drip-drip torture of Nick's slow descent.

The hearing which was to take place in Manchester was drawing near. It was due to commence two years almost to the day from when he had first received the letter that had taken him and Allison to breaking point. It was all Nick could think of, and the process was exhausting him. Over and over, alternative ways he could have behaved - but didn't - percolated around his brain. These did nothing to elevate his sense of self-worth, and he was increasingly fearful of a disastrous outcome: suspension, or worse, erasure. Arrest and imprisonment. Could he face any of this? The more he tried to shut these thoughts from his mind, the larger they loomed.

On the other hand, Nick's defence team, ably led by Bernard, was feeling confident that even though this was not a case that could be won, at least they could mitigate the sanction to a modest suspension of three months, the minimum allowed. No suspension at all would be sending the wrong message to the profession and public about doctors who dabbled with drugs, even one who had behaved impeccably over the past couple of years and met every condition that could possibly be required by the arbiters of the medical profession. In short, even though he had fully remediated, a punishment was required.

The lawyers at DIG were working overtime to find supportive psychiatrists who would give expert testimony. Two were traced. These did not include Dr Margie O'Connor who was only too happy to agree to give evidence against him, as were at least half a dozen local pharmacists.

'What chance have I got, Bernard? Even with those two psychiatrists batting for me, O'Connor's evidence will destroy whatever they've got say.'

'I wish I could say it will go well but one can't be sure. What is sure is that your conduct in Suffolk was exemplary, and that I will do everything I can to present the admirable you that I have come to know.'

Then, just one day before the hearing, they were rocked by q bombshell - no, bombshell doesn't come close – by an Exocet missile launched by none other than Susan McDonald. Bernard was informed that the Medical Practice Committee had decided to add two additional allegations, the first about possible intent to abuse alcohol, and the second and far more serious, alleging suggested sexual misconduct. These allegations had been made by his erstwhile surgery colleague.

McDonald had complained to the committee about an alleged statement made by Nick as he entered the staffroom after an operation, to wit: *"That was a bloody difficult operation, and what I need right now is a large whisky and a good screw."* She said that the second part of the alleged statement was made as he looked directly at her, belittling her in front of other members of staff.

One could not be sure who was more shattered, Nick or Bernard. 'Did you utter those words, Nick?' asked Bernard as the team gathered in his chambers eighteen hours before the hearing was to begin.

Nick could only laugh, funny though it was not. 'It's utter bollocks, Bernard. In the two years that I was in Suffolk I only had one operation where I encountered extreme difficulties: an older man who had fallen and cracked his jaw and neglected to inform us that he was on Warfarin. Consequently, he bled copiously and unendingly to the point where a transfusion was necessary, and we thought we might lose him. After an hour and a half we managed to stem the bleeding, and if I came into the staff-room and did say anything to that effect, which I can assure you I have no recollection of having done but very well might have, it could only have been made subconsciously and echoed my feelings *at the time* about the difficulties we had just experienced. In any case, she'd be the last person in the world I would ever think of having any form of sex with. A good screw with Susan Mc Donald is a contradiction in terms.'

Bernard glared at him. 'Please don't repeat that last sentence in front of the Committee, or you'll end up like Oscar Wilde.'

# Chapter 18

## Head beaten   Manchester 2011

The Committee was made up of four people. In the chair was Lady Felicity Duff, a former lawyer and career committee panellist; she would be supported by a maxillo-facial surgeon, a general medical practitioner and another ex-lawyer: according to Bernard, not a panel known for sympathy and definitely not one to be taken lightly.

To make matters worse, the prosecuting barrister was one Miss Shirley Leadbetter, known to all as Shirley Headbeater. Anyone who had been unfortunate enough to cross her path would testify to this as being the absolute truth. If Bernard was the master of the sharp-pointed rapier, Leadbetter employed the cudgel, albeit while wearing silken gloves. She was a caricature of an amply proportioned large woman with flaming red hair and deep booming voice. She was formidable, to which any poor defendant who had ever been head-beaten by her would attest. In boxing parlance, when she hit you, you stayed hit. She made Bernard look sweet. Bernard knew that she would milk the allegations by McDonald to the full, and indeed this was evident from the outset in her perfectly enunciated opening address to the panel.

Leadbetter began oh so sweetly. 'Madam Chair, the issue today is straightforward. We are here to decide whether Mr Nicholas Simpson is fit to remain a member of the medical profession. I will contend that he is not. We will present evidence that his conduct has been so egregious as to render him totally unworthy of so honourable a calling, the highest to which a person may aspire.'

She paused to allow her words to sink in before continuing.

'Nevertheless, I am sure that in due course, my learned friend will be producing evidence and testimonials galore attesting to Mr Simpson's skill as a surgeon. I will not be opposing this in any manner whatsoever; there are no issues likely to result in criticism of Mr Simpson's ability. Indeed, Madam, his record as a clinical surgeon is exemplary, and there is no one who will testify that he was not competent enough to be carrying out difficult and skilful operations to the fullest requirements and most exacting standards of the medical profession. He is a medal winner, a recipient of bursaries.' (*Damn her, thought Bernard, in the first two minutes she has just managed to make light of virtually our entire defence.*)

'Yet, here is a man who has taken all these gifts, ALL these God-given gifts, and flung them in the teeth of the profession that he so ably represents. He has been economical with the truth with a fellow member of his profession, Dr Margaret O'Connor. He has abused the use of medication, and worst of all, used the names and conditions of his patients to fuel that abuse.

'He has played fast and loose with the allied profession of pharmacy, and you will be hearing plenty about that, I can assure you. Yet he will deny being a mis-user of drugs; he will surely say that no-one, not even he, suffered any ill-fortune because of a temporary aberration of judgment.' (*Oh, Lord, why did it have to be The Headbeater?! Why couldn't it have been Ralph Simmons who is probably still recovering in a monastery from the mauling I gave him last month!*)

Leadbeater now began to wax lyrical: 'The immortal Oscar Wilde wrote, "*What made medicine fool people for so long was that its successes were prominently displayed, and its mistakes literally buried."* In this case, we will hear much about the former, but if he is allowed to continue, we are likely to hear of far more burials.' *Ouch!*

'In respect of sanctions regarding the drug-taking issues, the Council are seeking a long period of suspension to declare to the public that standards cannot be walked on with carefree abandon and have to be maintained at all times.'

Then, having downgraded what should have been the primary allegations of the hearing to mere incidentals, Leadbetter brought out the cudgel, this time without gloves. In her imperious manner that brooked no contradiction, she continued onto the public issues that would be reported in every Yorkshire newspaper and beyond:

'There are also conduct issues related to impropriety, over-familiarity with patients, and aloofness with staff. Mr Simpson does not believe that his actions towards his patients or staff were improper, and will no doubt say he kept his own sex life to himself. No doubt he will say that his nurses discussed their sex-lives freely in the staffroom, but not he.

'But, ladies and gentlemen, surgeon Dr McDonald and a nurse, from whom you will hear a great deal tomorrow, will testify that not only did he make a degrading *(she paused),* disgusting *(she paused again),* demeaning and very unprofessional statement for all to hear, but directed this at a female colleague who had been entirely supportive of him.

'She will say that on more than one occasion, his hands strayed and touched her inappropriately.' *(What?!! Where did she pull that one out?! This blow was so far below the belt that Nick's socks were at risk.)*

'Dr McDonald will say that he was hell-bent on being appointed head of surgery at their hospital and was determined to stop her from being promoted; that he belittled her performance as a surgeon at every opportunity.

She will say that she understood that he had been experiencing difficult times prior to coming to her hospital, and she had always tried to show empathy toward him, but she will say that he cruelly rebuffed her kindness in the nastiest manner he could manage.'

And then came the killer punch from Ms Leadbetter.

'We wish to make it clear that we will be applying to have the sexual abuse issues relating to Dr McDonald treated not as health issues but as misconduct of the most egregious type punishable by nothing less than immediate suspension followed by erasure.

'That, Madam, concludes my opening address.'

Bernard leapt to his feet. 'Madam, this is outrageous! We were only served notice yesterday about the alleged misconduct issues. We have not had the opportunity of preparing any sort of defence whatsoever. This is opportunistic, and to be very blunt, so far below the belt that my knees are shuddering. I wish to serve notice that this may very well prove valid grounds for appeal.'

The Chairperson frowned. 'I perfectly understand your concern, Mr Finch. This is indeed an extremely late introduction of some very serious allegations. Are you seeking to adjourn this hearing? If so, we will almost certainly allow it, but I must warn that there is no possibility of returning for at least eight months.'

'Thank you, Madam, I must now ask for an adjournment to take advice from my client.'

'Adjournment granted. We return at 2pm.'

To describe the atmosphere in the defence room as angry would not be coming even close. Sizzling like a roman candle, Bernard turned to Nick to ask him if and how he wished to proceed.

Nick was slumped in his seat. 'These past two years have been the most difficult of my life, Bernard. I hated working in Suffolk, but I endured it, and my contract there is now completed. I cannot go back there. I am extremely unlikely to find work elsewhere. My wife, despite being recently supportive, barely talks to me. I cannot return home. My recent earnings hardly cover my expenses. How can I possibly ask for a postponement for eight months without income? I have no choice but to go in later and hope that the Committee will believe my story.'

Bernard grimaced. 'So be it, Nick, but if you were a racehorse, I'm afraid I wouldn't be putting my money on you with this Committee. I cannot feel optimistic about your chances, but we're going to give it our best shot.'

## Chapter 19

## The Hearing

Leadbetter smiled to herself as they walked in at 2pm. No, smiling is nice. Leadbetter smirked contemptuously. She had assessed her victim's response correctly and was not surprised to hear that they would be continuing. She expanded her ample chest; she was going to teach this upstart Australian a lesson on British morality that he would never forget.

For the next three days, she dealt solely with the drug abuse issues. She called witness after witness; pharmacists, all of whom testified in strong terms how they had been deceived by Nick into filling out prescriptions for him; patients who stated how mortified they had felt by the misuse of their names on Nick's prescriptions.

The most damning of all was Dr Margaret O'Connor, who saw him as a person with no sense of morality whatsoever. 'He totally hid the fact that he was an overworked surgeon. Had I been aware of this I would have probably not treated him with medication. Instead, I would have warned him that physician burnout is a common condition that sadly has been linked to *(now pausing between each hammer blow)* poorer quality of care.... patient dissatisfaction.... decreased ability to express empathy.... total mood disturbance.... emotional instability.'

She hadn't finished yet. The hammer blows continue to thud against the coffin she was constructing for Nick. 'I would have warned him that he was putting his patients at risk…. I would've warned him of increased medical errors…. I would have warned him of the increased likelihood of lawsuits. What he needed was a long holiday, but he tried to convince me that he was suffering from depression to get me to prescribe the very drug to which he was addicted.'

Get out of that one, thought the smirking Leadbetter.

During this whole duck-shoot, Nick realised Margie had him on toast and was enjoying every mouthful. He desperately wanted to stop her and say to the Committee that, yes, he was beyond tired but that was nothing unusual for him, and he had never made a surgical error or a wrong diagnostic decision - but he dared not interrupt. All he could do was to give the appearance of being as unemotional as possible even though he was seething. It was not easy. He was fortunate that his jaw clenching and teeth gnashing could not be heard.

Only a person who had experienced such total character assassination could perceive the destructive thoughts that were running through his cauldron of a mind. Destructive not of anyone present but to someone two hundred miles away, someone who hadn't even appeared yet, a sub-human serpent who had poisoned the entire process,

The pharmacists then had their say, even more damning. When they returned to the Defence room at the end of the fourth day, Nick sat in his chair and could not stop himself from slumping forward. He looked drained and felt worse, much worse. In fact, he was catatonic. When eventually words started to return, all he was able to say was, 'What's the point of me continuing to attend? I'm fucked.'

Bernard assured him that this was a game of two halves, and his half was yet to come. This might have been reassuring, but there was an elephant in the room, a huge grey beast: the allegations concerning Dr McDonald were yet to be heard, and they would be heard as a separate hearing following immediately after the drugs issues had been completed.

Now it was time for the defence.

# Chapter 20

## The second half

Bernard, whose attitude had so often ranged from cynical and sarcastic to downright nasty, now found another face, a much more empathetic one. He was determined to fight as he had never fought before. He would be calling few witnesses. He would rely mainly on Nick's testimony and the written testimonials garnered by Allison including those from the two psychiatrists.

'These testimonials will show that here is a man who had been at the top of his game but who has made a catastrophic error of judgment. This has led to the loss of virtually everything that was of value to him. My client has seen and smelled the bottom of the pit but has remediated himself absolutely. Setting aside the alleged misconduct issues that he strongly denies, his dedication to duty for the past two years had been blemish-free and drug-free, and he has shown great insight in accepting the need for humiliating reassessment of his life and the necessity for absolute change.

'Madam Chair, I call Dr Nicholas Simpson to testify.'

As Leadbetter had said he would, Bernard lead Nick to present a panorama of the work he had done, the challenges he had overcome, and the gratitude of his patients. The story that had resulted in the building of the new glandular surgery unit at the Leeds hospital was reiterated. Nick performed brilliantly; he grovelled and apologised to the Committee for so badly letting down himself, his family and his profession. This having been said, he told the Committee, he had paid penance and had atoned. If given the chance to do so, would live his personal and professional life in a very different and more humble way in future, in keeping with the Hippocratic oath he had sworn twenty years before.

Despite Ms Leadbetter's best efforts to goad him and get under his skin when he was cross-examined, not once did he allow himself to be baited into losing his calm demeanour. He apologised when he needed to do so. He remained calm and focused, especially in the later part of the day where he seen Stanley Wethers come short. His testimony lasted for a full day, at the end of which he knew he had performed as well as he possibly could have done. But he knew the difficult part, the trial in public, was yet to come. A train crash was looming, one that could not be averted, one that would leave blood on the tracks.

His blood.

He barely slept that night.

# Chapter 21

## A Consummate Stitch-up Manchester 2011

The hearing room the next morning was conspicuous for two reasons.

The first was the presence of two reporters from local Manchester newspapers, and two more from Leeds - stories of medical sexual misconduct always read well.

The second was the absence of Allison. She had been prepared to support him on the drugs issue, but this for her was a bridge too far. Allison's earlier presence at the hearing may have looked supportive, but Nick knew that with or without her, the value of his stock in that room would very soon shrink to zero.

Dr Susan McDonald, when called to give evidence, was calmness and reason personified. Always looking straight at the Committee, she told how she had welcomed Nick's arrival, especially because prior to that she had been pressured by overwork. She had been sympathetic to his fall from grace at the Leeds hospital and was willing to play her part in his rehabilitation. She was willing to accept that he was more skilled and able than she, and never hesitated to seek his advice in the first year he was there.

As time went by, however, she found him becoming increasingly arrogant at work and was disturbed by the way he looked down on his very able nurses, often belittling them despite the hard work they put in trying to meet his over-demanding standards. As a senior staff member, he often chose to be insensitive to a junior member.

Nick was fuming – where was this rubbish coming from, this total bullshit? He could feel Bernard's arm restraining him from leaping up.

McDonald continued. When he tried to become a tad too friendly socially with her and invited her to meet him for a drink *(she emphasised the word 'drink')*, she drew a firm line: they could be work colleagues, but she was not about to get involved in any sort of relationship with another member of staff, least of all one who was married. After that, he became aloof and distant, and she had heard from others that his eyes were turning elsewhere but again without success. As far as she was personally concerned, he had seriously pushed aside every boundary of propriety. It was not for him to disregard standards, and he needed someone to tell him his impropriety was unacceptable.

Nick could feel his jaw muscles clench with tension and anger, but he had been warned by his team that to show any form of emotion, even a nod or shake of the head, was to be strictly avoided. He was to sit impassively and take whatever was dished out, and his turn would come to make his own case.

Sitting quietly became increasingly difficult for Nick as Susan McDonald spoke of the odd occasion – not often, she added - when she was walking towards the door of theatre after they had been working together and felt his hand on her posterior as he gently 'steered' her out. Nick wanted to leap up and shout 'You are a lying bitch!' but with commendable restraint managed to control himself.

Then, she said, came the moment when he walked into the staffroom and said quietly but very clearly as he looked straight at her that he could do with a stiff whisky and a fucking good screw. She did not over-emphasise these words, did not play to the gallery. Just a short pause to let those present hear her intake of breath and slight snicker. The am-dram group would have been proud of her performance. With deliberate emotional understatement, she said there was no doubt in her mind that the remark was made to belittle her in front of her work associates. This had had a significant impact on her self-esteem as she wrestled with how to deal with the emotional effect this assault on her femininity and morality had had on her, until she came to the inevitable decision that a complaint had to be made, and that a complaint to the Medical Practice Committee was her only recourse. She closed, leaving the inevitable impression that she was everything a genuine victim needed to be.

The local newspaper hacks could be seen scribbling furiously.

Although Bernard was tempted to have a go at breaking down the wall of granite, he considered that this was well-nigh impossible. He had learned from experience that the easiest witnesses to demolish were those who were most shrill, who embellished their stories in the hope of making their evidence seem more powerful; those who spoke in a small, still voice tended to gain sympathy. So, no cross-examination. Instead, he simply said, 'Madam Chair, we are in an invidious position. We have had no time to prepare our cross-examination.' He glared at Leadbetter. He scowled at McDonald. 'We have no questions.'

When the surgeon walked head held high from the hearing room, Nick's eyes followed her with venomous contempt. He prayed it would the last time that he would ever see her because were he to do so he was unsure whether he could hold himself back.

McDonald did not return to listen to the evidence of the young nurse who supported her to the full, not seeking revenge but needing to protect her colleagues from similar embarrassment and belittlement. The nurse had also spoken softly, unemotionally, clearly, not gilding the lily. This added to her dignity, to the impression that lurking under Nick's professional demeanour lurked a predatory monster. It was apparent to Bernard that she had been well-schooled and consummately prepared, but would the Committee see it that way? He thought not.

What really struck Nick was that he was sure he had never set eyes on the nurse before. He knew that she was simply the needle being used by his former colleague to stitch him up, and she was doing this with clinical micro-precision - only this wasn't taking place in an operating theatre but in a courtroom. If only her surgical prowess were as good!

Hell indeed hath no fury like a woman scorned.

Nick would have slit his wrists if he had been able to find the courage; never had he felt so utterly worthless and bereft.

When called for the second time, Nick said he could not begin to understand why McDonald had acted this way. He was never hostile to her career prospects – he had always intended to leave the hospital at the earliest moment possible. It was not within his power to get rid of her, even if he wanted to, and he most certainly did not. He denied her version of the social line that had been drawn. He was not generally a touchy-feely person, and certainly had no recollection of touching her bottom or any other part of her body.

He did not consider himself a sexual predator, as Leadbetter had alleged.

He had heard the allegations that there was serious misconduct and concurred that if he had made the 'good screw' statement, then this might well be considered offensive. But he had, at the time of the alleged remark, just carried out an operation where he had come very close to losing a patient for the first time in his career. At such times one may well say things that were lodged in the deepest recesses of one's mind. Nevertheless, he strenuously denied that he was one to make a range of crude remarks. Once again, he spoke from his heart, but his demeanour spoke of someone who knew the game was up.

Given the total lack of time to prepare the defence adequately, it had proved impossible to assemble an array of witnesses to speak up for Nick. The solicitors had managed to enlist just one. Speaking on his behalf, an older nurse said Nick was always professional and performed well as part of the team, and when they had earned it, he was the first to proffer praise. Receptionists and nurses responded well to him. She had never had personal concerns about his conduct. He often used humour to make a point, but hardly ever inappropriately or with impropriety.

She said banter was common among the staff but to the best of her knowledge Nick never participated. She did however recall that, after a difficult operation he had audibly announced in front of a group of staff that he could do with a good screw, which she thought totally inappropriate, but he did not seem to be directing the remark to any one person in particular - she thought he was simply voicing his stress.

She recalled an example of some nurses discussing a tv programme they had been watching called "Naked Attraction" about body features that had been presented in full uncensored glory. They had made comments that were less than complimentary of the male genitalia on display, but Nick had taken this lightly and understood that sexual banter was now normal conduct not just for younger men but for young women as well. She said that, although his nurses discussed their sex-lives freely in the staffroom, he kept his own sex life, if he had one, very much to himself.

The older woman told how he had completely and positively transformed the teaching curriculum in the department. He was popular and well-liked by student and staff alike and was a good mentor to junior staff. He was able to get the best out of students during viva exams. He treated her personally with consideration and respect. She told of the great burden the last couple of years had been to him. She said he was always very professional and never spoke inappropriately to staff.

Would that be enough to counterbalance the earlier nurse's evidence? If only.

The evidence had been presented. Nearly three weeks had passed, three weeks that seemed a lifetime to Nick. It was now time for the barristers to present their closing statements.

In her summing up, Ms Leadbetter did not speak at length about the misappropriation of medication. She accepted that the defendant had commendably remediated. Nevertheless, she said in respect of sanctions, although there were no submissions as to ongoing risk, she was seeking a period of suspension on the drugs issue to ensure that the good name of the profession had to be protected from falling into disrepute and it was imperative that high standards of conduct were to be maintained.

On the sexual misconduct issue, she spoke of how the psyche of a dedicated surgeon had been damaged, perhaps irreparably so. There was no comeback from this.

She was demanding nothing less than erasure.

Bernard Finch, in response, noted that there had never been a patient complaint of poor care. In his time in Suffolk Nick did not spare himself, even under the difficult circumstances that he had to endure. His conduct throughout was selfless - he was, and always had been, a kind, considerate and dedicated person. He was a brilliant surgeon and a remarkable and inspiring teacher.

In respect of the alleged remark, there were four possibilities:

The first, Nick had not made the remark at all and the whole scenario was a fiction concocted by a jealous and malicious woman aided by an equally malicious assistant; he did not think anyone would stoop that low, because if it were true, the wrong person was being tried.

The second possibility: it was a rude, inappropriate and malicious remark aimed at one individual and made by a hyper-sexed predator; if this were true, a long suspension would be appropriate.

The third - it was an off-the-cuff bit of banter aimed at no-one in particular - crude, yes; inappropriate, yes; malicious? Not, and punishable only by a warning on future conduct.

The fourth, it was a silly remark made under unusually stressful circumstances without intent and aimed at no one in particular but taken personally; if that were the case, he offered an immediate apology on behalf of the defendant doctor and this should be sufficient.

Intention was of importance, said Mr Finch. Nick's remarks, if any, were never intended to hurt. Was this the sort of case that cast such a long shadow that the practitioner would not be able to step out of it? Patently not.

Proportionality too was important: if there had been misconduct at all, it had not been serious misconduct. His conduct was remediable and had been remediated, as could be determined by his humility and following the evidence of the two earlier witnesses on his behalf.

Suspension would be entirely illogical, said Finch. The purpose of suspension was to punish an individual, *not* to send out a wider message. Dr Simpson faced huge hardship if found against. Did the public need protection from Dr Simpson? No, it needed his skills.

The Medical Conduct Committee sat *in camera* for two full days of deliberation, and they felt ten times as long to Nick. Despite the best efforts of his legal team to lighten the atmosphere, nothing could dispel the mood of impending doom that he was experiencing as he sat waiting for the Committee's decision. Nick knew he was in a deep hole, a hole he had dug for himself, and an unscrupulous someone else had cheerfully shovelled the gravel over him. He knew he was dead and buried.

At four-thirty pm the Clerk recalled everyone. It was time for the Committee to deliver its findings. Although Nick felt his heart pounding as never before, he tried not to show his emotions. After a lengthy preamble that seemed to Nick to go on interminably, the Chair announced their decision: first of all, that Nick's actions, by using and prescribing drugs inappropriately and dishonestly, had clearly amounted to egregious misconduct that could normally only be punishable by erasure. However, the Committee accepted that he had been honest in his evidence, had remediated himself beyond expectation, and had shown humility, all of which amounted to proper insight. Although guilty of allegations as charged, his current fitness to practise was not impaired.

A warning against repetition was considered appropriate and sufficient, and no additional sanctions were imposed.

This was an outcome better than any in the defence team had believed possible. For a brief few seconds, Nick experienced the relief of a man saved from the gallows. He heaved a huge sigh of relief and turned to smile at Bernard Finch. When he saw the look on Finch's face, his optimism was stillborn.

The Chair paused for a moment then continued speaking. In respect of the sexual misconduct allegation, they had found Dr McDonald and the nurse to be credible witnesses, and, based on this, believed that Dr Simpson had transgressed well beyond the bounds of decency expected from a medical practitioner, no matter how skilful. Whereas they had considered simply issuing a warning regarding the drugs related issues or at most a three-month suspension, they could not allow the sexual misconduct to go unpunished lest the message to the profession be that such conduct could be tolerated. Under normal circumstances they would have unhesitatingly ordered that Mr Simpson's name be erased. However, given that he had not had a full chance to prepare an adequate defence, the Committee was prepared to show a degree of leniency, and accordingly, Mr Simpson was to be suspended from any form of medical practise within the UK for a period of two years.

Preventing him from practising abroad was beyond their jurisdiction, and he was free to do so provided the Medical Board was informed, and he was also to inform the governing body of his chosen country of the hearing and its outcome.

The case had concluded. Disastrously. Like Icarus, Nick had flown too close to the sun and had fallen burning to earth.

Back in the Defence room, the mood was sombre. The feeling was akin to that of a hospital waiting room where a doctor had just come through to say that the patient, despite successful surgery, had died. Nick and his team were as glum, no that's not nearly strong enough, they were as shattered as any small group could be. The two solicitors silently completed the packing together for collection of the hundreds of files they had accumulated over the past two years. Bernard, the aloof man-of-a-thousand-cuts throat-slitting destroyer of less competent barristers, had lost a battle with the only barrister that, given the opportunity, he would cheerfully have shoved off a cliff.

But it was not for himself that he was concerned. He knew from experience that the disgrace of being found guilty of sexual misconduct could drive medical practitioners to self-harm, even suicide. He was in dread fear about the immediate intentions of his client. Yes, when he had first met Nick, his impression was that his client was arrogant and unfeeling, a man for whom ordinary rules did not apply. Yet, over the past two years he had seen Nick being humbled, humiliated to the point of self-destruction. He had witnessed the man's brilliant professional career dismantled piece by piece. Yet, with all that he endured, Nick, at the final hurdle, had stood strong and cleared the bar, only to be brought down with the finishing line in sight by the outstretched leg of an unscrupulous competitor. That is what Susan McDonald was: a competitor. She had competed for her position, she had competed for his affection. Yet when she saw that she was not going to get his affection, she had stuck out her leg and he had gone flying. Bernard put his puny arm around the distraught surgeon.

'Don't berate yourself, Nick, there's not a thing more that you or I or these amazing solicitors could have done. When you have time to think about this a little more dispassionately, you will realise that except for that disgusting woman's blatant lies, you would actually have been able to return to work tomorrow. When we first met two years ago, you were heading for erasure. Today, this Committee, hard-bitten as they are, has not seen fit to punish you with anything worse than a reprimand on the main substance of the case. You have been suspended, not because of an addiction, not because you had duped other professionals and patients; on all of those issues you have had the strength to rehabilitate and redeem yourself fully.'

Nick said nothing – he was barely hearing the words.

Bernard continued, 'You have been suspended because of the fabrications of a woman seeking revenge for a crime you had never committed. If it were possible, I'd have lodged notice of appeal immediately, but that would still take another year with little likelihood of success, if truth be told. All I can say is that you should walk out of here with your head high, reflect on what I have just said, take a holiday and then go abroad to work for a couple of years. You can still achieve great things for people who need your brilliant skills. You can still serve your profession honourably albeit not in this rain-plagued grey country. It has been a privilege to work with you, my friend.'

My friend? Grateful as Nick was to Bernard Finch for the stern efforts he had made in his defence, it was his fervent wish never to have to see this man again. This wasn't personal – he had learned that under that gruff exterior lay a kind and decent heart. No, it was the matter of the whole process that he had been through, the hours that he had spent in the barrister's chambers, the incessant whittling away of his confidence and self-respect - and all to no avail.

Nick walked out of the building. It was rush hour and hordes of people were scurrying by, heading for buses and trains. He did not see them. Nor did he hear the hooting of the vehicles or see the buildings that loomed above him. What he saw was a life damaged beyond repair. And he saw that it was he who had wrecked it, and he knew the nightmare had barely begun. There was a future to face – if he could find the courage.

# Chapter 22

## A Sad Farewell

What now? McDonald's lies had destroyed Nick's career, but unfortunately worse was to follow: Allison had found that the posting online of the Committee's decision on the McDonald issue was intolerable, worsened by the public humiliation that had followed publication in the Leeds Echo. Despite his repeated attempts to speak to her, she refused to have contact. Her secretary informed him that the continuation of their relationship was untenable and she had decided to sue for divorce.

From the time he had received that fateful letter to the present moment he had not heard a single word from his in-laws, nor from any of his former friends. He was an outcast. His life was in tatters.

Nick considered his options. A pattern in his life needed to be changed but he was not ready for that. No, far more preferable to falsify one more prescription for a drug that would send him away quietly as he swallowed a month's supply of anti-depressants with a glass of cold beer. Then he thought to himself that such an action would bring a small smile to the thin lips of Dr Susan McDonald, and that thought alone was enough to dissuade him from any such action. Perfect irony: it was the action of Susan McDonald that was driving him to take his life, and the thought of her satisfaction that would keep him alive.

Eventually, two realisations came to him at once. The first was that he was not and had never been a quitter; he had fought and beaten his addiction and fought his case to the bitter end when a lesser person might have given up.

The second realisation was that he had been suspended from medical practise in the UK only, and now that Allison too had dumped him, he was free to leave England and find employment to practise his craft in any other country he chose.

He considered going home to Australia, but there were too many bags to carry back, too many people to whom he would have to answer. He would carry his shame with him. Just as he had not informed Allison about his addiction issues, neither had he told his parents about the hearing and its outcome, and they had been kept totally unaware of the past two years of his unravelling. He wasn't about to open that bag if it could be avoided.

He spoke no Spanish, French or Italian nor at least twenty other European languages, so Europe was out. It would take too long to be permitted to practise in America, and anyway the USA had never appealed to him. India? Hong Kong? Those were indeed clear possibilities and he considered India at length. One problem: rugby was not an Indian sport and even if he could no longer play that game, it had to be part of his culture.

The one that he eventually chose was South Africa.

Why that country? Several reasons: he had observed in the numerous medical colleagues who had graduated in SA a work ethic similar to his own, standards of practise that matched his own, and a healthy attitude to enjoying life when not working; it was a country that played cricket, rugby, tennis and squash. Australian teams frequently visited South Africa. He had heard that it was a beautiful country with a climate that matched that of Australia. Most of the population were either English-speaking or could speak English, so he wouldn't have to learn a new language. The final thing that swayed him was that he would be in a country that offered wildlife viewing that was second to none.

On the downside, HIV/AIDS was a massive problem. He would have to be ultra-careful, but not once in his career had he ever suffered a cut finger or needle-stick injury and he had no intention of doing so there. The cities were also notorious for the high levels of urban crime, but at least he could play a positive role in mitigating the effects of this violence by repair of the wounded.

So Nick emailed a letter to the Health Council of South Africa explaining his circumstances in full, including the reasons for his UK suspension; he attached his previously impressive CV and begged them to allow him to practise facial surgery at any hospital of their choosing. This would enable him both to keep his hand in (literally) and also to give something to a country where a large proportion of its citizens were in need.

A response came quickly. Although South Africa had a decent number of surgeons, the overwhelming majority were in practise in the larger cities and towns, and no post was immediately available at any of the teaching hospitals in cities such as Johannesburg, Cape Town or Durban. If however he was willing to join the staff at a relatively small and very under-staffed provincial hospital in Mpumalanga, then a position was there for the taking as soon as he could get there.

Nick had no idea what Mpumalanga was - a state? a town? Nor where it was. A quick visit to his computer informed him that Mpumalanga was that province formerly known as the Eastern Transvaal in the far north-east of the country, that it was an area of extreme beauty but also of extreme poverty, that its population was predominantly black, and that it was in close proximity to the Kruger National Park and to Swaziland. Wildlife on his doorstep? Very appealing.

The letter informed him that the hospital on offer to him was in White River, that it was more than 200 miles and four hours by road from Johannesburg. He learned it was a very small town of predominantly white people with a very large local population of under-privileged black people living in townships nearby. The workload he would be expected to carry out would be onerous, the circumstances and facilities less than ideal, the heat at times intense, and the incidence of AIDS dangerously high.

The bait was that he would be head of surgery for a minimum period of two years with an option to review. He would have a small cottage, a personal assistant and a small car at his disposal. The remuneration would be pitiful but expenses negligible, and the work experience incomparable.

Nick hesitated only long enough to check that he still had two years availability and six empty pages left in his passport as required by SA border officials before responding that he would be there just as soon as he could arrange an international flight to Johannesburg and a domestic one to White River.

His last act before departing was to post a handwritten letter to Allison.

*My Dear Allison*

*I feel deeply saddened that you felt unable to see me after the hearing, but I fully understand the reasons. Nevertheless, with whatever little goodwill is left within you towards me, I hope you will at least find sufficient kindness to read this letter. I doubt it, but here goes anyway.*

*The past two years have without a doubt been the worst of my life, and I am quite certain, yours too. With the deepest regret, I accept absolute responsibility for this. I have unforgivably fucked up what I believed was a decent marriage, and this hurts me to my deepest being.*

*I was deeply hurt that you did not support me when I was down, and it took me a long time, too long, to realise that by my conduct I had made myself unworthy of your support. I have been dishonest, arrogant, headstrong and extremely foolish. Yes, I have learned those things about myself and am shamed by them. I learned that a relationship is only as good as the way it copes when all is not right, and ours crashed the first time it was tested.*

*On the credit side, I have emerged from it intact, and I have learned a great deal about contrition. I have learned that is entirely possible to be a failure at exactly the same time one feels most successful. Hubris runs wild, probably because success breeds arrogance and destroys humility.*

*I was fortunate to find a barrister who did not pander to my vanities and had enough perseverance to take me into myself and get me to reflect on my shortcomings and take responsibility where it was due.*

*The things for which I do not have to take responsibility are the lies of Susan McDonald, who, as Bernard Finch so perfectly expressed, stitched me up with surgical precision. If you believe nothing else about me, please believe that. Had it not been for her perfidy, I would have been back in a hospital somewhere in the UK, chastened but at work.*

*I have been completely drug-free for the past two years. That was probably the easiest part of rebuilding myself. The next stage of the rebuild will be in coping with life without you, and that will be much more difficult.*

*As I cannot work in the UK, I am going out to South Africa for at least two years. I will be at the White River Hospital, Mpumalanga. Yes, a very long way from Leeds, both in distance and hopefully in mind. That will be another big challenge, but one that I am looking forward to experiencing.*

*Should you wish to write or email, I will be grateful, but I'm not holding my breath.*

*Maybe one day, when the murk has cleared, we can meet again and share a drink on a veranda and have a laugh.*

*I will always think of you with love and warmth and remember the good times we enjoyed together. I wish you luck, love and happiness.*

*Yours, always,*

*Nick.*

# Book 2
## The Road to Redemption

# Chapter 23

## Johannesburg 2012

On a cold winter's night three weeks later, Nick boarded a packed South African Airways Airbus for the eleven-hour flight to Johannesburg. The past few days had been a whirlwind of preparation and he had looked forward to a relaxed flight. Fat chance. He found it difficult to sleep and being in economy did not help. His mind was a maelstrom of thoughts and questions – Allison, McDonald, Bernard Finch, Shirley Headbeater - could he escape from them? How would he cope in a new country? Would the challenge push him into another spiral of drugging?

Even though he was no longer bound by restrictions, he resisted the temptation to drink the wine offered with his meal or to request something stronger.

He could not but notice that the overwhelming majority of his co-passengers were white – businessmen, families going out for a holiday, returning residents. When he asked one of the crew why this was, the response was that despite having achieved majority rule and theoretically having ended apartheid, in practice the black population who outnumbered whites by ten to one had remained overwhelmingly poor. Travelling from town to town was an issue for them, let alone occupying seats on jumbos.

He had placed a book in the pocket in front of his seat, and as he rummaged for it, his hand found instead a brochure written by the South African Tourist Board. Well, it was as good a time as any to read about his destination. An interesting fact he picked up was that Johannesburg, the biggest city and business hub, had the largest man-made city forest in the world. He learned that, despite there being eleven official languages, nine of which were indigenous, all official announcements and notices were still made in the two European languages, English and the Dutch-derived Afrikaans. *Plus ca change, plus c'est la meme chose....*

He was aware that Nelson Mandela had managed to negotiate a peaceful transition despite having been incarcerated on Robben Island for 28 years. He was equally aware that the president who succeeded him, Thabo Mbeki, despite being highly educated, had been an AIDS denier. Mbeki believed that HIV was caused by poverty and not by a virus, and Nick knew this denial had cost hundreds of thousands of lives. But Nick knew little if anything about the current state of the nation. Well, he would make it his business to learn as much as possible over the next two years.

He also resolved to put every thought of his recent experiences out of his mind and use the harsh lessons learned to approach this new opportunity with open mind and positive attitude. He knew this would not be easy, because recent events had become so ingrained into his psyche that he no longer believed he knew quite who he was nor which Nick was the real one *(shades of Margie)*. Nevertheless, if reversion to his original self was possible, that was where he would choose to go, although with humility.

The flight arrived at O R Tambo Johannesburg International airport on a bright southern hemisphere spring morning. Oliver Tambo had been a hero of the struggle against apartheid and a former leader of the African National Congress (the ANC) who had been incarcerated with Mandela.

Nick was surprised by the cleanliness and modernity of the airport that carried Tambo's name. Nothing third world there! He was informed that this was a legacy of the 2010 football World Cup.

He was not due to transit to White River for a couple of days, so he boarded the brand-new Gauteng Express to Sandton, the luxurious predominantly white satellite town on the outskirts of Jozies, as Johannesburg was now colloquially known. This was in stark contrast to the poverty-stricken black townships with their zinc roofs and lean-to walls that he observed as he whizzed by on the train. Yes, some of these had been replaced by small newish brick bungalows, but the overall impression they emitted was of unremitting poverty. What a contrast to the airport, and on another planet altogether when compared to the Sandton CBD where all but the oldest buildings had been erected in the past twenty years. The architecture was futuristic, and the brilliant sun reflected off dozens of glass towers.

His stay over the two nights was at a plush hotel on Sandton Square where a large bust of Nelson Mandela was located for all to see and pay homage. Adjacent to the Square was Sandton City, a vast, sprawling shopping mall serving two classes of locals: the rich and the very rich.

He took a tour through the predominantly white suburbs characterised by large modern homes and huge gardens. These were fronted by manicured grass pavements with jacaranda trees and bougainvillea in full bloom that could barely be seen from the road because they were obscured by high fences bedecked with razor wire. Australia was never like this!

He knew that the following day would provide a very different scenario, because he planned to visit Soweto.

Soweto – the South-West Townships - was the largest of the black townships on the outskirts of Johannesburg;

in some areas more modernised than the shanty homes he had passed while on the train, but for the most part far from bearing any sort of comparison to even the poorer white suburbs through which his tourist minibus had passed en route. Indeed, many of Soweto's inhabitants had been forcibly removed to Soweto from these poorer Johannesburg white areas in the sixties. Their former homes had been expropriated, razed and replaced, and they were now forced to travel long journeys on overcrowded trains to work in the cities. What had changed in recent times was the growth of more luxurious areas in Soweto that were the homes of the emerging middle-class and more well-to-do black population, unfortunately still overwhelmingly in the minority.

Their first stop was at the Hector Pieterson Museum, named after a twelve-year-old student who had been shot to death by callous white policemen while protesting against the foisting on black schools of Afrikaans, the Dutch-derived language of their oppressors. The police tried to quell what had been a peaceful march, and the angry children responded with stones. An unnamed person gave the order to open fire, and within moments ten children lay dead and hundreds more had been injured. One of the first to fall was Hector Pieterson. An older student, Mbuyisa Makhubo, had picked up the critically injured boy and carried him through the streets looking for assistance.

A photographer, Sam Nzima, saw them coming towards him. They reached Nzima's car and he drove Hector to a nearby clinic where Hector was pronounced dead. No policeman was ever charged, but Mbuyisa Makhubo and Sam Nzima were relentlessly targeted and, in fear for their lives, were forced into exile. A photograph by Sam Nzima of the mortally wounded Pieterson being carried by Mbuyisa with Hector's older sister at his side was published around the world and has become iconic of what has come to be known as the Soweto Students' Uprising.

Nick was deeply upset by this, but that was just the hors'doevres.

He had heard from colleagues that at Baragwanath Hospital, or Bara as it was known to all, one would see every disease ever described in a medical textbook, and even more that were not. He was taken on a tour through what was the largest hospital in the southern hemisphere - 3000 beds - and even though he had braced himself, he was quite shocked by the overcrowding and shortage of beds. Patients lay in the passages. The hospital seemed to burn with frenetic activity. There were few white faces about and those that were all had white coats and carried stethoscopes.

He had heard that Jozies, once an orderly business hub, was now a violent and unsafe city, and Soweto even worse. He learned that Friday night was the worst because Friday was the day that the wages the workers had just been paid would be spent in large part on *skokiaan* at the local drinking holes called *shebeens*. As the night progressed it would become a surgeon's nightmare because of the huge number of stabbings and alcohol–related road accidents. Drink-driving was not so much a crime as a way of life. And death. Dante's Inferno brought to being.

The visit had shaken him to the core. The South African doctors he had worked with in the UK had not spoken much about the chasm between black and white in their home country, and it dawned on him that this was because they probably felt shame, or, like him, wanted to clear their painful memories.

The surgeons he encountered at Baragwanath spoke in awe of their former chief who had suddenly quit and disappeared. His skill with a scalpel was legendary, as was his ferocious demands for high standards. Nick could not know that a couple of days later he would meet the former head of Bara surgery who would become a valued friend and advisor.

Although never for a moment feeling personally threatened in Soweto, Nick was shaken to the core, and when he returned to Sandton, he felt quite relieved. This feeling was not because it was less dangerous, but because the tour for the most part had been a grim one, a portrait of man's inhumanity to man. Was this what was in store for him at White River? Was he strong enough to cope with pressures such as he had never before experienced?

His final thoughts as he drifted into sleep were for once not of a committee hearing-room but of a sun-drenched modern city of stark contrasts. He slept fitfully, images of Baragwanath (strange - a Cornish name for an African hospital) rampaging through his subconscious, but woke the next morning in a positive frame of mind. He had never shirked a challenge before and was determined this would not be the first.

His final memory of Sandton was of enjoying a large kudu steak marinated in herbs and grilled on an open fire at a large steak-house - probably the tastiest meat he had ever eaten. It was served with a porridge-like maize mash called *pap* beloved by the indigenous black people. It was accompanied by a thick sauce containing onions, garlic and tomatoes, Worcester sauce, ketchup, vinegar, chutney and heaven knows what else, but piquant it was. The concoction revelled in the name of monkey-gland sauce, but no one could tell him why.

# Chapter 24

## White River 2012

Back by Gauteng Express to the airport and onto the Kulula Airline 40–seater plane for the 90-minute flight to Nelspruit airport. A very bumpy journey it was, lightened only by the dark humour of the cabin crew for which Kulula was renowned, or perhaps more accurately, notorious. The cabin crew kept the passengers in laughter virtually from take-off. When passengers were finding it difficult to choose their unallocated seats, the flight attendant announced, *'People, people, this is not a furniture sale, just pick your chair and sit on it.'* During the safety briefing, they were told *'There's fifty ways to leave your lover, but only four ways out of this aeroplane.'* A little later, a senior air hostess informed the passengers that the lights were being turned down *'to enhance the appearance of your flight attendants'*; but best of all, as the plane taxied in, they heard a low voice from the cockpit bellowing *'Whoa, big fella, WHOA!'* Nick thought he was going to like this country...

During the short flight he scanned a brochure describing White River. The small town had developed as an agricultural and tourist site. Its produce was tropical fruits, veggies, flowers *(something to look forward to!)* and timber. There were three large irrigation dams in the area, which was one of scenic beauty, and it was the gateway to the Kruger National Park with its Big Five and lots of other animals too. Not to mention birds of species unknown to him .... Hmmm, mused Nick, I hope I get the time to enjoy any of this....

As he stepped onto the tarmac at the small airport, almost blinded by sunshine, Nick could just about make out the figure of a black man dressed in a brilliant white safari suit. The man made straight for him and with a smile as wide and white as his suit said: 'Dr Simpson, I presume?! You are most welcome, Sir.' Nick appreciated not only the warm greeting, but the colonial irony of the words certainly not accidentally chosen. The man introduced himself as Mr Nelson Ngope, chief administrator of White River Hospital.

With him was a sturdy young man in khaki who carried Nick's bags, one hoisted effortlessly onto each shoulder. The man's name was Samson – how appropriate! As they walked to the large black chauffeur-driven Mercedes car, Samson whispered to Nick that the only thing that made his employer unhappy was not to be addressed by his full name. He was Mr *Nelson* Ngope.

As they were driven through rolling hills clad by acre upon acre of pine forest, Mr Nelson Ngope told Nick how he had come by his Christian name; he had been born on the very day that Nelson Mandela had been sentenced to life imprisonment for treason and sent to Robben Island just off Cape Town. Mr Nelson Ngope had benefitted from Mandela's legacy by being in the first cohort of black students to graduate in hospital administration from Fort Hare University. That Eastern Cape university was originally for black students only, and it was there Mandela himself had gained his law degree.

Mr Nelson Ngope's mother was an unemployed domestic worker, his father long disappeared - he knew not to where - nor whether he was still alive. Certainly, no money was ever received from him. Two brothers, two sisters - he was the eldest. From a background of grinding poverty,

Mr Nelson Ngope had conscientiously worked his through school, university and up the professional ladder. Five years ago had been appointed CEO of the 75-bed 400-strong staff at White River. This would not have been possible before Mandela's time, so he was extremely proud to be named after so mighty a leader.

As they drove through the small and attractive town of White River, Nick noticed that the main street was more than twice as wide as the average British High Road and was pretty much the only non-residential street in the entire town. There was not going to be much in the way of nightlife happening here, that was for sure, not that he had ever had time for such frivolities....

Mr Nelson Ngope (*pronounced Ingopeh*), who was obviously well educated and extremely knowledgeable, provided Nick with a brief summary of the experience he might expect: 'When extreme poverty affects a large proportion of the population, as in South Africa, health is predominantly affected by a lack of access to the basic requirements for life - clean water, adequate nutrition, effective sanitation, reasonable housing conditions, access to vaccinations, childhood nurturing, good schooling, to name the most important. Unfortunately, these basic requirements are not yet with us, Dr Simpson. Redressing that, together with increasing the availability of jobs, will set the scene for improved health and longevity.'

Nick was impressed. Here was someone who cared about the community he served. Mr Nelson Ngope paused to draw breath.

'You will find that our surgeons are vastly overworked and understaffed, whereas the nurses tend to be the opposite. Most of the older nurses are very helpful and dedicated, but many of the younger ones are aggressively unionised. Well, that is their right. Unfortunately, sometimes they put *their* needs first and their patients second. Nonetheless, Doctor, I think you will find the challenge exciting.'

He explained that although the population within the town itself was only sixteen thousand, mostly white and mostly wealthy, the outlying townships numbered ten times that figure, entirely black, all poor. This, he said, was the legacy of apartheid. Nick had expected this. What took him by surprise was that the district was governed not by the ruling African National Congress, the ANC, but by the opposition Democratic Alliance who were doing their best to redress the situation. It was a slow process, but progress was being made.

The hospital was comprised of the clinical wards, a research institute and a small teaching unit, all of which fell under the jurisdiction of Pretoria University, some two hundred miles away. Once solely for, and the bastion of white Afrikaners, post-Mandela the university was now predominantly for black students.

Nick would be living in a small bungalow cottage within easy walking distance of the large white building housing the hospital. The white-painted, red-tiled cottage had a well-tended and colourful flowering garden - a profusion of hibiscus, 'firecrackers', roses and geraniums. The bungalow was basically but not uncomfortably furnished and was bright and airy. Adorning the walls were photos and drawings of the wild animals and birds Nick hoped soon to be seeing in the flesh. There was a rudimentary kitchen – all meals would be taken in the staff canteen - but a fridge, microwave, kettle and mugs were on hand for coffee or tea.

The bathroom was adequate and spotlessly clean, and he noted the toilet lid was always down. Samson informed him this was to prevent the ingress of unwanted critters like snakes and spiders and other smallish insects collectively called *goggas*. When Nick tried to pronounce the word *gogga*, Samson roared with laughter – these *Lekgoa* had no clue with deep-throated gutturals! Samson had also warned him always to check his shoes before putting them on lest he experience a close and undesirable encounter with a scorpion.

Samson was to be his valet, his personal assistant, and no sooner had the cases been deposited in the bedroom than Samson began to unpack for him. In the cupboard were three perfectly pressed white safari suits, and Samson suggested he try one on for size. To Nick's surprise the trousers turned out to be knee-length shorts to be worn with long white socks. 'Won't they think me strange wearing these things?'

Samson laughed, another set of perfect teeth gleaming. 'No sir they will think you strange if you are not wearing short trousers because it gets very very hot here.' Samson had guessed the size correctly, and as soon as Nick had donned the uniform, Samson suggested heading for the staffroom where Nick could meet the professional staff.

Nick was apprehensive. If the doctors he was about to meet had been informed of the reason he was there, would they have already formed an opinion about him? Words like addiction, sanctions, probation swam turbulently through his mind. He need not have concerned himself. The younger ones, all black and mostly male, seemed more concerned about how *he* would perceive *them*. Was he going to be another bullying white martinet such as they had experienced throughout their undergraduate training? Clearly unsure of their ground, they shook his proffered hand but said little. There was also a number of Indian-looking doctors and physiotherapists who seemed a little less apprehensive.

Nick would be one of only four surgeons who were white, two others being Afrikaners of Dutch descent and the third a Jewish part-timer (the only one not present, he was operating). One thing they had in common: they made Nick feel like the Messiah had just arrived. Nowhere had he ever been made to feel so welcome. Even if for a brief few moments, it was as if the unpleasantness of the past two years had just floated away in a big bubble.

After Samson had made the introductions, Nick commented that the CEO, Mr Nelson Ngope, seemed to run a tight but happy ship. Samson concurred.

It was still an hour before dinner, and the next pleasant surprise arrived in the form of a perfect African sunset. He and Samson walked around for a while amongst the overhanging purple flowers of the jacaranda trees and Azalea bushes. Not since he left Australia had he seen such a profusion of colour. As his eyes turned to the beautifully maintained lawn and garden, He noticed a creature that he had never seen before, not even in Australia. It looked like an oversized black cockroach but with a thick striped outer shell and whip-like antennae. It was the length of his hand.

"What's that creature, Sampson? It looks like a miniature dinosaur."

"Doctor, that is a Parktown Prawn."

"You're kidding me Sampson – a prawn? On grass?"

"No doctor, they are called prawns just because they look like prawns, but really they are king crickets. And they are Parktown because that's where they were first noticed, there in Johannesburg."

"What do they eat?"

"Doctor, they eat snails and slugs in the lawns after the lawn has been watered, but don't step on them because they also eat dogshit and dead beds."

"Beds, like you sleep on??"

"No seh, beds that fly in the sky like parrot beds and sparrow beds. But then the ha-de-da ibis beds come and eat them. Those ha-de-da beds going to wake you every morning with their terrible noise."

Nick grinned. He realised he had a great deal to learn, not the least being a whole new way of pronouncing his weds.

He was intrigued by Samson, whose face was characterised not just by that gleaming and ever-present smile but by a glass left eye. Samson would later explain to him that a few years ago, while chopping wood at his home in Zimbabwe, a large splinter had shot upwards and lodged in his eye forcing its removal. He had covered the socket with a black eyepatch. Unfortunately, the loss of an eye was considered an evil omen and Samson had been requested to leave his village, which necessitated leaving his wife and young children too. Employment in Zimbabwe was a rare luxury, so he headed south. His journey from home was one fraught with risk and entailed crossing the mighty Limpopo River where the small boat was at risk of being capsized by hippos.

Nick looked towards the large white hospital turning golden and then copper. They entered the communal dining room where, to his absolute astonishment, a huge group of nurses stood up to welcome him and burst into the South African national anthem, *Nkosi Sikelele Afrika*. As his ears filled with sound, his eyes filled with tears. This was indeed a new beginning.

# Chapter 25

## White River Hospital  2012

Nick slept more peacefully than he had in a long, long time, to be woken in the morning by an almightily raucous squawking noise. Of course, the ha-de-das! His nose filled with the smell of hot black coffee freshly brewed by Samson. Then into his white safari suit – he was so conscious of his untanned knees - and off to breakfast and the wards. Breakfast in the canteen was adequate if uninspired, but what excited him was the abundance of fresh fruit: slices of mango, melon and papaya; bowls of lychees, guava, passionfruit and huge green avocados, all fresh from the hospital's garden and trees. He learned to slice the ripe avocados with their distinctive nutty taste onto stone-ground wheat toast, then squeeze a drizzle of lime juice and add a fresh seed mixture, and this and a bowl of fruit became his staple morning meal.

What struck him immediately was, despite being over-crowded, the wards were spotlessly clean. One could see the sunshine streaming through the large windows reflecting off the polished wooden floors. He remembered the hospital in Ballarat – it all seemed so long ago….

He was introduced to Nursing Sister Anna Kunene, whom he would get to know well over the next two years. Another Zimbabwean expat, Sister Anna gave him a list of patients that he was to examine prior to their pending surgeries. The list was extensive, the reasons multiple: fractured lower jaw following a cycling accident; removal of a facial tumour the size of an egg; extraction of impacted wisdom teeth; repair of a leaking nasal sinus; suturing of a knife wound across the entire left face; resetting a fractured eye socket - on and on it went. He would be doing more operations in a day here than he was accustomed to doing in a week in England, and he couldn't wait to start!

After inspection, he went into the theatre section and once more he was surprised by the number of beds lined up and waiting. He entered what was to be his theatre for the day, unaware that the one next door was for his use too, to avoid wasting time in switchover. He would alternate between the two, where a patient and staff would be at all times be prepared and waiting. He met the nursing surgery team that was to assist him, and the anaesthetist, Dr Lucy Malherbe, a sweet-faced young Afrikaans graduate from Pretoria. He hoped she would be up to the job; as he was later to find out, she most certainly was. He found it interesting that quite a few of the staff were white Afrikaners and Nick took that they were willing to work in a black hospital as a positive sign of change.

His surgical colleagues were mostly ten years or so his junior and were keen to learn from him in matters of technique. However, Nick soon discovered that this was not a one-direction learning programme. Their knowledge of the management of cysts and cancers was far more detailed than his, for three very simple reasons. The first was their occurrence was much more common than in the UK because health homecare was so poor. Second, the fact that in English hospitals, patients were referred at a much earlier stage of disease progression, and so the lesions tended to be smaller and less widespread to other parts of the head and neck. The third was simply the sheer diversity of lesions; those in the UK could be easily identified by referral to textbook or computer, whereas here in South Africa, tumours and cysts occurred that had never seen the light of day in any textbook, UK or anywhere else.

Nick was to learn that one of the main reasons that many people were not presenting timeously at White River Hospital was that their first port of call was the local *sangoma*. Nick had no idea what a sangoma was, so he made a point of asking Nurse Anna. Anna considered how best to explain this to him. 'A sangoma is a highly respected healer among the Zulu people of South Africa who diagnoses, prescribes, and often performs the rituals to heal a person. Like other healers, they look at all aspects of what's going on: physical, mental, emotional, or spiritual.'

'Well, there doesn't seem much wrong with that.'

'Most of them do good work and help many people. Unfortunately, Dr Nick, there are a few rogues who are in it only for the money or the power that it brings, and they give the good ones a bad name.'

Nick smiled wryly – been there, seen it. 'I get this, Sister Anna, it's the same with all healing professions I suppose.'

'No, you don't understand, Dr Nick. The bad ones are very dangerous. They claim they can cure cancer with herbs (she pronounced it 'hebs') and they don't want people like us interfering with them. Unfortunately, no matter how many times the sangomas roll the bones or consult their gods or prescribe drinking the blood of a young virgin goat or even of a young girl, no cancer ever gets cured – they only get larger. And if the patient didn't have cancer to begin with, Dr Nick, the prescription of noxious hebs is quite likely to cause an illness, disease and even be the cause of the cancer.'

Nick realised that he could learn a great deal about treating patients in Africa from this very wise woman who had never been near a university. Knowledge is borrowed, experience is one's own.

Nick found that his team of six senior nurses schooled by Sister Anna were all industrious and competent. There was none of 'that's not my job' or 'I'm not working overtime'. They simply got on with whatever had to be done and were grateful to be employed. He was never short-staffed. His workload more often than not was thirteen hours a day, from seven in the morning till eight in the evening, with (if he was lucky) a short break for a snatched canteen lunch. Nick had three teams each of two nurses, one pair in each surgery, the third pair rotating as required. On an average day they would get through around twelve to fifteen operations. Some were relatively straightforward, others incredibly complex – excising tumours and re-uniting fractured facial bones (amazing what damage can be done with a wooden *knobkerrie* wielded by a drunken man). Dr Lucy Malherbe, whose energy and work rate was the equal of his, was a tireless anaesthetist who never put a foot wrong, so that was one less problem to worry about, and she was training a younger black doctor to stand in for her when exhaustion would eventually set in.

Nick became adept in repairing cleft palates and harelips, too many to tally. Not that he hadn't done his share at Leeds, but it was the sheer volume that staggered him. He would later train staff to make acrylic prostheses to close the palatal gaps when they were too large to close surgically, but that would have to wait.

When his colleagues were overburdened, Nick found he was also doing the work of a general surgeon such as removing an appendix or re-uniting broken arm bones. The work was onerous, often difficult but always worth the while. This was in spite of the fact that for the first time in his career, Nick would lose the occasional patient whose disease or condition was too far advanced to allay. The first time this happened he felt devastated but had the good sense to realise that he had done nothing untoward, and the outcome could not have been altered or averted.

At the conclusion of each working day, Nick was grateful, first, that he did not have to drive wearily home on a rainy night as he so often had to do in Leeds; and second that his bed would be turned over, snake-, scorpion- and *gogga*-checked, and supplied with a hot water bottle on the colder nights by the ever-diligent Samson. When he asked Samson what *goggas* were, Samson explained that they were what in England were called creepy-crawlies. Nick found these little and occasionally large creatures about as pleasant as he found the guttural pronunciation, the latter as if one was trying to clear one's throat of phlegm while adding some extra spit and gravel. This was so of many Afrikaans words, and he learned not to get embarrassed when he made a pig's breakfast of trying to use them with English inflection. Trying to pronounce names of towns derived from Dutch always brought peals of laughter from the locals.

He rarely had time to think about Allison and was very grateful for that. Indeed, had there been a woman there to share his bed, it would have been to no avail because he was just too tired to do anything but put on a soothing Beethoven or Dvorak cd and read two pages before the novel slipped out of his hand.

# Chapter 26

## Snakes alive! 2012

One morning, Nick awoke and was about to put his foot on the ground when he saw a large snake slither from under his bed in the direction of the bathroom. His scream could have caused a terror alert, a scream that was more than sufficient to bring Samson charging into the room. Completely unable to speak coherently, Nick pointed in the direction of the bathroom. Samson went through and emerged a few moments later holding a large and very lively snake by its neck. Nick was about to cause a second terror alert, but Samson assured him that it was just an Aurora house snake. It was absolutely non-venomous and did not bite – well, not very often.

Nick was about to ask Samson to eject it as far as humanly possible from his room, until he looked at the dangling creature and saw it for what it was – a strikingly *(no, perhaps that was the wrong word to be using in this context)* beautiful oleaginous creature. Samson said it was an immature snake and not full-grown. It was about thirty centimetres long, and Samson said it might get half as long again. Nick was instantly smitten *(rather than bitten).* It had a distinctive orange-brown stripe running the length of its back, and as its name suggested was deep golden in colour. As he would later learn, the gold would darken to olive green as it got older. Sensing that Nick was by no means fully convinced that it was non-venomous, Samson opened the front door and allowed the snake to slither away, although he told Nick it would probably return because it liked its habitat under the bed.

Nick remembered that he was now in Africa, and if he was going to encounter snakes under his bed, he needed to know that they were house snakes rather than a poisonous *boomslang*, the Afrikaans word for vipers that lived in trees but would occasionally make their way earthwards. So, on his next outing to White River, Nick bought a hardback copy of *Fitzsimmon's Book of Snakes of Southern Africa*, which is the definitive study of the 160 species and sub-species known to occur in the southern African sub-continent. The book was some 300 pages of text and exquisite photographs. It did not take Nick long to read and assimilate vast tracts of this encyclopaedic work.

The first thing he checked in the Fitzsimmons book was the provenance of the Aurora, and was relieved to find that it was indeed not likely to cause his or anyone else's early demise. Thank heaven for small mercies! The Aurora, he learned, is active at night, and its diet consists of rodents, lizards, and frogs, but only needed to feed once a week. Nick did not fancy the idea of a gecko being crunched under his bed while he slept!

The Aurora had become quite attached to his adopted home under Nick's bed. On the basis that it was better to have this creature at a safe distance nearby rather than that close, Nick decided they should build a house for it on the back veranda and provide its food there.

The next time they went into White River they stopped in at a hardware store where they purchased all the paraphernalia required: wood for the frame, nails, hinges, sturdy wire mesh. A day later, their pet had a new and hopefully secure home. The next task they faced was to get food for the creature, and Nick discovered he could purchase live baby mice from the research institute next to the hospital. As soon as he put the first of these in the hutch, the Aurora moved in, and Nick became the proud possessor of a pet snake named Andy that he felt perfectly safe in picking up and stroking, a snake that felt safe enough to let him.

Another experience of a close encounter with a venomous creature was when he had been walking along a path with Samson and by about a foot's breadth had narrowly missed treading on a sleeping snake as he scanned his route map. He was blissfully unaware of his near miss, but Samson was not, and had later informed Nick that he had almost stepped on a *boomslang.* Samson was pleased to report that the reptile had got the fright of its life and quickly slithered away rather than argue about right-of-way. Boomslang were definitely not to be trifled with, Nick now knew.

Samson suggested to Nick that now he had found a new interest, it might be an exciting challenge to collect a few other snakes that were non-venomous. Samson, who had never read a page of Fitzsimmons, knew a great deal about reptiles. On a rare day off, he and Samson had driven to a Snake Park about two hours away and were informed by one of the resident experts that snakes could be found in most un-built-up areas of surrounding veld. The best time to go was when it was hottest, when the snakes were most sluggish or asleep. So Andy turned out to be the first of several snakes that Nick acquired with Samson's assistance over the next few months.

Nick did have a couple of rocky moments, though. He used to do a roll-call every evening to ensure that all reptiles were present and correct. One night there was an inmate that wasn't. He and Samson searched everywhere and then searched again. They looked on the bed, in the bed and under the bed. Nothing. Nowhere. Although the reptile was non-venomous, it had the potential to grow quite large, and Nick didn't much fancy the idea of waking up one morning with a snake wrapped snugly round his ankles, or even worse, around someone else's ankles or neck.

Then, about six weeks after it disappeared, he had gone into the bathroom to collect a bath-towel from under the wash-basin. As he lifted if from the pile of towels, there was this large scaly fellow asleep on the towel below. It was swiftly returned to the cage, but the invective that issued forth from Samson's mouth made Nick wonder whether he had seriously misjudged this heretofore mild fellow's nature.

Did he regret the whole reptile adventure? Well aside from being considered (probably correctly) to be insane or at best highly irresponsible, he believed his interest was very beneficial to him as a rite of passage. He had never feared a snake since, but still felt queasy when he later thought of the live little baby mice he fed to them.

# Chapter 27

## The Lofty Giraffe 2012

The first three months had flown by. The work was relentless, but Nick was coping. The doubts that had assailed him early on were slowly dissipating although he still felt the odd attack of angst, especially when he was on his own. Compared to his recent feelings, however, he would have taken this any day of the week.

Every fourteen days, Nick would have to travel out to one of the surrounding clinics to carry out minor surgical procedures. The facilities there were generally pathetically poor, but those facilities made it possible for patients who could not afford or were unable to travel into White River to be treated. Sometimes, the equipment was so poor that it made Nick think of what it must have been like for surgeons and their unfortunate patients during the great wars of times gone by. Instruments were sometimes still being 'sterilised' in boiling water, and x-ray facilities were conspicuous by their absence. These excursions made him grateful for the facilities on offer at White River, while the first world cities of Sydney and Leeds seemed on another planet.

Just thinking about Leeds was enough to bring on unease, but he tried to bury these feeling by enjoying the luxury of seeing more of the countryside. Mpumalanga was rather beautiful. It was a province of rivers and dams, canyons and ravines, forests and plains, sunshine mostly and fog also often on the menu.

On one journey back to the hospital, with ever-present Allison drifting through his thoughts, Nick saw in the distance an enormous collection of wild animals for sale on the side of the road – not real animals, of course, merely reasonably facsimiles thereof, animals made of wire and wood. Towering above all the many hundreds of wildebeest, lions, hippo, rhinoceroses (rhinoceri?) and whatever else, were the creatures that the locals called *hoogies* ('lofties') – giraffes. And looming above all this vast herd was an eight-foot, loftiest-of-the-lofty giraffe. When Nick caught sight of this towering creation he swerved off the road, narrowly avoiding a full demolition job of the entire animal kingdom. His heart was pounding as he flung aside his seat belt, opened the door, and literally flew to the huge giraffe. This was indeed something special - how imposing would it look on his veranda! He had to have it.

Then began the process of negotiation. The vendor was an illegal immigrant from Senegal and spoke with a charming Gallic lilt. The Senegalese did not have much difficulty in realising Nick was also from elsewhere. Elsewherians weren't as tight-fisted as the locals.

'M'sieu is from England, oui?'

Nick ignored the question. 'How much is this guy?'

' 'e is twenty sousand rand only, but for M'sieu, I will charge only eighteen sousand, zat's about one sousand English.'

Nick offered R2,000 at which the Senegalese muttered something which sounded like 'Aaai, areyoucrazeee, for zis geereffe twosousand? twosousand?! Peh!!' and walked away, but not *too* far. Nick also walked away in the direction of his car and noticed that he had left the door open, not a very wise thing to do in South Africa where open doors were an invitation to anyone passing by to help themselves to whatever was in the car or even the vehicle itself. The good news was that the car was still there, and no one was sitting in it claiming that possession was nine-tenths of the law.

Both parties knew a deal had been struck, the only thing left to settle being the final price. So Nick waited. After a couple of minutes, the man from Senegal blinked first and walked towards hIm. 'I have six shildren to support, M'sieu.'

'You should be more careful,' responded Nick.

'I have tree wives to take care of.'

'That's three wives too many.'

'Ten sousand?'

'Four.'

'Eight sousand?'

'Six.'

They agreed at six thousand rand and Nick peeled back twelve notes from the wad he had clasped to his belly. 'Ayee, M'sieu must be more careful wiz showing his monay. Msieu is fortunate I am an 'onest man.' Nick instantly realised his error - revealing a wad of banknotes in South Africa was just an invitation for wealth redistribution. The honest man from Senegal smiled – he knew that even though it looked as if he had been roundly beaten down, he had just scored his biggest and most profitable sale of the day. As the Senegalese pocketed the cash, he said: 'Zere is a problem, m'sieu, ze animal 'e is not varnished.'

'No problem,' said Nick, 'you can varnish it right now and put it in the car.'

'Non, non, you do not understand, ze geereffe moost be properly varnished, ozerwize ee will crack. I moost take it to my ome to varnish and you moost come tomorrow afternoon to collect eem.'

'Not possible - I'm a surgeon at White River Hospital. I work till eight.'

'Zen I will bring eem to ze hospital at eight.'

'But it's twenty miles from here.'

'So what is ze problem?'

'I'm a bit concerned that *you* may have a problem and not pitch up, and then *I* will have a problem. Why don't you give back the money and I will pay you tomorrow when you deliver.'

'Does Msieu not trust me?'

It is a difficult thing to say to someone who is holding your possessions that, no, you definitely do not trust them, not in any way whatsoever. At this point Nick realised he had more chance of becoming a lion tamer than getting the smiling man in front of him to return the money. Better then to place his trust in human nature and his faith in God. So they arranged the meeting point for the following day and Nick returned to his car to continue his journey home. By the time he returned to his cottage, the thought had clearly dawned on Nick that he would be fortunate ever to see the Senegalese man or his *geereffe* ever again.

Samson had greater belief in the inherent goodness of man. 'Don't worry, Dr Nick, the giraffe will arrive, and it will be delivered on time.' And, sure enough when at eight the following evening Nick, more than a little exhausted, ducked out of the hospital to return to his cottage, there was the Senegalese with the giraffe standing proud and regal on his veranda, surrounded by a crowd of admiring people. He embraced the man who had kept his word, who bid him adieu and went on his way with an extra thousand rand in his pocket.

At Samson's suggestion, Nick named the giraffe Morota, the Swazi word for 'immense', and he never failed to rub Morota's neck each morning when he went off to operate, and every evening when he returned to the cottage.

# Chapter 28

## Bokkie 2012

During that early period, Nick had been befriended by the big, burly, and as he was later to find out, brilliant part-time surgeon that was Dr Boris Steinberg, who carried the nickname of Bokkie. To an outsider, Bokkie seemed a strange moniker to be carrying, but to a South African not at all unusual. Nick wasn't quite sure how this manifested, but he wanted to know why. What better way to find out than to ask?

How come you're called Bokkie?'

'Ha, when you've been here for a while, that name will became very familiar. A bok is the Afrikaans word for a buck, and bokkie means a 'little buck'. I am told that when I was a kid in the orphanage, I was always hyper-energetic, always running climbing jumping like a little springbok. I ended up in the local hospital on more than a couple of occasions, fortunately nothing ever fractured but lots of stitches. Maybe that's where my destiny was sealed. So all my life I've been called Bokkie or Mr Bokkie or Dr Bokkie. Very few people actually know my given name.'

Now seventy-eight years old, Jewish and widowed with three children living abroad, Dr Boris Steinberg had been head of surgery at Baragwanath Hospital in Soweto. After thirty years there, he had found the pressure at a hospital as manic as Bara becoming too much to handle.

'The administrators were overwhelming the doctors with petty edicts; the nurses were becoming increasingly demanding – it was turning into a shit-show', mused the venerable doctor. He had found uncaring staff attitudes not easy to tolerate. He might be ten minutes from completing a delicate operation, but it was not unusual for nurses to walk out because they had also run ten minutes beyond their allotted working hours.

After the death of his wife, he had tendered his resignation, sold his home and relocated to the one place where, because of its proximity to Kruger Game Reserve, he felt at peace with life - White River where he now worked part-time although often well beyond his allotted hours. Bokkie didn't do hours. He did patients, victims. When he wasn't working, he would be found indulging his love of nature.

'I spend the happiest hours of my life taking photos of big buck and anything else that moves. I might take fifty shots but when I get one decent photo of a bird in flight, that brings me absolute contentment. The digital cameras of today make everything possible.'

South Africa was not America, but there was no shortage of small firearms. Because of the inordinately large number of gunshot injuries that he had had to repair, Bokkie had acquired an interest in ballistics. Such was his experience and expertise in gun-inflicted injury, he was frequently requested to provide expert opinion in murder trials.

Bokkie had even learned to make his own bullets as a hobby. He would load boxes of these bullets, a high-calibre rifle and his enormous bull-mastiff dog into his pickup truck and head to the veld where he would enjoy a couple of hours of target practice. Not shooting down defenceless animals (he abhorred those who did), merely improving his ability to hit a careering balloon that he had pumped and let loose. For a person of advancing years, his eyesight remained remarkably strong. He was a man in full control of his faculties.

Nick would be invited to accompany Bokkie to these unspoilt rural areas. He would advise Nick on the most likely places he might find dormant anthills wherein snakes might be resident. There, they would knock over large ant-heaps, within which all manner of reptiles and insects would be taking refuge from the searing heat. After pinning the snakes with a forked stick, Bokkie would demonstrate to Nick (both with hands heavily gloved) how to pick up the sleeping creatures. Dangerous? Insane? You bet!! But Bokkie had long held the belief that the words "be careful" should not be part of his vocabulary, and felt it was his duty to support anyone interested in nature in whatever endeavours they chose to pursue. Nick soon realised that within this bluff exterior resided as kind a heart as one was ever likely to meet.

A great benefit of the friendship he had developed with Dr Bokkie was being able to accompany him into the Kruger National Park in his pick-up truck. Bokkie was expert in spotting lion, leopard and cheetah, not to mention the huge variety of buck, wildebeest, giraffe and zebra. He despised hunters, and Nick shared this abhorrence. Bokkie was also adept at spotting and identifying the huge variety of bird species of every conceivable hue and size, from the honey-suckers to the predators. Their safari would take place every second Wednesday and last an entire day. During that time, Nick added immeasurably to his knowledge of fauna and flora and learned where to spot a leopard or cheetah by observing its spoor from the vehicle, which they were strictly not allowed to leave under pain of imprisonment.

On one occasion, they were accompanied by an Afrikaans ex-soldier, Major Piet Myburgh. Piet told Nick that he had devoted his life to the fight against poaching. He explained that although almost all of the poachers were indigent black men who were prepared to expose themselves to the gravest of risks, it was callous whites who were behind the cruel killing of rhinos for their tusks, supposedly aphrodisiac, and elephants for their ivory.

Major Myburgh had successfully overseen the prosecution of several of these dealers but knew that retribution would surely follow. He knew he was a marked man and could only hope that revenge would still be a way away. Bokkie said that Piet Myburgh was nothing short of heroic, but felt that Piet, if he had any brains, should now be leaving the heroics to others and finding a new place to live in a different country as far away from White River as it was possible to go. Piet however was a fatalist – this region was where he had been born, and as good a place as any to die if that was what his stars decreed.

Those driving excursions were great, but the icing on the cake was to occupy the spare seat of the two-seater plane that Bokkie, a qualified pilot, housed at a nearby airfield. From the air and flying low, they could see vast herds of wildebeest, zebra and antelope heading for a water hole or on their migratory paths. On more than one occasion they witnessed a kill. This of course reminded Nick of the film he had seen while still in Oz, 'Out of Africa', when he had thought how much he would like to visit that continent but did not think his work would allow him to do.

Nick, who before this had never had more than a passing interest in photography, found himself developing a new passion using a 35mm camera with 200mm zoom lens. Soon, with the assistance of the hospital photography unit, the walls of his cottage were lined with his very own and very professional photos.

Bokkie and Nick occasionally flew further afield to Zimbabwe, Botswana and Namibia where Bokkie would land the plane with great expertise and they would find safe overnight accommodation and enjoy an evening barbeque (in Afrikaans, a *braaivleis* or just *braai*) with indigenous people. Nick was developing a great fondness not just for the African terrain below him with its rivers, swamps and deserts, but for Bokkie who had become a father figure to him without the complexities and hang-ups of parenthood.

Bokkie was a wealth of information on every conceivable subject from classical music to guerrilla warfare. Nick had never met anyone who knew more about nature, human pathology, Mahler's symphonies or indeed the frailties of human beings. And Bokkie could talk, boy could he talk! His reminiscences were endless, his stories fascinating.

For his part, Bokkie was more than pleased to have found a colleague who was intelligent, non-judgmental and his match as a surgeon; with whom he could chat easily; who, despite his prodigious talent, was always willing to upgrade his knowledge and his skills. Above all, Bokkie was able to sense that when Nick's mind seemed far far away, he would not ask what Nick was thinking but wait for him to return to the present. Nick would later learn that it was Bokkie who had urged Mr Nelson Ngope to bring him to the hospital in White River.

# Chapter 29

## The Hard Man

On one excursion, Nick decided it was time to find the person behind this hard-man facade, behind the bluff exterior.

'You haven't told me much about your earlier life, Bokkie. What's your story, mate?'

'My story? My story is a long and boring one. Why would you want to know, Nick?'

'Well, until I got to Uni, I had never met a Jewish person, but then I met dozens who were studying to become doctors or dentists. So I'm interested in finding out why so many choose medicine as a profession.'

'Simple, really - in Hebrew, we call it *tzedakah,* a sort of moral obligation. It's an innate desire to give back for being given life. Actually, there's a lot of people who think I should be given life', he chuckled wryly. 'But there's a more prosaic reason - it's a portable profession.'

'Portable?'

'Ja, let me illustrate with a riddle: why do so many Russian Jews arrive in Israel carrying a violin? Answer is, because it's easier to carry than a piano. We suffer from innate insecurity that at any moment everything we have will be taken away from us. Remember, I grew up during World War Two, when the only Jews who survived were those who were able move out of Europe quickly and settle elsewhere. South Africa, Argentine, anywhere. So, the need for mobility is etched into our DNA. Now our children, who are worried that the doodoo is about to hit the fan here too, are on the move again – England, Canada, Australia, Israel. If things were to go wrong here, I can practise medicine pretty much anywhere else. It's my violin, easy to carry. Law on the other hand would be a piano.... I couldn't, for example go to England and get a position as a lawyer – I'd have to re-qualify, learn a different legal system - it's not always easily transportable.'

Nick nodded. 'I'm beginning to get this.'

Bokkie continued, 'My parents came from Salakas in 1936, a small Lithuanian town near Poland, and settled in Johannesburg when I was two. They were uneducated and poor. I had a brother, Gerald who was 18 months older. My father was a shoe-maker and unfortunately for us he died a year later from a kidney infection. My mother could not afford to keep my brother and me, so she put us in an orphanage. She died a couple of years later of breast cancer, so now we really were orphans!

Anyway, we had no choice but to get on with it and fend for ourselves, and we learned to use our brains and our fists. Fortunately, my older bro never damaged his hands; Gerald was on the artistic side, could draw beautifully. He would later write a couple of good plays and eventually became a famous theatre director in New York until he died a few years ago of AIDS. Poor bugger didn't listen to my warnings.....

'The first bit of good fortune in my life came when I was ten, and an uncle who was a doctor in some hick country town moved to Jo'burg. I had only met him on a couple of occasions when I was very young and he visited my mother in hospital. He and his wife didn't have children and were happy to have us live with them. In those days, Jewish men did not want their wives to work, the implication being that the man of the house wasn't earning enough himself to support the whole family. They weren't wealthy but were rich with kindness and my aunt saw to it that we got a decent education. We tried to pay back by doing chores, but they said we would be better off reading. They encouraged us to take books from the library, boys' books, girls' books, adult books. Ayn Rand, Nikos Kazantzakis, John Steinbeck. There was no tv then, but they insisted that we listen to discussions on radio. That's how I acquired a wide general knowledge.'

Nick thought of his own upbringing, and how he and all his friends had taken having parents for granted. He was pleased he had invited Bokkie to open up about himself - it certainly brought some clarification as to why people turn out the way they do.

Bokkie continued, 'From the time of my mother's illness, I knew I wanted to be a doctor *(we have that in common as well, thought Nick)*, but when I applied, they said I was a year too young and should go and work for a year. I didn't fancy being a waiter or a shop assistant, so I decided to go and learn about life in London. My uncle loaned me the money to pay for my fare but would not ever accept repayment. I had no money but thought I'd find interesting work there. How wrong can you be! I was penniless and homeless after three weeks, and probably would have starved if I hadn't met a couple of recently qualified dentists in Earl's Court. I picked up they had SA accents and asked them if they could help me out until I found my feet. Without hesitation they invited me to stay in their rented flat for a few days until I found a job. I ended up staying there for the full year and working with the one guy as his dental assistant. I will be forever grateful to those two guys. I spent every penny I earned on cheap theatre or concert tickets and it certainly broadened my mind.

'On my return I got a scholarship to study medicine and was still the youngest student in my class. I sailed through and didn't hesitate to specialise. When I was in the orphanage I always had to use my hands to make my own toys and clothes and even repair my handed-down shoes. Tell you what, Nick, it's easier stitching a gashed leg than a broken pair of shoes. I developed respect for my late father, even though I had hardly known him. I found surgery a doddle. I got the surgery prize, and another grant with it, which I believe you did too.' Nick smiled knowingly and nodded.

Bokkie went on, 'I was always more interested in the job than the people I was carving up. I was hardboiled. I guess that came from being in the orphanage. The medical student I fell in love with was the polar opposite. Sharon was gentle and soft. They didn't come more sensitive than my sweet Sharon. She loved poetry and composed many lovely odes and sonnets. Fortunately, our three kids took after her and were all artistically gifted. Artists, actors, poetry.

'I wasn't overly loving to any of them, it didn't come naturally to me. I was rather boorish and just wanted to be with my dog and my rifle in the bush. Overall, though, we had a decent marriage, but it wasn't easy for poor Sharon - I was such a smart-arsed arrogant curmudgeon! I've never forgiven myself for not spotting her illness until it had become too advanced to treat. She had simply shown no signs, or if she did, I didn't see them. So now Sharon's dead, all three kids – kids?!! – all gone god knows where. I don't hear much from them, and they're always going somewhere else. Violin sickness!

'I got sick of the politics at Bara, hated the unions, and refused to pass incompetent students simply because they were black and underprivileged. It's one thing to overlook inadequate technique in an art class, but another matter altogether when you literally have someone's life at the end of a scalpel. I was asked, no, ordered, to change my attitude, and refused. I'm a selfish man, so eventually I told them all to get fucked, resigned, and found myself in this metropolis. Things have been much calmer here politically, but I can see the clouds massing. The times they are a'changin', Nick my boy, and my violin case is at the door.'

Nick heard these words but found it hard to believe that this gruff man, who had taught him so much about animal preservation, about bird habitats, about surgical technique, a man who would work 20 hours a day to prolong the lives of native people and fight for better conditions and pay for the hospital nurses, could consider himself selfish.

# Chapter 30

## Gardener Stories  2012

The longer journeys could on occasion be somewhat boring. It was not always easy to discuss matters other than those surgical. To move away from work issues, Bokkie would regale Nick with stories about his gardeners.

'During the years that I worked at Bara, Sharon and I and our three children lived in a suburban home on the outskirts of Jo'burg. We were 'comfortable' rather than wealthy, but sufficiently well-to-do, like all in our middle-class suburb, to employ a maid and a gardener. Some families' employees remained with them for many years and became as integral a part of the household as any who lived there. A story more familiar to us and others was that their domestic aides came, stayed for a year or two and then, for whatever reason, moved on.

'Most white-owned houses in South Africa were comfortable bungalows or double-stories, with a large garden and two or three sparsely furnished rooms to the rear that were occupied by the domestics living on their own and very rarely accompanied by members of their own families. So, it would be considered normal - normal??!! - for a black maid to have a husband who worked in another town and three children being reared by her parents in a village somewhere far away. The husbands would arrive once or twice a month for a weekend; the children might be visited four times a year.'

Bokkie and Sharon had employed a series of gardeners to care for their half-acre of property and also to carry out the heavier housework. One such was Franz. Bokkie was now into his story.

'Although in general I got on ok with our domestic staff, Franz was one for whom I did not care very much, and I was never sure why my Sharon insisted on keeping him on, other than she must have been terrified of sacking him – I'm sure she felt he would be capable of taking revenge.

'There was definitely something weird about Franz, he suffered from periodic mental delusions. The guy used to smoke far more than his fair share of dagga, and I'm pretty sure it addled his brain. One day we heard horrendous screaming from his room, as if he was being eaten by a lion. Not being scared of gardener–eating lions, I rushed to his room to find the guy sitting on his bed, still yelling his head off.

'What's wrong, Franz?' I ask.

It's my mother, he screams.

'What's wrong with your mother?'

'She's dead!!!'

'Well, no wonder the guy is screaming. So I ask him, when did she die? Today?'

'No, five years ago.'

'So why are screaming now?'

'She's come to haunt me, she's under my bed!'

'I look under the bed but there's no one there. And then the penny drops: many African people are very fearful of ghosts and spirits, and for this reason raise their bedsteads further off the floor by placing the legs on bricks. They keep the underside of their beds exposed and free of possessions, so that they can see a spirit or "tokolosh" should it be hiding under the bed. Well, I don't generally believe in tokoloshes, but his mother really did a number on him because by morning he was gone. But that wasn't the end of the story. He returned two days later.

'Now, here's the reason I'm telling you about Franz. I had a thing about old cars, which I used to repair and maintain myself. This was not something the average Jewish guy did, but I was never average. One sunny day, Franz was washing my old 1950s Studebaker car on the downward–sloping driveway of our home. He neglected to pull up the handbrake when he was finished, and carelessly left the car in neutral. He must have been having a bad *dagga* day, I guess, he really smoked a lot of the stuff.

'Our doorbell rings and the pleasant woman who lives on the other side of the street politely wants to know why my car is impaled on her fence. I look out, and there is the Studebaker, stuck on her garden wall like a big-game trophy.

'I looked for Franz, but he was gone, never to be seen again. Only in South Africa, Nick......'

Bokkie's stories always finished that way. Tales of his gardeners would become a great way of passing the time while they were flying, and Nick found them endlessly diverting.

# Chapter 31

## African Adventures

On one occasion, they drove in Bokkie's *bakkie*, his pick-up truck, to an isolated farm near Pretoria called De Wildt where a courageous and enterprising woman had set up a hospital farm for cheetah that had been injured by animal traps and careless hunters. Almost by accident she also discovered that cheetahs could breed in captivity. This had long been considered an impossibility, but the environmentalist had shown that, provided the roaming space for the animals was big enough, they could and did reproduce. Singlehandedly, she rewrote every textbook ever written about cheetahs and their reproductive potential. Even in a protected habitat, to view a roaming cheetah from close by was a privilege for the British Australian.

There was no doubt in Nick's mind that not only was Bokkie able to teach him valuable surgical techniques but was also providing him with a master's programme in wildlife. He realised how fortunate he was that he had not succumbed to the temptation of ending his life after he was dismissed, suspended, and cast out. He had found a whole new world, an exciting one, and the only thing missing was Allison, for whom he still carried a brightly burning candle. With each passing day he was beginning to realise their relationship was over and the candle would inevitably blow out.

There were still days when, despite the good times he was sharing with Bokkie and the satisfaction he was drawing from his work, he felt the need to reach out for that mind-numbing feel-good medication that had sustained him in those past dark days, but he was determined never again to succumb.

One glorious spring day they flew to Kuruman, a small town sitting just underneath Namibia, to see the Namaqualand daisies. These flowers, normally dormant, only come to life for a few weeks of the year in early spring; but when they do, they grow in such profusion that they occupy acre upon acre of otherwise barren and rocky ground. The most amazing thing of all is that the daisies segregate themselves according to colour; so, one vast field would be white, another yellow, yet another bright red, stretching as far as the eye could see. Bokkie's comment was, 'This is floral apartheid!' Overflying this was an incredible experience given to very few and caused Nick to wonder what Darwin would have made of this example of nature's brilliance.

They spent the evening at an old-fashioned hotel in the town of Kuruman, and, quite exhausted, went to sleep early. To be frank, other than going to the hotel bar, there was precious else to do in Kuruman. It was the one-horse town that gave the expression meaning. A good night's sleep? Not a chance.

Nick was rudely awoken by the sound of very loud bigband music. He looked at his watch - just past midnight. Strange – he didn't think there were enough people in the hotel to be having a party......

He tried to go back to sleep, but the loud music persisted. He made a mental note never to forget earplugs ever again. He pulled on his shirt and trousers and went to seek the source of the unwelcome but not unpleasant music. As it got louder, he found himself in a barely lit room with a huge dance floor, half the size of a football field, in the very centre of the hotel. In one corner of the floor was a shellac record spinning round on an ancient gramophone, the kind that one had to wind up. From this was issuing the sound of Duke Ellington's band playing 'It Don't Mean a Thing if it Ain't Got That Swing', a sixty-year-old evergreen. In the middle of the floor and dancing rapidly and elegantly was a couple doing a type of quickstep that took them from one end of the vast room to the other and back again. The woman was dressed in a long salmon-coloured ball-gown of a time gone by. She and the tall man in a long-tailed black dinner suit with white bowtie brought images of a more elegant age.

Nick was mesmerised. It was if he had been transported back to a time before he was born. He thought that this was possibly the most bizarre sight he had ever seen.

When the music finished, they spotted Nick and came over for a chat. In thick Afrikaans accents, they explained that in a former life they had been professional dancers and had taught at the Arthur Murray School of Dancing in Johannesburg but had now retired to Kuruman where they ran the bar in the hotel. After they had cashed up each evening, they would don their competition clothing and come and practise the *Kuruman vastrap,* their version of Fred and Ginger's quickstep. Once a year they would go to England where they still won the occasional seniors' medal at the Blackpool Tower Ballroom, which they both swore was the finest in the world.

A gracious Viennese waltz followed, after which Nick wished them well and returned to his room to dream of swirling across the floor with Allison.

Breakfast the following morning comprised a huge plate of steak and *boerewors* - spicy sausages - fried eggs and thick mealie-meal (maize) porridge with lashings of tomato gravy. The platter sizzled with protein. Bokkie said this was normal fare in older rural hotels. The health-conscious Nick considered this a prelude to heart surgery, but he put his conscience aside and allowed himself to savour the fare.

He described to Bokkie what he had observed during his midnight perambulation. Bokkie, of course, had slept right through the entire performance! After the sumptuous repast, they returned to their plane.

Soon after take-off, reports began to filter through of extremely turbulent weather in nearby parts of the country, and their small plane began to be buffeted about. Nick began to feel very queasy. Maybe boerewors for breakfast wasn't such a good idea. Just breathe deeply and look straight ahead, said Bokkie. Nick did, and the need to chunder passed. He was more concerned about their safety, or to put it more correctly, their lack of safety. White River Hospital could not afford to lose a single surgeon, let alone two. Bokkie didn't seem to be put out in the least, or if he was, he wasn't showing it. Nick was hugely relieved when, despite the worsening weather, they landed without mishap and were operating by 3pm and for the next eight hours.

Not for the first time, Nick was able to appreciate this second chance he had been given.

For the first few months, Nick had worked six days a week, only taking Wednesdays off and sometimes not even the entire day. The reason he worked over the weekends and on Mondays was that they were the busiest of the week: Saturdays because the local working men got paid on Friday afternoon and would head straight for the local *shebeens* where they would drink the homemade maize-meal brew, *skokiaan*. They would become progressively and aggressively drunk and attack any available male from a different tribe with pangas or *knobkerries*. At about ten in the evening the steady trickle of stab wounds would become a flood and continue throughout Saturday. Saturday evenings were equally busy but from an additional cause: *skokiaan*-fuelled faction-fighting would take place after the local football derbies and continue into Sunday after more such matches. Leeds United's home games were a doddle compared to this!

Sunday nights and Mondays were a nightmare because of the carnage wreaked every weekend by local taxi-drivers as they drove their overloaded vehicles with no regard to speed limits, vehicle maintenance or any form of traffic control. It was not unusual for a mini-bus designed for eight to carry twenty passengers, and one genius driver had even removed the steering wheel to accommodate an extra passenger. How did he steer the vehicle? Simple - he replaced the wheel with a large wrench that was far less space-consuming. So, when the guaranteed accident occurred, epic destruction resulted.

On the Saturdays that he worked, the staff for the most part were not the usual rota, and there was an interesting reason for this: many of the older black nurses belonged to the Christian Church of Zion and observed Saturdays, the Hebrew sabbath day, rather than Sundays as their day of rest. They were part of a very large sect who would go by bus to Zion City near Polekwane, formerly Pietersburg, a town not too distant that was the epicentre of their church. At Easter every year, thousands of buses carrying three million people would set out for Zion City to listen to and be blessed by the Bishop.

The nurses who did not belong to the Church of Zion tended to be of a younger generation, and as Bokkie had said they tended to be considerably more bolshie than the older women - bolshie about having to work on weekends, bolshie on pay, bolshie about having white doctors lording it over them (even if they didn't). The general opinion at the hospital was that, if problems were to arise, whether political or financial, these younger nurses would be its festering wound. The Jeremiahs were not wrong, but Nick was blissfully unaware of that at this time.

# Chapter 32

## Carotid blowout

When found early, many cancers in the head and neck can be abated with few side effects. Cure rates for these cancers could be greatly improved if people sought medical advice as soon as possible. Unfortunately, the local witch-doctor, the *sangoma,* was the person whom many indigenous people first attended for treatment.

If one took a generous view, sangomas might be very competent in predicting that rain would fall or not fall. If one were a little less generous and a lot more cynical, one would say that rain fell or did not fall, not because of anything that the sangomas said or did, but because of prevailing weather conditions which, to their credit, they were able to sense.

Their herbal remedies were useful in treating minor ailments and obviated the overuse of prescription medication. Nick more than most could appreciate this as a good thing. What the sangomas were not competent to treat were matters relating to serious health issues in general and cancer in particular. One could be certain that no matter what the witchdoctors said or did, a malignant tumour would worsen if it was left only to the tribal medicine-men to treat. The longer the patient went on being otherwise untreated, the worse the prognosis would get. That was, if the remedies the sangomas prescribed didn't kill off the patient prematurely anyway.

It was Nick's misfortune to be the surgeon on duty when a 45-year-old man with a 35-year smoking history was admitted to the hospital late one Friday evening with a bleeding mass the size of a bar of soap in the right side of the neck. The mass had been present and untreated except with the herbs and potions supplied by the sangoma for the last two years, but when the mass continued to grow and started to bleed, he eventually pitched up at the hospital.

The patient complained of great difficulty in swallowing and right-sided jaw pain. Direct visual examination left no doubt in Nick's mind that this was consistent with a clinical stage IV squamous cell carcinoma spread all over the shop.

Radiography confirmed this, and Nick realised that even with radical surgery the man had little chance of survival for more than a few days. That was bad enough, but the biggest problem lay in the fact that involvement of the carotid artery was diagnosed, and a carotid angiograph showed the cancerous mass being fed by the carotid artery system. One of the branches was bleeding through the eroded skin.

So far, so medical, but the bottom line was that Nick knew both he and the patient were faced with an invidious choice: if he didn't operate, the patient would die within days, even hours; if he did operate, there was every likelihood that the large and vital carotid artery would burst, an event described as a 'carotid blowout'. Nick was only too well aware that carotid blowout referred to rupture of the carotid artery and its branches. Although never having had to deal with such an event previously, he knew it to be one of the most devastating complications associated with therapy for head-and-neck cancers - when the artery blows, it does so with devastating force and with 100% certainty the patient will be dead within minutes.

Although a carotid blowout was unusual in other parts of the first world because of early diagnosis, in a South African hospital theatre it was not uncommon because of the delay in the sufferer seeking treatment. Nick had never experienced a carotid blowout, but he had seen *The Italian Job* and remembered Michael Caine's iconic words, *"You were only supposed to blow the bloody doors off!"* He did not relish the idea of the carotid exploding, so Nick did the only intelligent thing he could think of – he phoned and woke Bokkie.

Bokkie was blunt. 'You will almost certainly kill the patient but you have to operate. Just make sure you have a crew standing by with packs to mop up the blood, and make sure your face and eyes are protected and everyone else's too.'

'With respect, Bokkie, what's the point of me killing the patient? Why do I need to have his death on my conscience?'

'Have you discussed the risks with the patient?'

'Of course! I told him that he would probably never awake from the anaesthetic, but he is absolutely clear that he wishes me to operate - says he would rather die that way than by choking to death.'

'Witnessed and noted?'

'Witnessed by the staff nurse and noted by my supporting doctor.'

'Ok, so at this point it's no longer about the patient, Nick, it's about you. If you operate, and the patient dies, it's a clinical accident. If you don't operate and the patient dies then you will have gone against his wishes and will be held to have been in breach of duty. Your call.'

Nick operated. He proceeded very carefully and methodically to elevate the tumour. The operation was into its third hour, and Nick was beginning to feel that he might actually be achieving a miracle. He could see the carotid artery clearly separated from the cancerous mass now lying in a dish. The artery was pulsating, but it was intact. The hard part was done.

Boom.

Just at the moment he thought he had ridden the storm, the carotid burst. It burst with unimagined ferocity. Nick would never forget the eruption of blood hitting the ceiling, hitting everything in white scrubs within a metre, but worst of all hitting the operating light. The theatre became murky. To compound this, blood was dripping down the protective plastic shield that he was wearing to protect his protective glasses, causing the room to turn a grim red. The patient was clinically dead a minute later.

No, definitely not something that one forgets. Ever.

Ironic, he thought; I worked all those years in Oz and Leeds, and never lost a single patient as I operated. And here, where I'm doing some of the best surgery of my life, life is cheap as chips, and it's in my hands only to do the possible.

This particular episode unfortunately did not end there. Beauty Mzani was a junior nurse on duty, and she wasted no time in lodging a complaint first to the Matron and then to Mr Nelson Ngope that she believed Nick was drunk at the time he operated, and that had he not been, the patient would surely have survived. She said she could smell alcohol on his breath. Mr Nelson Ngope, who knew Nick was still teetotalling, could smell mendacity from a distance and realised instantly that the nurse's complaint originated not from herself but at the bidding of someone unknown.

A political move? A jealous younger surgeon? The likelihood of the latter was small, and in his mind a political cause loomed large, something that he had feared for some time. He was sure the answer would eventually present itself. As events transpired, it would not do so for nearly four years and when it did catastrophe threatened. For now, a hearing was looming.

Whatever he himself believed, Mr Nelson Ngope was forced to instigate an inquiry, and once more Nick knew he was being stitched up. He became convinced that it was his karmic destiny once again to be destroyed by a woman that he barely knew. Within himself the churning doubts about his ability to cope turned wilder, threshing about in the troubled waters of his brain. This time, however, he was not prepared to give in to his demons. He did not drug. He did not drink. How was it he was able resist this time? What had changed? Nick could not explain it, but changed it had. He carried on working, doing the very best surgery he was able to produce.

Fortunately, the inquiry process was not allowed time to fester and took place quickly. No evidence was found to support the nurse's allegations, and the glowing testimonial he received from sister Anna together with the signed records was more than enough to have the spurious charge thrown out. On the other hand, many of the younger nurses believed Beauty Mzani's story and believed that he was as guilty as hell and that white privilege had once again triumphed.

Coming so soon after the Suffolk experience, Nick found the saga debilitating and depressing and it was only Bokkie and Sister Anna that stopped him from walking. Nevertheless, he realised that he was skating on very thin water. There were venomous monsters in the deep below, and in future he would have to avoid the slightest presence of a current if he did not wish to be pulled down.

# Chapter 33

## Raichie's 2013

Nick had not shared his bed with a woman for as long as he had abstained from medication or not drunk alcohol. This is not to say that he did not miss sex greatly or a social drink (less greatly), but he did not trust himself sufficiently to get involved with any members of staff (and there were plenty of opportunities), for there lay the road to complications and he'd had enough of those. He still felt liable to spin out of control if he relaxed his guard. Nevertheless, Nick was feeling lonely.

Every now and then when one calls, even if subconsciously, life answers.

On alternate Wednesdays, when he wasn't going on safari with Bokkie, Nick would drive the small and fairly ancient Toyota car that had been allocated to him into White River to have breakfast and coffee at Raichie's. Raichie's was a well-run and frequently busy tea-room, popular both locally and with tourists on the way through to the nearby Kruger National Park. The owner was a petite, raven-haired and pretty Jewish woman (he knew this from the Star of David necklace she wore) who looked to be in her late thirties.

He learned that the restaurant proprietor's name was Rachel, but she was called Raichie by her family, her black staff and other regular customers at her eatery. She never dressed in anything other than jeans and a white t-shirt that, despite her bustling and energetic activity remained unsoiled. Although she spent most of her time behind the counter, after the first few occasions he visited Raichie's, it was she who came out to take his order. After a few more times, she had no need to ask what he would like but simply delivered his breakfast of soft-scrambled eggs, spicy mushrooms, slices of fresh tomato that tasted of tomato, home-baked beans, and the best chips he had ever eaten. This was always followed by a steaming mug of strong black coffee and a walnut and cinnamon muffin fresh out the oven, and Raichie would pause for a short but never intrusive chat.

This chit-chat was much appreciated by Nick, because Raichie had a nice sense of humour and an infectious laugh. He had to admit to himself that he found Raichie very attractive, but she was wearing a ring and was almost certainly married or attached, so he didn't think it worth pursuing.

It might have been the thought of Allison holding him back – they were of course still married – but he had reached the stage where he did not think much about her, if he thought about her at all. She had already passed into a hazy memory as if in an air balloon that had broken from its tether.

There was something, however, that caught Nick's attention one Wednesday morning. It was a notice to say that every Wednesday afternoon commencing the following week, a clinic to offer advice on AIDS prevention would be in operation in a side room at Raichie's, and this would include the dispensing of free condoms. When Rachel delivered his coffee, he found himself asking 'Do you have a doctor involved in this project?' She replied in the negative.

'Would you like to have a doctor on board? I'm happy to help if it's needed.'

'I didn't know you're a doctor *(actually she did)* - do you work at the hospital?'

'Yes, I do. My name's Nick Simpson.'

'Well, Dr Nick Simpson, I think that would be amazing, but I couldn't possibly afford to pay you, so thanks anyway.' With that she cleared the table. As she made to move off, he said: 'I don't need to paid and I'd like to help.'

He was as surprised as she was by this offer – what on earth had made him volunteer to work on his day off? Could his overworked self even possibly become more involved in the demands of being a doctor than he already was? He could only stretch his elasticity so far.

'Well, we need to discuss this, Dr Simpson, but this is probably not the best place – would you like to come over one evening, or better still come for Shabbat dinner on Friday night and sample some of my homemade chicken soup and special bread?'

'The short answer is yes I'd love to, thank you very much, but Friday nights are my busiest at the hospital.'

'No chance of getting a substitute?'

'I would have to get one of my colleagues to cover for me for a couple of hours before the stabbings start to come in around ten o'clock. If I could find someone, and it's a big 'if', I'd definitely have to be back there by 10pm latest. Can I let you know?'

'Sure, no problem; just call me here not later than three on Friday, because I have to prepare dinner and prepare my kids for the shock of seeing a man in our home.'

Her last words left Nick a little confused, and he asked her what she meant by them. Was her husband away? Was she divorced? He posed the question.

Raichie's face, normally a cheerful one, nosedived into sadness. He regretted asking.

'Do you mind if I sit for a few moments?' said Raichie.

'Of course not' replied Nick, upset that he had once again been insensitive.

'My story's a sad one. Do you really want to hear it? I'm sure that's not what you came in for.'

'I did ask. Please continue, I'm a good listener. Not much of a speaker, but my hearing's good.'

Raichie informed him that she was a widow, her husband Steven having died in a horrible motor accident some three years before. He had been driving his Mercedes from their nearby farm towards the town. As he reached the top of a hill he was forced to swerve off the road to avoid hitting a mini-bus taxi approaching at speed on the wrong side of the road. The driver had just overtaken a lorry on a blind rise. Steven's car hit a tree and burst into flames. Although there was little left to bury, the funeral on his farm had nevertheless been attended by over three hundred relatives, friends and his workers.

Raichie missed him awfully – her best friend, her lover, her rock had been ripped from her. Her life had become a meaningless blur once the immediate acute pain had been replaced by one that was dull and aching and then by an interminable numbness. Events and words became meaningless. Just waking and numbness and sleep. One thing she could not ignore was that she had three very young children to care for and bring up. Life was for the living, and she had to get on with hers and theirs.

Once Raichie's children were off to school, she had sold the farm (except for the plot where Steve was buried), bought a townhouse in a gated and walled estate (safer from break-in) in the local suburb, and opened her eponymous restaurant to take her mind off the tragedy. Within a short time, her industrious efforts and expert culinary skills had turned a once derelict shop into a busy haven of activity, employing twelve staff and open for breakfast, morning coffee, lunch and afternoon tea. Then she would close the shop and return home to welcome her children from school, ensure that their homework was done and that they were fed.

Nick's first reaction was a feeling of warmth for the bereaved woman, followed by the beckoning of an opportunity for friendship that both seemed to need, but this was quickly replaced by the ringing of alarms. Was involvement with a widow who might be as lonely as he be a bright idea? It was unlikely that she and her young family would want another man intruding into their lives. Besides, he was tainted, and nothing could expunge that stain. She might be a widow, but he was still a married man in disgrace.

Then he decided he owed Allison nothing. Let the dice roll!

# Chapter 34

## Shabbat Dinner 2013

Nick chatted to the other surgeons and found Dube *(whose name was pronounced Dubay)*, one of the more promising younger surgeons, willing to cover; his girlfriend had just dumped him and he was looking to take his mind off things. Nick knew the feeling, although he held back from getting into a discussion about his own past life with someone who had his own immediate problems. He settled for offering platitudes, saying he understood how Dube felt while knowing full well that one could never fully understand how another felt. He expressed his appreciation when Dube offered to stand in.

When he phoned Raichie, she suggested he should be there at 7:30pm after they had returned from the sabbath service at the small local synagogue.

'Do I need to wear a tie?'

'Only if you want my kids to fall over laughing!'

At exactly 7:30, Nick rang the bell of the townhouse in a complex on the outskirts of town. The door was opened by Kevin, a serious-looking, brown-haired, tall and wiry eleven-year-old. Peering under each arm were his two blond curly-haired sisters, Leanne aged nine and Alexis who was seven. Nick smiled as he greeted them, but they continued to stare at him and said nothing. He handed Leanne the large bunch of flowers from the hospital garden that Samson had picked and wrapped, and she scooted off to the kitchen. Raichie emerged, gave him a warm smile and introduced him to the children, but still they said not a word. Then he gave a box of candies to little Alexis and she mumbled a sort of 'thank you' before they all scurried away to inspect its contents.

Raichie offered him a whisky and was surprised when he refused, saying he had not had an alcoholic drink of any kind for the past thirty-six months and had kind of gotten out of the habit. On the mantelpiece stood a photo of a handsome blond man, and this did nothing to make him feel more comfortable. Perhaps he should have accepted the whisky...

She suggested they should head straight to the table that had been beautifully laid out. He particularly noticed two plaited breads covered by a beautiful silk square with strange writing decorating it. They went through the sabbath rituals: first she lit two candles in large silver holders, moving her hands in a circular motion with the girls following suit to bring in and welcome the sabbath.

'This ritual is normally carried out before we leave for synagogue, but tonight we have delayed it in your honour,' she informed him with a smile that made him feel special indeed. Then Kevin put on a small *kippah* or skullcap, handed one to him and said a short benediction in Hebrew over a small silver chalice filled with wine.

'This wine-cup had belonged to Steven, my late husband. It was one of his *bar mitzvah* presents, and Kevin's bar mitzvah is in two years' time', she said. Nick had no idea what a bar mitzvah was – he would find out soon enough.

They all offered a short blessing of thanks over the two plaited bread-loaves that had only come out of the oven a short while before, and then Raichie sliced one of the sesame-encrusted loaves. They all said another benediction and she handed each of them a slice. Nick had seen such breads in Leeds' delis, but never had the faintest idea that they had anything to do with the Jewish sabbath. It tasted more like a simple but delicious cake than bread. They wished each other and Nick *shabbat shalom,* a peaceful sabbath, before sitting at the table for a meal that Nick would remember for a long time.

It began with small fish-balls served with mild red horseradish and more of the delicious bread called *chollah,* the 'ch' being pronounced very gutterally, as in the word 'loch' rather than 'chill'. This was followed by chicken soup with noodles and small balls made of meal and yet more chollah. Rachel told him that the soup was called Jewish penicillin because ill people miraculously felt better on eating it. It certainly seemed nourishing and definitely delicious but he thought its healing powers might just be a little bit of a myth. But then, what did doctors know?

The main course, roast chicken and roast potatoes, was served with a stew of carrots and prunes roasted in honey, which she said was called *tzimmis*. He thought it an odd mix, but delicious it was! Finally, there were apples done in the oven with the core removed and filled with savoury nuts and raisins, and strawberry jelly for the kids. Apparently, all this was standard shabbat fare.

Raichie explained to Nick that her family was not particularly religious but felt it important that they continue some of the orthodox traditions that had been in existence for over five thousand years. These were exactly the same in South Africa as they were in Argentina or Russia or Canada or any place to which her people had been scattered over the past two hundred years until the state of Israel, of which they were intensely proud, had been founded in 1948.

She told him there had once been about fifty Jewish families in the White River area, although that number had dwindled now to less than half as families found the need to be closer to a city. The first of those families had arrived from Lithuania in the mid-nineteen twenties and set up a general store that supplied everything from sewing needles to bedsheets, from canned beans to newspapers. It was still in existence, run by the fourth-generation Goldberg family, and Nick remembered stopping there for a new toothbrush and paste.

In the old days, the townsfolk would come and either purchase all manner of goods or place orders for products not in stock. The founder proprietor Nathan used to drive to Johannesburg every month to stock up, a three-day event resulting in a car packed with goods of every description and its sole occupant driving slowly back to White River. Those monthly excursions only ceased when travelling salesmen, more often than not also Jewish, started coming from the opposite direction. These 'travellers' would often spend the evening or even stay overnight at one or other family's home.

Nathan's family was followed by relatives and friends, and within ten years a community had been established. Several of the families bought land and set up farms, and this was what the late Steven's great-grandparents had done. The children attended the local school where lessons were conducted in English and Afrikaans, and in the afternoons they would have lessons in Hebrew at the local *shul* that Raichie said meant the synagogue with small school attached.

On Friday evenings and Saturday mornings, the community would celebrate the sabbath. In recent years it had been led by Steven, but Alexis informed Nick that Uncle David was now doing it, although, she made very sure to say, not as nicely as their dad had done.

Then they all went to the lounge, where Raichie served tea with slices of lemon instead of milk, Nick's candies and a most delicious dairy-free cake she had baked. By this time the girls were very chatty, asking him where he had come from and why, and telling him stories of their school and memories of their farm. They spoke about how their dad had always made a point of finishing earlier on Fridays and had said the Friday night home blessings, but now that he was no longer there, Kevin had assumed the role at home. They never did homework on a Saturday (one of the Ten Commandments was not to work on the seventh day, they told him) but of late Kevin would often be away playing rugby for his school.

Up to that point, Kevin had said virtually nothing. Nick could understand this because Raichie had said he was the first male to visit them since Steven had died who was not an old friend or relative. Then it all changed. Kevin was thrilled to hear that Nick's schooling had also included serious rugby, and a bond was immediately cemented. Suddenly, they had much to talk about – the merits of their respective country's players and styles, bragging rights not excluded.

Raichie then excused herself while she put the children to bed, leaving Nick to ponder over the warmth of the evening he had just experienced. When she returned, he realised the AIDS project had still not been discussed. When he raised it, she just smiled and said coyly, 'There's lots to do but nothing to discuss, and I only used it as excuse to invite you for the first meal I could serve you without you having to pay.' Nick actually blushed. The attraction was obviously mutual. He offered to wash the dishes, but she laughed and said the maid would attend to them in the morning.

Raichie then said 'So now let me meet the Nick who never says much about himself, actually who never says much about anything. You're very *verklempt,* you know.'

'What's *verklempt?*'

'It's a Yiddish word meaning "bottled up." I know so little about you and I'd really like to.'

Oh well, it was inevitable. The moment he had dreaded, the moment he dreaded with everyone he was with, the moment that would utterly kill any potential for a friendship or anything else that the future might bring; the moment he would have to own up to his back story, would have to confess to being a drug addict who had been suspended by his professional body; to still being married. He knew that once he had become un-*verklempt,* that would probably be that. Why would Raichie want to have more to do with anyone stained with drug offences and sexual misconduct? Nick looked at his watch and realised he would have to leave soon to return to the bedlam of the hospital.

'Another time', he said.

'No, not another time, Nick. I need to know who you are, and I need to hear it from you.'

So Nick, as briefly as he could, unrolled the saga of his precipitous fall from grace, the saga that occupied his mind every waking moment when he wasn't working, the saga that made him forget all the good things he had ever done and replace them with the negative comments that had been dredged up by his peers; the thoughts that raged through his mind when all he wanted was silence.

When he stopped talking, he stood up. 'There. You have it. Now I need to get back and relieve Dube. Thanks for a really enjoyable evening.'

Raichie too stood and placed her arms on his shoulders. 'That must have been hard for you, not only the experience but sharing it with me. That took courage. Thanks for joining us, Nick. I hope it won't be the last. By the way, my kids really liked you.'

'Even Kevin?'

'Even Kevin.' Her smile was dazzling. She kissed him lightly on his cheek. Maybe there was hope after all. Maybe there was the possibility that she could see him as he was now, not how he had been in recent years. Nobody since the Allison of long ago and later Jesse had anyone made him feel so warm, and he hummed to himself (he never sang) as he drove back to the hospital. When last did he feel this way? The thought went through his mind that it was nearly three years since he had last had any physical contact with a woman, and aside from Jesse, the first time that he really wanted to.

When she delivered his breakfast ten days later at the coffee-shop, Raichie said: 'Thanks for the flowers, Nick – beautiful bouquet!'

When she returned with his coffee, she added, 'You made quite an impression on my kids – they haven't stopped laughing! No, seriously, Nick, all three seemed to find something to like about you. Kevin was impressed by your rugby stories, Leanne thought you were quite handsome – remind me to book an appointment for her with my optician – and Alexis says she wants to be a doctor. They want to know when you will be coming to us again.'

'When you next invite me. By the way, what was *your* assessment of your guest?', Nick somewhat disingenuously inquired.

'The less said the better. Your coffee is getting cold.'

Her departing giggle left him in no doubt that something very unexpected, and very welcome, was happening in his life.

# Chapter 35

## The AIDS Clinic 2013

Workwise re the AIDS project, he was happy to be able to see Raichie regularly over the next few months. He was impressed by her sense of humour, but more than that by her energy, enthusiasm and competence. She applied herself to her new project with the same vigour and desire to succeed that she was giving to her business. She ensured that word of the clinic was spread and disseminated, pinned notices in all the shops of the town, even stood with a loudhailer at a busy intersection. People began to trickle and then to flow into the clinic, and soon they were inundated with locals seeking advice and, for too many, treatment. They needed a hand, hands. They needed professional assistance.

'Wow, I knew there was a need for this sort of clinic, Nick, but I wasn't expecting an avalanche. And our effing government does bugger all. I think I've bitten off more than I can chew.'

'You certainly have, but Ieave it to me, I'll sort out something.'

Nick's enthusiasm for the project went into overdrive. It had been ages since he had felt so motivated. With the permission of Mr Nelson Ngope, he enrolled a group of nurses and, when possible, junior doctors from the hospital to attend the AIDS clinic, and set up a rota for them; and when he had free moments, pitched in himself. They gave advice, explained how AIDS was transmitted, dispensed condoms, and far too often diagnosed the possible presence of HIV in the attendees, encouraging them to seek treatment at the hospital rather than from the sangomas whose methods in this respect were nothing less than futile.

The clinic received anonymous threats, presumably from the disgruntled medicine-men, that the clinic would be burned down, so Nick took it upon himself to organise another rota, this time of night-watchmen. Samson's assistance proved invaluable. As the number of attendees increased, Nick suggested to Mr Nelson Ngope that the hospital might want to take over its management, and following discussions with Raichie, the clinic became a hospital outpatient extension. Raichie's role was now to raise funds from donors and pharma companies, and she did this with immense skill and charm.

It definitely wasn't all about work, though. Friday nights with Raichie's family had become a regular event and something to which Nick looked forward hugely. The issue of his past had not been raised again. He realised he had become captivated by the presence of the children, and even more so by their mother, and this made him think that had he and Allison had children of their own, he might never have gone through the depression that led to his downfall. Then he thought of former colleagues who were having problems with their children and realised maybe it would have happened anyway. The thought struck him that if that was the case and there had been children, how much bigger a mess would that have been to sort out? Water under the bridge .... Just be grateful that he was here with this family.

After the children had said their goodnights, the adults would chat over their lemon tea, something that intrigued Nick. 'Why do you prefer tea with lemon, Raichie?'

'Why, don't you like it?' (Bokkie had told him that Jewish people always answered a question with a question.)

'I don't mind it at all. To be truthful, I wasn't mad about it at first, but I now rather enjoy it. I'm just curious.'

'I like that you're curious. I like a lot of things about you, actually. Ok, so according to our kosher dietary laws, we never have any dairy products for a couple of hours after eating meat. It must have made sense thousands of years ago and it probably doesn't now, but I just respect it.'

Nick was quite surprised to learn that Raichie was not originally from White River.

'I was brought up in a small town called Randfontein about thirty miles the other side of Jo'burg, where my father still owns the main town pharmacy. Randfontein is a typical mining town, at the time overwhelmingly white, overwhelmingly Afrikaans, with enough Jewish families for us to have a decent-sized synagogue. Although we were a self-contained community, we got on pretty well with our neighbours – we used to call them Dutchies, they called us Yids. Randfontein was not a pretty town, fairly flat, bungalow houses laid out in a square grid, safe to play in the streets. It was a great place to grow up.'

'Sounds exactly like Ballarat.' He told her a little about his upbringing. She was interested to hear about his mother's work as a seamstress.

Raichie said 'My mother worked very hard too, but only in the home. Today you'd call her a domestic executive; at that time, she was a fulltime housewife. So my mother became a wonderful cook; I learned to prepare the food you've been eating here and at Raichie's from her. She's also an amazing baker, and it's surprising I didn't grow up twice the size. She's still very involved in Jewish charitable activities – women of her generation generally didn't work because they didn't need to, but she and my dad wanted their children to have professions.'

'Interesting, I've been learning the same thing from my colleague Bokkie.'

'I wonder how come I've never met him? He's kind of legendary here. You must invite him over.'

'I can, but I doubt he'll come – he's a very solitary person since his wife died, totally comfortable on his own, always out in the bush when he's not working. Anyway, you were saying?'

'Well, my two older brothers and I were taught from our earliest days that we should study, and we all ended up at Wits Uni in Jo'burg. Jeff's a doctor and his family have emigrated to Toronto, and Michael's a lawyer in London. The Jewish diaspora, always on the move. They don't return too often. My kids hardly know them, although we chat regularly.' Nick felt a pang in his guts. He needed to communicate more often with *his* parents.

'Sounds not unlike my own experience. What did you do at uni?'

'Do you mean besides look for a husband? I was studying psychology but spent most of my day in the student canteen, having a wonderful time socially, and that's where I met Steven. We were both boarders in the halls of residence, and he was majoring in zoology.'

The attraction had been mutual and instant, and they enjoyed university life to the full, with regular parties at one or other of the residence halls. Within three months of their simultaneous graduations, they married in a synagogue in Berea, a suburb of Johannesburg, with her brothers travelling back to join the celebrations.

'We had a wonderful honeymoon in Mauritius and returned to Steven's home and family farm in White River. Not much different to life in Randfontein, really, only much prettier. I had thought to set up a small psychology practice in the town on a couple of days a week, but then the kids came along and that was that. Steven's father passed away following a coronary not long after, and Steven found himself head of family, farm and community. He was a very special guy, was my Stevie.'

'So I have heard from many people. It's obvious your kids have inherited his genes and fortunately not yours. They're also very special.'

She leaned over and gave him a soft kiss. 'And so are you, big boy.'

Nick was aware of one huge change in his behaviour. From being laid-back and laconic, he couldn't stop talking when he was with Raichie and her kids. Rugby, work, Leeds, it all came gushing out. So different from Allison. If the reason that he found himself in South Africa bothered her, she certainly did not show it. If he had been errant in the past (and she found this hard to believe), comments she had heard from other doctors at White River Hospital suggested that such erroneous ways existed no longer. Nor was she in any way bothered by the fact that technically he was still married - she accepted that it was just a matter of time before that would change.

Their relationship had gradually developed into a physical one, and he found Raichie to be a passionate lover. She had been without another's touch for as long as he had. On the first occasion that he spent the night with Raichie he was woken by young Alexis jumping on him and smothering him with kisses, and he knew that something was significantly changing in his life.

# Chapter 36

## Enjoying Mpumalanga 2013

And so the first twelve months passed. All malignant thoughts in respect of Dr Susan McDonald had diminished and receded to a very small part of his brain, and Nick could not have been more grateful for the change in his life that had been forced on him by that spiteful woman.

The next few months were exhilarating but exhausting. There were times when he felt overwhelmed by the burden of responsibility that had been placed on him. At those times old doubts would return and he would develop a fear of false starts and even the sense that he could end up repeating previous destructive patterns. He also worried that perhaps things were going *too* well – *don't look for trouble, it will find you in any event.* He was grateful that these negative thoughts did not occur often.

At most times, though, he was thriving with the unending challenges being thrown up by his work. Far more than he had ever imagined, he was enjoying the experience of working in an unscripted, at times chaotic, environment that was as different from Leeds as Indian food was from Chinese, where innovation and improvisation replaced doing everything by rote.

He had decided no longer to work every Sunday but to take off one in three, which Mr Nelson Ngope said was a good thing to avoid burnout. On those free days he and Raichie and her kids would go out to the countryside for picnics, and Nick loved the experience of setting up a *braai,* a barbie in the wild. They would drive to different beauty spots, each more scenic than the last. Best of all were the Bourke's Luck potholes. These were cave-like erosions created by decades of swirling eddies of the Blyde River, a series of cylindrical rock sculptures that looked as though they would be more comfortable on the moon.

The Blyde River Canyon was one of the largest and greenest on Earth due to its lush subtropical foliage. The views of the Three Rondavels, huge, round rocks reminiscent of the huts of the indigenous people, and of God's Window with its sheer and awesome drop were sights Nick would not quickly forget. This, added to Raichie's innate ability to turn a picnic or a braai into a banquet, plus the joy and excitement of the young girls (and occasionally even of the laid-back Kevin when he wasn't sporting) made Nick realise that life was indeed to be enjoyed.

As his second year drew to its end, Nick was approached by Mr Nelson Ngope, the hospital CEO, and asked if he would consider staying on as head of department at the hospital, where his performance and diligence had exceeded expectation. Nick of course was only too pleased to accept, especially in view of his now very close relationship with Raichie and her children. He did question whether it might be better for them to appoint a black surgeon, and Mr Nelson Ngope had said that time would come but was not yet ripe for such a move.

Before he could accept the offer, and he very much wanted to, there was one matter still to be dealt with: he was now due to re-appear before the Committee in London, where hopefully his suspension would be terminated. This was by no means a certainty. What if additional complaints had been made against him by an unknown former colleague crawling out of the woodwork? Bokkie said he was just being paranoid, but Nick couldn't help feeling nervous.

He had been in touch by letter with the solicitors there, and through them with Bernard, and they were optimistic that this could be achieved without difficulty provided that he could show that during the past two years he had not partaken of drugs or alcohol, had not behaved improperly with his female staff, and had performed competently in South Arica. Based on his previous experience, however, he realised he could take nothing for granted.

A few nights before he left, he and Raichie saw an excellent film at White River's only cinema. 'The Deep South' recounted the largely true story set in the sixties of a black working-class New Yorker who by sheer dint of effort had taught himself and then been schooled to become a very cultured and accomplished classical pianist. His reputation had grown, and he had been persuaded to tour the southern states in America where his forebears had been slaves and where extreme racial prejudice was still very much the order of the day. Of course, the musician's expedition had not been without some rather distasteful incidents, but he had emerged intact and with reputation enhanced. The film left a deep impression on them both as they realised that the film could just as easily have been set in White River.

Bokkie poked his head past the door. 'Hey, Nick I've arranged a meeting with a colleague in Johannesburg; I can fly you to Tambo International airport, how's that suit you?'

'No thanks, I had actually been looking forward to another Kulula flight.' Bokkie thought maybe Nick's brain had become addled by too much chicken soup and was relieved when Nick said, 'Just kidding, that would be great. What's your meeting about?'

Bokkie didn't respond and chose not to inform Nick that the colleague would be performing a colonoscopy. He seemed unusually quiet and preoccupied that morning. Nick thought, he surely can't be sad to see me going away for a month. Well, he was somewhat incorrect about that, because as much as he had come to view Bokkie as a father figure, it went the filial way too.

No, aside from the impending procedure that would require a mini camera to be delicately passed through his rear-end orifice and into his colon, in itself worrying, something far more serious was on Bokkie's mind. With his voice choking with anger, he unburdened himself to Nick.

'The bastards got my friend Major Piet Myburgh yesterday. Four men ambushed his Toyota van at a crossroad and pumped twenty bullets into him. Amazing thing was they left his passenger untouched. It was obviously a revenge killing. I'm certain the police know who organised it, but they won't do a bloody thing.'

Bokkie explained that at a recent bail application by a group of white poacher ringleaders arrested by Piet, the judge had seemed only too happy to allow them to pay nominal bail and walk. Piet had paid with his life. Bokkie remained quiet for a long while. Nick was deeply saddened by Bokkie's news - this notion of revenge by execution was foreign to him but, it seemed, not unusual in South Africa. Corruption was the new cancer in the new South Africa, and there was no political surgeon with the courage to excise it.

# Chapter 37

## Slender Fingers, Deep Pockets
## 2014

Nick had chosen to fly via Schipol airport in Holland on KLM, which was offering the best fare. The flight was unremarkable. Between movies, Nick was able to reflect on his experiences over the past two years. Eventful, certainly. Rewarding – more than. He'd carried out more operations in the past two years than he had in the preceding ten and been appreciated for every single one. He'd had to deal with safari suits and snakes, giraffes and gardeners. He'd encountered dagga and daisies and the *Kuruman vastrap.* He'd formed strong relationships with Bokkie, Samson, Anna Kunene and Mr Nelson Ngope, and most especially with Raichie that he hoped would be lasting. The whole experience had been beyond expectation – *buitenverwachting.*

In those two years he had touched neither alcohol nor medication, proven by a recent test. He'd stopped carrying Leeds and Allison, Susan McDonald and Bernard Finch about with him, and had mostly managed to wipe the previous two years from his mind. Now he was on his way to close the circle, and aside from the odd moment of doubt was doing it with self-esteem riding high.

He found himself thinking about his experiences of being a white doctor in post-apartheid South Africa, where in the recent past no black person could dream of sitting at a white's table or using a whites-only toilet or travelling on a whites-only bus. Nick realised that he had been very fortunate indeed by being seconded to work in a non-racial hospital rather than, say, an upmarket private clinic in Johannesburg that only whites could afford. He was grateful that he had not had to be part of the apartheid experience.

At Schipol he switched to a BA flight for the short hop across the Channel. That flight proved to be the only time that he ever got upgraded, and he ended up sitting next to an elegantly suited and well-groomed man suitably dressed for smoked-salmon-class travel, whereas Nick was definitely geared for the sardine section. Nick was struck by the fine cut of the gentleman's lightweight grey suit and the crispness of his white shirt that was made to look even whiter by the obviously expensive silk tie and matching pocket handkerchief in red and black floral. But what really opened Nick's eyes (figuratively speaking) were the man's elegant long fingers with immaculately filed fingernails, fingers a surgeon would be proud to own, fingers that could make a scalpel sing arias.

They entered into conversation, and it turned out that Mr D R de Groot, as stated on his seat label, was actually Professor Dirk de Groot. He was a classically trained pianist who was professor of jazz studies at Beals, a private university in Massachusetts. Dirk had been born in Surinam; his family had emigrated to Holland when he was young. From his earliest days he had tinkled at the piano and with expert tuition grew into a talented classical pianist. He then went on to hone his talents at the Julliard school of music in New York, where he proved to be a reasonably good classical student, but outstanding at jazz improvisation of the classical repertoire. From New York he had moved on to a university down south near Atlanta.

Nick found the professor to be a charming and modest man who had overcome the prejudice and bile that was part of being a black lecturer at a predominantly white university in a predominantly white town in Georgia. His talent as pianist had carried him to places that would otherwise have been inaccessible to him, and he had finally acquired a professorship and tenure at Beals. The parallels with the film Nick had recently viewed were remarkable and he wondered whether the movie had been based on Dirk's experiences.

Dirk was on the last leg of a European-wide jazz tour with his two sidemen. His final engagement was to be at a large venue in Kent (the name of which was not known to Nick), but prior to that would be spending two evenings at an hotel in London. Nick was surprised to learn that, despite having travelled and given concerts all over the world, Dirk had never visited London.

'Tell me, Nick, how best do I travel not too expensively from Heathrow airport into the CBD?'

'It will cost you nothing. I'm going to be spending a couple of nights in London before I take the train up to Manchester for my hearing. You are welcome to share the mini-cab I've arranged to get me into the West End and it's only a short taxi-ride from my hotel to yours. You'll be saving around sixty dollars.'

'Wow, man, that's very kind of you.'

They chatted amiably in the cab, and Nick found himself warming to this refined and erudite man. When they arrived at Nick's hotel, he and Dirk spent a couple of hours having coffee and fresh croissants, chatting mainly about Dirk's music. Dirk was interested in Nick's impressions of various jazz pianists whom Dirk knew on first name terms. He had studied with Bill Evans and with Oscar Peterson, and also knew well the expat South African Abdullah Ibrahim. He was rather surprised to learn that Nick was also acquainted with the pianistic skills of the Jamaican Monty

Alexander who had jammed with Bob Marley, and also the Swede Esbjorn Svenson and his trio, EST. Nick had not completely wasted his time in Suffolk! Dirk suggested he would be happy to have Nick visit him at Beals.

On a whim, Nick invited Dirk to be his guest for dinner that evening, and the pianist had accepted without hesitation.

As Nick sat in the trendy Knightsbridge restaurant he had selected even though somewhat pricy, he was surprised to see Dirk enter not alone but accompanied by another younger man. An additional chair was arranged, and the younger man turned out to be a musician as well (a bass-man, also with long but less slim and much coarser fingers), and he too was well groomed and comported.

The evening and meal proved to be quite special, during the course of which it became obvious that the two men were more than just good friends. This bothered Nick not one iota, although the two bottles of fine wine they ordered made him gulp. When the bill arrived and de Groot showed no sign of offering to pay for the bassist, Nick realised that it was for him to settle the bill in its entirety. He would have to work for many hours when he returned to pay for the privilege of their fine company. Well, he had invited *Dirk*, if not *them,* and it had been a delightful evening, and some experiences are just worth the price.

Before they parted, Dirk handed Nick a leaflet advertising his concert in Kent the following evening and said he really hoped to reciprocate. 'Great idea', said Nick, 'My hearing's the next day but I'll do my best to be there.'

The concert was due to begin at 7:30pm and Nick took the 5:00 train down to Rye, from where he had to take an expensive thirty-minute taxi ride to the venue that turned out to be a large hall at a posh golf club. He was expecting to be Dirk's guest, so felt more than a little disappointed when his name was not found on the guest list and he was charged a £30 entrance fee. The concert, however, turned out to be rather wonderful and well worth the price of admission.

De Groot was a boundless musician whose wide-ranging ideas were executed with astonishing dexterity; his music was passionate, songlike, often poetic, and he was well supported by his two colleagues. The strength of his pianism and diversity of thought dissolved into uninhibited improvisation that reminded Nick of the greats whose cds he had enjoyed in his Suffolk bolthole. How was it that Dirk was not better known, that he played near Rye and not in London??

Nick barely managed to catch Dirk's eye all evening, not until he lined up with many other guests to obtain one of the cds that Dirk was selling and autographing. As Nick reached the table, Dirk rose and greeted him warmly, signed his disc and said he hoped to see Nick soon stateside - and charged him £15 for the cd.

A return taxi ride, train to London and taxi to the hotel meant Nick got to bed well after 2am. It had been a delightful evening, but also a very expensive one. When he debated whether he would ever contact Dirk, he decided he couldn't afford it. Nevertheless, he kept telling himself that the lapses on Dirk's part were mere oversights. He would listen often to his wonderful recording, put the negatives aside and think kindly of a most talented man who had long delicate fingers and needed them to reach into his deep pockets.

# Chapter 38

## Closure: Manchester 2014

Early the following morning, despite the acute lack of sleep, Nick took the train to Manchester for his hearing and was warmly greeted by Bernard Finch, the barrister who had become his mentor in the skills of life. Bernard was wearing the same suit and tie as he had two years before, but his white shirt was new and pristine. 'Good to see you again, Nick - so pleased to hear you've been making such a name for yourself. This is not going to take long. I'd like you to be my guest for lunch when we're done here, but in the meantime relax because it will all go smoothly.'

Nick responded, 'I wish I felt as confident as you, Bernard, but quite frankly I'm crapping myself.'

'That's not like you, Nick. When we first met, I thought you quite arrogant.'

'Perhaps so, but getting one's arse soundly kicked can have a salutary effect on self-confidence, and quite frankly the mere sight of this building makes me want to run.'

'Don't. I can assure you that you will leave here today a different person to the one who arrived.'

'As my mother used to say, from your mouth to God's ear.'

'Don't tell me you've found religion out there in the backwoods.'

'Let's just get this over, Bernard.'

Armed with a file full of testimonials and letters from Mr Nelson Ngope, Bokkie and several other doctors at the hospital, not to mention twenty-five certified letters from nurses, and character references from many grateful patients, Bernard addressed the same Committee that had suspended Nick. Nick was surprised when rather than ask him the serious questions they had raised on their previous encounter, they showed great interest in his experience of life at the nether end of Africa.

The large bundle of papers proved completely acceptable to the Committee. It was obvious to them that the doctor before them had completely exonerated himself, had remained free of noxious substances, and was never likely to be a threat to the public or his profession in future. The hearing lasted less than two and a half hours. As Bernard had foreseen, Nick's suspension was lifted without condition. He was informed he would be allowed to seek employment or go into private practice anywhere in the UK.

Each member of the panel came over to shake his hand, stopping short of what Bernard was about to do which was to wrap his puny arms around Nick's broad shoulders. Large tears were streaming down Nick's cheek. A four-year nightmare had come to an end, during which time he had experienced, fought and overcome adversity, and had found redemption. The weight on his shoulders, that millstone around his neck was gone, and only when it went did he realise how heavily it had weighed.

At the promised lunch at a fine restaurant nearby, Nick thanked Bernard profusely for his sterling efforts and presented him with two tickets he had managed to acquire (not without difficulty) for a performance of Don Carlo by Verdi at the Royal Opera House the following month. Nick would have loved to attend the performance himself, but his schedule did not permit such personal indulgences.

So he bid adieu to Bernard for what he believed would be the second and final time. The doctor was not to know that there were still more twists to this tale, but these would come some time later.

There was another matter to be cleared up. The following day Nick took the train across the Pennines to Leeds. He had left a message for Allison that he would be calling on her. When he arrived, he headed straight for her office. He was informed by her secretary that she was unwilling to see him but requested that he be kind enough to sign the divorce papers she had prepared. There was nothing to be contested and no blame was to be attached to either party. Allison would transfer to him half the value of their jointly owned property. Nick at first felt degraded by this final summary spurning and was tempted to walk out, but when he thought about it, he realised she was probably right – no point in raking over old coals. Seeing each other would only upset them both.

With only a moment's hesitation, he signed the offered document. He chatted briefly to the secretary who informed him, not without a smirk of satisfaction, that Allison was now dating another lawyer and planned to remarry as soon as the divorce came through. Nick did not bother to mention that he too was in a relationship and left as quickly as he could.

One final thing to be done: Nick stopped in at a travel agent to book a ticket from London to Ballarat via Denver, Sydney and Melbourne.

## Chapter 39

## Denver and Australia  2014

The flight was long, 22 hours in total with a stopover in Denver, Colorado. He had picked this particular flight because he had extracted from his wallet a card that had been nestling there since Puglia. Denver was an hour's bus ride from Boulder, and Boulder was where Jesse lived. He had e-mailed Jesse: 'If you're around, I am passing through and it would be great to catch up.' Jesse was about to head off to experience and write a critique of the premier restaurants of the city of Split in Croatia but responded she would be around for the couple of days he planned to spend there and couldn't wait to see him. She was indeed waiting at the bus station on the outskirts of Boulder, but this time she was not alone. Her husband Randy was a strapping big Texan with personality to match. He wrapped his massive paw around Nick's slightly smaller but far more delicate surgeon's hand, and Nick was grateful to have it returned with no bones crushed.

'Good to meet ya, Nick, Jesse's told me a lot about ya! I sho' hope you kicked those medical asses!'

'Well, they sure kicked mine two years ago, but it's all good now,' said Nick. He briefly described the original hearing and its bitter ending, and then told of his redemption. He told stories of his experiences in South Africa.

'You sho' are a good story-teller, Nick ma man, no wonder Jesse's so mad about you.' Jesse winked – it seemed they had sorted their problems. The big Texan had had his tenure at Colorado University Department of Architecture confirmed, and Boulder was where they would be for the foreseeable future. His financial issues had resolved, and his alcohol dependence was well under control.

She was really glad that they had been able to meet up so unexpectedly once more. Seeing her stirred something in him, but he was pleased they had not allowed their relationship to proceed too far because she and her Texan seemed a good match. She in turn was thrilled to hear about Raichie.

They drove Nick around Boulder in their big old Cadillac and explored a futuristically-styled private art gallery Randy had designed. They took him on a tour of the university campus, where 20,000 students enjoyed fantastic facilities, and then the threesome headed for dinner at a gourmet downtown steakhouse with a view of the Flatirons, the mountains at the foot of the Rockies. Nick had got used to eating large steaks at *braais* in SA but his jaw dropped when the monster-huge T-bone steak with jacket potato and onion rings recommended by Randy was set down before him. He thought back on the amazing kudu steak he had had in Sandton Square when he was first setting out for White River, but even that paled into insignificance by comparison. The accompanying glass of Napa Valley Zinfandel was the first wine he had had in four years. Why did he change tack? Simple. Because he could. His life was his own once more and it felt good.

He spent the night at a luxurious new hotel, the first bit of creature comfort he had permitted himself in four years aside from Puglia and a night in Sandton. What a treat not to be concerned that there might be a snake or spider or tarantula or scorpion under his bed! After a gargantuan breakfast together at a restaurant nestling under the Flatirons on the following morning, Randy and Jesse drove him to Denver airport for his connecting flight to his former home. Nick did a great selling job of Mpumalanga, and though they promised to visit 'sometime rill soon', he knew he shouldn't hold his breath. They seemed genuinely sad to see him leave, and he would value the time he spent with two people whose friendship he would always treasure, even if their paths did not cross again.

During the flight, Nick thought how strange life could be. When he lost Allison, he thought a gap had been created that would not readily be filled, but since then he had met not one but two amazing women. Jesse was not an option for the future, but he couldn't wait to see Raichie and her family once again.

His parents were at Melbourne airport to meet him. He was shocked to see how they had aged since his wedding to Allison when his whole world had been before him. He had visited them a couple of times, but not for the past five years. As they drove back to Ballarat, he recounted exactly what had taken place in the recent past and apologised profusely for letting them down. They were of course terribly upset, but most about Allison and that they had no grandchildren and would almost certainly never have. Gladys's response was typical (and she cited Forrest Gump): 'Shit happens....'

He stayed in their small house in his once upon a time bedroom for two weeks, spending all his time with them. He envied the simplicity of their lives and was grateful for their undiminished love. Although inquiring about his old-time mates, he contacted not a single one. His old buddy Jason was married with four kids and a job selling insurance that he seemed to do very well. Nick's life had taken a very different direction to theirs, and he was content to keep the memories of them as the happy ones of his youth. His folks were of course full of questions: what was Raichie like, did he regret losing Allison, was Africa like

Australia. He was pleased to be able to show great photos of Raichie and the kids; photos of Bokkie and his pickup and his plane; photos of snakes and wildebeest and lofty giraffes; and photos of Samson, Anna and Mr Nelson Ngope and White River.

Gladys's seventieth birthday was coming up. As a special treat to celebrate the event, Nick drove them out to Dunkeld, just two hours south straight down the road. There they enjoyed a spectacular taster-menu meal with matching wines at the Royal Mail, once a postal sorting office at the centre of the gold rush, now a luxury hotel with a brilliant restaurant – well, it was the chef who was brilliant. The eight-course tasting menu was the best he and certainly his parents had ever experienced (and it was indeed an experience!) The wine-pairing selection was equally impressive, chosen from a massive repository across the road. For Gladys, all her dreams came true at once: a different town, a sumptuous meal, superb wine and the small family together.

She was tickled by what people in the restaurant were wearing: a couple who had flown in from Darwin two thousand miles away to celebrate their 50th anniversary were respectively dressed in full long dress and black tie regalia *(shades of the Kuruman vastrap)* whereas the cobbers at the next table were in khaki shorts and t-shirts – and no-one cared a hoot. It dawned on Nick how much he missed the egalitarian nature of Oz society and how different it was to race-ridden South Africa, though it did not pass without notice that there was not a person of colour in sight.

They stayed overnight before enjoying a long walk in the hills with dozens of kangaroos in attendance. He realised just to what extent his parents had missed him and how much they loved him, and by the same token he them, but knew that he had to return to White River, the hospital, and most of all to Raichie and her children.

When they drove back to the airport, Nick promised that at the first opportunity he would send them tickets to visit him in South Africa, but he left with grim foreboding that he would see neither of them again, and found the thought painful.

This was to prove very prescient, for within three months a lawyer's letter reached him to say that both had been suffering from terminal cancer when he visited and had resolved not to say anything to him. Not long after his departure they had passed away within a few days of each other after 49 years of marriage and had specifically requested that he only be informed after their funerals. They had said their goodbyes and did not want him to go the expense of flying out again. They left him their house. The only thing that lessened the sadness that Nick felt was that he had seen them that final time, shared a caring couple of weeks and a wonderful evening, and that their farewell had been warm and loving.

# Chapter 40

## Randfontein 2014

It didn't take long before his workload once again overwhelmed his waking hours, which helped considerably to take his mind off the recent sad events: divorce, loss of parents, end of the past. However, another important event was on the horizon, this time a most pleasant one.

Young Kevin was approaching his thirteenth birthday. This was the age when a Jewish boy celebrated his *bar mitzvah*, the coming-of-age ceremony 'to mark his passage from boyhood to manhood'. On a forthcoming Saturday morning, he would be required to be called up to the altar at the local synagogue in the presence of all his relatives, family, friends, and his own mates. He would be required to sing a short portion from one of the first five books of the bible, and then a fairly long portion from the biblical prophets. Kevin had spent six months in preparation of this important event, learning his portion in Hebrew.

This would be followed in the evening by a grand party. Raichie's brothers would be flying in to celebrate the occasion, and her excitement was building by the day. There was so much to organise: outfits to be chosen, accommodation for the guests to be booked, caterers to be selected and briefed.

As the big day drew near, an important issue required attention. 'Listen, Nick, I need to ask a big favour of you and I don't want you to give me a hard time because you have to do this for me', said Raichie, wagging an imperious finger. 'On the big day, the young man traditionally sits next to his father, but since Kevin does not have his dad, I would be very pleased if you would do my son the honour of sitting next to him in synagogue.'

Nick was completely taken aback - he did not know what the inside of a synagogue looked like. 'But why me, Raich? Surely your brothers or your father should do it.'

'Sure they could, but Kevin barely knows them, and he wants you there. He idolises you, as if you didn't know.'

When Kevin himself came to ask him, Nick realised there was no way he could refuse. Yet he was concerned - how would her brothers feel about it? Nick chatted to each of them by phone and both said they had no problem. But Nick was only too aware that another very difficult bridge had to be crossed – how would Raichie 'out' her *goy,* her gentile partner? She put his mind at rest to some degree when she said that she would inform everyone that he would be there as a 'very good friend.' Since very good male Jewish friends were hard to come by for a forty-year-old woman with three children in a small town like White River, she was confident that he would be welcomed, even if he wasn't Jewish – yet.

However, there was also a dragon to be bearded, and that dragon was Raichie's mom. So Raichie phoned her mother in Randfontein.

'What do you mean he's going to sit next to Kevin? That's *meshuggah*, absolutely crazy! He's a *goy*! What will the Rabbi say?'

'Mom, the Rabbi won't say anything, nor will anyone else. It's what Kevin wants, and that's all that matters.'

'But what about Jeff and Michael, can't *they* sit on either side of him?'

'Sad to say, but he barely knows my brothers. It's not about them, Mom, it's about Kevin. He wants Nick next to him. Michael can be on the other side. So it will be Dad, Nick, Kevin, Michael and Jeff in the front row, and to make up for not sitting right next to him, Jeff will stand next to Kevin when he sings his portion. I've spoken to them, and they're both cool.'

'And us? Are we going to meet this Nick before, or are we going to play 'spot the *goy*'?'

'Of course you must meet him! How's about we drive down to see you and Dad next Wednesday? Nick's not working, and he's arranged cover for Thursday morning so we can stay over.'

'What, you're sleeping with him already?'

'Mom, I'm not a little girl anymore!'

'Will I like him?'

'What's not to like? He's a doctor – every Jewish mother wants a doctor for a son-in-law.'

'You're talking marriage already?!'

'Not much chance of that – he's still married to someone in England.'

'You're telling me he's a philanthropist?'

I think you mean philanderer, Mom.'

'Don't be such a smart-ass, my girl. So I didn't go to university...... Anyway, what's good for you is good for me too, but I'm more concerned about how your Bubbe is going to take it - she's getting a bit past it. Most of the time, she thinks she's back in the *shtetl* in Lithuania being attacked by the Cossacks and trodden on by horses. She may think Nick's a Cossack and have a heart attack!'

'Don't worry, Mom, there isn't a woman around whom Nick can't charm – except his wife!!'

'Listen, Bokkie, I need you to teach me a few choice Yiddish phrases so that I can make a favourable impression on the parents and the granny'.

'Not so easy, boychik – Yiddish expressions are either rude or insulting and usually both. It's perfectly possible to insult someone in 365 different ways, one for each day of the year.'

'Give me an example,' asked Nick.

'Tell the old girl she's an *alte yente.*'

'Wozzat mean?'

'An old busybody.'

'I'm sure that will really endear me to her! Any other bright suggestions?'

'Well, you might tell her you heard she's a *shloomper,* that's an untidy, slovenly woman.' He smiled mischievously as he envisioned the old girl's response and ducked as the book Nick was holding flew in his direction.

The following Wednesday morning, Raichie collected Nick at the hospital in her BMW and after seeing his small but pleasant cottage for the first time and having a brief tour of the hospital, the family set off for Randfontein, minus Kevin who was playing rugby for his school. The journey for the most part was un-scenic, but Nick spent the time telling the girls stories about his surgical dramas, which fascinated them all including Raichie and stopped the little ones from annoying each other. When that began to flag, he attempted to practise the few Yiddish expressions he had learned from Bokkie, and that had everyone in fits of laughter.

When they arrived, while the grandparents were fussing over their daughter and granddaughters, Nick was left to face the stern old lady, who was staring at him as if he had just slithered through the grass. Oh, well, he thought, best get this over with. If I'm going to give her a coronary, it might as well be now. 'Hullo, Bubbe.' She glared at him towering above her small frame and said nothing. He continued, 'I'm pleasantly surprised, you seem quite normal.'

'So vot vere you expecting?', Granny replied in a distinctly European accent.

Too late to turn back. 'The way Raichie spoke about you, I was expecting an *alte yente,* a bit of a *shloomper,* but you seem quite nice.'

If she had been staring before, now the venerable little fireball was positively glowering.

Undeterred, and not necessarily wisely, Nick continued, 'I bet *you* were expecting a *shaygitz.*'

Granny looked at him, saw his smile. The venomous looks ceased, and she burst out laughing. 'A *shaygitz* is a *little* rascal, but you're a big one! You're a very naughty boy!'

The ice had been broken, the citadel breached, and they got on really well after that.

They had a cold lunch of salad and chopped chicken liver that looked revolting but tasted delicious. The salt beef slices served on bagels with sweet'n'sour pickled cucumbers could only have been bettered in New York. For dessert, there were potato *latkes* (not unlike hash browns) served with stewed apples sprinkled with cinnamon that were mouth-wateringly scrumptious. Nick took an instant liking to Sam and Leah, and they to him. They too were fascinated by his stories of hospital politics and surgical dramas.

Later, after some small talk with the family over lemon tea and apple strudel baked by Bubbe, Raichie had intended to take Nick for a drive around nearby Robinson Lake, in her day one of Randfontein's few beauty spots. From there they would be able to see the many mine dumps, remnants of the gold-mining bonanza in which JB Robinson had made his fortune a century before. Sam wasn't having it. It appeared that following dumping of uranium waste in the dam, it had become seriously radio-active. Raichie was upset, because the lake had once played a significant part in her life. That evening, Nick would learn the reason.

Instead, they strolled around the town centre. Nick could see that it was indeed not physically that different to Ballarat. Both towns had grown up on reefs of gold, but whereas Ballarat had become a thriving university town, Randfontein had retained its mining heritage. Its population was being swelled to a small extent by increasing numbers of black people who had joined the ranks of the middle class, although most still remained impoverished. Indeed, the town was not that far from Soweto, the largest of the country's black townships. They strolled past Sam's pharmacy, still elegant despite so many shops surrounding it seeming decayed.

The tasty dinner was a treat for Nick: pot-roast beef in gravy with roast potatoes and green beans, followed by *lokshen* pudding, a calorie-laden feast of noodles and raisins. How different to the simple hospital food to which he had become accustomed! He saw where Raichie had acquired her cooking and baking skills, because her mother was still the reigning queen of matters culinary.

The women went off to put the girls to bed and Nick was left to chat with Sam. Nick learned of the Jewish experience of immigration from Europe, mainly Lithuania, in the nineteen-twenties and thirties; how the first generation had become shop-keepers, peddlers and traders and acquired modest wealth, and how they had invested that modest wealth in their children's education and seen them become professionals or captains of business. Not to have an education was like not having a passport, Sam explained, it limited one's movement and options.

Sam soon got onto the topic that was at the forefront of every conversation in every white home in South Africa: the future. Nick found him quite philosophical, almost stoic. 'Building up a black middle class is a very good thing for the country, because the middle class doesn't start revolutions. All that we can hope for is that the poorer people don't get tired of waiting for promises that will never be kept by their corrupt leaders and start land-grabbing and driving us whites out.'

Bemused, Nick asked 'Doesn't that make you feel very insecure?'

'There's an apocryphal Yiddish expression, a Jew should go to bed with one shoe on - ready to run. It's like being on the top deck of the Titanic - we know the ship is going to sink, just not sure when or how long it will take. It's late for us to leave and start again in another country. So, we just hope the Titanic will stay afloat for long enough for us to live out our lives. Anyway, I suppose we are luckier than most because if God forbid we did have to leave suddenly, we do have options; we could go to one or other of our sons in England or America, but we don't want to be a burden on them. Or we could even go to Israel, but there's a language barrier. But leaving would not be our choice – we are part of two communities here, the smaller Jewish community and the larger Randfontein one. They are part of our lives, and we're part of theirs. Although we as a people are accused of being Jewish first and South Africans second, we are in fact extremely grateful for the lives we have led in this country and are intensely patriotic.'

At that moment, Leah, Bubbe and Raichie returned with lemon tea accompanied by small doughnut-like pastries covered in what looked like glazed toffee.

Raichie saw Nick hesitate, and said 'Go on, try one. These little babies are called *taiglach (again the gutteral 'ch')*. They're my Bubbe's specialty crowning dish. They're made of dough boiled in syrup and ginger and allowed to harden and glaze. I promise you, they're better than sex.'

Leah's eyebrows raised, and a bemused Bubbe said,'Vot did she say?'

Nick bit into the proffered taigel, licked his ginger-tingling lips and commented, 'You're right Raichie, definitely better than sex - with you.'

Leah's eyebrows raised a little higher and Bubbe said, 'Vot did he say?'

'Raichie says you work far too hard, Sam. Do you plan to continue working indefinitely?'

'I'm in two minds. My pharmacy is the oldest established one in this town, and even though my Indian assistant is dead keen to buy it from me, I wouldn't know what to do with myself. I suppose a sensible option for me at this stage of my life would be to sell to him, he's a good man, and then continue to work as his associate, and I am thinking seriously of doing just that. '

'That seems like an ideal solution'

'For us, yes. Our problem is Raichie and the grandchildren. Would they want to leave South Africa? Interrupt the kids schooling? Where would they go? In your case, you're lucky because you could return to England or Australia.'

'You know, Sam, I have found a new home here and a new family that has come to mean a great deal to me, so if it came to it, I would never just walk away from them. They have become a very important part of my life, and I love them all. My options could easily become theirs if the need arose.'

'I'm grateful to hear that, Nick, very grateful. You seem a real *mensch*, and I can see why they like you so much.' He stretched upwards to put his arm around Nick's shoulder and Nick in turn hugged Sam. A bond had been forged. Although Nick had no thoughts about going anywhere at that time, he knew that the political situation in South Africa was volatile and could change in a flash.

As they cuddled in bed that night, Raichie suddenly burst out laughing.

'What's tickling you, kiddo?' asked Nick.

'If I tell you, I'll have to kill you, because I've never told anyone this story before, not even Steven.'

'I'll take my chances.'

'No, on second thoughts, I won't tell. You're such a strait-laced puritan *you'd* probably want to kill *me*.'

'I might kill you anyway if you don't get on with it.'

'Tread carefully, Nick; this could be the end of a glorious friendship. Are you prepared to take the chance?'

His hand moved towards her throat.

'Get on with the bloody story!'

'Ok ok, so I'm seventeen, innocent as buds on a tree, and my matric dance is coming up at my school. I have a little problem: my boyfriend Francois is a big blond Afrikaner about whom my parents know nothing. My folks would have imprisoned me if they knew that I wanted to be with him and not with some nice Jewish boy, but there were not many around. What to do? Your clever Raichie has a solution.

'I phone my gay cousin Joel who lives in Jo'burg, and who is also in matric, and I invite him to come to Randfontein to be my partner. Joel is only too happy because he adores me and wishes he could wear my clothes. But I don't tell Joel what my devious plan is.'

Nick interjected. 'I sense where this is going, and I suggest maybe quit while you're behind.'

'No, listen to the rest of the story. Joel comes to Randfontein by train. My parents collect him from the station, big hugs, and they drop us at the school hall.'

'And then you leave Joel at the school hall all alone with this bunch of Afrikaners who probably eat gays for breakfast and go behind the gym with Francois and surrender your virginity. Am I right?'

'You're wrong only in one respect. We didn't go behind the gym because there were too many others there. We drove to Robinson Lake in his father's Buick.'

'Ooh, big back seat. Nice.'

'Bingo. So I wanted to show you the exact spot at Robinson Lake where I became a woman.'

'Perhaps it's just as well you didn't.....What about Joel?'

'What about Joel indeed! He went behind the gym and had a snog with the captain of the rugby team! Love at first sight! No, I'm kidding. Joel was cool about the whole thing and had everyone at the table in fits of laughter with his gay stories. They'd never met a real *moffie* before and there he was telling stories that would make their parents' hair fall out. Of course, I had to tell him what I'd done, but as far as I know he's never split on me.'

Nick got up and started to pack his small case. 'I suppose you expect me to be impressed? I'm utterly disgusted!! I'm leaving you. Now. Immediately.'

'How're you going to get back?'

'I'll drive.'

'It's not your car.'

'I'll walk. I'll hitch.'

'It's three hundred kilometres. At night.'

'Ok, maybe not.' He got back into bed and smothered her, first with a pillow, then with kisses. And then he went travelling where Francois had been the first to go.

The following morning, Nick reflected on the three sets of parents he had come across on three different continents. His parents were uncomplicated, unambitious, decent and kind; Allison's, cultured, respectable, but, like Allison herself, ultimately cold; and now Raichie's folks, living in their own closed world but giving and loving and warm. It was that warmth that stood out, that was new to him until he met Raichie, and now he had seen where she had acquired it.

The visit was everything Raichie hoped it would be, and as they walked to her car, Bubbe gave Nick a huge hug - well, as big as she could manage. 'You're such a *zhulik!*'

He asked Raichie, 'What did your granny just call me?'

'*Zhulik* means rogue. Smart woman, my Bubbe."

Raichie's mother said quietly to her only daughter, 'He seems a very nice man and I can see he's mad about you. I promise I'll never refer to him as a *goy* ever again.'

Leah then took Nick's hand and said, a little louder, 'Thanks, my boy, for caring for my family', and kissed his cheek.

The dragon had indeed been bearded.

On the way home, the girls quickly fell asleep.

Raichie explained what would take place at the synagogue. 'The orthodox Jewish religion is patriarchal, and men and women are separated by an aisle. That's the reason why Kevin will need a good friend next to him, why it can't be me. Sam will be too occupied with organising stuff. Seven selected male relatives or friends get called up to the altar in a prescribed order for the reading of the law from the parchment scroll, beginning with Sam, culminating in Kevin doing the main bit at the end. It's a ceremony that goes back to Abraham.'

Rachel described the simple celebratory lunch that would follow afterwards and the lavish party planned for the evening. She even gave him a few pointers about each of the individual members of her immediate family so that he would find it easier to converse with them. Nick was initially filled with trepidation but was now quite looking forward to what would be a novel experience.

'Oh by the way, If you'd like to invite your colleague Bokkie, he'd be most welcome to be our guest.'

'That's so kind of you, Raichie; I will mention it to him but there's little chance he will accept. It's just not his scene. He's a Jewish agnostic.'

He was right. Bokkie informed him that the last bar mitzvah he had attended was his younger son's forty-five years ago, but to thank Raichie for her kind thought.

# Chapter 41

## The Bar Mitzvah  2015

Nick too had to think about what he would wear on the day – definitely not a white safari suit! The only proper suit he possessed (actually the only suit) was fine for Leeds but far too heavy for sultry White River. Thinking of Dirk de Groot and of Bernard Finch who were polar opposites in matters sartorial, he opted for the de Groot look of elegance and decided on a new lightweight suit. He chose one in charcoal with smart white shirt and magenta jacquard tie from a local outfitter (unsurprisingly a good friend of Raichie's family) which Raichie and the girls approved without reservation.

Nick arranged to be covered at work for the entire weekend. On the Friday evening, he arrived early to accompany Raichie, Kevin and the girls for a short walk to the shul. Each of them commented that a suit suited him well. He was introduced to Jeff and Michael who had arrived with Sam. They were pleasant enough, in fact surprisingly warm to him.

When he walked into the synagogue with Kevin and sat in the front row opposite Raichie, he felt the eyes of everyone upon him. He wanted to move out as quickly as his athletic legs would carry him, but when Raichie smiled, he relaxed a little. The tension waned almost completely when the young Rabbi, Mike Katz, who had travelled from Johannesburg to officiate and did not look anything like

Nick's image of a Rabbi, came across to welcome him with some reassuring words. 'Feeling nervous, Nick? Listen, man, so am I. I'm also a stranger in those parts. Let's both be big boys and do the best we can.'

He was followed by several of the fifty or so men present who came over to shake hands first with Kevin, Sam and the brothers and then warmly with him, saying they had heard what a superb job he was doing at the hospital. Raichie wasn't one to leave anything to chance!

Kevin only had to sing the Friday evening blessing and one of the psalms and did so with confidence and reportedly in tune. That however was only the *hors d'oevres* - the main course would be served the following morning.

When the short Friday night service concluded, the men came up once more to shake Kevin's hand and his, and by now were addressing Nick by his first name and not as Dr Simpson.

Fifteen or so close family members came over to Raichie's townhouse for Friday night dinner. The meal, even by Raichie's high standards, was sumptuous, and she had prepared everything herself. Nick felt quite overwhelmed by the joy the large family shared in being together, not something he had ever experienced, certainly not on this scale, and soon felt at one with them. Nick was surprised that whisky, but only whisky, seemed to be imbibed copiously by the men. He learned that not all alcohol was kosher. Nick had a thimbleful of scotch, and it went straight to his head. Go easy, boy...

The only underlying note of sadness was the presence of Steven's mother Anne and her small family, but they made every effort not to dampen the mood. Difficult as it must have been for Anne, she embraced Nick and he felt chuffed when she told him that she too was pleased he was bringing happiness to the family she loved.

He spent quite a while chatting to Raichie's older brother, the doctor, comparing notes on what it was like to be a practitioner abroad. And as for Bubbe, they virtually had to tear her away from Nick. He was her man! Eventually they all departed, if reluctantly. Nick too was preparing to drive back to the hospital, but neither Raichie nor Kevin would hear of it.

Saturday dawned bright and sunny, and once more Nick was woken by kisses, this time from Leanne. The family dressed, had breakfast and walked to the shul where once more the Rabbi greeted them. This time he handed Nick a large black-and-white prayer shawl, showed him how to drape it over his shoulders and led him to the seat next to Kevin. Once more the male congregants all bedecked in prayer shawls came to wish Kevin *mazel tov,* good luck. Nick looked across at Raichie, and she blew a kiss to him. He had never seen her look so beautiful as she did in her brand-new lemon dress, wide white hat and Italian shoes, looking as if she was at the races at Ascot (not that he'd ever been, but he had seen My Fair Lady).

After a long and boring first part of the service, during which the men chatted to one another, the moment came when Kevin was called up to sing his portion. The congregation fell silent. Nick squeezed his arm and gave a reassuring word in his ears – 'Go knock 'em dead, mate, stick it between the posts!' Kevin ascended the steps of the altar, stood there for a moment as he composed himself, took a deep breath and proceeded to deliver his sung portion in a clear, loud voice and with total aplomb. Not that Nick would have been able to discern, but Kevin sang in perfect tune and without error.

When he finished twenty minutes later, everyone shouted *mazel-tov* again and as Kevin descended and walked along the aisle towards the Rabbi, what seemed to Nick like a mini-riot broke out. The women were showering Kevin with sweets. This was to wish him a sweet life as an adult, and as the candies noisily hit first him then the floor, dozens of young children scampered out to collect the goodies. The adults cheered. Nick thought, church was never like this, not that he had spent much time in too many. How they all seemed to be participating in the enjoyment of the occasion!

The congregation stilled to silence as the Rabbi addressed Kevin standing before him. Mike Katz was speaking eloquently about how Raichie and the late Steven had kept the Jewish traditions going, as their forebears had done for thousands of years. But now that his late father was there only in spirit, Kevin had taken the baton. How fortunate he was to have a wonderful mother, a strong family and a special friend to support him on his journey. Nick looked up to see Raichie holding a tissue to her eyes. Tears were not far from his either.

A few more exuberant tunes sung with great gusto by the cantor and congregation, and it was all over save for dozens of congratulatory handshakes and hugs. Kevin felt seven foot tall – look Ma, I'm on top of the world! - Raichie not far short.

The lunch that followed was quite informal. Many of the foods were unknown to Nick, especially the variety of herrings, few of which looked appetising; but when it was insisted that he taste all, he was surprised to find each one different and most palatable, especially when washed down by a wee dram of Scotch. Although not the first drinks he had had since his summons, he approached with caution, but still they went to his head.

It was mid-afternoon. In no state to drive, Nick felt obliged to call Samson to collect and drive him back to the hospital to check his patients, which he was in no state to do either. As he arrived, he was approached by the Matron. 'I am so happy to see you, Nick, it's all gone crazy here - so many trauma accidents. The surgeons, they can't cope. So change quickly, we've got a man with a knife through his head and he's ready to be operated on immediately.'

'You can't be serious, Matron, I've just been at a celebration, no way can I operate. I'm not sober. I've had about six whiskies – you know I had that complaint from Beauty Mzani when I wasn't drunk – well, now I am.'

'However much you've had to drink, it's far less than the patient has had. He doesn't need anaesthetic. You have to operate, Nick, if you don't the man will surely die anyway. There's no one else available so please get to work, Doctor.'

Nick called Raichie. 'I'm sorry my darling, I have to carry out an emergency operation.'

'But you're tipsy! You're not safe to cut bread!'

'Too true, but there's no one else. Barring unforeseen complications and assuming I don't kill the patient, I'll be back with you well in time for the evening's celebrations.'

She understood and wished him luck. She had her doubts but as she had done in the past would just have to get on with it. She managed to control her composure, but Kevin was, to put it mildly, really pissed off. Raichie muttered, 'Why can't they find someone else to operate?'

They can't and that's just the way it is,' said her brother the doctor.

Nick scrubbed up. The victim had tried to pull the knife out himself and had succeeded only in breaking the blade. With the assistance of a strong black coffee, two nurses and the anaesthetist, and feeling surprisingly clearheaded, Nick set to work on removing the broken 5cm blade firmly embedded below the eye. A centimetre higher and the eyeball would have been pulped. Fortunately, the direction of thrust was downward and not into the brain, and nothing vital had been pierced.

Nick remembered the Portuguese goalkeeper in that operation that seemed a lifetime ago. This one was child's play by comparison. His hand was steady, his mind focused. He completed the procedure two hours later, and the patient was still breathing. The wound required thirty stitches, but there was little bleeding and Nick was pleased with the result.

A short while later, Nick was dressed in his newly-acquired dinner suit (*If you could see me now, Dirk!*) and sitting at the main table of a fashionable restaurant in a luxurious hotel a few miles from White River. Raichie looked a dream in the black full-length dress she had bought at a super-smart Johannesburg boutique. It had cost a fortune, but as she said, this was the only time she would ever celebrate her son's bar mitzvah. The two girls also looked gorgeous, but the star of the show was undoubtedly Kevin, who was wearing a suit for the first time in his life. In the speech he had prepared himself, he spoke eloquently of his memories of his father and what an inspiration Steven had been. There was not a dry eye in the room, and Raichie and Anne wept openly. Kevin praised his mother for the support she had given him and the success she had made of herself, her family and her business. It surprised no one when he thanked Nick for being there for him that morning when he was feeling very nervous indeed, and if not replacing his father, had nevertheless become a respected role-model, especially on the rugby field.

The four-course meal was sensational, and Nick noticed that unlike the functions to which he was accustomed, the emphasis was more on the repast than on drink consumption. The band that had travelled from Johannesburg began with a spirited medley of Israeli songs that had the crowd singing, dancing, and throwing Kevin into the air in celebration, and then rocking to great soul songs. To huge applause, Kevin and Raichie performed the swing routine they had practised, and then Bubbe swung into action with her man, the zhulik. Sam and Leah were doing the twist. What a party! More whisky flowed, much more. The joyful festivities went on till midnight when the fleet of taxis arrived to take the guests to their homes or hotels.

On the way back, Raichie snuggled against Nick's chest. 'You know, I missed Steven's presence most awfully, but I'm sure that he would have approved of my partner on this important day. Thank you, my darling.' Nick in turn thanked her for a wonderful day, for a new experience and for allowing an alien stranger to become part of their lives. Even in his hazy state, he knew without a shadow of doubt that he loved this woman as he had never loved anyone before, loved her family, and would never leave them.

When Nick returned to work on the Monday morning, the first person he bumped into was sister Anna Kunene. 'You're looking happy, Nick. You were so sad when you first arrived here. I think married life is good for you.'

'Well, I'm pleased I'm looking ok, but I'm not married, Anna.'

'Well, you should be, because since you met that lady, the sun is shining out of you. They say she has nice children.'

'Who says?'

'Ha, we are all watching what is going on in the town.'

'Hmm, I'd better be more discrete. So what's on the list for today? How's my emergency man doing?'

'He buggered off yesterday.'

'What! He was supposed to stay in for seven days!'

'You don't understand, Nick, he had urgent business.'

'Like what?'

'Like to stab the *tsotsi* gangster who stabbed him.'

The *tsotsi* turned out to be Nick's first patient that morning, with a knife sticking out of his head.

# Chapter 42

## Samson 2015

The more time Nick spent at the hospital, the more he came to like and respect Samson. Samson, like many black people in the area, had illegally crossed the Limpopo River border from Zimbabwe to find work when the despot Robert Mugabe forgot the people who had put him into power. Mugabe had systematically turned what was once the breadbasket of Africa into a dustbowl of poverty and unemployment. White farmers, who had long run their farms efficiently and provided grossly underpaid but reliable employment for the local people, found these farms repossessed and handed to Mugabe's cronies.

Had these new owners continued to run the farms profitably, one might have argued that the white farmers got what was coming to them. Unfortunately, the new owners did not have a clue and within a very short period of time the cornfields and tobacco crops lay fallow and the workers found themselves with neither work nor food. Those that could migrated to the bigger towns and found some degree of work, but many crossed illegally into South Africa where they quickly found jobs as domestic servants or gardeners, or in hospitals or factories, or working as waiters in restaurants. From there, they were able to remit most of their again underpaid salaries to their families they had had to leave behind back in Zim.

These migrants, besides being most pleasant by nature, were extremely industrious and hardworking, and it

THE ROAD TO REDEMPTION   CHAPTER 42

wasn't long before they began to rise to more senior positions within whatever organisation they worked. Every month, they would go to their banks and transfer sufficient money to their families back home to keep them in food.

Their progress caused substantial jealousy, envy and enmity amongst the local indigenous people that was to have calamitous consequences later, but at the time all was peaceful.

Samson was one such man. He had had to leave his young wife (a domestic assistant at a Harare home), and two small daughters in the care of her unemployed parents.

Crossing the Limpopo River into South Africa was illegal and risky. Some of the overcrowded boats and rafts that had attempted the crossing previously had been capsized by hippos and lives were lost.

Samson arrived penniless at the White River Hospital where he found work in the kitchens as a dishwasher. He impressed the supervisor by his intelligence and work application and was upgraded to be the valet of several of the medical staff living in their little cottages adjacent to the hospital. It was his job to ensure that the cottages were cleaned properly, kept in good repair and snake-free, and supplied with basic domestic products. Although he seemed older, he was not yet thirty when Nick came into his orbit.

Samson rarely left the vicinity of the hospital, spent almost nothing, and remitted sufficient money from his salary and the bonuses handed to him each month by Nick and the other surgeons to take care of five people at home.

Not long after the bar mitzvah, Nick began to notice that Samson seemed far less cheerful than usual and seemed to tire easily.

'What's going on with you, Samson, are you feeling ill in any way?'

Sampson played it down, saying' No seh, I'm just suffering from an upset stomach.'

Nick might have been foolish in the past, but in this matter he was not - he knew Samson's problem was not just an upset stomach. He insisted that Samson see one of the hospital physicians.

Then the terrible bombshell that Nick had feared: Samson came in the next morning to inform that he had contracted HIV some time back, and this had now developed into full-blown AIDS. Because he was scared of losing his job, he had not reported it, and was by now quite seriously ill. With difficulty, Nick managed to persuade him to become a patient at the hospital where he worked – what irony! – but tragically Samson had delayed too long. The anti-retroviral drugs that could have saved his life were not available because of the blinkered decisions of the previous president of South Africa and his Minister of Health who both believed AIDS was an apartheid illness caused by poverty that could be cured by eating healthy vegetables. Samson said he would have to return home, probably to die, and nothing Nick could say would make him change his mind.

Nick was heartbroken; not only had Samson taken care of his every need, he became the younger brother Nick had never had. He wanted to accompany Samson to his home near Harare, but neither Mr Nelson Ngope nor Samson himself would hear of it. So it fell to kind-hearted Bokkie to be the last non-family person to see Samson alive as they said farewell at Harare airport when he stepped out of Bokkie's plane.

The news reached Nick not long after that his dear friend and valet had succumbed to the illness that was taking so many in Africa. Nick asked Bokkie to make yet another trip to Harare, which as ever Bokkie was willing to oblige if not happily on this occasion. Nick was accorded the honour of reciting the eulogy at the funeral. Up till then, he had only seen photos of Samson's family, but meeting his grieving wife and children ripped his guts apart. He faltered frequently as he paid respect to his beloved friend.

There was no conversation, no banter on the return journey – there was nothing one could say except to lament that what they had experienced that day had been and would continue to be experienced in Africa millions of times.

These were difficult days for Nick. His parents gone, now Samson. From the depths of his mind, he dredged Shakespeare's words: *"When sorrows come, they come not single spies. But in battalions."* He hoped loss wouldn't come in threes. He tried desperately to think about how he could make something good come of this. Then, as if ordained, an answer presented itself. He received a letter from his late parents' attorney to say that probate was now completed. The house had been sold. Nick arranged with the Australian lawyer and executor of his parents' wills that the proceeds of the sale be sent directly to Samson's family.

## Chapter 43

### The Eye  2015

Following Samson's death, Samson was replaced by James, an older and rather dull man. Although his attention to duty was beyond reproach, James lacked that spark that had caught alight every time Samson entered Nick's room. The hard thing for Nick to digest was that nobody was ever likely to match Samson. Samson was gone – get used to it, he kept telling himself, but he continued to feel the loss keenly every morning as he awoke, each evening as he returned to his cottage. Nick's spirit began to spiral downwards. Losing Samson was bad enough but once again he became unnaturally concerned about being concerned, and worried most of all about the impact his incipient depression would have on his relationship with Raichie.

This time he did not keep his feelings to himself. When Raichie explained to him that she had gone through the same spiral when Steven died, he understood that such feelings were not unique to him but part of the human condition.

At the same time, unfortunately, Raichie was experiencing problems of her own. Her relationship with Leanne was going through an extremely difficult patch. The teenager was probably experiencing what every girl of that age was going through; a virtual tsunami of raging hormones, acne, gawkiness, feelings that her older and younger siblings were getting more love and attention than she, that her friends were more popular. Surliness and sullenness followed about not being allowed to stay late at parties, limits on make-up. There was nothing Leanne seemed unable to say 'no' to. The psychologist in Raichie understood exactly what was going on but the mother in her was finding it difficult to tolerate.

When Nick tried to discuss the issues with Leanne, she responded, 'You're not my father!' and slammed her door.

Insensitive Nick who had become supersensitive realised that that elephant was always going to be in the room. Despite his best efforts to support Raichie, their relationship was suffering. Nick was becoming aware that old feelings were recurring and badly needed something to quell his negative thoughts. Raichie the psychologist suggested that he record his feelings and thoughts in a journal and use this to reframe the negative thoughts into more positive ones. He found this helpful, and concluded he needed a new project to distract him from his morbid feelings.

Once again, his thoughts went back to Leeds, but Nick was not about to repeat his folly. He would have to work through this without benefit of medication.

And then he remembered his time at UCH London. One of the dental fields in which Nick had become involved as a post-graduate student was the art of maxillo-facial prosthodontics. This mouthful involved creating new facial parts made of latex. When facial areas that had been lost to facial trauma or cancer were too large to repair by plastic surgery, the only solution to closing the surgically created facial cavities was to replace them with latex prostheses that were pasted onto the defective area. When Nick had first honed his skills, the prostheses had to be glued into position using a special medical adhesive, but the *modus operandi* now was to use precision attachments that locked onto the implants placed in the remaining healthy bone surrounding the defect.

Although Nick was usually on the hole-making end rather than the hole-filling one, the creative experience involved in making an incomplete person whole once more excited the latent artist that was part of him. Rebuilding a nose lost to cancer or sealing a cleft palate with a prosthesis had provided satisfaction for him and tremendous gratitude from his patients.

Sadly he remembered a motorcycle policeman who had been involved in a collision and fallen, unconscious, his face hitting the hot exhaust. The unfortunate man had lost an entire ear, gone up in smoke. Nick had created a new ear in latex held in place by modified spectacles held in place by an implanted connector.

It had been years since Nick had last replaced an entire eye-socket and nose eroded by a virulent cancer, but the hospital administrator, Mr Nelson Ngope, had reacted positively when Nick suggested purchasing the necessary materials and equipment to create a small laboratory. This would be a challenge to his creativity and flair, and he was well up for it. Fortunately, it was not a high-cost project, so funding was not as big a problem as he anticipated, but it turned out to be a slow and consuming process. Many of the materials had to be sent from England, but Nick managed to find sufficient supplies in Jo'burg to get the project started.

Nick sought, found and trained a young black laboratory technician named Lucky how to fabricate the prostheses. Initially they were very crude, due to lack of experience and inadequate materials, but Lucky had shown an amazing aptitude to develop the skills necessary to create life-like eyes, noses, lips and jaw parts. Lucky in turn trained an assistant to do the preparatory work.

For Nick, the loss of Samson began slowly to fade in the excitement of his creation. He was in constant touch with the unit, which had initially occupied a room the size of a small bathroom but was now relocated to two large rooms. Soon the unit was carrying out work not only for their own hospital but for smaller outlying clinics as well, and it was part of Nick's long-term dream (if he was going to be there for the long term) to turn this unit into a full department.

Lucky thrived in telling stories of the people he had reconstructed, and never tired of recounting one particular tale.

An elderly man had been referred by Nick to see him, a man who had lost an eye while chopping wood and been left with a gaping eye-socket crater. This was considered to be an ill omen by his Swazi community, and he had been asked to leave before he brought bad luck to others. He was now an outcast. When Nick heard his story, he felt a shiver running through him – was Samson revisiting? This man was born many years before Samson, but the similarities were uncanny. Chopping wood seemed a very hazardous occupation unless one wore protective glasses.

Lucky had taken an impression of the man's eye socket using alginate that set quickly and was easily removable. Utilising this impression, his assistant cast a replica model in plaster-of-Paris, and Lucky set about replicating the skin tissue of the eyelid and cheek using wax. When he was satisfied that he had got the shape right (a laborious process), he had to then create an eye. Lucky cast the facial surrounds in latex and the eye in acrylic that then required painstaking and time–consuming painting by hand.

The whole [hole?] process had taken about ten appointments, and each week the older man had arrived two hours early and sat in the garden outside having a smoke (which had probably caused the cancer in the first place) and waiting patiently to see Lucky. Finally, the prosthesis was ready for fitting, and Lucky was justifiably proud of what he had created.

The local press had been invited to attend on the morning the eye was due to be fitted, and a reporter was present. Lucky realised to his consternation that the patient had not arrived. The party was on, but the birthday boy wasn't there. Lucky knew that something serious had happened because he had never been late before. He phoned the man's home, sadly to learn that the elderly gentleman had passed away peacefully in his sleep the night before. Lucky was devastated. He began to worry that maybe he was not so lucky after all and kept the old man's eye in his pocket as a protective amulet wherever he went.

On the positive side, this sad story was reported in the White River local newspaper and made readers aware of Lucky's activities, and this brought increased respect for the hospital.

# Chapter 44

## Expert Witness 2016

Just when Nick's negative feelings and Leanne's raging hormones were subsiding and everything seemed to be flowing more smoothly, Nick had the misfortune to fracture the middle finger of his left hand. *"When sorrows come, they come not single spies. But in battalions."* You might try to guess how this happened - playing rugby with Kevin? - but you'd be wrong. The accident happened as Nick was playing alien soccer / football in the annual staff versus students match. Nick went in for a tackle, found himself turned inside out by a lively fourth-year student, and ended up flat out on his butt. While in this undignified position, one of his own team-mates had trodden on Nick's hand while trying to apprehend the slippery student. Unfortunate? Definitely. Serious? Not at all, unless you're a surgeon. It was enough to put Nick out of surgery for a month while waiting for the digit to heal in its plaster-of-Paris casing. How ironic this was, thought Nick; he'd played rugby, a far rougher game, for years and never suffered injury except for the knee incident.

Nick realised he was heaping pressure on his already overburdened colleagues. He went to see Mr Nelson Ngope, who was seriously unimpressed because he knew the load on the others would substantially increase almost to breaking point; Nick could only apologise, but what was done was done. He offered to try to continue operating, but Mr Nelson Ngope wasn't having it. He explained that the hospital was already in deep trouble with a locum dentist from an Eastern European country with an unpronounceable name. She had been drafted into the dental department for work experience, but as things turned it was Nick who was to get the experience. The woman had got herself into difficulties, a patient had died, and she was facing an inquiry.

'Well, maybe I can speak to her and give her some tips, Mr Nelson Ngope.'

'Hmm...... that may not be the worst idea you have ever had. In fact, you can be her expert defence witness.'

'Please don't make jokes, Sir. The mere words make me go catatonic. My mouth goes dry and my temples pulsate. I'd be happy to give her some advice, but expert defence witness? No way!'

'No, I'm serious, Nick. She's up to her neck in *kak*, and it's making my hospital smell. We are about to have an official inquiry, with a committee of three assessors arriving in a week's time. They will have the power to suspend or erase her, but much worse for us, they may close her department as well.'

He handed Nick a file of notes and records and said 'Go and prepare, because her legal team arrives in two days' time.'

'Who is the defence advocate? Is it Barend van Jaarsveld?' asked Nick, thinking of the charismatic Capetonian who was always in the news.

'Actually, it's not, he wouldn't touch this case. Because of the seriousness of her position, her indemnity organisation has imported an English barrister. He's from London, a Mr Bernard Finchley, and he'll be arriving with the assessors.'

Nick turned ashen. 'Nonononononono! Do you mean Bernard Finch?'

'Yes, that's the one.'

'Include me out!'

'I am afraid not, Dr Simpson, you've just been included in.'

When Nick's temple stopped throbbing and he had drunk two glasses of water, he explained to Mr Nelson Ngope the reason for his extreme reaction, how just hearing Bernard Finch's name again had immediately brought flooding to the fore those dark memories that he had managed to force to the furthest recesses of his mind. As for the prospect of seeing him again.....

Mr Nelson Ngope listened, placed his hand on that of his senior surgeon and said, 'I can understand how you feel, but perhaps it's no bad thing to confront these issues face-on and finally cleanse yourself of them. You can do this, Nick.'

Nick sat quietly thinking and then said, 'I can see why the authorities placed you in charge of this hospital – you have wisdom beyond your years.' Then he picked up the very large file, went to his cottage, poured a coffee and started to read.

Dr Maria Cantarac had qualified as a dental surgeon in Dushanbe *(a city? a province?)* in Tajikistan and was 43 years old when she felt a change from her Eastern European roots would be beneficial in assisting her to forget one or two unmentioned but unfortunate work mishaps. Although he had not yet met the woman, Nick immediately felt sympathetic. Dr Cantarac had applied and been accepted for work experience in a seriously understaffed clinic in Rametsu, about forty kilometres from White River Hospital but under its jurisdiction.

She had practised there without problems for a couple of months until a 66-year-old patient, Mr W, attended in pain at the Rametsu Clinic and was attended by Dr Cantarac. She observed a lower molar tooth to be mobile, and extraction was advised.

Mr W attended again a week later and was given a mandibular block injection of local anaesthetic. Dr Cantarac used a short needle as she had been taught to do in her home dental school, although in South Africa one always used long needles for lower jaw injections, as was also the custom in most Western countries.

When the patient did not appear to be going numb, she lifted the syringe to deliver some more local anaesthetic and noticed that the steel portion of the needle had separated from the plastic hub. It was nowhere to be seen. She immediately informed the patient and her nurse, searched his mouth, prayed that he had not swallowed it and sent her nurse to collect the clinic manager.

When nurse and manager returned a few moments later, they continued to search for the missing needle on the floor and in the patient's clothing, but to no avail. The manager said an x-ray was required, and departed. Dr Cantarac then delivered some more LA using a new short needle and continued to complete the extraction, which did not take long. Only then did Dr MC expose an x-ray, which, although not very distinct, showed a very thin horizontal object about 2 cms long behind the molar region of the left lower jaw.

Then followed a note in the records that made Nick wince - she "told Mr W to return the following day." Nick gulped – *what was she thinking?! This should have been dealt with immediately!* When Mr W returned the next day, a second x-ray was exposed which clearly showed the fractured needle no longer in the jaw but in the left cheek. *Getting worse!* Nick noted from the clinical records that she discussed this with the patient and had given him a letter referring him to the White River Hospital. The records did not however state he should attend "immediately as a matter of urgency".

Nick felt that Dr MC had acted correctly by asking for support from colleagues after she was unable to find the needle, but she should have referred the patient to a hospital without delay immediately the needle fracture occurred, not twenty-four hours later. She should have stressed this was urgent. There was a real risk to the patient's life if the needle was still in the patient's jaw. And, as he and most other surgeons knew only too well, it was capable of movement.

The White River Hospital surgery consultant wrote back saying that, by the time the letter arrived, Mr W had already attended to have a foreign body removed from an area at the base of the skull, but none was found. He was placed in a ward, and further x-rays were exposed for the next ten days, with no sightings, but because of bed shortages he was discharged. *This is getting worse and worse, thought Nick.*

Meanwhile, the clinic manager told Dr MC that he had sent the remaining needle batch back for testing and they had found no fault with them.

He then informed Dr MC that he had previously received complaints from patients about her, and he had intended to have a meeting to discuss these, but the incident had intervened. Since then, there had also been complaints from the other dentist at the clinic relating to treatment planned and carried out by Dr MC. Dr Cantarac was upset, as this was the first she had heard of any alleged complaints.

A week after Mr W was discharged, his brother telephoned the clinic to inform the manager that Mr W had suddenly collapsed and was dead. Later at his autopsy the needle was found lodged in his heart.

Knowing how fastidious Bernard Finch was, Nick wasn't about to blot his escutcheon by not preparing fully. The following morning, before the arrival of the legal team, Nick met Dr Cantarac. She was a large woman who perspired copiously. She had a profusion of carrot-coloured hair, no two of which seemed to follow the same direction. The silver crowns on her lateral incisors reflected the heat of the day. She said she was not particularly concerned about the impending inquiry, because she could not see that what she had done could actually be labelled negligent. Nick's immediate thoughts? *'Not taking responsibility for her actions, lack of insight'*. He, who not so long ago had been in a similar situation, had a certain degree of sympathy for her, but he had learned, and his task was to make this woman learn too.

Nick was surprised by the warmth by which Bernard greeted him, but there was little time for discussion of matters past. In their pre-hearing discussion, Bernard expressed his foreboding - this woman was in serious trouble. The two-day hearing began in a large air-conditioned room at a nearby hotel. Despite Bernard and Nick's best efforts, Dr MC performed wretchedly, blaming everyone else at the clinic and even the patient - "he kept moving around as I was giving the injection" - for her own incompetence.

The assessors found that, although the breaking of the needle was an unfortunate event, to have left the needle *in situ* for a prolonged period and not referring him to a hospital immediately was a breach of the duty of care that imposed serious risk to the patient. The broken needle could have travelled through the bloodstream to another part of the body (including the heart) that could have had fatal consequences, and in this case inevitably did.

Dr MC's practise was found to be currently seriously impaired, as a result of which she was placed under full suspension and her name removed from the Register of Health Practitioners in South Africa. They did not however recommend that criminal charges should be placed, as there had never been intent to cause harm. Their decision to erase was not vindictive or to punish Dr MC, but simply to protect the public because they could not be sure she would not make stupid decisions like this in the future and were not prepared to take the risk.

The clinic manager, not having responded timeously to serious issues and for not informing Dr MC of the complaints against her, was also censured and warned about his conduct.

Dr MC stated she was intending to return to Dushanbe immediately, no doubt to continue practising there, and thanked the assessors and her defence team, all brought out at great cost, for their attention. She had no intention of returning to South Africa.

Despite his earlier reservations, Nick was pleased, if not with the outcome, at least with his own role that he had conducted with feeling and sensitivity. He was congratulated by Bernard whom despite his misgivings he was very pleased to see once more. The Bernard Nick was now getting to know was far more chilled than the London Mr Finch and in fact had a marvellous sense of humour.

For his part, Bernard was delighted to hear via Mr Nelson Ngope that Nick had made a new life for himself. After the initial hearing in London, he had feared that Nick might top himself, although he thought topping Susan McDonald would have been far more appropriate.

Nick arranged with Bokkie to give the barrister a flight over the Kruger National Park. Bernard, who rarely left England, said this was the most exciting thing he had ever done. Bernard matched wits with Bokkie on a number of issues and later told Nick that Bokkie was the possessor of one of the sharpest brains he had ever encountered. This did not surprise Nick, who had often had cause to appreciate the wisdom and barbed humour of his friend and mentor.

Bernard was invited by Raichie for dinner and for once Bokkie came along as well, and for once the children never got a word in edgeways. Raichie was stimulated by their company and made Bokkie promise to return, although she knew the chances of that happening too often were slim.

Nick mentioned Bernard's comment to Bokkie, who just shrugged. 'Shall I tell you something, *boychik*? Once upon a time I used to be considered clever and intelligent. I may even have acquired the aura of wisdom that age and experience brings, but medically speaking I have become a dinosaur, a part of history. I am no longer relevant to my profession except to remove the odd tumour without killing the patient. I am the past. I have been overtaken by technology. You, Nick, are the present, and Dube and Sipho are the future.'

Nick pondered these words and realised that his friend was almost certainly correct. In this new age of high-powered medicinal drugs, computerised diagnosis, power politics and social media, he too was probably already on the downward slope and he was sure it would happen quicker than he could anticipate.

Bokkie was happy to fly Bernard to Tambo International near Johannesburg the following day, and by the time they arrived, a firm friendship had been cemented. Once again Nick had said farewell to Bernard in the firm belief that he would never have cause to see him again, and for the third time he would be mistaken.

# Chapter 45

## *Schadenfreude* 2016

Some six months after the hearing, Bernard telephoned and requested that Nick come to London for a few days to attend a hearing. He would not give the reason, save to say that all expenses would be borne by Bernard himself and that it was a matter of honour that he attend. Nick thought this sounded bizarre and declined the invitation, but Bernard was insistent and following more phone calls, Nick arranged to fly to London with Mr Nelson Ngope's surprising blessing, given how busy they were. Bokkie was more than happy to fill in for him. All very mysterious…..

He suggested to Raichie that she travel with him.

'I would so love to, my darling, but the kids are all going to be in the middle of exams, and it's peak tourist season. So, regretfully, no. But I promise the next time leave is due to you, I'm not going to let you bank it again and we are going to take Europe apart.'

On arrival at Heathrow, Nick made his way by taxi to Bernard Finch's somewhat unsalubrious chambers in Middle Temple off Fleet Street. The drab rooms were completely in harmony with the clothes the man wore: utilitarian, no more, no less. Bernard then revealed the reason he had insisted that Nick fly six thousand miles each way: he, Bernard, was acting at a hearing that was approaching its climax and he was acting for the prosecution. The reason for this was simple: the defendant was none other than Nick's nemesis.

It appeared that Dr Susan McDonald had once more tried to perform her dark arts. It was her anaesthetist who had complained to the Council. Bernard was invited to act for the prosecution, an invitation he rarely accepted. On this occasion, though, he was more than happy to take on the brief. McDonald had requested Shirley Leadbetter to act for her but Leadbetter had refused. Even she realised how nefariously McDonald had behaved on the previous occasion they had met and wanted nothing more to do with the bitter woman. A bit hypocritical, one might think, because Leadbetter had not shirked from using the woman's testimony to win her case.

Nick scanned through the papers Bernard had provided for him. During a routine surgical operation, McDonald had made a serious error of judgment from which the patient, a young woman, was fortunate to escape with her life (if not her body) intact. Instead of owning up to her error, McDonald had blamed her anaesthetist. The latter was not one to take this lying down (the patient did not have this choice) and had lodged a complaint first to the hospital and when this appeared to be going nowhere, to the Council.

Nick smiled, but his smile was sardonic – he could see what was looming for Susan McDonald, but the mere thought of seeing her made him want to throw up.

'I can't go in there with her, Bernard. I've spent years getting over it and now it's all gone fucking live again.'

'I'm not surprised you feel that way, Nick; all I can say is, trust in my experience and judgment.'

Trusting Bernard was one thing, seeing McDonald another matter entirely. She had occupied so much space in Nick's mind, he had struggled for so long to get her off his shoulder. With time, he had managed to eradicate her, and he did not want her to return. She had become a distant figure, a figment of the past, a nasty fiction. He wanted to keep it that way, but since he had physically travelled so far at Bernard's expense, he had little choice but to go along with the barrister.

As he entered the hearing-room Nick was fervently wishing he was somewhere else, anywhere else. Preferably in the toilet throwing up. His guts were churning.

The hearing began. The nurse who had given evidence against Nick was called to provide testimony. This time she turned against McDonald, and she did so with vicious intent - she had had enough of McDonald's sarcasm and lack of gratitude. She was quite happy to shop the surgeon whose supercilious attitude had brought the nurse to the verge of giving up her profession, and she was about to join a friend in a florist venture. She dished the whole story not only of McDonald's surgical cock-up but of how she had been enrolled and bullied by McDonald to perjure herself against Nick. McDonald had tried to get her to do the same thing against the anaesthetist, but this time she wasn't having it.

Bernard Finch was tough when in defence, but always caring. Not this time. Revenge might be a dish best served cold, but Finch was stoking the coals and doing so with relish. He was merciless, first shredding the nurse then macerating the surgeon. He has said to Nick there would be tears, and there were by the bucketful. When the Chair asked him if it was necessary to be quite so vicious with the two women, Bernard replied with just three words: 'Madam, it is.'

The case dragged on for the best part of four days, during which time Nick began to unwind as he willed himself to be dispassionate. Then it was done, and the Committee returned to deliver their verdict. The nurse of course was suspended for a period of thirty months, which mattered little to her, but McDonald's name was ordered to be erased from the medical register. A notice to this effect was to be posted online with immediate effect.

When asked by Bernard whether she wished to say anything to Nick who was sitting opposite her, she bowed her head and in a still voice said that she deeply regretted her actions in besmirching his name. Her head was still bowed when she left the room.

As a consequence of the hearing, all the previous findings against Nick were ordered to be expunged from the records. So, not only had Nick's suspension been lifted but the stain against his name had been completely washed away.

What did Nick feel as he left the hearing room? One would have expected him to have felt elation at his reputation being restored, elation at the biter being bit, indeed being chewed to shreds. One might have expected him to be jubilant, but he left the hearing room feeling strangely flat. People like McDonald weren't worthy of any emotion at all, not even *schadenfreude.*

Bernard was surprised by his lack of emotion and began to suspect once more that Nick was on the Asperger spectrum, but when Nick explained his lack of feeling, the wise barrister got it completely.

Now exonerated, Nick was told if he wished he could seek substantial financial compensation through the civil courts, a case he was now certain to win. This however was the furthest thing from his mind, as it would mean reliving all the unpleasantness of that earlier trial, a trial in every sense of the word. He forced himself to suppress any feelings of vengeful satisfaction – to desire more would have meant bringing her back to life.

After bidding Bernard farewell for the fourth time, he returned to White River. This time he did not speculate on whether he would see Bernard again and hoped that if he did it would be for social reasons, for he now regarded the barrister worthy of a place in his small pantheon of heroes.

Although not asked to do so by Nick, Bernard wrote to Allison (now Mrs Beasley) informing her how her former husband had been shafted and subsequently cleared. Allison did not respond. *Quelle surprise...*

# Chapter 46

## Winston Rabada 2016

Nick's tenure at White River Hospital thus far had been almost idyllic, but the idyll was about to be rudely shattered.

He had just completed a fairly complex removal of a laryngeal tumour from a fifty-year-old woman. The operation had involved carefully dissecting the squamous cell carcinoma from the woman's voice box, a procedure full of risk that could literally have left the woman speechless for life, but it had gone without mishap. As he was changing out of his scrubs and looking forward to coffee in the staffroom, he received a note from Mr Nelson Ngope asking him to attend his office urgently. He washed up, dressed and headed upstairs to the CEO's suite on the fourth floor. There he found the Administrator and Sister Anna in animated conversation.

'Dr Simpson, you know that many of the Zimbabweans and illegals from neighbouring Mozambique are being physically threatened by local residents, who perceive the immigrants to be the cause of their unemployment. The mood is turning more violent and soon there will be many casualties, which will put considerable pressure on our already strained resources. This xenophobia is not accidental, it is being stirred up by people who have their own rather than the country's interests at heart. Have you heard of Winston Rabada?'

'Of course! He's the guy who has been causing a lot of issues for the government and many of the big businesses. Didn't he set up the strikes at the Thabazimbi iron mine where forty people got killed a few months ago?'

'Exactly, Dr Simpson. Forty dead black miners mean nothing to him. A small price in the scheme of things. He is the one who is stirring up the locals, and now we believe he is coming to speak to our staff', said Anna. 'He is targeting higher wages, better working conditions and the need for more black doctors.'

She was not surprised when Nick replied, 'I'm in favour of all of those aims, Anna.'

Mr Nelson Ngope then added quietly, 'He is also targeting immediate replacement of white doctors with blacks, and the two people he is specifically gunning for, and I choose my words carefully, are the two Jewish doctors, Dr Bokkie and you...'

'That's absurd – first of all, Bokkie is the finest surgeon I have ever encountered, not to mention being a brilliant teacher. Second, I'm not Jewish – '

Anna intervened, 'Yes, but the young nurses know about your relationship with the coffee woman.'

Nick snorted but continued, 'Third, one of my main missions here has been to help train the young black surgeons. Sipho and Dube have made fantastic progress, and others are coming up too. When they are ready to take over from Bokkie and me, we'll be only too happy to make way.'

Mr Nelson Ngope looked at him. 'Nick, there are few at this hospital who do not appreciate what the two of you have done, but we are dealing here with a bigoted racist who does not care what or whom he destroys in the cause of black nationalism. He is determined to avenge the iniquities of white apartheid that his people have suffered, and he has found fertile ground amongst our younger staff who seem only too happy to support him.'

'Ok, I get that. Look, my friends, it has never been my wish to be the source of problems, so if it makes things easier for you, I will resign with immediate effect and be forever grateful that you gave me another life.'

'That's the last thing we want and we will not agree to that under any circumstances. But we must prepare ourselves for some rough times very soon. Right now, I have to say that it will not be safe for you to be there when he addresses the staff next week because he is not afraid to stir up violence. The man has no respect for human life and his henchmen have less. We fear blood will run, and we do not want it to be yours.'

'There is no way I will not be there – if he's got something to say about me, let him say it to my face. Does Bokkie know about this?'

'Dr Bokkie is still operating, but we will appraise him later.'

'I would be very surprised if Bokkie's response is any different to mine.'

Nick wasn't wrong.

All hospital activities were cancelled for the Monday afternoon, creating a backlog that would take a week to resolve. The entire staff of four hundred gathered on the football field behind the hospital. It was searingly hot, the atmosphere as much as the weather. There was nowhere to sit, and the crowd shuffled from leg to leg. Little groups exchanged comments and viewpoints, but all that could be heard was a loud hum. Tension grew, expectancy grew. The heat was insufferable but not a single person moved away and miraculously no-one fainted.

A group of armed policemen arrived, but Mr Nelson Ngope asked them to leave as he felt their presence would incite rather than allay violence.

Winston Rabada arrived thirty minutes after the advertised time, followed by a forty-strong entourage, all members of his political party, The Freedom Lions. Wearing scarlet overalls with orange berets, they marched their way onto the hastily erected stage, a stage without a roof or any form of covering. They stood with chests puffed, legs apart and rifles in hand - to say their presence was intimidating didn't begin to cut it.

Rabada looked at the audience. A section of the staff applauded and as he acknowledged this he seemed to give a nod to someone in the front row. Nick scanned the audience and saw a now-familiar figure – Staff Nurse Beauty Mzani smiling broadly and cheering the tall man in scarlet. In an instant, Nick realised with absolute clarity that the source of the complaint following the carotid blowout could have been none other than Winston Rabada.

Rabada, an impressive figure, solidly built, tall of stature and with a deep booming voice, began by reminding everyone of how their forebears and indeed many of them too had been oppressed under white rule, and this was greeted by tumultuous booing. His henchmen pointed their rifles in the air and fired a salvo of bullets. 'Our time has come!' Uproarious cheers, more rifle fire. 'Higher wages!' Biggest cheer of all. 'We don't need white doctors.' Silence, except for the firing rifles.

Rabada looked directly towards the two white doctors and yelled: 'That man' – he pointed at Bokkie – 'that man is infamous at Baragwanath where he thought he was God. My people, he is not God - he is a tyrant who abuses our women and does not allow our doctors to progress. He must pay for this.' Nick shuddered as he heard those women in the front row cheer – the mob was baying. Did they really want Rabada's men to kill Bokkie and maybe him too? Nick's blood ran cold and despite the heat he shivered.

Rabada carried on spewing his poisonous spittle. 'Jewish doctors have been suppressing our progress for years;

they are the spawn of those who have owned our banks and factories and mines for hundreds of years and made their wealth on the backs of our people! It is time for them to go – it is time for us to remove them!'

The rifles were no longer pointed upwards but towards the two surgeons. Were they really going to fire? Nick's hand clenched Bokkies's arm. Bokkie stepped in front of Nick. Nick tried to pull him back. The crowd turned completely silent. They sensed that the guns were not there just for effect. At that moment, something remarkable happened. Sipho and Dube, who had been standing next to Nick and Bokkie, moved in front of them. The sigh of relief from the two white men was audible. Bokkie's tanned face had turned white. Nick felt his knees buckle but managed to remain vertical. He could feel the perspiration running down his sides. His mouth was as dry as a desert. He needed water but whatever had been available had long disappeared. He remembered the same feeling when that letter arrived. He was certain shit was about to happen now as it did then. Trouble had found him once more.

Mr Nelson Ngope strode forward and grabbed the loudhailer from Rabada. Rabada immediately drew his revolver and shoved it in the face of Mr Nelson Ngope. The Chief Executive did not flinch. 'We have heard your views, Mr Rabada, and we respect them, but now hear ours.'

The rifles pointed towards him but were stilled by Rabada's downward-moving hand. 'We understand the grievances about low salaries, but our hands are tied by the government led by Mr Zuma. If we could improve them, we would. Going on strike won't bring higher wages but it will hurt the people. It will bring hardship to the nurses and their families. It will bring less bread to their families' tables, not more.

'The working conditions at this hospital are better than any other comparable hospital that I have seen, and I have seen many. Yes, many things can be improved with more money, but we do not want things to get worse, and I fear that by inciting change that is what will happen.

'The two evil white doctors you have threatened with your guns are paid the same as and not more than our black doctors, and they work as hard, probably harder. Since their arrival, our standards of surgery and sterility have improved. They exploit no-one. They deliver brilliant honest service. They are good teachers. More people, black people, are receiving surgical attention and more are surviving. Teaching has improved. We have opened new departments. We are fighting AIDS without the help of the government. So, Mr Rabada, instead of undermining the model of progress that is White River Hospital, we suggest you put your guns away, or take your guns elsewhere to the people who are presently milking this country by corruption and greed, who are black and not white and not Jewish. If you want power, get the people to vote for you. We have heard your message, thank you for coming, but we now have work to do.'

Time seemed to stand still, but only a minute had passed, and then the rifles turned away and once more fired into the air.

With the exception of a small group of young nurses who remained behind chanting their approval of Rabada and his Lions, the crowd quietly dispersed, The four musketeers, Nick, Bokkie, Sipho and Dube walked away with their arms about each other's shoulders. They knew their problems were far from over and Rabada or someone else would be back sooner or later, but while they could be together, so they would choose to remain.

That evening, Nick recounted the events of the day to Raichie. She shuddered in horror when she heard about the rifles being pointed. 'You were bloody damn stupid to attend that meeting. Rabada has a reputation that a mad dog with rabies would be proud of. Do you not think they would have fired? I would have gone insane if they had killed you.'

'At first I doubted it, but Mr Nelson Ngope thinks they well might have. I was crapping myself, not so much for me but for Bokkie. I can tell you, it's not a nice experience to have forty rifles pointing in your direction. We were fortunate to have Sipho and Dube next to us. I owe them big-time.'

Raichie took his hand and embraced him. 'They owe you big-time for the selfless way you work with them. They are fortunate to have you next to them. You're a good man, Charlie Brown!'

# Chapter 47

## Sipho & Dube  2017

'I'm really grateful for your support, guys, and we probably owe our lives to you two', said Nick the next day as he sat in the staffroom sipping black coffee with Sipho and Dube. The morning's operation for a work accident victim had been really demanding, all three being involved. A crate had fallen from height and smashed into the victim's face, crushing the orbit and nasal area. That the man had survived at all was miraculous, because several facial bones had been fractured and he could barely breathe. The operation had proceeded brilliantly, the prognosis for the still unconscious patient looked promising, but the surgeons were exhausted. The accident brought back vivid memories of the Portuguese goalkeeper. How much water had flowed under the bridge since then!

The normally uncommunicative Nick suddenly started to raise the question of professional motivation.

'What does being a doctor mean to you, Dube?'

'It means I have a lot of power, Nick.'

'What, power to rule people who are not as educated as you?'

'No no no, you don't understand - as a doctor, as a surgeon, I have the power of life and death over my patients. If I get the diagnosis right, if I do competent surgery, I am able to prolong someone's life or make someone's life easier and more comfortable. Like today – that man is dead if we are not there for him. On the other hand, if I cock up an operation, I can turn a reasonably healthy person with a minor problem into a vegetable with just one slash of my scalpel or with a poor decision.'

'So why did you want do medicine in the first place?'

'I was quite ill when I was about fourteen, and my family didn't know how to make me get better. So they took me to the local doctor, who prodded my guts and said I had appendicitis and needed to go into hospital pretty urgently. By this stage I was throwing up and my pain was level ten. They rushed me straight into theatre, and the next thing I remember, I had this pretty nurse talking my pulse, and my pain was down to level four and I had an erection. Then the surgeon and a house doctor came in to check me and the pretty nurse spoke to the surgeon as if he was Jesus Christ reborn and to the house doctor as if he was one of his disciples, which to a large extent he was. So I liked this whole notion that I could get rid of pain, get the respect of pretty nurses, and teach younger people. My parents didn't have money to put me through medical school, but I worked every spare hour I could as a waiter or in a supermarket, and here I am!'

How like his own experience, Nick reminisced.

'Ah, Dube,' said Sipho, 'but that's all about you and the power you get to control other people's lives. I have different motivation. I want to be of service to the community. I want to do a job well, do it as well as I can do it and as well as it can be done. When I was a child, I could make toys for myself out of the most rubbishy refuse *(Nick thought of how Bokkie had created similar things)*. I was never interested in making as much money as I could, although that too requires skill and judgment. Of course, I could have done something less stressful, for example become a carpenter or an electrician, they're both creative in their own way, but I get a real buzz out of taking risks not for its own sake but in order to bring about a successful outcome. That's me. What about you, Nick?'

'I think I am more in Sipho's camp on this one although like Dube, initially I was turned on by the 'power of healing' thing. I was blessed with sensitive and creative hands, a calm temperament and incredible energy and powers of concentration, so that made it much easier. But when push comes to shove, it's not about success, or power, or being admired, it's something much simpler – it's about creating order out of disorder, it's about catching something that's going over the edge and pulling it back. I hate failure much more than I enjoy success. When I remove a large tumour successfully, I don't feel elated, I feel satisfied. I don't go home thinking about it. When I cannot achieve what I set out to do, I feel frustration and spend hours going over and over in my mind what I could have done to achieve a better result. I have always been driven in that way, and it would have made little difference whether I was a doctor, accountant, schoolteacher or sportsman, my main objective would have been to get the job done flawlessly. If I happen to save someone's life in the process, that is a bonus.'

'So,' said Dube, 'which of us would you choose to be your successor?' This question was very much on both the young men's minds.

'That's a very simple decision. I would choose Diphe. No no, on second thoughts, maybe Subo. Or maybe somebody else completely! I know an excellent Australian doctor who wants to apply to be the *baas*. No, just jokin', fellas. Actually, the choice will not be made by me but by Mr Nelson Ngope and his advisors of whom I hope I am not one. Perhaps, considering the recent Rabada event, this should be sooner rather than later but it's completely out of my hands. Anyway, enough of this idle chit-chat, let's discuss this morning's case.'

# Chapter 48

## The River  2017

Nick's relationship with Raichie and her family was strengthening by the month. Both girls were bright and were developing into vibrant adolescents. This is not to suggest that they weren't capable of giving Raichie a very difficult time, but what else were teenage girls meant to do? Each complained that the other was getting more attention, and both complained that Kevin was getting the most.

Leanne was still stroppy but was no longer being disrespectful to her mother. A sort of peaceful truce had broken out. The dark cloud on the horizon was that whatever was bugging Leanne had transferred itself to Alexis. Raichie was learning what having teenage daughters was like. She tried to remember how she had been but did not remember being like either of them. Perhaps having a real father might have mitigated her behaviour. Then she remembered Francois. She would have to keep a close eye on the girls and be there to support them when it mattered.

Raichie was extremely pleased to have Nick around to act as referee, arbiter and peacemaker, and of course he carried no family baggage. The problem was that for much of the time he wasn't there, so when he did come over, as well as keep the peace he had to pacify Raichie, which was probably the most difficult task of all. He learned that she had a frightful temper and could swear like a longshoreman when provoked. Leanne and Alexis knew exactly how to set each other off and in so doing set Raichie off, taking great delight in doing so. They were prickly nerve-ends all over and stung like cactus. Nick was not exempt from their barbs.

When she discussed this with her mother, Leah cited a Yiddish expression she had learned from Bubbe: "Small children disturb your sleep, big children your life."

Kevin, on the other hand, was thriving. After the bar mitzvah, Nick and Kevin had become especially close. Maybe the girls were reacting to this. Kevin, now grown into a solid and strong young man, was nearing midpoint of high school. Not all had gone smoothly there either. In the early days there he had been picked on and isolated by the local Afrikaans kids because he was Jewish. When he discussed this with Nick, the doctor had advised him to be proactive. 'The next time someone says anything to you, deck him. You may end up getting a mauling but at least it will show them you have guts.' Kevin took this at face value and although he took a few, soon showed he packed as a good a punch as any of them and better than most, and the bullying more or less stopped.

But his real acceptance came when, despite being only fifteen, he established a place for himself in the open rugby team as a very fast and tough-tackling centre. Nick, of course, had been an outstanding rugby player in his Australian schooldays and at university, and was still very fit and strong. He was happy to spend hours coaching Kevin. When Kevin learned to tackle Nick without fear, he would be unlikely to hold off tackling a sixteen- or seventeen-year-old. Another very valuable lesson he learned from his medical mentor was how to avoid injury, to learn what the body would and would not tolerate.

Kevin did not know it, but he was even being mentioned in dispatches as a potential future provincial star. There is an oddity within South African rugby that having a Jew in your team was an omen of very good luck. This went back to the days of the great Okkie Geffin who had booted South Africa to victory against the touring All Blacks from New Zealand in 1949, and Hoerskool Wit Rivier, White River High School, was happy to buy into that belief.

Raichie was not slow to recognise how Nick's relationship with Kevin was strengthening. The girls too adored him, and when Kevin wasn't around Nick was happy to be playing netball with them at a nearby field or assisting with their homework.

Chatting after dinner one night, Raichie snuggled close. 'You know, Nick, when we first met, I kind of imagined you as, how shall I put it, someone who could satisfy my frustrated libido. I'll put it another way, a replacement for my Rabbit. What I never in my wildest dreams imagined was that you would become a father figure to my kids, and I cannot tell you how much I appreciate it, how much we all value it. You're a top man, Nick.'

One day, Nick happened to be reading a nature magazine and saw a write-up about a group that specialised in white-water rafting and kayaking expeditions. It was an activity he had wanted to pursue since arriving in South Africa but had never found the time. Nick knew that although the group he could be accompanying were known for their safe practise, injury or worse was a real possibility. Here was an opportunity, but he did not want to do this on his own.

'Raichie, how would you feel if Kevin accompanied me on a river-rafting expedition along the Orange River? It's not far from Kuruman, a place I remember well.' He showed Raichie the article he had been reading. When she had finished it, she raised an eyebrow. Hmmm....

Nick added, 'Think carefully, because the trip will not be without risks.'

'Tell me more about this, Nick, it sounds a bit hairy. Not just for Kevin, for you too.'

'I'm sure it will be, but it'll be exciting, and you know I'll look after Kev.'

'Of course, but who'll look after you?'

'I'm a big boy now, and I'm sure it will not be as dangerous as facing Winston Rabada. Anyway, give it some thought.'

Raichie did what she always did when she was unsure: she asked her late husband what he thought. Steven in this case did not hesitate – he knew and trusted Nick enough to feel confident about letting Kevin go.

When the fifteen-year-old Kevin was asked if he would like to accompany Nick, the younger man went whooping wild. 'Do I want to? *DO I WANT TO*???!!!' He went racing out of the townhouse and they watched as he reached the garden, jumping up and down with excitement like a puppy that had been given a tasty bone. Then he came racing back in. 'Yes yes, I swear this is the best thing that's ever happened to me!' He and Raichie flung arms around Nick, and the only ones who didn't were the girls because they too wanted to go. They made very sure that Nick was aware that if he only took Kevin he would owe them big-time and they weren't likely to let him forget this.

The excitement that was building up over the next three weeks was matched only by the envy of Kevin's burly schoolmates. Massive! 'What happens if you drown, Kev?'

'Simple. I'll come back and haunt you all and you'll never win another rugby match ever.'

The rugby season was over. Early on a warm spring morning when Kevin was on school holiday, he and Nick set off on the long drive to Kuruman in Nick's hospital car. Nick drove with great care and concentration because he knew that his cargo was at greater risk on the road than

## TROUBLE WILL FIND YOU

he would be on the river. By mid-afternoon the terrain had changed from hills of green pine to flat brown and arid plains. Large quiver trees typical of the area dotted the landscape more and more. The unusual trees had received their name because their branches were used by the ancient San hunters to make quivers for their arrows. Later in the afternoon they reached their destination within sight of the majestic and powerful Augrabie Falls that would provide the momentum to carry them downstream and across the rapids in their kayaks and rafts.

The group of 14, nine males and five females, set up camp alongside a shallowish pool adjacent to the storming Orange River, where they spent the evening around the campfire getting to know one another. Excitement and apprehension were felt in equal measure. There were five teenagers in the group, of whom Kevin was the youngest. Nick was his taciturn self but was outmatched by Kevin.

The next day they were given intensive training in the use and management of a kayak and an inflatable rubber raft by the trip leader, Will and his eighteen-year-old son Jack. It turned out that Jack had already won two national kayaking championships, but still had two to go before he caught up with Will. The group were in awe at the way the two leaders were able to make their kayaks spin, turn, rotate, flip, and come to a standstill in less space than it took to set up a tent. The group were expecting Will to be skilful, but if anything, he was outdone by young Jack. Not surprising, since he had been kayaking since the age of four when the word 'fear' did not exist in his mind.

They were instructed in how and when to correct an overturned kayak while they were still in it, and how to exit from it when they could not correct. By the end of the day, everyone felt confident that they could manage the simpler rapids, but the more difficult ones were still to be tested. Said Will, if they felt they could not or did not wish to manage the worst of them, they could carry their kayaks forward on dry land.

The final stage of their preparation was in the use of inflatable eight-seater rubber dinghies, a skill requiring clearly defined teamwork. Will said they would probably need this on the biggest rapid of all that they would encounter on the final day. They learned how to adjust their weight to determine which path to follow, and practised using techniques of slowing the craft when in too-fast free flow.

Exhausted, they sat around the campfire that evening to be addressed by Will. 'Listen up guys, you're going to experience some wild and difficult white-water rapids and currents later on, but if you stick to the rules and carry out the procedures you learned today, I guarantee you will come to no harm. Just don't get too smart because you're going to end up very wet or worse. Either Jack or I will lead and the other will follow at the rear. You are about to have the experience of your lives.'

They were issued with safety vests to keep them afloat, and helmets similar to those of motorcyclists.

The next day dawned red and gold and very chilly; the group had already been up for an hour, preparing the fire for the fry-up they were going to cook in anticipation of a hard day of action. This was the first time Kevin had been camping and he was keen to assist wherever possible. He was assigned the task of collecting water from the edge of the pool and bringing it back for boiling. Although this in itself was an energy-sapping task, his extensive and at times obsessive rugby training stood him in good stead, and his enthusiasm was quietly admired by Nick and Will, expressed with an arm around the shoulder and a short 'Well done, Kev.'

At that moment Nick realised how fond he had become of this young man who had suffered the loss of his father but got on with the business of moving his life forward in the manner his father would have wished.

After breakfast, they all dragged their kayaks to the main body of the river, which was flowing well. Will and Jack were pleased about this. Had it not, many more rocks on the shallow riverbed would be obstructing their passage. The two leaders had chosen the route with great care: easy going to begin, more and more intense as the days progressed. While some of the time it was a case of propelling the kayaks along and simply going with the flow, there were sufficient minor rapids and rocks to be negotiated to provide the participants with the expected thrills. The water was cool rather than cold. More than one kayak had overturned, to be righted by observance of the techniques they had practised the previous day.

A former army transport truck carrying all the tents and inflatable rafts followed their route and they met up at the agreed site for their third night together. By nine o'clock, after a good barbeque meal, a short singsong and an exchange of amusing stories, every last one of them was happy to bed down in their sleeping bag and drift off with the satisfaction of a day well negotiated.

As Kevin tucked into his sleeping bag, he looked at the night sky and the myriad of stars in contrast to the dark infinity above. He thought about his father, how good it would have been to have Steven there as well. And then he thought about the use of the words 'as well.' He missed his father so much, but he had grown to love Nick 'as well'. Nick, who treated him not as a boy but as an equal.

The following day they encountered what Will described as 'little sweeties', meaning rapids that were testing but, given the perfect weather, not too demanding. They were all feeling pretty confident by now, but were sobered when Will said, 'Don't get overconfident, guys, you don't know what you don't know. Rapids have a way of teaching you some difficult lessons, especially if weather conditions alter.'

Will must have known something the group did not know, On the fourth night, the weather changed. It does not rain very often in that part of the world, but when it does, it buckets down. That night the heavens opened, and then stopped as suddenly as it started, leaving pools of water everywhere. Nick, who had been deep in sleep became aware of a floating sensation, as if he was on a waterbed. There was a reason for this. His blow-up mattress was actually floating! How eerie it all looked in the moonlight. As he looked around, he saw that Kevin too was floating, but the teenager was completely oblivious to everything around him. Some of the others were stirring too but went back to sleep as the waters were quickly absorbed into the parched landscape. When he told Kevin that he has slept through the entire flood, the teenager laughed and in the South African vernacular said 'Ag, quit chaffing, Nick.'

The next two days' kayaking were to prove much more challenging with the size of the rapids increasing due to the heavy downpour of the previous night. The skill level required became more demanding. At each rapid, Jack would demonstrate the technique required, while Will would point out which large rocks to aim for and use to bounce off. They became aware that there was always one pathway that would provide smoother passage, and they learned how to recognise and guide their kayaks along that path of bubbling water. Failure to do so would require much greater energy–draining skill levels to negotiate, with a far higher risk of capsizing and banging against the rocks.

The entire morning was spent negotiating rapids that were getting bigger and stronger, but they all applied their recently-gained experience and coped well.

One of the participants, a wealthy builder from Pretoria, got too gung-ho and ended up having to be rescued by Will and Jack. Had they not been quick to spot his folly, he might well have drowned. As it was, he was quite badly bruised, the worst being to his inflated ego. When they camped that evening, Will did not belittle him, but simply reminded all that there were always many hard ways to negotiate a rapid but usually only one channel that was easier. Nick thought this was a very fine metaphor to describe his passage through the medical council three years before. He thought of how the advice Bernard gave to him was similar to that being imparted by the experienced Will, and realised that for all his verbal spite, Bernard had been a wise counsellor, without whose skills Nick might be doing a very different job of work in a very different part of the world.

The final morning on water was to provide the biggest test of all. Although almost all the rapids they had encountered thus far could be negotiated by kayak, a mode they were by now well skilled in employing, the final one was a monster. It was called the Dolly Parton, because they would have to navigate between two huge rocks in fast-flowing and very turbulent waters and avoid the huge stony protuberances as they passed through those big rocks. Tricky currents were all over the place and the risks of smashing into the massive rocks was high. A few years earlier, a local man, drowned when his kayak overturned – should he have been in one in the first place? He was sucked into an eddy, pulled along a flow-path under the rocks and found dead two hundred yards downstream. A sobering and frightening thought!

The group was given a choice of three possible ways to get to the other side: walk over the bankside rocks around the rapid (no shame in that); attempt by kayak (easy for Will and Jack, extremely difficult for the rest); or they could split into two teams of eight led by Will and Jack and attack the rapid in the large dinghies. They all opted for the dinghies, and after breakfast packed their kayaks onto the truck and unloaded and inflated the two rubber rafts.

'So listen up guys,' said Will, 'Whatever you have learned over the past six days will be tested, and failing the exam could be very painful if not catastrophic. Don't underestimate the risks you will be taking. Each of you will not only be carrying your own life in your hands but also the lives of the other seven members in your craft. This is a time for bravery and courage, but most of all for common sense. Just don't do anything stupid, hear me? Follow the rules, think caution, and you will all have an incredible experience that you will never forget.'

Now it was time for Dolly Parton. Nick had to think seriously about whether he should allow Kevin to participate but realised Kevin would never forgive him if he were denied this final challenge. Nick turned to Kevin and said, 'Are you ok with all that? There's no shame in opting out.'

Kevin's response was unequivocal: 'This is what I came for. No way I'm not doing this!'

He asked himself what he would advise if Kevin were his own son, and the answer was crystal-clear: let him do it.

They paused their dinghies as Will and Jack explained to their crews what to expect. They would approach on a high wall of water and aim for a large rock on the left which they would use to propel their boats to the right; repeat this in the opposite direction; zig-zag through a path of manageable obstructions until they came to the biggest challenge of all: they would hit a huge wall of back-flowing water at speed and the dinghies would literarily fold in half, so if they were in the back four they would have to lean back as far as they could in the anticipation of being thrown forwards and vice versa if in the front four. If, as was entirely possible, they were thrown out of the dinghies, they would end up in a huge eddy current swirling around them. Fighting this eddy would only draw them deeper in, so they were simply to wait as the eddy drew them up and down until it expelled them.

Now it was all systems go.

First Jack's team entered the rapids; each member performed brilliantly and they negotiated the enormous swirling waters, bouncing off the rocks without mishap, pumping their fists in the air as they reached the clear still water on the other side two minutes later.

Now it was Will's team's turn; Will was in the back row of four on the outer left; in the second last row to the right was Nick. To Nick's left was Kevin, and in front of Nick sat the property developer, James, now recovered and chastened. Will repeated the instructions and then they were off - into the fast-moving swirling waters. They could barely see through the spewing foam that was being thrown at them with unnerving force. There was no time for fear, only for absolute concentration and commitment. Do what you have to do. Don't be smart.

First big rock on the left, negotiated; the bigger rock on the right, bounced off. Into the smaller rapids - so far so good. Then through the foaming waves they saw the wall. They leaned back in anticipation of hitting it, but nothing could have prepared them for the force of smashing against it. Although he remembered Will's warning, Nick was astonished at the strength of the impact; he remembered being thrown forward with great force and immediately feeling is if he had been kicked in the chin and then remembered nothing until he became aware of a chilling stillness and a feeling of bobbing up and down like a cork in a dry space. He had absolutely no memory of being ejected from the dinghy, but realised he was no longer in it. He was alone. He could see water swirling all around him but not touching him. Was he dead? Was this what being dead was like?

He realised he was in a huge eddy. His first instinct was to force himself upwards and then he remembered Will's words and he relaxed. It was eerie, just bobbing up and down. He felt strangely calm, but became aware that his jaw was aching, as if he had been punched – hard.

Will later explained what had happened: as the dinghy hit the wall of water with tremendous force, the dinghy jackknifed and literally folded in half. Being in the front half, James's head was thrown back. Newton's First Law. Simultaneously, sitting in rear half, Nick's head was thrown forwards, resulting in James's helmet connecting with Nick's chin in as perfect an uppercut as was ever delivered by Mike Tyson, propelling Nick upwards and out of the dinghy. Kevin had tried to follow Nick into the swirling waters but had been held back by Will's iron grip. To lose one member of the group would be calamitous – to lose two, catastrophic.

What Nick did not realise was that when he was thrown unconscious from the dinghy, he had been pulled for a hundred and fifty yards downstream by the fierce current until he got sucked into the huge whirling eddy where he bobbed until he regained consciousness. His body, he later realised, had been battered all the way by the unforgiving rocks, but astonishingly nothing had broken. He was intact and alive. Had he been conscious he almost certainly would have tried to fight the current and would almost certainly have drowned.

The rest Nick could remember – bobbing up and down in the eddy, the eerie silence.

The dinghy had followed him downstream. As the dinghy, still being propelled with speed, shot by next to Nick's floating body Kevin leaned out to pull him up. Will ordered him to sit back and not put himself at risk, but Kevin wasn't about to listen to anyone. Nick's safety was all that mattered to him, Nick who wasn't his father but was his best friend - he wasn't going to go home without him. After what seemed an eternity but in reality was no more than thirty seconds, Nick became aware of rising up and then of an arm reaching down in front of him; he grabbed the arm and it pulled him upwards. As he broke free of the eddying waters he realised the arm was Kevin's; but now other arms were pulling him up and back into the dinghy. He was safe. He was alive,

Every one of them, but most of all Nick, congratulated Kevin on his courage. James was very apologetic, but Will assured him it was totally accidental.

An hour later they stepped onto dry land - the expedition was over. What an adventure it had been! Glorious scenery of Northern Cape on the one side and Namibia on the other; acts of foolishness and bravery; new skills learned and courage gained – a rite of passage for Kevin and even for Nick!

Getting his aching body into his car required body manoeuvres that would have filled a contortionist with pride. As they drove home, they said little to each other but both were aware that this had been a bonding, the likes of which few get the chance to experience. Far from Nick having to care for Kevin, Kevin had had to take care of him – and Raichie and the girls were overjoyed to have both back in one piece even though one piece was damaged goods.

The next morning Nick's body felt as if had been passed through a mangle then a wringer and then been run over by a minibus. Every bone in his body ached. His head was a volcano waiting to erupt. Yet, for all of that he felt elated, liberated and above all alive, even if only just.

When Nick returned to work the following morning, the pain had abated into mere discomfort. That notwithstanding, he still managed to remain on his feet for fifteen hours of cutting and scraping and wiping and stitching, all the while feeling another corner had been turned, even if by floating unconscious down a raging river.

# Chapter 49

## Shleps 2017

African people historically have wide smiles revealing beautiful strong and regular white teeth, for the most part unaffected by decay because of their coarse diet. However, as sugar intake increased in that part of the world, dental caries came to be an increasingly prevalent disease. When restorative treatment is not possible, it is usually in the remit of dentists to carry out extractions, but when one is not available, the options are for either a doctor or medical student to do it. Or DIY. DIY was not a good idea, but if doctors could be trained to do basic extractions or refer them if they were complex, then a lot of critical delay and pain could be avoided.

Based on the notion that many needy people *could* not attend the hospital (too scared, too ill, too far), or *would* not (pressure from *sangomas* not to go), Bokkie then came up with the idea of extending the basic hospital service by creating mini clinics that would attend particular outlying areas once a month. If the people could not come to them, they would go to the people.

So Nick and Bokkie and Mr Nelson Ngope appointed an administrator to contact outlying smaller hospitals or clinics to set up an outreach programme. This would involve packing a half-dozen medical students into a minivan, travelling to a local missionary or doctor's practice, and setting up a half-dozen chairs where students could diagnose illness, treat minor problems such as abscesses or carry out dental extractions.

A month later, the first batch of medical students set out for the Mliweni mission hospital 40 kilometres away. After being traditionally greeted by the local staff with a welcoming song, they set up the lightweight and basic chairs they had brought with them and waited. Word had spread of their presence by bush telegraph, and after an hour the first patients trickled in. The trickle grew into a torrent within another hour.

Bokkie demonstrated to the medical students how to give a dental injection and how to use a pair of forceps with minimum force and maximum skill. Soon each of the students had experienced the satisfaction of extracting their first decayed tooth (in one case, even a healthy one, but that's how it goes). Only when they were in difficulties did one of the two men step in to assist. By the end of the day, each student had treated a number of infections, extracted about 10 teeth each and had a useful and interesting away day in the country. By the end of their third day out, each student was sufficiently competent not only to extract a tooth in its entirety without breaking off and leaving roots behind, but also to remove broken roots themselves without having to call on their mentors for assistance.

On one occasion, however, things did not go to plan. A young female student was involved in the extraction of a very mobile lower premolar tooth that seemed to be surrounded by an abscess. She had no way of being certain of the exact cause, given that there was no possibility of an x-ray. Anyway, she gave her injection of local anaesthetic, waited for numbness, and then applied the forceps to the tooth. The tooth came out easily enough with minimum effort, but half the woman's jaw came with it, the remnant of which then proceeded to snap in half and buckle in front of her.

The young student screamed, and when Bokkie reached her she had already fainted. When she revived a few minutes later, Bokkie informed her that what she had extracted with the tooth was a very large and very malignant bone tumour.

The patient was driven by ambulance to White River, where unfortunately she died two days later. The student was utterly distraught, and even Bokkie's most sympathetic assurances that the cancer was so far advanced that death was inevitable anyway and that she was in no way to blame, nothing would stop her from packing her bags and returning home to become the artist for which she was temperamentally far better suited. As Mr Nelson Ngope was later to comment, 'So it goes....', and there really wasn't much else one could say. Shit happens.

As this facility grew and expanded, Nick enrolled Raichie to approach some large medical and dental supply companies to donate out-dated equipment and overstocked materials to each of the six mini hospitals they attended. Eventually she even got one major company to sponsor a minivan that could be converted into a proper dental surgery-on-wheels attended by local dentists working voluntarily on a rota. It became known as the Shleps Van. To 'shlep', Nick had learned from Bokkie, meant to pull (or extract) in Yiddish. (Nick was still learning a number of other Yiddish expressions that varied from crude to disgraceful but were always humorous.) The van was equipped with a dental chair, a dental light, a compressor, a small autoclave/steriliser and multiple sets of diagnostic and extraction instruments. So successful was this programme that they were able to persuade the sponsors that a second van was necessary, which was given the name of Shleps Too.

Once more Mr Nelson Ngope had cause to be thankful to the quiet modest doctor that he had acquired. Nick quiet and modest? He might have been arrogant in an earlier life, but his chastening experience with the Medical Practice Committee had profoundly altered him, and very much for the better.

# Chapter 50

## Cape Town 2017

Five years had elapsed since Nick arrived at White River to begin a life-changing odyssey that was still far from over. Not for a single moment had he regretted his inverted 'Grand Old Duke of York' journey. He had been up - Head of Department at a grand British hospital. Then, through his own ill-judgment and rank arrogance, he had spiralled downwards to the point where he had lost everything of value to him and was contemplating ending his life. Now, after the Grand Old Duke of York had marched him to the bottom of the pit, he marched him up again - and up was where he was determined to remain. He had re-established his career, had regained his self-respect and the respect of others. He had lost an adopted country but had adopted another; lost a wife but found a family that he loved with a depth of feeling that he never knew he possessed.

Then, once again for no particular reason, Nick began to experience those same feelings of self-doubt that had led to his downfall in Leeds. However, there is no better teacher than experience, and he was not about to make the same mistake again. He reasoned that the only possible cause of his negative feelings was burnout. He was simply making demands on himself that could not be sustained. He knew he had leave due to him and it was school holidays, so he asked Raichie and the girls (Kevin was on a school cricket tour in Kwa-Zulu) if they cared to join him for two weeks in Cape Town.

'Dare leave without us!' responded Raichie, as the two blonds jumped gleefully up and down. The girls were now eleven and thirteen respectively and had been on few holidays since Steven's untimely demise, and one was well overdue.

Nick booked two rooms at a boutique hotel in Clifton, just above Fourth Beach. Nick had heard Clifton was beautiful, but the reality took his breath away. The white sand of the four beaches separated by huge boulders (he remembered Dolly Parton!); the Twelve Apostles gigantic in the background to the right and Table Mountain bedecked in its cloudy tablecloth to the left, with Lion's Head separating them. Much as he loved his Aussie beaches, there was nothing to compare to this. But every upside has one going down, and that was the icy Atlantic Ocean, which was cold enough to turn uncles into aunts. He and the girls found they could just about run in, get sorted by a big roller, and then rush out again breathless but refreshed. Raichie didn't even consider it.

They could have ascended imposing Table Mountain by cable car but chose to walk up (a testing climb that took about two hours) and stroll along the top – the views were breath-taking. They spotted the little *dassies* running along the rocks, little rabbit-like creatures that were closer genetically to elephants than any other creature. How strange is nature! They could see Robben Island in the distance, Nelson Mandela's home for 28 years. On their climb down they meandered through Kirstenbosch Gardens with its amazing protea and aloe plants growing wild in profusion.

They went for fresh fish to the small port at Kalk Bay which they then cooked on a barbecue. They walked for miles along Muizenberg beach, so different from Clifton, but at least they could swim there because it was the warmer Indian Ocean and not the wretched Atlantic. As they strolled, Raichie would hold one of Nick's hands and the younger girl the other – Leanne thought she was too old to be seen doing anything so childish.

How different were girls, Nick thought, so much more demonstrative in their warmth. He was well aware that, being an only child and not a father himself, he had had little experience in family relationships, and was enjoying this more than he could express. After the girls had gone off to their room after dinner to read and watch tv or play on their iPads, Raichie and Nick would sit on the terrace sipping wine, saying little but feeling complete with each other and enjoying the last rays of sunlight as it sank golden-red into the sea.

When they boarded the Kulula flight to return, all were sad. Even the offbeat dark humour failed to lift them. *'Thank you for flying Kulula, it's been a pleasure taking you for a ride!'* Nevertheless, they were now a family, and his dark feelings had gone. Without the help of drugs.

Then another letter in a buff envelope arrived by surface mail. The only times Nick had ever received letters was when his mother wrote, or when the late Samson's widow wrote to inform him how the house-building was progressing. This letter had the return address of the Department of Health and Education in Pretoria. Nick felt sick to his stomach. Was this to be another kick in the guts? His hands shook as he tore open the envelope.

Dear Sir,

It has come to this Department's attention (Nick gulped) following a report from Mr Nelson Ngope (Nick gulped again and felt dizzy) that you have been carrying out some outstanding work in surgery at White River Hospital and also developed an excellent curriculum for the students there.

> You may be aware that some years ago we completed the building of a new hospital and state-of-the-art medical school named Medical University of South Africa [MEDUNSA] near Pretoria. We are now recruiting for staff.
>
> We feel honoured to offer you the position of Head of Department in Surgery at the new MEDUNSA Hospital together with the post of Professor of Surgery at MEDUNSA School of Medicine.
>
> Terms and conditions are attached, as are full details of your proposed remuneration package. We would be grateful if you could consider this and respond to us within the next few days.
>
> Yours sincerely and with great anticipation,
>
> Professor Simeon Masinga
>
> Dean of Faculty MEDUNSA

Nick re-read it. His head was swimming. This was a once in a lifetime opportunity to rise to the level his talents merited. The salary was more than twice what he was currently receiving. A few years ago he would have grabbed the offer with both gloved hands, but now....... if he accepted the offer, he would almost certainly have to go alone. Be alone again.

He handed her the letter and waited as she read it.

Raichie said just one word. 'Congratulations!' She tried to smile as she held back her tears.

'What do you think I should do, Raichie?'

'Do as your heart tells you, Nick. It's a wonderful reward for a talented person. But it's not nearby. Do you know where this place is? It's close by a large black township forty miles from Pretoria and two hundred from here. It's in the *gramadoelas,* the middle of nowhere.'

'I would have to leave here. How would you feel about that, Raichie?'

'It would break my heart. It would break all our hearts.' She turned away to hide her sobs.

Then she faced him again.

He looked at her as he said, 'I've made my decision.'

'I wish you luck, Nick. You go with my blessing.'

'I'm going nowhere, sweetheart. I couldn't possibly leave the woman I love, the children I love.'

She threw herself into his arms and wept with joy.

The letter he wrote in response was met with disappointment at MEDUNSA.

There was no way he could imagine being without her, and he was certain that she felt the same for him. Marriage however seemed unnecessary. Yet, there was one piece of the jigsaw not yet in place: defining his relationship with the rest of her family. If there was one thing Nick had added to his life, it was sensitivity, and he was acutely aware of the difficulty young Leanne and Alexis were experiencing: they both adored him, but he was neither their father nor their stepfather. They knew he was their mother's 'best friend', but as far as they knew from their Calvinist teacher, best friends did not (or should not) share the parental bed.

Then, one day, their teacher had used the term 'scarlet woman' in the context of a story she was reading to the children at assembly, and when they got home, Alexis had asked their mother (in Nick's presence) whether she was a scarlet woman, and if so, why wasn't she redder? Why weren't they married? Raichie had merely laughed and reassured them that she wasn't scarlet in any way, and the only reason why she and Nick weren't married was that they were both too busy at work to find the time to organise a wedding.

Nick did not find this totally satisfactory. The issue needed to be sorted out, if not for themselves, then certainly for the girls. So, later, when the two young ones were asleep, he asked 'Raichie, tell me truthfully, how do *you* feel about being a scarlet woman? Embarrassed?'

Would she be happier if they were married? For that matter, did she want to marry him at all? As he asked these questions in turn, he realised that deep within him, he expected, even hoped the answer would be 'yes' to each. He then gulped as he realised he had poked a hornet's nest, the bag had closed and things might never be the same again.

'My darling,' she said, 'when Steven got killed, I thought the end of my world had come. We had been so happy together that the thought for me of being with another man was about as possible for me as becoming an Olympic athlete. I started my tea-room, not to be able to support myself – Steven's insurance policies and the farm have ensured that I and the kids would never want for anything – but to take my mind away from thinking of him every waking second. The longer time went on, the more I realised that the chances of meeting another man that I could love, that could love me and also take on the burden of three young children, was very unlikely.

'Also, it had never entered my mind that I could have a relationship with a man who wasn't Jewish, because you are by now well aware how important that is to me. The chances of finding an unmarried Jewish guy while living in a small town like White River are as high as finding rocking horse poop. And then hey, guess what, this guy comes into the tea-room; he's very good looking – no, I'm not talking about you, big-head! - who is always alone and always looks lonely, who doesn't give me a second look, who doesn't try to chat me up like all the local white married men do, or eye my pretty black waitresses with intent.

'Then, one night soon after I saw you, I went to bed and for the first time in five years the man's face in my mind was not Steven's. I masturbated like a pubescent schoolgirl that night and felt wonderfully guilt-free when I came – and that wasn't the only time. I started asking questions, learned you were a surgeon at the hospital making quite a name for yourself, and that you were more celibate than a monk. Then, when the opportunity arose about the AIDS clinic, well, you know the rest....'

Nick thought for a moment before responding. 'Fine, but that doesn't deal with our future relationship - where to from here?'

Raichie's response was surprising. 'While Steven was alive, I loved him very deeply, and always will. In the last few years you and I have both suffered loss, found ourselves, and found each other. I have now grown to love you very deeply too, and I hope I always will. It seems to me the most natural thing in the world that one can love two people, and that the one love doesn't diminish the other. But my new love is a delicate flower that's growing beautifully, and I don't want to do anything that will cause that flower to wilt. At the moment, we are under no great pressure. We are together when we are together and you go off to work or anywhere else when you have to or want to. I am perfectly content with that.

'Marriage, however, changes relationships - this is the psychologist in me talking. It introduces more responsibility and greater expectations, and replaces co-dependency with dependency. I don't want to be dependent on another person ever again, not even to make the girls feel more comfortable.

'Then there's another question. I am Jewish; you are, as far as I can tell, agnostic. Where would we get married? In a registry office? Not appealing. In a church? Not a chance. In a synagogue? You'd have to convert to Judaism, and I simply won't ask that of you. I am totally content where we are right now and wouldn't want to change anything in the name of greater security or more acceptable morality.

'So, my darling, we should not worry about the future; we have to 'seize the day' and enjoy each one as it comes, and my children will have to work it out as best they can.'

Nick stared at her. She had, in a few emotional phrases, summed up their relationship in a way that his brilliant but one-tracked clinical mind could never have done. Yet it still hadn't answered the question: what was he to the girls? So Raichie asked him what he was to her. 'I am your lover,' he answered. She laughed: 'That is exactly what I tell the girls to answer when someone asks who you are: they are to say you are my lover - and that, my dear simpleton, is all I ever want you to be. I have had boyfriends; I've had men trying to get into my pants. I have had a husband, I've had a support-system. I've never had someone with whom I can absolutely be myself, who asks nothing of me but gives me everything of himself. So there you have it, Nick Simpson, and if you ever get tired of it, you are free to move on without a backward look. Listen to Bob Dylan, "Don't think twice, it's alright."'

And, in that moment, Nick knew he would never have to look back or away, in any direction ever again.

# Chapter 51

## Lunch with Vultures  2018

Two more years had elapsed, two years of incredibly hard work for Nick, two years of cementing his relationship with his acquired family. Raichie's restaurant was thriving, and sadly the AIDS clinic was booming as well. So, when Bokkie suggested spending a day at a vulture restaurant, that was probably the last thing on Nick's list of priorities. But if he had learned only one thing in his time at the hospital, it was that if Bokkie made a suggestion as to how that time might be spent, it was well worth the listening.

Thus, when Bokkie said he was planning on flying over to the Magaliesberg mountains to feed some vultures, and a space was available for Nick to accompany him, Nick was not about to say no, even though feeding vultures seemed to Nick to be a very odd thing to be doing on one's day off. So, after breakfast on the Wednesday, the two doctors headed for the local airport and took off for the 90-minute flight going west. Speaking into the little microphone, Bokkie attempted to explain the purpose of their mission.

'Consider this, Nick: local farms are vulnerable to having their livestock attacked by predators. A lion will kill a cow on a farm and its pride will take what they need to feed their family. What is left behind is cleared up by local jackals that pick every last bit of meat off the cow's carcass, even to the extent of crushing the bones of the cow into small chips in order to extract the juicy marrow from the bones.

'Then down fly the vultures and vacuum up the bone debris, which is all that the jackals have left behind but which is full of calcium. The bone bits are then transported by the parent vultures and fed to the baby vultures in the heights of the steep hills. The nutritional calcium will be absorbed into the little wings of the mini-vultures so that they can grow strong, enabling them to fly when they grow a bit older.

'Just think about it, one cow provides food for lions, jackals and vultures. This is nature's cycle. But there's a problem – farmers are interfering with that cycle. Farmers don't like losing cows, so they get licences to shoot lion. They also poison the jackals and electrocute the vultures as the birds rest on high-tension electric wires before doing their house-keeping chores. The young vultures don't get the crushed bones and the calcium, their wing bones don't develop, and they literally fall off the mountain when they attempt their first flights.

'What we are going to do today is find a carcass, crush some bone, take it up the mountain, and serve it to the vultures without the farmers interfering. Should be an interesting day.'

They arrived at Lanseria airport, where they met up with the other six people who would be on the expedition. Waiting for them was Russell Friedman, a wildlife conservationist who had been instrumental in creating the first vulture restaurant in South Africa. As they headed off to the mountains in Russell's combi-van, he passionately explained the reason for the vulture restaurant's creation.

'The vulture population is diminishing at an alarming rate, Now, anyone who has ever stared a vulture in the face might say this is no bad thing. Rarely has a less endearing creature made its way through the evolutionary cycle. I'll put it another way – they're fucking ugly. You might think the sooner they were eliminated, the better. But you'd be wrong. Vultures are of great value as scavengers, especially in hot regions. Their stomach acid is exceptionally corrosive, allowing them to digest putrid carcasses infected with toxins and bacteria like cholera and anthrax that would be lethal to other scavengers. The vultures remove these bacteria from the environment.

'Besides being scavengers, grown vultures are also pest controllers. They keep the local population of vermin in check as they pick off excess rats, mice and rabbits. Their naturally well-filtered and very nutritious poop also provides excellent fertiliser for the farmers' crops. So, ugly as they are, we need them. They are an integral part of nature's cycle. But we are killing them off.

'To combat the loss of carcasses, carrion can be deposited with farmer co-operation in non-functional areas of their farms for the endangered vultures to feed on to provide a safe source of food.'

Russell ensured that everyone had sufficient water not to dehydrate and provided them with high-powered binoculars. Fortunately, they didn't have to begin by smashing up the carcass bones – this had already been done by farmers' staff and the chipped bone placed in small sacks; but they would have to carry the sacks right to the top. There were two of Russell's strong men carrying heavier bags of carrion flesh. Fortunately, the carrion was hygienically wrapped, because the smell could have killed anything (except vultures) within a hundred metres. The climb up the mountain was not difficult, but it was hot, so it was essential that they drank copious amounts of water, which also had to be carried up. The two men pushed on ahead to empty the carrion, so by the time the party reached the top, the worst of the smell had dissipated.

The ascent took about 45 minutes, and when they reached the flattish plateau, the view of the surrounding hills was spectacular. But this was not what they had come to see, so the process of scanning the hills with their binoculars began, and Nick quickly became adept at spotting vulture nests on the hillside. They made their way towards these nests and when they were as close as they could safely reach, they emptied their sacks of crushed bone shards. Soon the adult vultures, with their acute sense of smell, began to fly towards the 'restaurant'.

The vultures were now close enough to be seen clearly in all their natural ugliness, and the amazing thing for Nick was the more he looked, the less ugly they became, and he felt towards them as he would to any patient in need. Via his powerful binoculars, he noticed that the vultures appeared to be urinating down their legs. Russell explained: 'The uric acid kills bacteria accumulated from walking through carcasses, and also acts as evaporative cooling.' Nick was amused – many were the times he would have welcomed such a mechanism in theatre! Darwin would have found this interesting.

Within an hour, dozens of vultures had scraped up every vestige of carrion flesh and chipped bone and flown back to feed their young. Russell explained that this process took place every week with the assistance of local volunteers or members of the Vulture Preservation Society. Nick was filled with awe at what Russell and his group were achieving and was about to become their newest member.

The climb down was significantly easier – no bones, less water. After enjoying a packed lunch themselves (bones not included) it was time to return to base, and Nick was sure this would not be a one-off experience. Then Bokkie said something really odd: 'I wonder what it would feel like if one was flying towards a mountain, say this one, and not be able to stop before crashing……' This thought being rather unpalatable considering they were about to fly home, Nick was unable to find an intelligent response, so intelligently said nothing. He did sometimes wonder, though, how Bokkie's mind worked.....

# Chapter 52

## Bokkie 2018

Nick had only just finished a tricky operation to rebuild a patient's jaw that had been partly shot away in an attempted robbery. It had entailed grafting bone from the victim's hip onto what was left of the mandible. The operation had lasted ten hours, and he was utterly exhausted. His energy levels were definitely not what they used to be! As he came into the staffroom, (this time without saying he could do with a stiff whisky, or anything else), he was requested to go directly to Mr Nelson Ngope's office. Was Wilson Rabada causing trouble once more? Were the junior nurses acting up again? Had Bokkie also been summoned?

He knocked and entered. Mr Ngope was standing with Sister Anna, Dube and Sipho, but no Bokkie. All were sombre, and sister Anna was sobbing.

'We have some terrible news, Nick. It is about Dr Bokkie.' Mr Nelson Ngope had to pause while his voice faltered and tears filled his eyes. Sister Anna wailed. Mr Ngope stuttered, 'I deeply regret to tell you that he had a terrible accident today. The police have just been here to inform me that while flying back from Johannesburg, he crashed into a mountain. He was killed instantly. I am so sorry, Nick, we are all so sorry. We are just grateful that you were not with him.'

Nick went ash-white and sank down onto the carpet. Sister Anna rushed forward with a tumbler of water, knelt next to him, placed one arm around his shoulder to support him, used her other hand to force him to drink the cold liquid. Nick could not, did not attempt to contain his emotions, setting all the others weeping as well. Minutes passed. The wailing ceased, and Nick stood up. Sipho stood by him on one side, Dube on the other. Mr Ngope handed him a tumbler of brandy, and then a second one. The four musketeers were now three.

'Do they know how it happened?' eventually whispered Nick.

'Yes, Nick,' said Mr Ngope. 'While you were operating, Bokkie told me he was flying to Johannesburg to visit a Dr Stephenson. On his return flight apparently the weather suddenly turned very bad and there was a violent electrical storm and Dr Bokkie crashed into this mountain in the Magaliesberg'. Nick had experienced a few of these storms earlier that summer while driving and he knew how quickly they could develop and how intense they could be. The driving rain could make visibility practically impossible, and it was entirely plausible that the electronic guiding system on the plane had been knocked out by lightning, thus sending the plane veering off course and careering into the mountain. But then Nick remembered those strange words of Bokkie when they were on their vulture expedition.....

Nick took it upon himself to inform Bokkie's three children in their various countries abroad, and although the Jewish tradition was to have the burial as quickly as possible, the funeral in Johannesburg was delayed until their arrival. Although all the White River doctors and many of the staff wanted to attend the funeral, urgent duties rendered this impossible, and only Mr Nelson Ngope and Nick were driven up to West Park cemetery in Johannesburg. Nick had experienced a bar mitzvah not long before, now he was to experience a Jewish burial. The funeral was a profoundly visceral experience, depressing and sad. Both Nick and Mr Nelson Ngope requested that they be allowed to say a few words. Mr Nelson Ngope spoke eloquently of Bokkie's skill as a surgeon, the contribution he had made to the hospital and the dignity with which he conducted himself after the death of his late wife. Nick spoke of the insight he had gained from Bokkie that enabled him to appreciate everything that his beautiful country had to offer but above all, how to be a *mensch*.

Many of Bokkie's former colleagues at Baragwaneth Hospital were present, and they were interested later to hear of his activities at White River. Nick was surprised to learn that in those earlier years, the undemonstrative man he knew and loved was a veritable power-house feared by all, clashing with all staff, students and authority that failed to meet his exacting standards.

Despite the circumstances, Nick enjoyed meeting Bokkie's grown children. They too were pleased to meet someone who held their father in such esteem. He spent a lot of time talking with them while they sat in mourning and learned that despite Bokkie's misgivings about being a poor father, they held him in great respect and affection. They resolved to keep in touch with Nick, a promise that was kept, if not often.

Mr Nelson Ngope and Nick decided to pay a visit to Dr Stevenson, and were shocked to learn that the reason for Bokkie flying to him on that fatal day was for blood tests and a biopsy diagnosis, both of which confirmed inoperable intestinal cancer. This of course begged the question: did Bokkie die accidentally or did he choose to fly in dreadful conditions knowing he would never make it back? They would never know for sure but once more Nick heard Bokkie's voice ringing in his ears...

They could not inform anyone of the medical disclosure, nor did they wish to set the cat amongst the pigeons in respect of the pending insurance pay-out. The man had paid his dues....

A couple of weeks later, a memorial service was held at the hospital, attended by the four hundred staff and illuminated by the words of Mr Nelson Ngope, Nick, Dube, Sipho and Anna. This was followed by the singing of traditional Church of Zion songs and *Nkosi Sikelele Afrika.* Bokkie would be missed, and by nobody more than Nick. It took several weeks for his sorrow to lift. He had now lost two very wonderful friends, a younger then an older man, both virtually brothers to him; one to AIDS, the other to cancer.

What comforted Nick most during this period was his adopted family. Raichie and her children had also suffered grievous loss and had learned just how valuable the support of others could be.

# Chapter 53

## The Birthday Party   2021

The next couple of years passed predictably. Nick was more or less a permanent fixture in Raichie's home, staying over at his cottage only when necessity demanded. He was a father to the children in everything but name. They adored him no less than he loved them. To Kevin he had become a father figure. His presence made the teenage girls the envy of their friends. As the days went by, Raichie wondered whether she had missed a golden opportunity by not snagging Nick when the chance presented itself. By the time she got round to discussing the matter again, he made it clear that he had taken her earlier words on board and thought there was no longer a need to get spliced. This of course made her all the more determined to get him to change his mind, but Nick was not for turning.

Kevin had distinguished himself in his matric exams, spent a year on a kibbutz in Israel where he taught kayaking on the dam, and was heading off to Raichie's *alma mater* in Johannesburg to study economics and finance, and looking forward to furthering his rugby talents. The girls too were good students and excellent netball players.

Raichie continued to own her little restaurant but had appointed a top-class black manager, Martha. This created the opportunity of resurrecting a career as a psychologist, but much of what she has studied at uni had been superseded by new research. Further study was required to acquaint herself with current ideas. How notions had changed! For example, genetic researchers had mapped human genes with the aim of isolating the individual chromosome responsible for mental dysfunction, and this looked like an area worth exploring. Psychologist Daniel Kahneman, whom she thought a brilliant mind, was awarded the Nobel Prize in Economics for his research on how judgments are made in the face of uncertainty. These ideas were not around in 1990 when she graduated.

She needed to make herself currently relevant, so she enrolled with UNISA, the University of South Africa, to do a distance-learning revision programme, and was enjoying the stimulation it provided. There was research to be done, essays written and projects completed. Alexis took great pleasure in saying 'Mom, there'll be no dinner till you've finished your homework!'

Nick's career had prospered despite the unpleasant political environment that seemed to blight everything. The despised Zuma had been replaced by a moderate and intelligent if somewhat ineffectual new President, Mr Cyril Ramaphosa. Unfortunately, alongside this came the ever-increasing spectre of Winston Rabada. Mr Nelson Ngope, with Rabada breathing down his neck, did wonder how much longer Nick could remain in charge. Both Dube and Sipho had developed into fine surgeons, but it was Sipho who had shown the greater leadership qualities. When Nick offered to stand down for the umpteenth time, Mr Ngope accepted the opportunity to make a momentous change. Sipho was appointed Head of Department, which Nick was pleased to accept as he thought it proper in the context of black empowerment.

At his own request, Nick's fiftieth birthday had come and gone quietly and celebrated only with a family dinner; and when he came to think of it, he had no other family than Raichie's. He had specifically asked for no presents, and they reluctantly concurred, but did give him a new edition of *The Birds of Southern Africa* to sit next to his one of snakes. The family also made a sizeable donation to the Sick Nurses' Fund, and Nick was more than pleased with that.

Another milestone was approaching - Raichie's fiftieth. Unlike Nick, Raichie had a huge extended family, and wanted all to share her big day. She booked a room large enough for sixty people at Laletchwe, a large game reserve a few miles from White River with a restaurant that specialised in celebratory functions. They were reputed to have a kitchen second to none, spearheaded by Carl Van Rooyen, considered the region's finest chef, who only used locally sourced ingredients and created miracles with them. Raichie was not one to mess around with second best, as she kept reminding Nick. And then she would add, 'I do occasionally make a mistake...'

Of course, a big party necessitated a trip to the chi-chi boutique in Hyde Park Johannesburg for a new outfit, because you only ever celebrated your fiftieth once in your life. This was combined with a visit to Randfontein not too far away. Her parents were still in good health. They were delighted with the idea of a celebration and would be driven to White River by cousin Joel. Bubbe, although technically still with the living, said nothing but was always smiling, as you would do too if the Cossacks had gone away and there were fairies all around. Joel, by his own proud admission, was also with the fairies but of a different sort. He was much loved by all the family with the exception of his father who still had very old-fashioned ideas.

Then came the matter of speeches. Raichie said 'Nick, I'd like you to propose the toast to me and say some kind words, difficult as that may be.'

'Sorry, sweetheart, but I'd be far too nervous to stand up in front of all those people and make a speech. I'll be happy to assist the kids prepare theirs.' And thus it was.

Raichie did ask herself how it was possible for a man to have the courage to kayak down the Orange River or to take on Winston Rabada, to perform life-saving operations but be too chicken to say a few nice words, but she knew not to pursue it.

Came the day of the party. It was mid-January and mercilessly hot. Guests began arriving from noon. Every room and chalet at Lalechwe had been reserved, the air-conditioning full blast. As the sun was dropping on the horizon, it became a little cooler, and the ten reserved open Land Rovers arrived to take the guests for a sunset safari. They saw lion, giraffe, zebras galore, but were especially thrilled by the rhinos that charged between the vehicles as if trained to do so *(they actually had been)*. Vincent van Goch had been commissioned for the sunset. By the time they settled down at their tables, everyone was in the best of spirits. They were more than happy to let the band of local African musicians make them do things they hadn't done for years, that is to move it and shake it and let it all hang out – especially Bubbe!

If Raichie had looked like a princess at the bar mitzvah, on this occasion she was a Roman goddess. Her gold and navy dress clung to her still fine figure like a second skin. Nick wasn't used to seeing her in anything but jeans and a t-shirt, and often much less. Holding court, she moved about the room from one guest to another, making each feel special. Even by his own fine standards, the chef had excelled himself, and his salmon *en croute* was executed to perfection. Nick too moved around comfortably, for by now he knew and had been totally accepted by most of the guests. He felt part of the family and extremely proud of his lovely partner.

The girls shared a lovely speech saying the sort of things Raichie wished Nick would have said as well as written for them. Kevin added a few humorous lines, and old man Sam proposed a toast to his only and very special daughter. Raichie responded, remembering Steven, and thanking everyone for making the long journey, but especially Nick who had made the longest and most difficult journey of all. He had filled a gap in their lives that they thought was impossible for anyone to do. She did comment though that unfortunately Nick had failed to heed the words of Beyonce, *"If you like it, put a ring on it."* She invited everyone to drink a toast to her Bubbe, parents, children and her best friend, and was about to ask the band to continue when she saw Nick approaching the bandstand.

What was he doing? The answer came soon enough.

The band struck up, and Nick began to sing. To sing! Nick, who had not often sung in his life, not in the shower, not when alone, not when happy nor when sad, Nick began to sing. To the tune of a very old Andrew sisters ballad based on a Yiddish song, he sang, not in a great voice, not in a strong voice, but in his own voice:

'Of all the girls I've known, and I've known some

Until I first met you, I was lonesome;

Bei mir bist du schon, please let me explain,

Bei mir bist du schön means that you're grand.'

Bubbe, who had not said a word all evening, suddenly began to sing, too, picking up the Yiddish refrain, '*Bei mir bist du schön.*'

Then everyone joined in '*Bei mir bist du schön means that you're grand.*'

When they quietened, and it took a while, Nick continued to sing a story he had put together using short verses from pop classics including Beatles' favourites, Bohemian Rhapsody, Paul Simon's lyrics and many of the Gershwin oldies, weaving a story about a woman who wanted to get married: *"Some day he'll come along, the man I love (with a ring)"*, and her guy who couldn't afford to;

*"I'm just a poor boy, I don't do diamond rings; I'm just an old guy,*

*Empty as a pocket, no diamonds on the soles of my shoes."*

Nick hoped Paul Simon would forgive him.

These were by no means the only verses that forced their way past the tonsils of the intrepid crooner. Raichie was beginning to wonder where all this was going. Was this Nick's idea of fun? She didn't think so. That was not his style, but then nor was singing. The audience however was enjoying it and joining him as he sang each verse.

And then 'she' said (within the context of the song, of course,) *"It don't mean a thing, if it ain't got that ring."*

To which 'he' responded, *"All you need is love, babe, love is all there is."*

Was that really all there was, thought Raichie. This didn't seem to be heading to a satisfactory conclusion.

On went Nick: 'She' said: *"Take me to the chapel, cos I want to get married."*

'He' said: *"Wise men say, Only fools rush in."* (Raichie thought, it's only been seven years, definitely you don't need to rush....)

'She' said: *"Tomorrow will be too late, it's now or never..."*

It bloody better be, thought Raichie.

Nick stopped singing and began to recite a little poem he had composed:

*'I think I've waited long enough, let enough time slip away,*

*To know what I need in my life, and it's not to say "no way".*

*So tonight, my lady fair, I ask you this on bended knee*
*Will you be my wife, my life? Will you marry me?'*

Thirty men burst into cheers, thirty women burst into tears. Raichie did neither. She just stood there with her mouth open, her hands on her face. She did everything possible to imitate Edvard Munch's "The Scream." Then she put her arms around him, and everyone waited. She whispered in his ear, 'Swine, upstaging me on my birthday!'

Alexis and Leanne rushed to them. They threw themselves on Nick, then on Raichie. 'Say yes, Mom, say yes!' Still she said nothing. Then, a still voice rose above the crowd as Bubbe came floating up to them: 'So, what you're waiting for, Raichie? He's a *zhulik* but he's also a nice boy!'

Raichie said not a word, she couldn't, but knew she didn't need to. She already had it all worked out: the Queen Mary liner on the way to New York with the Captain conducting the ceremony, her three children in attendance and her parents as witnesses would fit the bill very nicely indeed.

# Chapter 54

## The Best Laid Plans

The next morning, Alexis and Leanne were up at sparrow's chirp. Unable to contain their excitement, they came rushing into their mother's room and jumped on Nick's prostrate body. 'Nick, Nick, you were amazing! Has she said yes yet, please please say she's said yes.' Nick did not respond.

Raichie stirred slightly – not too much, because she had the biggest hangover she'd ever had. This wasn't too surprising, because she very rarely drank much more than a glass of wine. Last night however everyone, absolutely everyone, had insisted that she share a *l'hayim* with them, a toast 'to life'. She vaguely remembered saying to the first few that she had not yet accepted Nick's proposal, and after that her memory appeared to be in inverse proportion to her hangover - the more her head ached, the less she remembered.

She searched for a pillow. The girls had snatched them. She tried to take Nick's, but he was holding on to it for dear life.

As they sat down for breakfast and her head began to clear a little, she looked at the person she took to be Nick. 'I did not see that coming, I just didn't see it coming. Why have you never told me you can sing?'

'I didn't know I could. Still not sure that I can! But listen, seeing as you haven't said yes yet, I'm going to withdraw the offer.'

THE ROAD TO REDEMPTION   CHAPTER 54

'Then I'll sue you for breach of promise.'
'I'll plead temporary insanity while under the affluence of incahol.'
'And I'll cut off your crown jewels.'

Her 50th birthday party and the proposal were the talk not only of White River but of Johannesburg and Randfontein and god knows where else. The next few days were a blur for Nick, but not for Raichie. She was busy. Non-stop phone calls from family, from friends. Dresses to be chosen, itineraries to be planned. The more she thought about the Queen Mary, the more appealing the thought became. The travel agent in Jozies informed her that there was availability on a Queen Mary cruise departing Southampton in July for New York. Six months to wait and plan. Perfect. It would be school holidays for the kids, a perfect time to get away from a South African winter to a northern hemisphere summer. Seven days on the elegant liner, three in New York, then a luxury bus tour to Philadelphia and Washington. It would cost two arms and a leg, as the current vernacular had it, but you only got married once for the second time.

She was so excited. The kids were over the moon. Even her parents were enthusiastic. And the most joyful of all was Bubbe, who had dreamed of becoming a great-grandmother since the day Raichie was born.

Then, once more, the shit hit the fan.

As Robbie Burns had said:
"*The best laid schemes o' Mice an' Men, Gang aft agley, An' lea'e us nought but grief an' pain, For promis'd joy.*"

The shit hitting the fan on this occasion could not have been seen coming. In fact, it couldn't be seen at all. But it could most certainly be felt, in White River, in all of South Africa, in every country of the world.

It was called Corona virus, Covid-19.

It began as just another rumour. They said a problem had occurred in China, and a number of Chinese from Wuhan had died, and it would spread like wildfire. Others said it was not dissimilar to Sars and Eboli and the millennium clock, just a nasty type of 'flu, something for the newspapers and television channels to feast on. Everything would be ok as long as you washed your hands and kept your distance and wore masks.

Why worry, Wuhan was far away, wouldn't affect them in Africa or Europe. And then Europe began to panic, because a disproportionately high number of cases with a significant number of deaths emerged that seemed to stem from Italy. The UK did not panic, nor did the USA and definitely not Sweden.

In South Africa, they said it was 'a white peoples' disease' because a number of whites who had been abroad and returned were the first to come down with the disease. Cruise ships seemed to be heavily affected and so it was obviously then a rich peoples' disease. Winston Rabada said it was a disease caused and spread by Jews, because several cases had followed a bar mitzvah in New York that had been attended by South African relatives. So now it was a rich white Jews' disease. How convenient for Winston Rabada….

South Africa did not over-react. Not at first. But then they did. As in every country all over the world, people started dying and everyone else began panicking. Two words became part of the lexicon: 'pandemic' and 'lockdown'. A third word applied to those people who could not stand two metres apart and could not buy masks and hand-sanitizers, people who lived in squalor and did not have work and could not buy food: carnage.

Even before the pandemic, unemployment was running at around 50%. Now few had jobs and thousands were starving. The hospital was becoming crowded then overcrowded.

THE ROAD TO REDEMPTION   CHAPTER 54

All staff were under massive pressure. Understandably, Nick was in sombre mood. Raichie was particularly concerned. 'I'm really scared for you, Nick. I understand you have to be there, but can they afford you getting ill?'

'Raichie, this isn't going to be an easy time for anybody, least of all medical staff. At the best of times there are insufficient facilities to cope. There is not a single hospital that is adequately prepared for a pandemic. All the cash resources that should have been available for dealing with it are sitting in the Guptas' bank accounts in Dubai. If this really takes off, we are going to be overwhelmed.'

There was nothing Raichie could say. All thoughts of a cruise and a wedding simply evaporated. There were much bigger issues to deal with, and at the epicentre locally would be Nick and the other doctors at White River Hospital.

Raichie's phone buzzed. It was Nick. 'Mr Nelson Ngope has told us that we have to stop everything but the most urgent trauma operations, and just deal with the Corona cases, and they are flooding in. They're in the passages, on the verandahs, on mattresses when there's insufficient beds and then on the floors. ICU's going full blast 24/7. I'm going to have to be here all the time. I'm on the front line now, so I can't come back to you. We're all in quarantine, will be for weeks.'

'I understand, Nick, but who's going to take care of you? I'm trying not to show panic in front of the children, but to tell the truth I'm shitting myself. I've heard you have no protective equipment.'

'None of us have. We've just got to do the best we can. People are dying.'

'I know, but I don't want you to be one of them.'

'I don't either, but I don't get to vote on this. I could walk away but then everything that Rabada and Beauty Mzani and the other nurses have said about me will become the truth. I can't, I won't run.'

Raichie paused as she drew a deep breath. The news was rife with statistics of the risks faced by medics. However, she was a realist, and understood that nothing she said or felt would change the situation. She decided that all she could do was face the immediate future with a positive attitude and place her faith in higher powers.

'I get that, my darling. Just take care of yourself. I don't want to be a widow all over again. Once was once too many.'

'We're not married.'

'That's the worst cop-out I've ever heard! We will be once this crap is over.'

'I can't wait! Give the girls a big kiss from me. On second thoughts don't kiss anybody.'

'So when will I see you?'

'It may be weeks. Or months. This thing isn't going away quickly.'

'Call when you can.'

'I will. I'll be ok, so don't worry, sweetheart.'

'That's like a dentist saying this isn't going to hurt.'

'I'll video-call.'

'Thank heaven for WhatsApp. I love you, Nick.'

In his worst nightmares, Nick could not have envisaged the dystopian world they were about to endure. Patients were flooding in. They couldn't breathe. There was no oxygen. There were hardly any ventilators. If the staff managed four hours sleep a night, they were the fortunate ones. They had run out of rubber gloves and masks and were having to wash and re–use everything they had.

There was no testing. They did not know who had the virus, who were carriers, who had developed immunity. Within days the staff themselves started going down with Covid-19. Within a few more days the deaths began. First some of the older nurses. Then, even the younger ones.

# THE ROAD TO REDEMPTION  CHAPTER 54

The first month went by. Sister Anna succumbed and this broke Nick's heart. When Dube passed away, Nick was beyond pain. Just unutterably numb. Raichie could only offer platitudes on the occasions he managed to phone. She knew how much Nick had loved those two. They were two vertebrae in the backbone of the hospital, and now the hospital would have to manage without them and dozens like them.

The people in the black townships were locked away, isolated, prevented from leaving by police and army. The shops had run out of food. They were literally starving.

For Raichie, there was much to be done. Her restaurant was closed but not inactive. Raichie and the girls phoned everyone they could find, friends, family, strangers: 'Please, guys, whatever surplus food, tins, packets, whatever; blankets, clothes, bring it all to Raichies. Join us in creating food parcels to distribute to the townships. We can't help everyone but we can help some.'

The response was overwhelming. Not just goods, but people, willing hands, working 14-hour days. Neighbouring shops also became depots. Social distancing was a big problem but somehow they managed. Cars and vans were commandeered to ferry the packages to the townships where they were systematically distributed.

But then the deaths stopped rising, reached a plateau and began to fall. Nick's calls and texts were beginning to sound less negative: 'I saw only eighty patients yesterday instead of the more than a hundred last Tuesday. Promising.' It was beginning to look like the worst was over.

Fat chance.

Raichie had had no word from Nick for two days. It had been six weeks since she last saw him. She knew that he was overworked and tired, but it was unusual for him not to make contact. She tried not to transmit her anxiety to the children, but they were not insensitive. She was beginning to experience that dread fear that can only come when you know the next call would be bad news, and the fear was getting worse with each passing hour.

Then her phone buzzed.

'Hullo, Mrs Raichie, this is Mr Nelson Ngope.'
'No, no, please don't say something's happened to Nick.'
'Unfortunately I do have bad news, but it could be much worse. I have to tell you that Nick is in intensive care.'
'Shit!! I'll leave for the hospital immediately.'
'That will not be possible, Mrs Raichie. You cannot come here, this place is like a war zone. Dr Simpson is in strict quarantine. He is experiencing difficulty in breathing but is coping. But he is conscious and he is strong, and we are hoping and confident that he will recover. All the staff are praying, Mrs Raichie, the doctor is very highly respected and very important to us, we cannot afford to lose him. We will phone you every six hours Mrs Raichie.'

Raichie had dreaded this moment, and that she could not be with him only made it worse. She began to experience very dark thoughts. Memories of Steven came flooding back, her grief at losing him, how she thought her world had ended. Time had allowed some healing, Raichie's had helped, but it was not until this quiet man had walked into her restaurant that she had begun to live again. She and her children had believed that Steven was irreplaceable, but Nick had provided a new and unique dimension, a man they could all love not instead of but alongside Steven.

And now was she, were they, about to lose their rock for a second time? No!! Steven was not able to fight his fate, but Nick was strong and he would come out of this. She had absolute faith he would.

Mr Nelson Ngope held to his promise, and three times a day Raichie would receive a call from the CEO or one of his staff. At first it seemed that Nick's condition was worsening: he was racked with cough, he was beginning to lose consciousness, and when he was awake he was barely able to stand for longer than a few moments. Those were not good moments for Raichie, let alone Nick.

'Nick seems very confused,' said Mr Nelson Ngope. 'Sometimes he is delirious and ranting and shouting about Dr Donald. He seems very angry with this person but we don't know who he is, certainly no-one at this hospital. It's taking two people to restrain him – I think he would like to kill this Dr Donald. It's not like Nick at all.'

Raichie could not but wince – then, despite her upset and fear, smile wryly – suppressed anger never disappears, and she felt sad that that dreadful woman was still haunting Nick when what he needed was love and tranquility.

They were desperately worried but they weren't giving up hope, and Mr Nelson Ngope said they had assigned a nurse to be with him at all times.

After three days when each phone call Raichie received stoked her worst fears, the tide began to turn. The coughing was easing. He was no longer losing consciousness. He was taking food. He seemed to be recovering but the danger had not yet passed, not by a long way.

Two weeks since he had taken ill and two months since she had last seen him, Nick phoned. Raichie couldn't speak, but he could hear her body heaving with relief. Then Leanne took the phone from her and shouted 'Are you ok Nick are you ok?' and heard him wheezing, barely managing to speak: 'I'm going to recover, my sweetheart, I'm improving each day. The worst is over. I can't wait to see you all.' No one said anything more. There was nothing more to be said. Their adopted father, her future husband, was going to return.

# Chapter 55

## White River 2022

Three weeks later, the man who had been a strapping former rugby player returned to their home, his home. He was an emaciated shell barely able to walk nor to breathe without a ventilator. He had lost a third of his body mass. Now, with three loving nurses on hand, the fighting back was about to begin. The ventilator disappeared, the kilos gradually increased until he was back to his target weight. The only issues that remained were tiredness after exercise, and training sessions with Kevin were out of the question. Then there was brain fog, where he would struggle to remember small events from two days before. Raichie would tease him, and thankfully his sense of humour was still more or less intact.

Gradually the fog lifted and the energy levels began to return. Under the care of Raichie, Leanne and Alexis, the old Nick slowly reappeared. It would take six months before he would feel 'normal', and that normal would never be quite the same as the normal of the past, but unlike many others, he had survived, he had recovered.

Despite Mr Nelson Ngope's strictest instructions that he was not to return to work, Nick could not keep away. On his first day back, Mr Nelson Ngope and the staff welcomed him once more with the national anthem, sung in the melodious tones that Nick knew were unique to its black peoples. Was this Australian Englishman now a

South African too? He certainly felt it.... When they reached the quiet of his office, Mr Nelson Ngope asked Nick who this Dr Donald man was that Nick wished so fervently to kill. When Nick looked at him somewhat blankly, he described Nick's rant. Nick responded rather cryptically that she was an ex-doctor who was only very distantly related to proper moral conduct, someone he would not wish to think of ever again. Mr Nelson Ngope, remembering why Nick had arrived at his hospital in the first instance, understood that there was a relationship between 'Dr Donald' and his suspension but was wise enough not to discuss the matter any further.

Nick began to carry out short procedures, then longer and more complex operations. A half year later, his mind clear, he was back to working full-time. There was one difference that everyone was aware of, not least Nick, and that was he was only managing only about half the number of operations. But, as Sipho said – he was now Head of Department - half of Nick was better than the whole of most others, and things were improving with each passing week.

Leanne was 18 and a first–year student, following in her mother's footsteps in psychology; Alexis was 16 and in her penultimate year of school. Both were smart, pretty as any model a magazine could produce, personalities to match. Rugged Kevin was in his final year, and a star of the university rugby squad who had already been selected for Mpumalanga Province. Nick felt as proud of them as any natural father might have done. He had much to be grateful for but should have learned by then that trouble would find him in any event.

Nick may not have been aware of another very nasty cloud returning on the horizon, but Mr Nelson Ngope certainly was. Yet again, Nick was summoned to Mr Nelson Ngope's office.

'Please sit, Nick.'

'I don't like it when you ask me to sit, Mr Nelson Ngope. It usually prefaces some bad news you have for me.'

'Perhaps, but not necessarily. You remember how Winston Rabada arrived here at what seems a lifetime ago with his followers, The Freedom Lions? Well, as our government has continued by stealth and corruption to enrich itself at the expense of our people, public services have seen their resources dwindling. Health Services have been hit hard, not directly, but by becoming collateral damage – there is not sufficient money in the kitty to repair buildings, upgrade equipment, to purchase materials. We suffer from regular electricity outages and dwindling water resources. And Mr Rabada is cashing in on this. More and more of the people are listening to him and seeing him as the solution rather than part of the problem. Our younger doctors and nurses are becoming increasingly militant.'

'I'm well aware of that, Sir. Unfortunately, things have got much more difficult with the huge cost of Covid.'

'Precisely. And whom is Mr Rabada blaming for this? Number one, the corrupt black ANC government who have taken control of every public utility to their own benefit; number two, the whites in general for creating the poverty of apartheid; and number three, the Jewish conspiracy who allegedly control everything from the gold-mining industry to food supplies and are the group really bleeding the country dry.'

'But that's complete bullshit!'

'I agree. But those are all generalities. Getting to the specifics, I hear from one of the black doctors that Rabada is still smarting from losing face at his previous visit here when together we stood up to him. He is looking to avenge that. You are going to hate what I am about to say, but I fear for your life. For your own good, I think you should resign.'

'I'll do no such thing. You want me out, fire me.'

'I will do exactly that if you force me to. That you must leave Is no longer under discussion, but I think it would look much better on your cv if you resigned. Go now, go to your home and discuss it with Raichie and her children.'

'I think he's absolutely right, Nick. I've buried one husband, I don't want to bury another. Hundreds, thousands of my people have made the decision to pull out of SA, and when the Jews start moving out, especially from the smaller towns, be sure that the writing is on the wall.'

'Where would we go, Raich?'

'Australia, of course.'

'But you've never been there!'

'Then it's time to broaden my horizons. I've got loads of friends in Sydney, Melbourne and Perth, and they've all settled in fantastically.'

'The children? Their education?'

'Nothing that they can't pick up elsewhere, Don't think I haven't discussed it with them, and they're very excited about going to Oz, as long as they can be near the sea. Quite a few of their friends are already there. Kevin reckons he's got more choice of playing rugby for Australia than for the Springboks.'

'Not so sure about that!'

'Well, if he doesn't make it, it won't be for lack of trying. You know, Nick, when you took him on that kayaking trip, he was quite scared of not being able to manage it.'

'Manage it? Kevin saved my bloody life!'

'My point exactly. That experience was the making of him. His mantra is "If I can survive the Orange River, there's nothing I can't achieve." '

'You know what, I'll buy that. He's the most determined person I know – besides you, of course! But what about your parents?'

'They'll stay put, but hey guess what, airplanes are still flying between Oz and SA. My folks haven't travelled much, and they find the idea of spending a couple of months a year in Oz a very exciting thought. I'll probably get to see more of them than I have in recent years because I was so committed to Raichie's.'

'So that's my next question: what will happen to Raichie's?'

'Martha, who has been virtually running the place for the past six months, is perfectly capable of continuing to run it. They don't need me. So I'm going to give her the deeds and the keys. How's that for black empowerment!'

The mere thought of writing that letter was painful for Nick, but write it he did, giving six months' notice of termination. At the same time, he sent an email to the Sydney Medical School and was delighted beyond belief when they offered him a post as Professor of Facial Surgery. The wheel had turned full circle. Now there was much to be done, and Nick was amazed at the enthusiasm with which his adopted family set about preparing for the huge change in their lives.

The cruise on the Queen Mary never happened. People were still reluctant to commit to being on a ship - a second wave of Covid-19 that could send shockwaves through the world was still a strong possibility, but at least a vaccine had apparently been developed and was being tested.

The wedding did take place, a few months later at the same hotel where they had celebrated Kevin's bar mitzvah. All family members were present including Sam, Leah, Raichie's brothers and Bubbe, who was about to reach her personal century. In spite of her venerable age with all its attendant risks she was still unscathed as yet by the virus. It was not a time to be celebrating excessively, not when the country was still riven by strife and distress. But low-key or not, that day was the happiest of

Nick's life. The same Rabbi, Mike Katz, was there to conduct the ceremony, on this occasion a non-denominational one.

Raichie for the third time in Nick's memory had gone shopping to Hyde Park, but on this occasion more for Leanne and Alexis. Came the night they both looked gorgeous. At Nick's request a chair had been set aside for Steven. Mr Nelson Ngope proposed a toast to South Africa, Israel, the King and Australia, and added a few words about how fortunate the local hospital had been that Nick had come their way. Led by Sipho, the small throng of black staff present sang Nkosi Sikhele Afrika, reducing Nick to tears. Sam proposed the toast to Raichie and also to Bubbe and officially welcomed Nick into the family.

Raichie responded, saying how fortunate she was to have been blessed twice in her life with powerful, admirable, handsome men, and three times with wonderful clever and beautiful children. She was joined by all three as she thanked Nick for filling their terrible void and praised him for having the strength to recover when all feared they would lose him. She did however sound a note of foreboding that she had nicked (pun not intended) from Oscar Wilde:

*'How can a woman expect to be happy with a man who insists on treating her as if she were perfectly normal human being.'*

On this occasion Nick did not sing, thus allaying the dread fear of all present, but he did make a very short speech. He remembered his parents. He remembered Bokkie, Sampson, Sister Anna and Dube. He remembered those who had not survived the pandemic and paid tribute to all who had. But most of all he thanked his courageous and extraordinary wife and her three exceptional children for showing him love, warmth and appreciation and giving him a second chance in life when he had pretty much given up on the first.

'How lucky was I that it was to Raichie's I went for breakfast and not Emilio's across the street! I, we all, have been severely tested for the second time, and for the second time we have come through. I have found a determined, wise and beautiful woman and a very special and loving family, and with them I am ready to face whatever else life might throw at me, at us. For all our sakes, I hope it will be sweets.'

The next few months were frantic. Papers to be completed, visas to be stamped, possessions to be packed or given away, the town house to be sold. Trips to Johannesburg and Randfontein. Activities at the hospital had to be wound down, goodbyes said. Nick and Mr Nelson Ngope were unable to speak nor to make eye contact, so they just stood there holding each other, shaking. Then Nick walked away.

# Chapter 56

## Epilogue  Sydney 2023

Arriving in Sydney in a sense was home-coming for Nick. The transition from the cauldron that was South Africa to the peaceful environs of suburban Sydney was almost a shock in itself, albeit in a very pleasant sort of way. The first thing they all became aware of was a relative lack of people of colour – relative but not absolute. There were many more immigrants from the Far East yet everyone looked the same, dressed the same, spoke the same as everyone else. There were no tin shacks with zinc roofs, nor were there large mansions with huge gardens and razor-wire on the outside walls.

The newspapers were filled with parochial news and sporting victories, not with stories of tragic road accidents and corruption and electricity outages. The hospital did not see stab wounds or skulls fractured with knobkerries or virulent cancers or exploding carotid arteries. It was blissful calm after the turbulent storm, but Nick missed the thunder, the *sturm und drang*.

The house they found was much less luxurious and spacious than Rachie's town house at three times the price, but it was more than adequate, and the view of the bay was an improvement on razor wire.

The young adults established new friendships very quickly, loved their universities, and were already making their sporting marks. Would Kevin get to play rugby for

Australia? At first it seemed highly unlikely, but he was improving noticeably, and the possibility was beginning to look more and more like a probability.

Raichie found unpaid employment as a counsellor in a charitable psychology unit and was enjoying putting her recently attained UNISA graduation certificate to use. She found Sydney a stimulating environment, made friends easily and couldn't get enough of the botanical gardens and Sydney Harbour. The local accents never failed to intrigue her. Even if the news was insufferably boring, at least it didn't fill them with anxiety. Going out to the Blue Mountains and to the Hunter Valley wineries was a treat to be shared with Nick, and it was wonderful that he was no longer occupied on weekends.

Did she feel homesick? Every day, especially for a small plot of ground on their once-upon-a-time farm and of course her mom and dad and amazing grandmother. However, with the aid of WhatsApp she spoke to her parents daily and to cousin Joel occasionally. They would all be visiting soon, including Bubbe as a special hundredth birthday treat, if they could convince her they weren't going back to a place where there would be Cossacks riding horses headed in her direction.

Raichie spoke periodically to the new owner of her eponymous diner and was assured that although they missed her so much, high standards were being maintained.

Nick would not be doing fifteen operations each day six days a week but would still be doing enough to keep his hands finely tuned. He had more than paid his dues, and mentoring the next generation of surgeons would become a priority. He would chat from time to time via Zoom with Mr Nelson Ngope and to Judge Bernard Finch, and think often of Bokkie and Samson and Nurse Anna Kunene but only rarely of Dr Susan McDonald and of Allison Beasley.

He was scheduled to fly to Melbourne periodically to deliver lectures or act as an external examiner and he resolved he would drive out to Ballarat to visit his parents' graves, remind himself of his roots and show them to Raichie. The countryside did not have giraffes or vultures, just a whole lot of kangaroos hopping about and lots of eucalyptus trees and occasional possums and koalas. This was a country at ease with itself, and England, dear old blighty, seemed a long way away. Nick's journey had gone full circle.

For Raichie and her children a new story had only just commenced.

*The beginning.*

# Acknowledgements

I thank my editors, Shyama Pereira and Felix Hodcroft who encouraged me to believe that I could become a writer and provided the tools that enabled me to do so;

I thank my wife Adrianne Morris for her forbearance, patience and encouragement;

Thanks to Matt and Gavin for their support and interest, and to my friends who had the kindness to read and comment on the story.

# About the Author

Ed Bonner was born and educated in Johannesburg, South Africa where he graduated as a specialist prosthodontist in dentistry. He has lived in London for many years. He is an expert witness in medico-legal cases and has given evidence in court and at tribunals on many occasions. This combined with his extensive experiences in South Africa form the backbone of this story.

Printed in Great Britain
by Amazon